FALLING FOR HIS UNLIKELY CINDERELLA

REBECCA WINTERS

BETTING ON A FORTUNE

NANCY ROBARDS THOMPSON

MILLS & BOON

First Published in Great Britain 2020
by Mills & Boon, an imprint of HarperCollinsPublishers,
1 London Bridge Street, London, SE1 9GF

Falling For His Unlikely Cinderella © 2020 Rebecca Winters
Betting on a Fortune © 2020 Harlequin Books S.A.

Special thanks and acknowledgement are given to Nancy Robards Thompson for her contribution to *The Fortunes of Texas: Rambling Rose* series.

ISBN: 978-0-263-27878-1

0520

MIX
Paper from
responsible sources
FSC™ C007454

This book is produced from independently certified FSC™
paper to ensure responsible forest management.

For more information visit: www.harpercollins.co.uk/green

Printed and bound in Spain
by CPI, Barcelona

FALLING FOR HIS UNLIKELY CINDERELLA

REBECCA WINTERS

To my darling, devoted Rachel, who's a dear friend and a saint besides being a spectacular wife and mother to three adorable children. Over the years we've talked about everything under the sun. As you can guess, the poor thing has had to put up with me telling her about my ideas for new novels. With her expertise as a voracious reader, marathon runner, nurse and carpenter, she has supplied marvellous suggestions that have helped me develop characters in my books.

What would I do without you, Rachel?

CHAPTER ONE

Monday, December 1

IN A STATE of euphoria, Raoul Fontesquieu left the apartment at the Château Fontesquieu in Vence, France, and headed for his office. He was now officially on vacation from work. Once he'd gathered up a few things and had talked to his cousin Dominic, he had big plans. But on the way, he heard his cell ring. It was only six in the morning!

A grimace marred his features when he saw his father's name on the caller ID before picking up. *"Qu'est ce qui se passe?"*

"I'm calling from the Sacred Heart. Your *gran'pere* was transported to the hospital a few minutes ago. He's in room 407 and isn't expected to live past the next hour. We expect you here *now*!"

Matthieu Fontesquieu, Raoul's intransigent father, didn't know how to do anything but demand obedience. Being his parents' only child, he'd borne the emotional scars of such treatment for as long as he could remember.

Over the last week the family had sensed this day was coming. Armand Fontesquieu, the eighty-five year-old, impossibly autocratic CEO of the Domaine Fontesquieu in Provence-Alpes-Côte d'Azur, was drawing his last breath.

News of his death would ring throughout Provence and the wine world, but Raoul wouldn't mourn him. As a little boy he'd tried once to establish a relationship with him, but had been shot down and had never tried again.

"I'll be there as soon as I can."

Once he'd hung up, Raoul turned his car around and drove out of the Fontesquieu estate for the hospital. Upon reaching it, he took the elevator to the fourth floor and strode down the hall. His mother and father had been watching for him. She seemed particularly anxious, which was not a good sign. Something was up. He just didn't know what.

"Your *gran'pere* is waiting for you," his father murmured.

Waiting? While he was on the verge of death?

Raoul frowned, looking around for Dominic. Neither he nor his dozen other cousins were here. "What's going on?"

"You'll understand in a minute. Let's go in."

Raoul entered the hospital room filled with his aunts and uncles and saw his grandfather lying in the bed hooked up to IVs and oxygen.

His father nudged him. "Tell him you've arrived."

He was sick of his father's orders, but now wasn't

the time to defy him. He walked over to the bed. "Gran'pere? It's Raoul. I'm here."

The old man didn't open his eyes. How sad that even now, Raoul couldn't conjure any feelings for someone so cold.

"Raoul?" He spoke in a loud enough voice to reach everyone. "I want the family to hear from my own lips that *you* are now the CEO of the Fontesquieu Domaine." In another minute his grandfather, plagued by liver disease, exhaled and was gone.

His father took hold of his arm. "The family has arrangements to make," he whispered. "Stay available. We'll talk later today about your new position and get you installed."

He sucked in his breath. The last position Raoul would ever want would be CEO of the Fontesquieu family wine business. He was already busy with plans for a future that had nothing to do with the family.

Before dying, that grasping excuse for a human being had colluded with his favorite son Matthieu to put Raoul in charge for one reason only. By making him the CEO, it was their last bribe to bend Raoul to their will.

They assumed this grand gesture would force him to call off his divorce to Sabine Murat. Both families had been fighting it to preserve all the Murat millions with the Fontesquieu fortune. Both fortunes together enabled the families to continue to buy more assets.

But no coup could have accomplished what they'd hoped for. Raoul had never loved Sabine. Now it was over and finished, *grace à Dieu*. His divorce from Sabine Murat had been finalized yesterday afternoon. That was all he'd been waiting for.

This morning Raoul was free to embrace his new life with his precious eighteen-month-old son.

Overjoyed that Alain's existence no longer had to be kept a secret from the world, Raoul left the hospital for the modern Fontesquieu office building where all the family head offices were housed, including his own as president of marketing and sales. It was located behind the immense seventeenth-century château on the estate of the famous Fontesquieu vineyards drawing tourists from around the world.

He phoned Dominic. They were closer than brothers. It was Dominic who'd insisted Raoul stay with him in his suite at the château throughout his two months' separation from Sabine. During that period Dominic had gotten married and moved out for good. Now it was Raoul's turn to leave the château and never come back. This morning he had so much to tell Dominic, he was going to explode if they couldn't talk right now.

To his relief, Dominic, the funds manager for the Fontesquieu corporation, had opened the door of his own office suite to wait for him. "Come on in. I only heard the news about our grandfather a little while ago. It seems wrong not to mourn him, but I don't have those feelings."

"Tell me about it," Raoul muttered. "I got the call at six. Papa ordered me to get to the hospital. I arrived just in time for our grandfather to announce to the room that *I* was the new CEO before he took his last breath. You and I both know the reason why."

Grim faced, his cousin nodded. "Even with death approaching, they planned it down to the last minute."

"He and Papa don't give up, but as you know, I would never have taken over, and before long I'll be leaving the family business. The good news is, last night I got a call from my attorney Horace. The divorce decree was granted yesterday at the end of the day. I would have called you, but the news came too late to disturb you. Dom—I'm a free man and can live like one!"

"Raoul—" Dominic hugged him so hard he almost knocked him over.

"It wiped out a good portion of my assets, but it was worth it."

"If you need help, I'm your man."

"I know that and am grateful, but my new business is growing and I'm already recouping. Papa said he'd call me later in order to install me, but I have news for him. When he phones, I'll refuse to accept it and wish him luck in his new position—the one he's always coveted. Now he can be both comptroller and CEO."

Dominic nodded. "We might have my father, three uncles and two aunts, all Fontesquieux, who are more than capable of taking over Grandfather's empire, but you and I both know *your* father is the one who'll run everything now. He's made in the old man's hardboiled image with my father a clone of both of them."

Raoul stared at him. "Good luck to him. Little does he know I'm resigning soon. Already I've gathered new clients for the company I've started. Over the last two months the list has been growing."

"You're a genius."

"Great Uncle Jerome was the genius who gave me the idea before he died."

"Nevertheless, I can't imagine the company without you."

"I've been wanting to leave for years."

"What do you mean?"

"I was bound by a secret and couldn't tell you the real reason why I didn't join you in Paris. But with Grandfather's death, I no longer have to stay silent. The truth is, I would have joined you in Paris when I turned eighteen, but by then Jerome was diagnosed with lung cancer."

"You're kidding—"

Raoul shook his head. "He swore me to secrecy and didn't even tell Danie. You know what he was like. Because he was a scientist, he handled his health care in his own way and turned to alternative medicine."

"How did he do it exactly?"

"He used holistic interventions of supplements, herbs, enzymes, plus he changed his diet and he prayed. Knowing he would eventually die, I couldn't leave him because I loved him too much. But it was hard not being able to tell you the truth at the time."

"I understand totally. Gran'pere Armand never liked or acknowledged him, but Jerome had you and loved you like the son he could never have." Dominic eyed him solemnly. "What's so sad is that your father has to know he lost you years ago."

"Amen," Raoul ground out. "Before the day is out everyone will have heard about the divorce being granted, but that's irrelevant. Right now, I've got to see about getting my villa furnished, starting with the nursery. Alain needs a crib. Want to come with me for a couple of hours?"

"What do you think?" an elated Dominic cried. "I'm all yours for now." He gave some instructions to his assistant Theo, then turned to Raoul. "Let's go!" They left the building and climbed into Raoul's Jaguar.

At 8:00 a.m., twenty-six-year-old Camille Delon, known to her friends as Cami, packed a lunch for her and her mother. Together they left their apartment on the main floor of the eight-plex located in the lower income area of Vence, France. They walked toward the van parked around the side with the company logo, Nettoyage Internationale.

A chilly breeze would have blown Cami's shoulder-length black hair around if she hadn't formed it into a chignon. Her blue pullover sweater felt good over her T-shirt and jeans as she got behind the wheel. From the time she'd started working with her mother seven years ago, they'd agreed Cami should do the bulk of the driving since her mom didn't feel that comfortable maneuvering the van in heavy traffic.

She closed the door and drove them to the house-cleaning office in the heart of Vence to get their next assignment. NI, a premier housecleaning and house-keeping service, had offices all over Provence and were great employers.

"Bonjour!" the manager, Helene Biel, greeted them when they walked inside her office. Three other full-time coworkers, Jeanne, Marise and Patrice, who usually worked together, had come in another company van and were already assembled.

"Now that you're all here, I'm sending the five of you out on a lengthy assignment. The new owner of a property with a large, ultra-exclusive villa needs a total housecleaning: walls, ceilings, woodwork, windows, thorough scrubbing of kitchen and bathrooms, main rooms, fixtures, vents, floors, fireplaces, patio, you name it. The only room you're not to touch is the study on the main floor, which will be locked.

"He wants it spotless before he can start furnishing the place. After visiting the site, I estimate it will take you ladies four to five days. I'll let them know you're on your way now. That's it. This is the address."

After hearing its location, Cami eyed her mother wordlessly. This villa was located in the most elite, prestigious area of Vence. Only billionaires could afford to live on the top ridge of hills that overlooked the whole spectacular landscape stretching to the Mediterranean.

With an address like that, it had to be near her favorite fairy-tale-like Château Fontesquieu, one of the wonders of Provence, set in the middle of its world-famous vineyards. The thought brought incredibly happy memories associated with her father. When Cami had been little, her dad, who'd been a taxi driver before his fatal car crash, had driven her and her mom to the estate every fall to see it and she'd never forgotten.

She must have been five years old when he'd first taken them on a tour through the vineyards at harvest time so they could watch the workers picking the grapes. Every year after that during the harvest he did the same thing, stopping each time for them to take in the sights.

One particular incident stood out in her mind and had always lingered there. At the age of twelve, she'd seen an older man walking through the vineyard with a young dark-haired man, maybe fifteen or sixteen. He was so handsome, she'd put down the back window so she could lean out and look at him a little better. They appeared to be supervising the workers before they reached the man's elegant black car with the gold hood ornament. As the younger man turned to get in, he caught Cami staring at him and smiled.

A thrill ran through her young girl's heart and she smiled back before the other car drove off. When she asked her father about the ornament, he said it was the emblem of the royal Fontesquieu family, which had existed for hundreds of years.

Cami sat back. In her mind's eye the younger man had to be one of the royals, the fictional prince who lived at the château. Nothing could have delighted her more and caused her to dream about living in there with him one day as his princess.

But in November of that very year her father had been killed. The pain and shock of losing him stripped her of such a foolish fantasy. No more trips to the vineyard or anything else. By the time she'd turned twenty-one with a brief, failed marriage behind her, she'd been forced to face another personal crisis.

Her doctor had said that in time the genetic heart murmur she'd been born with would have to work too hard. He explained to her that she had a bicuspid aortic valve. The surgeon ran tests and decided to put off surgery until the symptoms began to affect her life, possibly when she turned twenty-six. By then the technique would have been perfected and become less invasive, possibly avoiding open-heart surgery altogether.

She was allowed to do her normal work, but there could be no running marathons or doing any physical activity that raised her heartbeat to too high a level. To make certain she was taking care of herself, she had to go in for regular checkups. The doctor said she could continue to clean houses, but to do no heavy lifting.

This last October the doctor scheduled her operation for mid-December. The heart surgeon had plans to leave the country over the holidays, so the operation had to be done before that time.

There were no guarantees where her recovery was concerned. As the time grew near, Cami had to live with that prospect, even though the doctor sounded reasonably optimistic. But the alternative of not undergoing the surgery meant her days would be numbered.

Except for their extended family in Nice, Cami and her mother had never told anyone that she had to have an operation, not even Helene or their coworkers. She was lucky to have this job and needed it too much to lose it. At her last doctor's appointment, they had set the date of the operation for December 18, giving her the holidays to recover.

But what if she didn't?

As the doctor had told her, every surgery held a risk. In order not to dwell on it, Cami worked harder than ever and determined to make the most of her life—until she couldn't.

"You're to park in front and go to the front door," Helene explained. "Call me if there's any problem. Now off you go."

Since they had all the equipment they needed in their vans, they filed outside under a semicloudy sky. Cami got in the van with her mother and they started driving toward the verdant hills in the distance. The other van followed them. Slowly they wound their way serpentine style to the summit. How would it be to live up here in this glorious paradise?

As they passed by the entrance to the Fontesquieu estate and vast vineyards open for tourists, she eyed the impressive grilled gate with its gold ducal crest. Her mother noticed it too. "You probably don't remember what your father said the last time he drove us around there years ago."

"No, but I do remember all the times Papa took us there." Passing by here reminded her of that special day when the handsome young man had smiled at her. "Tell me what he said." She'd loved her dad and had suffered after he'd died.

"The Fontesquieu family lives at the footsteps of the gods." Her mother shook her head. "I can't comprehend their kind of wealth and never want to. All that money doesn't bring happiness."

"Probably not," Cami murmured. At least that's what you told yourself when you didn't have it. Her wonderful mother had worked so hard all her life, turning to housecleaning after high school to make a living. She'd never stopped.

Cami had just graduated from Sophie Antipolis University in Nice with honors in business and finance. If all went well with the operation and recovery, she'd start work in January at La Maison de Chocolat Gaillard in their finance department where she'd interned during her last semester.

Guaranteed an excellent starting salary, she was determined to pay back the small balance left on her student loan and take care of herself and her mom. No more housecleaning for either of them! Of course, that all depended on the outcome of the operation.

After several turns, they finally reached their destination. The rose-colored two-story villa appearing through the lush greenery was so beautiful, it didn't look real. Several sections of steps rose up the terraced landscaping to the main entry.

Cami pulled the van to a stop in front, thinking that the family who would live in this villa shared those same footsteps her father had once talked about. Feeling as if she'd arrived in a wonderland, Cami got out and started up the stairs with her mother. Before she had a chance to knock, the door opened.

An attractive blonde woman, probably a little older than Cami's mother, smiled at them. "You must be from Nettoyage International."

Her mother spoke first. "I'm Juliette Delon. This is my daughter, Camille." Patrice introduced the others.

"Wonderful. I'm Arlette Gilbert. Thank you for being so prompt. Please come inside."

Cami and her mother followed the woman into the foyer with its fabulous parquet flooring. A graceful winding staircase divided a salon on the right, empty of furnishings, and the sitting room on the left. The interior contained only two chairs and a modern-looking couch. Both rooms were set off with elegant wood carved French doors.

"Won't you be seated?"

Cami sat on a chair next to her mother. The other three sat on the couch.

The blonde woman studied them. "The owner will be in and out. In the meantime he's put me in charge and I'll be here all week. I assume your manager has explained what needs to be done. I'll take you on a quick tour of the villa and let you decide how to divide up your workload.

"After the tour, I suggest you drive your vans up the driveway where you can park in the rear between the garage and the outdoor swimming pool. I'll unlock the back door so you can bring in your equipment. If you need me, you'll find me here in the sitting room."

Within a half hour they'd moved their vans in back and had made decisions of what areas to tackle first. Cami and her mother chose to clean the four bedrooms with en suite bathrooms upstairs, estimating it would take them several days. All five of them agreed to save washing the windows inside and out until their last day.

They carried their cleaning supplies upstairs. As far as Cami was concerned, this villa was a small palace. What would it be like to live here, to wake up every day to such luxury and beauty, to be able to decorate it the way you wanted and not count the cost?

Her mother shook her head as she looked around. "Just the upkeep on this place would cost a king's ransom. I'm glad it's someone else's headache."

No one could bring Cami down from the clouds faster than her practical mother. With a resigned smile, she noted that the villa had higher than normal ceilings. The owner had provided a substantial ladder. Being up high made it easy to clean with no extra stress on her heart.

Because Cami's mother had arthritis in her shoulders, Cami insisted on cleaning those, plus the walls and moldings. That left her mom to do the hardwood floors and bathrooms. Their system worked and they got busy.

At noon they walked out to the van to eat their lunch like they always did on the job. Her mother turned on the news. They both liked to know what was going on. The radio would do when there was no TV.

After listening to the world headlines, they heard the announcement that France had lost one of the great vintners from Provence.

"Today France is in mourning over the death of le Duc Armand Fontesquieu, who will be laid to rest on Thursday on the Fontesquieu estate in Vence."

Cami and her mother eyed each other in surprise. They'd passed the famous estate on their way here earlier this morning. What a coincidence!

"The renowned CEO and vintner died at eighty-five years of age and left a dynasty of billions to his family. The future now lies in the hands of his grandson Raoul Fontesquieu, married to Sabine Murat of the Murat industrial millions. Today it was announced he is the new CEO of the Fontesquieu empire. The grandson—"

Her mother turned it off. "I've heard enough."

Cami understood what was going on in her mom's mind. The news was a reminder that 99 percent of the population couldn't relate to a world like the Fontesquieux or billionaires like the owner of the villa they'd been cleaning.

"Let's go in and get started again."

After grabbing lunch, Raoul had driven Dominic back to the office. He turned to his cousin. "Thanks for coming with me this morning. Only you could know how happy I am to be done with the secrecy about Alain. I've almost gone out of my mind having to keep all knowledge of him quiet leading up to the divorce."

"Despite all the problems, you've carried it off."

"But he won't be a secret any longer. As you know, the psychiatrist advised me that Sabine was fragile after losing the baby. No heart trouble had run in her family or mine. It was devastating. That's why I didn't want her to hear of Alain's existence until the divorce was finalized."

Dominic looked at him. "You were fragile too, even though little Celine turned out to be some other man's daughter."

"Nevertheless I loved that baby, but it's all behind me now."

"Nothing could make me happier for you, Raoul."

"My son is going to find out what it's like to have a father who loves him and is free to give him all the attention he needs. If you and Nathalie would get busy, maybe he'll have another little cousin to play with soon."

Dominic grinned. "Who says we haven't been doing our best?"

A chuckle came out of Raoul who felt a new happiness envelop him. Dominic's wife, Nathalie, had been the one who'd united Raoul with the son he hadn't known anything about. She and Alain's mother, Antoinette, had been stepsisters.

When Antoinette had died of a staph infection ten days after he'd been born, it was Nathalie and her mother who'd looked after Alain in La Gaude, a town fifteen minutes from Vence. But it wasn't until this year's grape harvest that she'd come to the vineyard looking for the nameless father of her nephew. By a miracle she'd found Raoul!

"I'm on vacation from the office for two weeks now. When everything's ready, I'll resign and bring Alain home to the villa. The housecleaning service I engaged on Saturday should be busy there cleaning by now. Arlette volunteered to be in charge."

"Where's Alain?"

"Minerve is tending him during the day while we get the villa ready. By the time the cleaners are through at the end of the week, I'll be leaving your old suite for good."

"Don't worry. We've moved out permanently. Nathalie and I have our own home we're in the process of furnishing. There's no hurry."

"Oh, yes there is. I want nothing more to do with life at the château. Thank heaven for Minerve who's been Alain's nanny since he was born. She's going to come with Arlette to help me with him during the transition. When Alain and I are on our own, I don't want him to miss them too much."

"It'll all work, and Nathalie will help too, but Minerve will be difficult to replace."

"You can say that again. I'm working with an established nanny training service. On Wednesday some women will be sent out for interviews. Arlette will help me vet them."

"She's the perfect one to help. I've got some good news too, Raoul. Arlette couldn't be a better mother-in-law to me and has hired another pharmacist so Nathalie only has to work part-time or not at all. From now on she can help you more when you need it."

"That's terrific."

"Who's going to run the marketing while you're on vacation?"

"I've been grooming our cousin Jean-Pierre to take over for good. He's effective without being pushy. Naturally Papa doesn't approve, but once I've left, Jean-Pierre will be there to save the day. I have great faith in him."

Another smile broke out on Dominic's face. "Then that settles it. Jean-Pierre is the right choice."

They said goodbye and Raoul drove to the villa, eager to take another look at the size of the room he planned to turn into the nursery. He wanted to paint it and needed to estimate how much to buy.

Full of excitement, he entered the villa and bounded up the stairs, but stopped short of entering the room because his breath had caught. An absolutely beautiful woman with a stunning figure was up on the ladder cleaning. She was probably in her midtwenties and totally engaged in her work.

He couldn't remember the last time any woman had caused him to forget what he was doing or thinking for a minute. Not since Antoinette… The same thing had happened with her. He'd taken one look and was so drawn to her, he'd approached her as if in a trance.

Now here he was again three years later, captured by the sight of this stranger. It threw him. He leaned against the doorjamb for a moment before entering.

CHAPTER TWO

AFTER LUNCH, CAMI was back to the second bedroom down the hall from the curved staircase. With her safety glasses on, plus her rubber gloves, she'd climbed the ladder she and her mom had placed on top of the drop cloth.

First, she'd removed the light fixture in the center of the room in order to clean it. Then she vacuumed the cobwebs off the ceiling and cove moldings before scrubbing everything.

As she started to climb down to wash out her flat board mop, she caught sight of a tall, black-haired male lounging against the doorjamb at the entrance. It surprised her so much it caused her to stumble. "Oh—" she cried.

Like lightning he sprang forward on those long powerful legs and saved her from landing on the hardwood floor with a bang, like the mop. "I'm sorry to have startled you," he said in a deep voice, lowering her carefully. She felt his warm breath on her skin.

"It was my fault. Thank you." She stepped back,

marveling at his speed and embarrassed to have been that clumsy in front of him.

"I should have knocked on the bedroom door to let you know I was standing there."

She took in the sight of this man who was probably twenty-nine or thirty, dressed in a black cashmere sweater and gray trousers. With those alive black eyes, he was so incredibly attractive, Cami struggled to gain her composure.

"I was deep in thought and probably wouldn't have heard it. Madame Gilbert mentioned the owner would be in and out."

He nodded. "I had something else on my mind too. This room is going to be my son's. I was trying to think what color to paint it tomorrow."

All the bedrooms had off-white walls with white moldings. "How old is he?" She was still trying to recover. The faint tang of the soap he used in the shower lingered.

"Alain is eighteen months."

A father with a toddler. She wondered if he resembled his gorgeous papa. "Then you must be planning to turn this room into a nursery."

"I was at a furniture store earlier picking out everything and fell in love with a white crib and dresser."

That made her smile. "Is he into trucks or cars?"

A light entered his eyes. "Both. And boats."

While Cami chuckled, trying not to study his striking masculine features through her safety glasses, Madame Gilbert appeared in the doorway.

"Raoul, the gardener is downstairs waiting to talk to you."

"Tell him I'll be right there."

After she disappeared, he plucked the mop off the floor and handed it to Cami. Their hands brushed, causing an unbidden current of electricity to dart through her body. She could still feel the imprint of his hands on her arms. "Forgive me for interrupting your work."

She shook her head. "Thank you for saving me from a crash. All I need is a broken leg."

"Heaven forbid," he murmured. This close he was so handsome it hurt. She'd heard that expression before, but for the first time in her life she felt the truth of it. "It was the least I could do after all your hard work. I can see differences already. We'll definitely be seeing each other again tomorrow," he said with a smile that made her legs go weak before leaving the bedroom.

Long after he'd gone, his smile stayed with her. Something about it haunted her, as if she'd seen it before. Her heart kept thudding. She'd forgotten it could do that.

Struggling to rein in her thoughts, she worked harder than ever, but couldn't forget what had happened. When she'd finished everything and had cleaned up, she carried her equipment to the third bedroom and spread the drop cloth on the floor in preparation for the next day. She put her safety glasses in her purse.

After pulling on her sweater, she walked to the

master bedroom to collect her slender, brunette mother who was cleaning the bathroom's exquisite Provençal floor tiles. "How's it going, Maman?"

"How it always goes," came the typical response, then a wry laugh escaped. "I'll be ready to leave in a minute."

"No hurry." Cami looked around. It made total sense that the owner's bedroom was next to the nursery. She wondered why his wife hadn't been here to let them in this morning. But anything to do with him was none of her business. Cami needed to put a governor on her thoughts.

Unfortunately his image remained in her mind and she had difficulty taking her own advice while she helped carry her mom's equipment to the third bathroom so they could begin first thing in the morning. Her mother deserved an easier life. Cami was determined to make that happen for both of them. But the operation might not fix what was wrong. That was the big imponderable.

Soon her mom had finished and their day's work was done, but they'd be back tomorrow. That meant Cami would be seeing *him* again. Her heart did a little kick she seemed to have no control over. Ridiculous when the man had a family, even if she hadn't seen a wedding band.

His fabulous villa had to be worth millions. Though it had sat idle for a while and truly did need a good cleaning, everything looked in excellent condition.

Again she tried to imagine owning a home like his,

the kind you'd see in one of the posh interior design magazines from Provence. Imagine living in it with the right man, making a home with him, never worrying that your heart might give out just when life was getting wonderful...

But that was pure fiction. If she wanted any kind of a future for herself and her mother, she would have to work by the sweat of her brow for as long as life and her heart allowed her to draw breath. She had learned never to depend on anyone else.

They asked Madame Gilbert to make sure the ladder was moved to the third bedroom with the drop cloth, then they left. On their way home, she pulled in to their favorite deli to pick up dinner so they wouldn't have to cook. After coming back out, she started up the van and soon she'd parked at the side of their apartment. "We worked hard today. Let's go in. I'm hungry too, Maman."

After walking around the property with the gardener while they discussed what needed to be done, Raoul had gone to the kitchen for a soda. From the window he'd happened to see the housecleaners leave and couldn't help focusing his gaze on the sensational-looking woman who climbed in the driver's seat of the first van.

When he'd started down the upstairs hall earlier in the day, he'd seen her up on the ladder. She had to be five seven, possessing a shapely figure. For a brief moment he'd caught her against his body to prevent her from hitting the floor. Even now he still remembered how she'd felt and the scent of her flowery fragrance.

With her glistening black hair pulled away from her face wearing those safety glasses, she cut a picture that refused to leave his mind. In all his experience he'd never met a female with eyes the exact hue of the tassel hyacinths that grew on Fontesquieu property near the vineyards.

Her coloring was a marvel of nature like Provence itself. It shocked him that he'd become so physically aware of this female when Antoinette's memory had filled his heart for close to three years.

That woman had been the love of his life, but before he could marry her, Sabine Murat, the woman he'd broken up with a month before meeting Antoinette, had come back into his life. He'd slept with Sabine once, but realized he didn't love her. To his shock, Sabine had been to the doctor and was pregnant with Raoul's baby.

His world fell apart. He did the honorable thing by giving up Antoinette and marrying Sabine, but he'd lost the woman he'd loved and concentrated on the coming baby, only to learn after its birth that the baby *wasn't* his and had died of a bad heart within the first month of life.

Sabine had lied to him about the baby's paternity. The news meant he'd been forced to endure needless pain during a soulless marriage, and he divorced her.

He had only recently learned through Antoinette's stepsister Nathalie that she'd given birth to Raoul's son whom she'd named Alain. Now his life had turned to joy so he could start a new life with his boy. Raoul couldn't wait for everything to be done and left for La Gaude.

Arlette, Alain's grandmother, had already gone home in her car. En route he dropped by his former suite in the north wing of the Château Fontesquieu where Sabine had remained during the separation. There were two averaged-sized framed oil paintings of significance to him, plus a set of two journals he wanted bequeathed to him by his great uncle Jerome. They represented the life work of a master vintner.

It didn't surprise him to see that before Sabine had returned to her parents' château in nearby St. Paul-de-Vence, she'd literally cleaned everything out, including those items she knew he valued most. He grimaced as he looked around. Somehow he'd find a way to get them back. As for right now, he had the satisfaction of knowing the whole ghastly ordeal had come to an end.

Raoul tossed his key on the kitchen counter and closed the door literally on his old life before walking back out to his car. Being with his son had made him feel reborn. He left the estate, eager to be with Alain.

Tomorrow the man who'd serviced the swimming pools for the former owner would be coming to the villa to check out the indoor pool and get it ready. The outdoor pool had a cover over it. He'd worry about it in the spring.

Now was the time to teach Alain how to swim. Raoul planned that he and his son would get use out of it every day. In time they'd be going out on the

Mediterranean in his sailboat. It was vital his boy be able to handle himself in any kind of water.

When he thought about tomorrow, the knowledge that the cleaning people would be at the villa for a few more days was an added plus. He intended to find out the gorgeous woman's name and more.

By 8:00 a.m. Tuesday, Madame Gilbert had opened the back door of the villa to let the cleaners in. Cami and her mother walked upstairs. Today they would tackle the third and fourth bedrooms and bathrooms.

Maybe the striking owner and his wife had other children who would be occupying these bedrooms, though he hadn't talked about any. The sight from the third bedroom window looked out on the property's greenery and outdoor pool. What a wonderful place to grow up.

When the owner had mentioned his son, she'd felt such love coming from him. A father's love was a great thing. She missed hers and turned away from the window to get busy.

After lunch in the van, her mother finished the third bathroom while Cami started on the fourth bedroom. As she was setting up, she heard a knock on the open door and turned her head to see the owner.

"I thought I'd better announce myself first before you saw me." That deep masculine voice of his curled its way through her insides. He brought in the ladder from the other room, which he set up for her.

"Thank you. My mother and I were going to bring it in."

"Now you don't have to. I'll move it wherever you wish. Just ask."

No man had ever looked so good wearing thigh-molding jeans and a T-shirt that covered his powerful shoulders and chest. This time it was her pulse that raced of its own volition.

She smiled. "I appreciate that. Since I wasn't up on it, I've been saved a trip to the hospital this afternoon." Before long she'd be going there for something that had nothing to do with a broken bone.

He laughed, exhibiting a refreshing sense of humor. "I should have asked your name yesterday."

"It's Camille Delon, but those who know me call me Cami."

He flashed her an answering smile. "*Bonne après-midi*, Cami. We weren't officially introduced yesterday. I'm Raoul Fontesquieu."

Raoul Fontesquieu? It couldn't be. But it had to be. There could only be one. She'd heard his name clearly over the radio.

Cami swallowed hard as reality set in. She clung to the side of the ladder where she stood. "I heard about the death of your grandfather. I'm so sorry. I never knew either of mine. You and your wife were lucky to have enjoyed him this long."

Her comment seemed to bring a subtle change in his demeanor, causing her to realize there were hidden emotions swirling inside of him. Prompted by his silence she said, "Let me congratulate you for being named the new CEO of your family's company. It was all over the news yesterday."

In an instant a frown broke out on his striking features. "I'm afraid bad news travels fast when it's false."

"What do you mean?" The comment had taken her back.

His lips twisted. "I'm divorced, and won't be accepting the position as CEO. In time, I won't be associated with the company at all. However, I'm assuming that the truth will be corrected before the week is out."

"Those are pretty colossal mistakes for the media to make." She was still trying to take it all in.

"Indeed." A strange smile appeared. "I came in here to ask if you would take a look at the nursery and tell me what you think about the color I've painted it. Is it too deep, or not light enough?"

It surprised her that he wanted her opinion at all. She couldn't help be excited. Everything about him had fascinated her even before she'd learned his identity. "Since I haven't started cleaning the ceiling yet, I'll come now."

Cami followed him down the hall. When they reached the entry, she took in the soft blue that had covered the off-white walls of the room. "It's perfect, monsieur. You did an excellent job. Are you sure you didn't head a house painting company in a former life?"

It was an outrageous comment to make knowing who he was, but she hadn't been able to resist. Not after realizing he was one of those royals her father had told her about years ago, even if their titles were defunct.

His laughter resonated in the room. Almost at once his body and expression relaxed, turning him back to the charismatic, virile man she'd hadn't been able to forget during the night.

"Call me Raoul, and tell me the truth."

"I promise you I just did," she assured him with a smile. "The blue color you've chosen has created a soothing ambience any child would love. With the white cove moldings, I can picture the white furniture you picked out fitting in beautifully."

His black eyes gleamed. "Thank you. Now that I have your seal of approval, I'll have everything I've bought delivered on Friday. By Sunday I'll bring my son home to live with me permanently."

She could hear his excitement. "Where is he?"

He shifted his weight. "You've met Arlette Gilbert. She's his grandmother and has taken care of him from birth."

She blinked. But where was Madame Gilbert's daughter? According to the report on the radio, Raoul had been married to a woman named Sabine Murat. Cami was so confused.

By now she's learned enough to realize there were volumes of information he'd left out: like why his son hadn't lived with him from birth; why the divorce; where the birth mother was; what the reason was for the false news report that went out to the whole world.

But she didn't have the right to ask those questions.

Cami was one of the cleaning ladies. In another couple of days, she'd never see him again.

"Your son is blessed to have a father like you who loves him so much and has painted his room. That's a story you can tell him when he's older. I lost my father at twelve."

"I'm sorry to hear that. You were so young."

"It was awful. For a while I thought my life was over. Hang on to the relationship with your son for dear life. Nothing's more important."

"I agree." Again, the emotion in his tone conveyed he was a man of deep feelings.

She turned to leave.

"Are you married, Cami?" With her gloves on, he wouldn't have noticed if she wore a ring or not.

She paused and looked back at him, surprised at the question. "I was married at eighteen and divorced at nineteen."

He studied her for a moment. "Do you have children?"

Cami shook her head. One month into her marriage proved she'd made a mistake and she was glad she hadn't gotten pregnant. "I've been working ever since. Now I'd better get back to my cleaning."

His eyes played over her, sending darts of awareness through her. "Then I'll see you later."

For the rest of the afternoon she worked her head off. When she and her mother left the villa at five, the owner was nowhere in sight. On the way home she told her mom what she'd learned about him and the nursery he'd painted.

"So...he's a Fontesquieu... Like I said, money doesn't ensure happiness. A divorce? A little boy he's never lived with? Why on earth would he buy that large villa for the two of them when his home is the royal Fontesquieu Château? It doesn't make sense."

"Neither does the fact that he turned down the CEO position," Cami murmured. Most successful businessmen clamored their whole lives to achieve that status, but she already knew he wasn't like other men.

Raoul Fontesquieu was his own person. After telling her in a quietly fierce tone that the media had spread lies about him, he could no doubt be formidable on occasion.

Still, a tremor shook her body. Something had happened to her today, something she hadn't thought possible. His jaw-dropping appeal had taken her by surprise in a way that made her feel—oh, she didn't know—thrown off course when her path had been set for so long.

After they arrived at the apartment and ate dinner, Cami went to the store for a few groceries in their old black Citroën 2CV. It was on its last legs and looked like an umbrella, but it ran. She hoped it would help her find a way to clear visions in her head of the most devastatingly attractive man she'd ever met in her life!

Raoul met the pool contractor Wednesday morning. He walked him down the corridor from the kitchen. They passed the locked study and continued to the end of the house. The square-shaped tiled pool was sealed off with a sliding door.

The contractor brought in the supplies; a water kit, balancers, conditioners and chlorine tablets used to test the water. Raoul worked with him so he could do it himself from now on, then saw him out.

Before the applicants for the nanny job started to show up, Raoul took the staircase two steps at a time. He saw Cami in her safety glasses midway down the hall. Behind her he glimpsed one of the other workers cleaning a linen closet.

Cami was up on the ladder scrubbing the ceiling and moldings. Her loose-fitting hunter green T-shirt couldn't conceal the lovely shape of her body.

Afraid to startle her, he stayed where he was. When she saw him she waved with her free hand. "Bonjour, Raoul. It's okay to approach," she teased.

Amused, Raoul strode toward her. "I came to see how things are progressing. You've transformed the villa. It sparkles."

A smile broke out on her face, beguiling him. "That's good to hear. Our boss will be relieved."

He liked the way she fastened her black hair in a chignon that suited her oval face and high cheekbones. "Is she a slave driver?"

"Yes. Don't you agree, Maman?"

His gaze darted to the older brunette woman who'd just lifted her head and glanced at him from the closet. He saw the facial similarities and smiled at her. "You're all such hard workers, I'm impressed."

Both women chuckled. "Raoul? Meet my mother and best friend, Juliette Delon."

"Bonjour, madame."

"Bonjour, Monsieur Fontesquieu. It's nice to meet you. My daughter's right. Our boss cracks the whip, but she's nice."

"She's terrific," Cami chimed in.

Raoul admired their loyalty. "How refreshing to see a mother and daughter who work well together." He couldn't think of a single positive instance within the difficult female circles of the large Fontesquieu family. Years of living together under the roof of the château had done its damage. "I'm glad to have met you, Madame Delon. I promise to give all of you a top rating."

"We couldn't ask for more than that. It means work for another day," the pragmatic older woman commented before getting back to cleaning the shelves.

He couldn't imagine his ex-wife doing manual labor like this, let alone worrying about where her next euro was coming from. Naturally the comparison wasn't fair, but he couldn't help but be impressed by the Delons' work ethic.

"Don't let me keep you. I'll see you tomorrow." Already he knew he'd like to take Cami out to dinner so they could get better acquainted.

"Isn't your grandfather's funeral tomorrow?"

She'd remembered and had shown concern for his loss though he hadn't felt it himself. After living around his austere relatives, her natural warmth was like a healing balm. "Yes, but I'll be back in the afternoon."

Cami's thoughtful gaze met his briefly before he walked away. He'd have preferred to stay and talk, but not while she was working with her mother.

After going downstairs, he met with two applicants for the nanny position. Neither he nor Arlette were impressed.

Raoul had been guilt ridden over having to give up Antoinette, knowing the pain he'd caused her. He hadn't been there for the pregnancy he'd had no knowledge of.

Once he'd found out, he'd felt responsible for her death and the anguish he'd caused her and her family. On top of that he was well aware how deeply Arlette missed her daughter. Though she could have blamed Raoul, she'd never been anything but accepting and wonderful to him.

His latest worry was what kind of a father he was going to be. Could any nanny he chose measure up or tend Arlette's grandson with the love and care she and Minerve had provided?

This was a difficult decision for him to make, in truth the hardest of his life. He decided he'd made a mistake by not bringing Alain to the villa today. During the interviews, Raoul needed to watch the women interact with his son on a first meeting simply to see if there was any chemistry at all. If not, it might be a long time before he found the right person to take care of his precious boy.

Raoul could only hope one of the applicants sent to

the villa tomorrow after three in the afternoon would stand out. He was also looking forward to spending more time with Cami. Besides her having an intrinsic charm that was growing on him, she had a way of encouraging him, of making him feel he could be a good father. Somehow he felt instinctively he could talk to her and connect.

CHAPTER THREE

THURSDAY HAD ARRIVED, which meant attending the funeral. Raoul climbed in the Mercedes. "Thanks for picking me up, Dom. Why isn't Nathalie with you?"

"We both felt the funeral was no place to introduce her to the family for the first time."

"I hear you."

"She wanted to go to Arlette's and help tend Alain. Arlette will be bringing him to your villa in time for the nanny interviews."

"What would I do without them?"

Dom flashed him a glance as they headed for the church. "They're so thrilled you two have been united, and that you're his father. They'd do anything for you. They love you."

"I don't deserve it."

"Never say that again. As far as I'm concerned, what Sabine did to you and Antoinette was evil."

Raoul agreed.

They pulled in the parking lot of the church where the hearse was parked. "I've been dreading today," Dom admitted.

Raoul groaned. "Tell me about it. Let's get this over."

The Fontesquieu family was laying a despotic patriarch to rest with all the grandeur of burying a king. Raoul couldn't take much more.

Both of them had dressed in black. They slipped in the back behind everyone else, refusing to join their individual families. Sabine, also in black with a veil, sat next to Raoul's parents with her family as if there'd been no divorce. They were all in denial. She turned her head when she saw them come in.

"Sabine never gives up, does she?" Dom said under his breath.

"Of course not," Raoul bit out. "I'm still waiting for Papa to inform the press of the truth. It's been five days..."

"He's waiting for you to come around."

Raoul shook his head.

Once the services were over, he and Dominic escaped out the back of the church with relief and walked to the Mercedes.

Between his cousin's private wedding where no Fontesquieu had been invited, plus the infuriating news that Raoul's divorce had gone through, not to mention his refusal to become CEO, they'd outraged both sets of parents and couldn't leave fast enough.

Everyone else would go on to the family cemetery on the eastern end of the estate to bury Armand Fontesquieu. All Raoul could think about was seeing Cami again. He couldn't wait to see her again and learn more about her. She was like a breath of fresh air.

Dominic dropped him off in front of the villa. Arlette had probably come and parked in back. The first thing Raoul did was hang his suit jacket and tie in the sitting room closet. After loosening the top buttons of his white shirt, he searched for Cami, nodding to some of the cleaners on the way.

Raoul found her in the large room he'd designated for a playroom where Alain could bring his friends. It was down the same hall near the indoor pool. She'd put a drop cloth on the floor and was kneeling while cleaning the vents. He couldn't be more pleased to find her alone. Her mother had to be somewhere else cleaning.

"Mademoiselle Delon?" he said softly. Their eyes met. It made him glad to think she'd taken her maiden name, which meant she'd chosen not to keep her married name after her divorce. Obviously there'd been trouble in a marriage she'd chosen to forget. He and Cami already had something in common.

"I take it the funeral is over."

"*Oui*, thank heaven." He sat down by her and settled against the wall, resting his hands over his raised knees. "At least you weren't up on the ladder when I walked in."

She chuckled.

He undid the cuffs of his shirtsleeves and pushed them up to the elbows. "Can I help?"

"I'm almost through here." She lifted those heavenly eyes to him. "Are you all right?"

"I am now." Knowing she'd be here after the funeral had made his day. "I'm expecting a new applicant for the nanny job in a little while. Until then, give yourself a rest and put me to work."

"The way you're dressed, I wouldn't dream of it. This isn't a normal day for you. I'm aware you've just buried your grandfather and have turned down the CEO position. None of it could be easy for you."

He studied her for a moment, marveling at her capacity for understanding, even if she didn't know what was really going on inside of him. "This is probably going to shock you, but this has been a liberating day for me in so many ways you can't imagine. That may sound harsh to you, but I'm telling you the truth. Today I'm happier than I've been in years! My son's coming to live with me and a whole world has opened up. Since I feel like celebrating, I have an idea."

"What would that be?" Her engaging smile lit up his insides.

"If you're finished, why don't you come to the kitchen with me? We'll grab a drink and go into the sitting room to wait for the next woman to show up. You can help me vet her, maybe give me a signal one way or another what you think."

"As if I'd dare," she answered with a teasing tone.

"Why not? Once we're in there we'll have something comfortable to sit down on while we talk. All the furniture I've bought won't be delivered until tomorrow."

At his suggestion, she removed her gloves. "You once lived at the château, right?"

"All my life until now."

"What about the furniture you brought with you?"

"It went with my ex-wife." Including the two paintings Jerome had done years earlier and given to Raoul before his death.

She looked surprised, but didn't comment on it. "So in order to fill this villa, you've had to purchase *everything*?"

"That's right."

Her fabulous eyes widened. "You must have been shopping for ages."

"And having the time of my life. It's been a treat buying modern furniture that wasn't invented when the château was built. Alain wouldn't feel comfortable—"

"The way *you* weren't comfortable?" she surmised sotto voce. "I'm sorry. I shouldn't have said that."

"Don't be sorry. Your instincts are right." Cami was amazingly easy to talk to. They seemed so keyed into each other, it had caused him to let down his guard when he was with her.

"Still, please forgive me."

"There's nothing to forgive. You were only speaking the truth. The first time my cousin Dominic and I were throwing a ball around in his family's suite, we broke a statue by accident. Needless to say, that never happened again. Life at the château was never meant for children, let alone lively ones. The paintings and tapestries covered up what I always thought was a gigantic prison where children couldn't be themselves."

"And here I've found myself envying you."

"I've ruined your picture of life at the château,

haven't I? But I'm afraid it was built and furnished for a very different period of time that was hard on children." Not waiting for a response from her, he got to his feet and put out his hands to help her stand.

"Thank you."

Together they walked through the house to the kitchen. He pulled two colas out of the fridge and left for the sitting room. She sat on the couch while he chose a chair.

"I haven't seen your mother, Cami."

"I think she and Marise are out cleaning the back patio. You didn't notice them?"

"My cousin drove us to the funeral and he dropped me off in front."

She nodded. "I hope this next interview for a nanny will produce the desired result."

He examined the features of her well-shaped nose. That enticing mouth was shaped like a budding rose. He longed to kiss her and it was starting to drive him mad. Again, he was shocked by his strong attraction to her. But it was too soon to be experiencing these feelings.

When he remembered how quickly his desire for Antoinette had taken over his life before fate stepped in to end their relationship, it worried him that history could repeat itself. Raoul needed to be careful not to rush into anything with Cami that could hurt her.

"That's my hope too. I'm excited about my new life." Right now, he was making a home for his son and establishing a new business. At least that was what he kept telling himself, but Cami was a raving beauty and her charisma had rubbed off on him. He found he couldn't be with her long enough to satisfy him.

"Everything you're doing has been based around your son in order to make him happy. He'll be a very lucky little boy," she asserted.

"Once I find the right nanny, one of my biggest worries will be solved. It's the worry about being a good father that gives me anxiety."

She flashed him one of those encouraging smiles. "The fact that it's your first thought guarantees you'll never fail. Papa always made me feel important."

The way Raoul's father and grandfather never did. Her hopeful, comforting words coincided with the ringing of the doorbell. Disappointment swamped him for being interrupted. "That will be she. Just a minute."

He walked to the front door. "You're Monsieur Fontesquieu?" the brunette woman asked after he opened it. She kept staring at him.

"I am," he said. "Come in." He walked her into the sitting room. She was probably Cami's age. By now Cami had gotten to her feet.

Their eyes connected as they remembered what they'd said about vetting her. "Mademoiselle Delon? Let me introduce you to Mademoiselle Herve."

"How do you do, mademoiselle?"

The woman stared at Cami. "Does this mean *you're* the new nanny?" she blurted, surprising Raoul. "I thought the position hadn't been filled yet."

"It hasn't," Raoul declared, bringing the other woman's head around.

"If you'll excuse me, monsieur, I have a floor to clean. *À demain*." Cami had been surprised too and couldn't escape fast enough. Raoul couldn't blame her.

He watched her leave the sitting room, already regretting the fact that she'd gone back to her work.

Unfortunately he knew he hadn't found the right nanny for Alain yet. He hadn't yet put into words what he really wanted because he needed to be cautious when it came to getting involved with Cami. Again, after what had happened with Antoinette, he couldn't bear for Cami to be injured in any way because of him, but he could tell he was falling for her.

Cami's mother awakened on Friday morning, with a lot of pain in her right shoulder. "That does it, Maman. Yesterday you overdid it cleaning the patio and porch. Today you're staying home and taking care of yourself. There'll be four of us washing windows, so you don't need to worry. I'll see you tonight and bring dinner."

She kissed her mom and took off for her last day of work at the villa. After today she'd never see Raoul Fontesquieu again. It shouldn't matter to her, but she couldn't lie to herself. From the first day when he'd miraculously caught her in his arms, she hadn't been the same.

A man like him was unforgettable—and as out of reach as the stars in a distant galaxy whether she had a heart problem or not, which she did. He was the stuff that had made up her fantasies after visiting the Fontesquieu estate with her parents. She was supposed to have given those up.

You fool, Cami Delon.

When she reached the villa, she noticed a furniture truck out in front. Three men were unloading. Two of them carried a large box. She saw Madame Gilbert at the front door conducting traffic. Alain's grandmother held a trusted place in Raoul's heart. Naturally she did when he'd loved her daughter enough for a child to be born.

Experiencing a pang she shouldn't be feeling, Cami turned the van to head up the drive. As she passed, one of the men smiled at her with male interest, but no man could compare to the owner who'd already slipped past her defenses to make chaos of her emotions.

After parking around back, she entered the villa and found her coworkers in the kitchen. For their last job, they paired up. Cami and Patrice worked on the downstairs windows inside and out. By one o'clock, every pane in the villa had been cleaned and they were free to go. Madame Gilbert thanked them for their outstanding work before the four of them walked out in back to go home. Patrice and the others left first.

Cami got behind the wheel of her van. She'd brought a lunch, but since they'd finished work early, she would eat after she got home. After finding the keys, she started the engine. But Raoul suddenly appeared, blocking her way. Her heart jumped to her throat.

Shaking, she lowered the window. "I could have run you down!"

Laughter escaped. "I'm a little faster than that." His chiseled jaw and sensuous smile melted her bones. He came closer. With that black hair and those gleaming black eyes, he looked too marvelous in a navy pullover and khaki chinos.

"This is the first time I've seen you without your safety glasses. Has anyone ever told you those eyes are the exact lavender blue color of the flowers popping up in my family's vineyard?"

Heat surged to her cheeks. "Never, but then I don't know anyone who's had an intimate knowledge of your vineyard."

"You know *me*."

Cami couldn't believe they were having this conversation.

"Before you go, I'd like you to see the nursery and tell me what you think. The furniture company delivered everything while you were cleaning windows this morning. Do you have time?"

How could she turn him down when he sounded this eager? Cami had to be honest with herself. She'd drawn closer to him so fast, she'd been disappointed to leave without at least seeing him once more to say goodbye.

"After telling me what you'd picked out, I'm curious to see the finished product."

He seemed happy with her answer and opened

the door for her. They walked in the house. Several times their arms brushed, bringing a new awareness of him as they climbed the elegant staircase to the second floor.

"Oh—" she cried when they reached the nursery. She'd never seen a more delightful sight in her life!

The room contained the white furniture he'd talked about including a stand for diapers next to the dresser. There was also an adult rocking chair and a toy box. She spied a collection of toy cars and trucks in a basket with some other toys. Blocks filled another basket.

She loved the blend of the blue walls with white woodwork and white window shutters. A sand-and-ivory rug covered part of the pecan floor. All the wall prints and books in the bookcase added vibrant colors.

Cami chuckled over the French bulldog placed in a child's rocking chair. On a shelf in the bookcase she saw a blue-and-white toy sailboat.

She smiled at him. "This room is utterly enchanting, Raoul. What little boy in the world wouldn't want to claim it for his own?"

"I hope he'll learn to be happy here. I've spent part of every day with him since the grape harvest, but he's never lived with me."

Why? "To live morning, noon and night with his own papa who loves him? Surely you couldn't have any doubts." Yet Cami knew that he did and it tugged at her emotions to feel his vulnerability.

The sweetest sight of all was an exquisite quilt of

nursery rhyme characters hanging over the end of the crib. She moved closer to examine it.

Raoul followed. "Alain's grandmother made several quilts before he was born. The other day she gave me this one for the nursery."

"It's absolutely beautiful!"

Cami looked up at him. *Where was the boy's mother?* She was dying to know.

"Antoinette died ten days after Alain was born." Raoul had read her mind after seeing the question in her eyes.

"Oh, no—" Cami put a hand to her heart. "How tragic." All this time she'd assumed Alain's mother was still alive somewhere.

"That's her picture on the dresser."

She glanced at the propped eight-by-ten framed photograph of a beautiful brunette woman.

His former lover.

"I want him to see her face every day."

"Of course." The man had to be in love with her memory. His words brought a lump to Cami's throat.

"I didn't learn through Antoinette's stepsister Nathalie that I had an unknown son until this fall."

Unbelievable. Was the baby the reason for his divorce to the Murat woman? There was so much she didn't know about him. It was getting more complicated all the time. "How amazing and wonderful to be united with him."

His black eyes fused with hers. "You have no idea."

"Judging by this room you've created, I think I do."

"Thanks to you and your mother, plus the other

women cleaning the villa, it's ready to be lived in. You'll all receive a bonus for your hard work and doing it so fast."

"It was fun." She flashed him another smile to hide what was going on inside of her. He still had to be suffering over the loss of the woman he'd loved. "We don't often clean a place as beautiful and exclusive as this. I'm sure you're going to be very happy here with your son." After a pause, "Did you hire Mademoiselle Herve? She seemed very eager for the job."

"You know very well I didn't. I'm afraid she was too eager and too impressionable."

"She was probably nervous about the interview." Though it was none of her business, Cami let out an inward sigh. The woman hadn't been able to take her eyes off Raoul. Not that Cami could blame her since she suffered from the same affliction. "Someone else will come along who's right for you and your son. Now I'm afraid I have to leave. My mother wasn't feeling well today."

"I'm sorry to hear that."

"It's her arthritis that acts up in her shoulders. I need to pick up some dinner for her and get home."

"Then don't let me keep you. I'll walk you out."

"You don't have to do that."

"What if I want to?"

His comment sent an unbidden dart of excitement through her. They went downstairs to the kitchen and out the back door. En route she discovered that while they'd been in the nursery, the kitchen furniture had been delivered. She'd spied a high chair, a table with six chairs and two stools placed at the island.

They continued walking outside. He opened the car door for her, then spoke to her through the open window. "What does a woman who cleans for NI do on a Saturday?"

"Clean the apartment."

He broke into rich male laughter. "The proverbial busman's holiday." She nodded, enjoying their conversation way too much. "Do you live alone?"

"With my mom."

His eyes studied her features for a moment. "Unless you have other plans tomorrow, would you help me clean my study? Naturally I'll pay you for your time. I'll do the ceiling if you'll do the walls."

She wondered why he hadn't left the room open while all of them had been cleaning during the week, but it wasn't any of her business. "I could come in the morning, but I have an appointment after lunch."

"Thank you. I appreciate it more than you know. We'll be done by noon. Now I'd better let you go. When you come tomorrow, park here and I'll leave the back door open." He backed away from the van so she could drive down to the street.

Each time she passed the entrance to the Fontesquieu estate, she thought about him. But this time it conjured up his comment about her eyes being the color of the flowers that grew there.

Cami didn't want to believe he was the kind of man who flirted with every woman he met, but maybe he was like that and had picked on her because it was so easy. Any woman young or old would be wildly attracted to him. Mademoiselle Herve had been a case in point. Cami wished *she* weren't. In fact she was upset that she'd agreed so easily to help clean his study in the morning.

There were some troubling facts about his past already staring her in the face. He'd had an affair with one woman that produced a child, yet he'd married another one. Now divorced, he was taking on the responsibility of fatherhood with the son of his lover.

Where did a cleaning lady fit in this scenario except to provide a momentary distraction for him? That was all she was or could be. Maybe he flirted in order to deal with his pain over losing Antoinette and could be forgiven. Who knew?

Cami had fallen out of love long before her divorce had been finalized. Any pain had more to do with her disgust for being such a bad judge of character. Since then she'd only gone on a few dates, but no man had interested her enough to get involved, not when she was facing heart surgery.

The only thing to do was be polite to the complicated man who'd given her and her mother a job for the week. Grateful for tomorrow's extra money, she'd do the cleaning and leave. Once out of sight, out of mind.

But to her chagrin Raoul wasn't out of sight during the night. He filled her dreams. She tossed and turned, and awakened on Saturday feeling restless and sick with excitement at the thought of seeing him again.

She climbed out of bed to get ready and fastened her hair back with a tortoiseshell clip. Once dressed in jeans and a blouse, she found her mother in the kitchen and told her she'd been hired to clean his study.

"That man is interested in you. What's nice is, you're interested in him too. Have a good time."

Cami ignored her mother's comments. "I'll be back by one to get you." The two of them were going to do some shopping for friends and extended family. This was one of the few free times left before her operation. "It will be my *last* trip to the villa."

"Are you sure of that, because I'm not," she quipped.

Cami left the apartment afraid her mother was right. If he happened to ask her for another favor, she probably wouldn't be able to resist.

Saturday morning Raoul opened the back door when Cami's car appeared. Every time he saw her, it was like the first time. She had an inner and outward beauty that appealed to him on every level.

"Bonjour, Cami. Thanks for coming to help me." He walked her inside and headed for the study. He'd lined up the furniture and boxes along the hallway.

They made their way past everything to enter the room where he'd placed a drop cloth and ladder. There was a door at the end of the room that led outside to the driveway.

"I was up early and finished most of the ceiling.

You're free to start the walls. I don't think this will take us long."

Her lavender-blue eyes were charged with excitement. She put on the safety glasses and gloves to get busy. "You've done the hardest part."

"This is nothing compared to what you and your co-workers accomplished this last week. When I bought this place, I knew it needed a thorough going-over and felt sorry for you."

"It wasn't bad, Raoul. The people who lived here before left it reasonably clean. Try cleaning a half-burned house. That's a real nightmare."

Her life hadn't been easy. "I can only imagine." Once done, he climbed down and put the ladder out in the hall.

As soon as she finished the last wall, he rolled up the drop cloth and cleaned the floor. "We make a good team," he announced at last. They stood in the doorway. "The room is ready to furnish."

She eyed the oak desk. "You're going to need help moving this."

"I'll do it. Leave the heavy lifting to me."

Cami had no choice because of her heart condition, but it didn't matter. His tall, hard, fit body could handle anything and was probably the envy of most men. No woman could keep her eyes off him.

While he brought in the furniture and told her to sit on the love seat, she was able to watch him. He also brought in a file cabinet and more chairs before he pulled a framed picture out of the desk and set it on top. At the first sight of the two people in the photo, she let out a cry.

He turned to her. "What's wrong?"

"I don't believe it," she whispered and got up to get a closer look. "That's *you* with that older man!"

Raoul chuckled. "Yes, but what do you mean?"

She stared up at him, incredulous. "*You're* the young man I saw at the vineyard with this older man years ago!"

"You saw *me*? With *this* man?" He tapped the picture.

"Yes. I was twelve. I was in the car with my mother and father. We'd stopped to watch the grape pickers. You and he were walking through the vineyard talking to the workers before you headed toward a big black car waiting at the side of the road. It had a gold hood ornament."

"That was a special day for me."

"For me too. I asked my papa about the emblem and he said it meant you belonged to the Fontesquieu family. You happened to smile at me before you got in. Good heavens! *That's* why your smile seemed familiar to me on Monday when we first met in the nursery."

Raoul stared hard at her. "*You* were the pretty girl with the long glossy hair watching me from the back window. You reminded me of a black-haired Rapunzel. I couldn't figure out what you were doing inside a taxi."

She laughed. "My twelve-year-old self decided then and there you were the young prince who lived in the château."

"That's incredible." He rubbed the back of his

neck. "Even though you're grown up and your hair has been caught back, it must explain why I felt drawn to you in those first moments. We had a connection."

"I agree," she murmured. "Who's the man in the picture with you?"

"My great uncle Jerome, the man I've talked about. It was my birthday. I'd just turned fifteen and his wife took that picture of us when we returned to the château from inspecting that particular terroir in the vineyard. They'd planned a surprise for me that evening. It was one of the happiest nights of my life."

She nodded. "Seeing that photograph takes me back to a time of great happiness with my parents too. From the time I was five, Papa always took us to the vineyard in the fall. It was one of my favorite things to do with him, but because certain roads were blocked off, we could never get close enough to the château to suit me. Then he'd drive us around Vence and relate stories about its history."

"Give me a for instance," Raoul urged her. "I love hearing about your childhood."

"I remember him saying that Francis the First, the knightly prince who furnished the ash tree that still grows near the fountain in the city, loved his mother so much, he knelt before her whenever they talked."

Raoul cleared his throat. "I didn't know that fact about his mother."

"Do you think it's true?"

"We'll never know, but it makes a tender story."

"Yes. Papa loved history and knew a lot of things.

He should have lived for a long time." Her voice wobbled before she sat back down.

"His legacy lives in you, Cami. Your words have touched me to the core." He walked out in the hall and started bringing in the large boxes containing a computer and printer. Then he brought in the smaller boxes.

"Shall I help unpack those? I'm still on your clock for another hour. Let me be useful."

"Your work ethic is as unmatched as your energy. Make yourself comfortable and we'll go through them. Before we do though, I'll bring us some coffee and then we'll get started."

"That would taste good about now."

CHAPTER FOUR

ENCOURAGED THAT CAMI didn't want to leave, Raoul hurried to the kitchen and made a fresh brew. His mind kept going over the things she'd told him. The mention of the knight's mother made him realize he needed to call his own mother and try to make things better between them.

He hadn't sat next to her at the funeral, but that was because Sabine had been right there. Even if his mother understood, he wanted to explain and Cami's words reminded him he shouldn't put it off.

Filling a plate with pastries, he carried everything to the study and handed her a mug. The pastries he put on the desk, then he pulled up a chair.

She reached for one and bit into it. "Um. Just what the doctor ordered."

Raoul swallowed his coffee, then studied her for a moment. "I can tell you're wondering why I kept this room locked while you and your coworkers were cleaning."

A fetching half smile appeared. "Am I that transparent?"

"You know that old saying about eyes being mirrors of the soul."

"Afraid I do. I'll keep them closed from here on out."

Low laughter rumbled out of him. Raoul knew he was in terrible trouble where she was concerned. It was too soon to be this enamored, but he couldn't help it and decided it was time to do something about it.

"If you remember, I told you I wouldn't be accepting the CEO position."

She drank her coffee slowly. "I remember everything you told me."

"That's because I've gone into business for myself, but it's still a secret. I put these boxes in here last week and locked the door. I didn't want anyone coming to the villa and getting curious." He opened the first one and pulled out some files.

"Why are you telling *me*?"

He gave her a long side glance. "After what we've just shared, I trust you."

"That's a real compliment. Are they in alphabetical order?"

"No."

"Would you like me to arrange them?"

"Please."

She took them one at a time and made a pile next to her. "That was easy. Why don't you open another box?"

Once they got started, there was no stopping her. Soon all the boxes had been emptied and she'd put all the files in the cabinet.

"You did that fast," he commented.

She flicked her gaze to him. "Are these boxes from your office?"

"This *is* my office."

"You know what I mean."

His lips twisted into a smile. "I'm head of Fontesquieu Marketing and Sales for only a few more days. Then my ties will be severed from the whole family business."

She bit her lip. "Doesn't that disturb you a little?"

Her insights were a revelation. "If you want to know the truth, I can't wait. I've started a new company and have sent ads throughout Provence. From here on I'll be doing all business here at the villa."

"So *that's* why you didn't accept the CEO position."

One dark brow lifted. "No. That's not the reason. I would never want to be the head of the family business under any circumstances. At this point I intend to be my own man. One of the reasons I chose to buy this villa was because this study has an outdoor exit and parking around the back for clients."

"I noticed."

"It makes everything convenient without involving the rest of the household."

"Of course." She cocked her head. "Do you mind if I ask what your new business is about?"

"For years I've wanted to build a consultancy firm for people who desire to start their own vineyard, but don't know where to begin."

Cami blinked. "Kind of like their own private expert."

He smiled. "That's one way of putting it."

"You'd rather do something like that than continue to work for your family?"

"In truth, I've wanted to do it for years."

"Your knowledge will be invaluable!" she cried.

Her excitement sent chills over his body. "Maybe."

"There's no maybe about it."

He stared at her. "Why do you say that?"

"Every time I've ever driven past your family's vineyard, I've wondered how it got started and how your family continued to make it flourish over the centuries.

"To me it seems like an impossible project that would take someone brilliant to start a whole new vineyard and make it work. But you know all its secrets! No one would ever go wrong consulting you. There'd be no risk."

"There are risks, Cami, and it takes a lot of work."

"But they'd be learning from your genius."

"My great uncle was the genius. I need the journals he kept to help me, but they're with my ex-wife. One day I'll get them." A dark brow lifted. "Anytime you want, you're welcome to head my advertising department."

A gentle laugh escaped before she glanced at the cabinet. "So those files represent the people who've already responded to your ads."

"That's right."

"You've received a lot already."

"We'll see how much it grows. I've advertised under an old family name Degardelle that has no connection with the Fontesquieu family. I won't be giving away any family secrets, but I know enough about the art of raising grapevines to help others. I want something that my son can get involved in one day, if it's what he wants."

Her eyes lit up, intensifying their unique color. "He'll want to do everything *you* do, I promise you. As you now know, my papa was a *chauffeur de taxi*. As a little girl, I had a dream of owning my own taxi."

"After what you've told me, that doesn't surprise me."

"I imagined driving all sorts of interesting, fascinating people around. That was until Papa drove us to your family's estate and I saw the château for the first time from a distance."

One black brow quirked. "What happened then?"

"I thought we'd come to the land of enchantment. As I told you a few minutes ago, I imagined being the princess who lived inside with her prince."

Cami had no comprehension what this conversation was doing to him. In an earlier time, he would have loved living in the château with her. "How long did that dream last?"

"After Papa died, it stopped, but he always had the most influence over me. I'm sure your son will want to follow in your footsteps. That's how it works. Now I have to go." She stood up.

Enthralled by her conversation, the last thing he

wanted was for her to leave. She had yet to tell him about the rest of her life, her failed marriage, but now wasn't the moment to detain her. She had an appointment.

"I'll walk you out."

"Please don't bother. You've got all your computer equipment to put together. You have no idea what a pleasure it's been to work here for you. I'm glad we met and I wish you all the happiness in the world with your son."

That was a goodbye speech if Raoul had ever heard one, but he had news for her and followed her through the villa to her car. "This may be your last workday with me, but I want to go on seeing you. Tomorrow I have to run by my old office on the estate and would like to take you with me. You'll be able to see the château up close."

He'd caught her off guard. "You mean it?"

"Knowing how much you loved your father, I'm certain another visit there will have special meaning for you. I'll be with my son part of the day, so I was thinking five o'clock. I'd really like to do this for you. All I need is your address."

He could hear her mind working, but was having a heart attack waiting for her answer. Finally, "How can I possibly say no to an invitation that would mean the world to me? I'll be outside at five. I live in an eight-plex at 130 Almond Street."

Relief swept through him. "I'll be there." As he helped her get in, he brushed her lips briefly with his own before shutting the door.

* * *

Raoul's quick kiss had come as a breathtaking surprise. The touch of his mouth on hers had kept her restless all night. She was still shaken when she got up on Sunday.

Cami could no longer pretend her deepest feelings weren't involved. Meeting this man who was bigger than anything life had really thrown her. He'd created feelings in her she didn't want to have, let alone feelings she didn't believe were hers to have!

Her mom had gone out with friends earlier. Cami left a note that Raoul was going to show her the château up close this evening, but she wouldn't be late. He had his little boy to get home to. Her mother's prophecy had come true. Cami couldn't stay away.

After washing her hair, she used the blow-dryer and left it loose and curly around her shoulders. While she put on her makeup, she realized she was a far cry from Rapunzel, the golden-haired princess high up in the tower.

She put on a wraparound blue skirt and matching sweater. After grabbing her jacket, she left the apartment a few minutes early and went outside to wait. When she saw the gleaming red Jaguar pull up in front, she sucked in her breath.

Raoul got out and helped her in the passenger side. He wore a burgundy-colored pullover sweater and dark gray trousers. One covert look at him and he'd become the embodiment of her fictional, dark-haired prince living at the château.

His black eyes played over her. "You should wear

your hair long more often. It's stunning," he said before driving them down the street toward the main route leading up into the hills. His compliment had her trembling.

Cami whispered her thanks, but found it hard to comprehend that when she'd thought she'd never see him again, he'd invited her to come with him this evening. If they were headed for a relationship, her feelings for him were already over the top.

"How is your son? Did you bring him home?"

"I did, and we've been having the time of our lives. Nathalie is with him now."

"I'm thrilled for you."

Within a few minutes their drive brought them to the gate of the famous Fontesquieu estate. He turned in. Suddenly it was déjà vu. In the distance the fantastic château came into view.

"I can't believe this has been your home all your life."

"It was like living in a large zoo under one roof. In comparison, my villa is paradise."

He'd packed so much emotion into those statements, Cami felt saddened and stirred in her seat. "Every time my father brought me and my mom here, I wondered about the people who lived inside."

Raoul darted her a glance. "Besides your prince?"

Cami laughed quietly. "I was a child with a big imagination and can be forgiven."

"I assure you no prince or princess lived here. We were the same, difficult, ordinary people who live in apartments and houses throughout the world with the same flaws and imperfections that make up part of the human family."

"Please don't destroy all my illusions. I'd like to keep a few."

He chuckled. "The public isn't allowed inside, but I'll drive us around on those forbidden roads so you can see it up close."

"Where were you when we needed you?" she teased.

He reached over and squeezed her hand. It shot warmth through her body before he slowly let it go, leaving her bereft. Soon they'd come to the private road that circled next to the base of the magnificent structure.

"Does your whole family still live here?"

"You mean my grandmother, my parents, six aunts and six uncles, eighteen cousins, twelve nieces, ten nephews and a load of great grandchildren?" He pulled the car to a stop and flashed her that heart-stopping smile. "Then yes. In fact every one of them except for my cousin Dominic and myself."

She couldn't imagine it. "Does that mean you two are the rebels?"

"The family considers us the black sheep. Is it any wonder I've found pure peace at the villa?"

More than ever Cami realized what an enormous change he'd gone through to separate himself from the world he'd been born into. Her eyes took in the architecture that made the château so spectacular. "Where was your room when you were young?"

"On the third floor in the center right up there." He pointed.

She didn't want to ask where he'd lived with Sabine. "There have to be so many fun places to explore."

"Fun, yes, but I paid a price when I got caught."

Cami frowned. "Why?"

"My grandfather ruled supreme and everyone obeyed him. He wouldn't tolerate a child being a child, especially me or Dominic whom he called the ringleader since he was a year older. No noise. No friends allowed inside the château. Any play had to be done outside under supervision, and those friends had to be handpicked by our fathers because they considered us serious problems who needed discipline."

"No wonder you're so fond of Dominic."

"He and I grew closer than brothers to survive our childhood. If we did something wrong, we were separated for a week from playing together. We were also locked in our rooms without food for twelve hours so we would come to our senses."

Cami was scandalized. "Are you kidding me?"

He lifted his hands. "I swear."

"My father was so sweet to me, I feel terrible for what you had to suffer."

"That was a long time ago. If you've seen enough, I'll drive over to the office. It'll only take me a minute."

To her surprise it was housed in a large modern building behind the château. Being a Sunday, the parking lot had few cars. She marveled over the incongruity of new and old in the same panorama sweep.

He parked in front and got out. "I'll be right back."

She watched him stride inside on those strong powerful legs. No man could ever measure up to him, inside or out. He had hold of her heart.

Sure enough he returned quickly. After he climbed in behind the wheel, his smile made her feel all fluttery inside.

"Did you get what you came for?"

"I needed this." He showed her a thumb drive before putting it in his shirt pocket. "This contains valuable new client information I couldn't find earlier and didn't want anyone else getting hold of. On our way out of here I'll drive you through one of the vineyards where tourists come to taste our wine. We'll stop there for a bite to eat too. How does that sound?"

"You know how much I'd love it." Cami would have gone anywhere with him for as long as he wanted. Her moment of truth had come. She was absolutely crazy about him. It was hard to believe a man like him existed.

The rows of vines were perfectly aligned and didn't look real. It thrilled her to think he was going to help would-be vintners to choose the right property and soil in order to grow grapes. His expertise would guarantee he'd make a huge success of his new company. Cami had no doubt he'd be touted forever. It was a privilege to know him.

Her eyes widened when he slowed down near a château much smaller than the main one that offered the delights of the Fontesquieu vineyard to the public. There were dozens of cars surrounding the structure.

"One of my jobs growing up was to run this place one summer."

"Did you like it?"

"Let's just say I learned a lot toward my later job of becoming head of Sales and Marketing. It surprised me how many people, women and men, love to talk about wine, the dreams they have about the perfect wine and what they prefer. Some of them wanted to start a vineyard of their own. I gained insights I wouldn't have had otherwise. But enough about the past. It's time to feed you and enjoy a little wine."

Little did Raoul know it, but he'd fed her in so many ways today, she never wanted any of it to end.

He led her around the side to a private entrance that took them inside a tasting room with arched ceilings and all sorts of signs with writings about wine. She found it fascinating.

Raoul found them a table, and an aproned man at the bar walked over. "*Eh bien*, Raoul. What can I get for you?" The man's gaze kept eyeing Cami.

"Your tapas and drinks from my special *bouteille*."

"*Tout de suite.*"

"Auguste couldn't keep his eyes off you," Raoul whispered after the other man had gone.

"You're imagining things." But his comment excited her. She started looking around and began laughing when she read one of the signs near their table.

Raoul smiled. "Which one amuses you?"

"The Baudelaire quotation."

Without looking at it he said, "One should always be drunk. That's all that matters. But with what? With wine, with poetry, or with virtue as you choose. But get drunk!"

They both laughed. When it stopped, the way he was looking at her made her senses swim. For the next half hour they ate delicious fish hors d'oeuvres and sipped his favorite rose sherry.

"Try it," he urged her, studying her mouth.

"All right." She drank a little. "Um. It's really delicious."

"Can you detect the rich, ripe fruit flavors of vanilla, strawberry, pomelo and tangerines?"

"I think I can taste strawberry."

He smiled. "I find this particular vintage at it's perfect sweetness." He leaned closer to brush his lips against hers. "Almost as sweet as your mouth glistening from the sherry."

His kiss turned her body to liquid and she was so entranced, she forgot the time. But it had to come to an end.

Raoul took her to the car and they left for her apartment. Filled with good food and wine, she couldn't bear to have to say good-night, but his son would be waiting for him at the villa. Cami knew Raoul was anxious to get home to him.

He cupped her elbow as he walked her to the apartment door. She raised her eyes to him. "Thank you for the private tour of your estate and the delicious dinner. I'll remember it always."

"I'll never forget this Sunday evening either. Expect a call from me tomorrow. We have a lot to talk about." In the next breath he lowered his head and gave her a lingering kiss she couldn't help but respond to before he strode swiftly to his car.

Cami stood there shaking from the sensations he'd aroused in her before she found the strength to go inside. Her mom still wasn't back yet, but it was only ten, which was just as well. Cami wanted to go to bed and savor what had happened this evening.

Raoul returned to the villa, aching with desire for Cami. He had plans for them tomorrow, but when he sat down at his computer before going to bed, he faced a mass of emails from clients he'd serviced over the years. They were waiting for him to get back from vacation so life could return to normal with him overseeing everything.

Raoul should have anticipated that reaction and realized it was time to clarify his situation. First, he called the Fleur-de-Lis Hotel in Fréjus. After reserving their largest conference room for tomorrow afternoon and evening, he reserved two rooms for Monday night.

With that done he phoned Jean-Pierre to tell him what was going on. It was time to make his cousin's position official as head of Sales and Marketing.

Between the two of them they sent emails throughout Provence to as many clients who could come. Those who couldn't make it would hear about it. Though it was short notice, he decided it was better to put out the fire ASAP. The move would be a fait accompli by the time his father heard about it.

On Monday morning he got up early to feed Alain and swim with him. Nathalie had stayed the night and agreed to stay for the day After the three of them had lunch, he packed and left for the thirty-minute drive to Fréjus.

En route he sent Cami a text that he'd gone out of town, but would call her on Tuesday to make plans. She'd be cleaning so he didn't want to bother her with a phone call. It was hard to have to wait another day to see her, but he needed to get this out of the way.

Jean-Pierre met him and they set up the large room. Before long the clients trickled in. The place was soon filled, which was very satisfying to Raoul. These were men and women he'd worked with for years.

When it was time, he walked up to the microphone. "Thank you for coming on such short notice, but my life has completely changed and you deserve to know what's going on.

"I have a son named Alain who's almost nineteen months old. He's come to live with me for good while I've been on vacation. I've entered a new phase of my life as a single man and can no longer work for the family business. He needs my full attention. But I know you're going to approve of my successor. After dinner is served, we'll both be on hand to talk to all of you."

He turned to his cousin. "Jean-Pierre Fontesquieu? Come on up here so I can officially introduce you as head of Marketing and Sales for the entire Fontesquieu Company. Not only are we cousins, we've worked together for years. He's been in charge while I've been on vacation and is the man who has my backing 100 percent."

As everyone stood and clapped, Raoul patted him on the shoulder. "It's your turn," he whispered with a smile.

No one could know what it meant to have this over and done. He truly was free now to embrace his new life with his son and the woman who was already necessary to his existence.

CHAPTER FIVE

ON MONDAY AFTERNOON Cami received the disappointing text that Raoul was out of town and would call her tomorrow. That must have been a sudden move on his part. She hoped he was all right. Somehow she got through the rest of the day, but couldn't wait until she saw him again.

Her sense of loss had grown acute by the time she and her mom returned to the apartment at the end of the day. No sooner had they walked inside than their neighbor Suzanne, the widow next door, was at the door.

"These flowers arrived for you. Just a minute. There are more." She was back in a minute. "Lucky you! Now I have to run, but I want to hear the story behind these later."

They thanked her and put the flowers on the coffee table. Cami took the paper off the first one. A gasp escaped her lips when she saw a vase filled with a dozen long-stemmed lavender roses, so exquisite they took her breath.

Another cry came from her mother who'd discovered a basket of yellow daisies called marguerites that looked like summer. She looked up at Cami.

"Is there any doubt where these came from?"

Cami smelled the roses with their heavenly bouquet. At this rate, that bad heart of hers needed an operation tomorrow. "No."

"That must have been quite an evening you had at the vineyard with Raoul Fontesquieu last night."

"He took me to see the château up close and then we had a meal at the wine-tasting château."

Her mother smiled. "And on Saturday you helped him clean his study."

Cami nodded.

"He not only looks the part, he's every woman's idea of perfection."

Don't remind me, Maman.

She reached for the card inserted in the roses.

"What does it say?" her mom asked.

"*'You've brought light into my life. R.'*"

A little shiver ran through her body before Cami glanced at her mother. "What did he write to you?"

"*'Thank you for an outstanding job despite the pain in your shoulders. Raoul Fontesquieu.'*" She eyed Cami with uncommon interest. "He says and does everything right, doesn't he?"

"Yes. But what you've just said makes me suspicious. It's all happening too fast."

"Why do you look so troubled?" her mother prodded. "Does this have anything to do with your ex?"

"Maybe somewhere deep down I don't trust my own feelings after my bad marriage."

"Then talk to me. Come on."

Cami sank down on one of the chairs, remembering the last kiss Raoul had given her. She still trembled from it. "He walked me to the door and said he'd call me today. Then he sent a text that he'd gone out of town.

"Now I see these roses. I feel like I'm spinning out of control and still have so many questions about him."

Her mother sat down opposite her. "Like what?"

"For starters, he has a toddler son he only learned about this fall. In the nursery he's put a picture on the dresser of his lover who died after the baby was born. He's barely divorced. I have no idea if he was unfaithful to his former wife or not.

"I can't help but wonder how many other vulnerable women have been left in his wake—women hoping for life everlasting with a man like him. The nanny who came for an interview couldn't take her eyes off him. Her behavior reminded me of myself."

"Give it time and you'll learn a lot more about him."

"I'm afraid to learn more and then find out I was a detour along the way." Cami was already disturbed at the thought of his losing interest in her. "It might be better if I never see him again, that is if he calls me again." He would haunt her dreams forever, but she didn't dare open herself up for possible heartache when she was already facing a personal health crisis.

Her mom walked over and hugged her. "Christophe hurt you."

"At first, Maman. But after I realized I'd made a terrible mistake to marry him, I was no longer in pain. He was a child and always will be. With hindsight I realized I'd gone into that marriage so young because I'd wanted security after losing Papa. Christophe was too immature to handle any crisis, especially the fact that my heart murmur wasn't getting better."

A wince marred her mother's brow.

"On the surface, Raoul Fontesquieu appears to be heaven's gift to women and has more money than most of us can imagine. But because of my former experience, I need to be aware of the warning signs— like that picture of his lover—and not get any more involved with him.

"Soon my life will be going in a brand-new direction. Depending on a positive result of my operation, which I worry about, I'll be working at Gaillard's, and be able to take care of both of us. You need a rest."

"That's not your job, Cami."

"Why not? You've sacrificed for me all these years. It's my turn."

"But there will come a time when—"

"I don't think so, Maman," she interrupted her. "I have to get through the operation first and find out the chances for survival. Forget thinking about a mythical man in my future. He would have to be the antithesis of someone like Raoul Fontesquieu with his complicated life and background.

"His type comes from another planet, let alone a different cultural postal code from mine, and has so much family baggage you can't wade your way through it. I have to face reality. If a man does show up—that is if I have a future—and he isn't trustworthy or can't add richness to the solid life I'm planning to establish, then I don't want him under any circumstances."

She kissed her mom. "I'm going to get ready for bed and read for a while. We're facing another workday tomorrow. Get a good sleep."

"Don't you want to put the flowers in your bedroom?"

"It wouldn't be a good idea."

Cami went back to her bedroom deep in thought. At eighteen she'd thought marriage would make her blissfully happy. How wrong could she have been? Shouldn't she have learned some lessons that would prevent her making another serious mistake?

On Saturday while she'd been arranging those files in his study, for a moment she'd found herself fantasizing about the tall, dark, prince-like Raoul Fontesquieu on the opposite end of the spectrum. There was no question he seemed to be and have everything she'd dreamed about after her father had taken them to see the château and grounds. But there was a glaring divide that excluded her.

He was born to that billionaire class of people and culture who could have whatever they wanted, who'd recently divorced with a love child in tow from the beautiful woman whose picture sat on Alain's dresser.

Raoul was obviously estranged from his family and the stories he'd told her explained why. Any day now he expected to cut himself off from them. There had to be serious trouble inside that dynasty for the media to print news about him that wasn't true. Since their conversation, she understood why he didn't want to live in the château that was a treasure of France, an iconic symbol some people would sell their souls to inhabit.

Even with her empathy for him, could she bring herself to trust a man like Raoul Fontesquieu? How would he react if he knew about her heart condition? Right now he was attracted to her. Would his attraction for Cami be fleeting until he found another woman he wanted to be with? Possibly one from his own strata?

Cami had made up her mind that until her heart gave out, she needed to survive in her own strata. If she couldn't become independent on her own, then she would have no one to blame but herself. With her father gone and a marriage dissolved a long time ago, she'd be a fool to go on trusting her growing feelings for Raoul if he didn't feel the same way. Part of her felt like she didn't have the right to his love.

On Tuesday Cami left for work with her mom. Raoul said he'd call her today. Maybe, maybe not. She missed him horribly and began to wonder if those roses had been his way of saying goodbye to her, just as she'd feared.

While she and her mom sat out in the van to eat lunch, her phone rang. It made her jump before she pulled it out of her purse and discovered it was Raoul. Just the sight of his name started her heart thumping.

"If that's who I think it is, I'll go inside while you answer it." Her mother was out of the car in an instant.

Cami clicked On. "Raoul?" She tried to keep the tremor out of her voice.

"I hope it's the right time to phone you."

"Of course. I'm eating my lunch."

"I would have called sooner but I've been out of town and just got back. The villa isn't the same without you being here. Are you free tonight? I thought we'd take a drive along the *côte* and eat dinner somewhere. There are things I want to talk about with you."

Her body reacted as if she'd suddenly been hit by a bolt of electricity. "I'd love to do that." Despite all her fears, she realized there weren't many more days before her operation. She had to admit she wanted to spend every free moment with Raoul.

"How soon can you be ready?"

"By six thirty."

"Perfect. *À tout à l'heure, ma belle.*"

He'd never used an endearment like that with her before. She hung up so excited, her feet hardly touched the ground as she went back in the house to join her mother. On their way home at the end of the day, Cami told her that Raoul was taking her out for the evening. She could tell her mother was happy about it.

Before he picked her up, she showered and washed her hair, leaving it loose. After blow-drying it, she picked out a skirt and sweater in shades of tan and white and spent time doing her makeup.

This time Cami waited until he came to the door. She invited him in because her mother wanted to thank him for the flowers. Once he'd ensconced her in the car, she turned to him.

"As my mother told you, she loved her marguerites. No one has sent her flowers since Papa died. You couldn't have done anything nicer for her."

"That's because I'm grateful for all your hard work."

"Those lavender roses are so exquisite, they take my breath away."

"I have the same reaction when I look into your eyes. I'm glad you like them. If the hyacinths in the vineyard were in bloom, I'd have sent you an armful."

"You're much too generous."

He started the car and they headed for the main route out of Vence. "You have no idea how I've been living for this evening. I thought we'd drive to Beaulieu and eat dinner on the water at a wonderful little spot that serves delectable cod croquettes you'll love."

"I was already hungry before you told me that."

"Good. The whole time I was in Fréjus, I was planning out what we'd do when I got back."

"What were you doing there?"

"News of my leaving the family business has reached all our clients. Some have been upset, so I arranged for a conference to meet with many of them and introduce them to Jean-Pierre."

"How did it go?"

"Very well."

She eyed him steadily. "No one could ever measure up to you, Raoul. I'm not surprised they're upset."

"No one boosts my confidence the way you do." He reached for her hand and held it all the way to the sea. His warmth spread through her body.

The delightful little restaurant in the coastal village looked magical with its patio heaters. The place was crowded, but Raoul had reserved them a table overlooking the water. True to his word, the cod was out of this world, as was the Fontesquieu wine he'd handpicked.

"I have a confession to make," he said after they'd finished their meal.

Cami had no idea what was coming next.

"I almost phoned your manager at NI on Saturday to ask her to talk to you on Monday about being my part-time housekeeper until you left for the holidays on the sixteenth."

Cami was stunned by the news.

"I planned to tell her I needed one and wondered if you'd like the position. It's true that I need someone on the premises now that I'm working at home. Not all day every day. Maybe twice a week. Arlette served that purpose for the last two weeks, but she's back working at her pharmacy now."

Somehow that was the last thing Cami would ever have expected to hear. She averted her eyes. For a moment she was speechless. *And hurt.* She'd thought— oh, she didn't know exactly what she'd thought, but it wasn't to take over for Arlette!

She'd thought it odd when he'd asked her to help clean his study on Saturday. What did he *really* want? Cami had done nothing but think about him since Sunday night. Now this—What was going on?

"Raoul—"

"Don't say anything," he interrupted her. "I only

told you this to let you see how desperate I am to be with you morning, noon and night. Surely by now you must realize you're the woman I'm so attracted to. I only want to be with you.

"For the week you were cleaning, I knew I'd see you every day. But after it was over, I didn't want it to end so I thought up the idea of asking you to be my housekeeper. But of course, that's not what I want at all. Now you know the truth of my feelings."

In the last minute he'd taken her emotions on a giant roller coaster ride. While she was still trying to catch up to the fact that he wanted a relationship with her, he said, "I hope it's clear that I need to be with you as much as possible, but I know you have to work during the day. The only solution is to be with you every evening and on weekends or I'm not going to make it. Please tell me you want the same thing."

She took a deep breath. "I wouldn't be having dinner with you tonight if I'd wanted to stop seeing you."

"*Dieu merci* for that. Come on. I'll drive you home because I know work comes early for you in the morning."

They walked back out to his car. She felt like she was in a dream. He reached for her hand once more and clung to it all the way to the apartment. At the front door he drew her into his arms and kissed her thoroughly. Cami couldn't get enough of him.

"Thank you for this evening, Raoul. I do love being with you."

He buried his face in her hair. "Tomorrow will

you come to the villa after your work and bring your bathing suit?"

"Is your indoor pool ready to use?"

"Yes. You can help me christen it with Alain."

She finally eased away from him, but it was almost impossible to stop kissing him back. "That's exciting. I'll probably get there by five thirty."

"I'll leave the back door unlocked for you. I can't wait," he murmured before walking out to his car.

Cami went inside and closed the door.

"Cami?"

She reeled around. "I'm home."

Her mother walked into the salon in her robe and sat in a chair. "How was your evening?"

Cami couldn't lie to her mom and sank down on the couch. "Wonderful." She told her what he'd said about wanting to hire her for his housekeeper before admitting to the real reason why. "Sounds like Raoul is infatuated, and has been totally honest with you. Have you told him about your heart condition?"

"No."

"That's because of your ex's reaction."

The problem with talking to her mother was that she knew Cami's fears and secrets way too well and was about as subtle as a sledgehammer.

"Christophe knew I had a heart murmur, but he never thought about it until after we were married and he wanted me to do one of those fun run marathons with him. When I told him I couldn't, he freaked out when he heard the reason why and wouldn't even talk to me about it sensibly. He didn't treat me the same after that. We'd been divorced over two years before my symptoms indicated I'd eventually have to undergo an operation."

Her mom leaned forward. "Even more reason why you should let Raoul know your situation the next time you're with him. He's fallen for you."

"What if he freaks out too?"

"Raoul Fontesquieu is a strong man who won't fall apart. But if you don't tell him and he finds out you held back, then he might not trust you. That could doom your relationship."

"I'm already doomed."

Her mother scoffed.

"Maman—have you forgotten I have to get through the operation? We don't know if I'll be able to live a full life or take that job at Gaillard's. I might not even leave the hospital," her voice faded.

"Nonsense. I know you're going to be fine."

"No—you *don't* know! None of us, not even the doctor can predict what will happen."

"That's true," she came back. "But the thought of losing my precious daughter is something I refuse to consider. So please do me this favor and tell him the truth soon."

On Wednesday morning, Raoul woke up to play with his son, relieved that Cami would be coming to the villa this evening. Last Saturday while she'd worked alongside him, Raoul had found himself enamored of her. It was no longer just a physical attraction.

In meeting Cami, he'd started to come alive again.

As he'd told her, he'd been developing a new consulting business to do with wine not connected with Fontesquieu. Raoul knew his father was enraged over the divorce and for his noncompliance as CEO, but that didn't worry him.

Now that he'd cut himself off from the family business, Raoul already had his own resources to do something that would bring income and a sense of pride over what his great uncle—a scientist, vine culture expert and artist—had envisioned years before. He wanted to build this into a legacy for Alain.

Cami not only applauded his ideas, she'd assured him his son would follow him anywhere. Just remembering what she'd said put a smile on his face. To envision her driving around Vence in her own taxi came close to giving him a heart attack. Her engaging personality was like no one else's.

Feelings and desires that had been buried for the last few years had come back. His mind told him he wasn't practicing enough caution with Cami, but at this point his heart was driving him and trumped everything else.

Frustrated that she wouldn't be coming to the villa anymore to work, he'd asked her out to dinner last night so he could express his feelings. To his joy she'd agreed to come swimming. Tonight, he would open up his heart to her.

At five, he went upstairs to shower and shave. Cami would be arriving any minute. Alain was in the playroom with Nathalie. He came back down to the kitchen. Through the window he saw her Citroën approach.

His pulse went into high gear. He loved her hair flowing, but once again her lustrous black tresses had been caught back in a chignon. She got out wearing another pair of jeans and an ivory-colored pullover that revealed her lovely shape. He opened the back door to let her in.

She entered and looked around. The room was cluttered with boxes full of all the things needed to supply a functioning kitchen. They needed to be opened.

Through her black lashes those hyacinth eyes met his. "What's all this?"

"Nathalie and Arlette picked out all these items at the store. It needs to be sorted and put away. I'll get around to it when I have time, but I'm afraid that living at the château all my life didn't teach me to deal with these logistics."

She smiled. "The fact that you were asked to be CEO proves your talents were better spent outside the kitchen."

"I guess we'll never know. The coffee's hot. I've poured you a mug."

"Thank you."

"Just give me a moment and I'll be right back."

Cami had to pinch herself to believe she was here again when she'd thought she'd seen the last of him. While she was sipping the hot liquid, she heard footsteps. Suddenly Raoul entered the kitchen with the cutest little boy she'd ever seen in her life.

With curly black hair and a lean build, his son Alain couldn't belong to any other man and would grow up to be impossibly handsome like his striking father. Both were in jeans and T-shirts. Alain wore a light blue one with a bulldog on the front.

Raoul flashed her a smile and hunkered down by him. "Alain, this is Cami."

Her heart melted as she leaned toward him and smiled. Talk about the perfect child! What she would have given for a son like this, but not when she'd been in a bad marriage.

"Bonjour, Alain—" *You darling boy.* Obeying an impulse, she touched the dog on his shirt. "I like your *chien.*"

He didn't hide from her. Instead he stood very still, staring at her through piercing black eyes exactly like his father's.

"I'm planning to get him a bulldog as soon as I can find the right nanny and she gets settled in. We'll all train it together."

"They're a lot of work, but they're wonderful."

"I wanted one all my life, but there was a no pets rule while I was growing up."

"Really? More than once I heard my father say a child needed a dog."

"Not all parents feel the same way."

She frowned. "That's no fun, Raoul. We had two dogs while I was growing up. I'd get home from school and play with them for hours."

He smiled. "Lucky you."

"I know I was, especially because I didn't have any siblings. When the last one died, we didn't get another one because by then I was married. Then after the divorce, I started working with my mom. We didn't get a new dog because we couldn't give it the attention it deserves."

"That's not going to be our problem around here," Raoul murmured.

"A boy and his dog. Could anything be cuter?" She reached for her purse on the counter and pulled out the little present she'd bought for his son at a toy store on the way here. "You were so excited about Alain coming home to live with you, I wanted to get this for him in celebration. This is for your nursery collection." Cami had noticed he didn't have a white toy car.

Raoul's eyes thanked her as he took it from her and unwrapped it. "Look, Alain. A white Porsche Cabriolet. You couldn't have bought him anything more exciting."

Alain's attention fastened on the car before reaching for it. In the next instant he got down on the floor with it and started pushing it around making funny sounds she was sure his father had taught him. That brought laughter from both of them.

"I can tell you've already been teaching him the important things of life, Raoul." His eyes met hers in amusement, causing her heart to beat faster. "I don't know what it is about men. They all love sports cars. I have to admit I love them too." But she'd never had the fun of driving in one. Her friends and acquaintances couldn't afford them.

His burning black eyes played over her, sending sensations of warmth through her body. "I'm hoping he'll love to swim too. I'm giving him his first lesson in our indoor swimming pool."

"Are you sure you want anyone else there while you're teaching him?"

He cocked his dark head. "I'm thinking if he sees someone else swimming, it will give him courage."

"That's a thought, but I'm only an average swimmer." The doctor hadn't told her to curtail her normal activities, but he'd cautioned her not to overdo. As well as instructing she should do no heavy lifting or running marathons, he'd said she shouldn't take part in swimming meets either.

An enticing smile broke the corner of his mouth. "All it takes is a little practice."

"I'm sure that's true." This could be the last time she ever went swimming in her life, let alone with this man she adored. Raoul had to be the most eligible, hunky male on the planet. "How about I just dangle my legs over the edge of the pool."

Raoul's eyes flickered. "You won't get any complaints from me."

Why did she have to say that?

"After our swim we'll have a meal in the kitchen that you and your coworkers have made shine."

She hadn't been imagining it. Last night Raoul had told her he wanted to be with her all the time, but it could be a very short-lived relationship. It all depended on the result of the operation.

"Come upstairs with us first and I'll get him changed. Then we'll go down. We want company, don't we, *mon gars*?"

It was crazy, but there was nothing in the world she wanted more than to be with him like this. "Let's go."

When they reached the nursery, Raoul put the Porsche on the dresser and pulled a little swimsuit out of the drawer with baby sharks on it.

Cami chuckled. "Did you buy this?"

There was a glint in his eyes. "I couldn't resist." He lowered Alain in the crib and put a clean diaper on him like he'd been doing it forever, then followed with the suit. Alain kept staring at her.

"I'll take him to my bedroom while I change. You would know there's a bathroom off the hall with towels outside the indoor pool. You can change in there and we'll meet at the pool."

She hurried off with a throbbing pulse and discovered the luxurious bathroom that now contained every amenity and a supply of beach towels. Someone had been busy adding all the furnishings. Cami removed her jeans and blouse. She's brought her modest blue bikini.

On her way out the door she reached for three towels and went to the pool.

Raoul had beaten her there and was pushing his son around on a blue inflatable raft. Fully clothed or in a swimsuit, he had to be the most exciting-looking male alive with a dusting of black hair on his chest.

She felt those matching black eyes appraise her as she walked to the shallow end. After putting the towels on a deck chair, she sat on the top step of the pool.

Alain saw her and pointed. "That's Cami," his father said. "Can you say Cami?"

"Cam—" he blurted to her delight.

"That's right, Alain," she cried. "I bet you're having fun with your papa." Her gaze darted to Raoul's. "Has he ever been swimming?"

He pulled Alain off the raft and moved closer. "Nathalie took him to a pool a couple of times during the summer, but that's the sum total of his experience."

She noticed how tender he was with his son, swishing him around in the water at the shallow end without alarming him. In a minute she slipped in the warm water and swam by them. Raoul urged him to kick his legs. Cami stretched out alongside and kicked her legs too. Pretty soon Alain got so excited Raoul's laughter resounded in the pool room.

She swam over to them. "Shall we watch your papa?" Cami instinctively reached for Alain.

CHAPTER SIX

RAOUL WAS EXCITED to see that his son went to her
willingly and didn't cry for him.

"Let's see how big a splash *he* can make," she said
to him.

Raoul sent her a smile before he starting swimming on his back. His legs and feet created a geyser
that fascinated her and Alain. "Papa—"

"That's right, Alain. Your papa didn't tell us he
was an Olympic champion!"

More laughter escaped Raoul's lips. It was all too
fun. In another minute he joined them and put Alain
through another series of kicking exercises. She swam
to the raft and pushed it over to Raoul. He lifted Alain
onto it so he could move him around again.

She followed them while Raoul made figure eights
and circles. Alain was loving it. So was he. In fact
this was the most fun he'd had in ages.

"You really are an amazing swimmer. Did the château have a swimming pool?"

"No. I wish there'd been one. On occasion I was
allowed to swim on the estate of a friend my family

approved of. In my midteens Dominic and I swam in the ocean when we finished our vineyard work. That's another reason I bought this villa. My son is going to be able to swim whenever he wants."

"He's taking to it already."

Raoul pushed Alain on the raft toward her. "I want him to love his life growing up. I wasn't as happy at home or at school."

Cami pushed Alain back to him, causing him to laugh. "Why didn't you like school? I love hearing about your life."

"You already know a lot. The private school I attended was structured the way my grandfather ran everything."

"In other words, you didn't get a break."

"Not until college."

"Where did you go?"

"I went to the Institute of Vine and Wine Science in Bordeaux."

"Bordeaux? So you really got away from here. How did you manage that?"

He smiled. "Jerome's wife, Danie, was born in Bordeaux. Decades ago Jerome went to a wine conference there and happened to visit her family's vineyard. The two met and married. In time she inherited a small château. They visited it once in a while.

"When I turned eighteen, they prevailed on my grandfather and father to let me go live with them while I studied at the institute. It was understood we'd all be back to live at the château and I would work for the family. Living with them during that time was one of the happier periods of my life."

"So the Degardelle name comes from her side of the family."

"Your mind doesn't forget a thing, does it? Yes, that was one of her family names that goes way back. I'd love to tell you more, but Alain is starting to fuss and it's time to go in. We've been out here long enough and he's hungry. I think we all are. I'll meet you in the kitchen and feed him before putting him down."

He watched her hurry out of the pool and wrap a towel around her beautiful body before she disappeared.

"Alain must have gone down easily," Cami said as Raoul came in the kitchen soon after.

"Yes. He ate fast and all the exercise wore him out." A minute later he'd put salad and sandwiches on the table and joined her.

"He's wonderful, Raoul, and so well behaved I'm impressed." Cami started eating.

"That's Arlette's and Minerve's doing."

"If you can't find the right nanny, would this Minerve agree to go on doing it?"

"No. She lives with her family in La Gaude. I'm in the process of looking for one who lives in Vence."

She sat back in the chair. "Since she's been with Alain from the beginning, that's not going to be easy."

Raoul shook his head. "I've already interviewed five candidates, but no one seems right yet. Especially not the last one." They both smiled in understanding. He finished one sandwich and started a second one.

"It must be difficult to trust another person to take care of your son. I don't envy you."

He focused his attention on her. "I haven't thanked you for the Porsche you gave Alain. As you noticed, he loved it."

"He was so cute. What I could see was the bond you two have. I'm happy for you. It won't be long before he's swimming circles around you. Now I have to leave."

"I know you have work tomorrow. Cami? Do you ever want to do anything else that isn't so physically demanding all the time?"

"Why do you ask?"

Raoul thought she'd paled a little and noticed the troubled look that crossed over her features. "I'm sorry if I offended you, Cami. It's just that you work so hard every day, it seems like you rarely get a break. But I didn't mean to impl—"

"You didn't offend me," she broke in. "You would never do that. It's just that your question surprised me because I'll actually be starting a new job after the holidays."

"What do you mean *new*? Is it with a different cleaning company?"

"No. I'll be working in the finance department at La Maison de Chocolat Gaillard."

Gaillard? It was probably the biggest historic candy company in Southern France with headquarters in Nice. One of their branches was here in Vence.

Fabrice Gaillard, the CEO, was a friend of Raoul's father. They were the same kind of formidable men who belonged to the same exclusive bridge club only a few elites were permitted to join.

He sat forward. "Now you've got me mystified."

A smile broke out on her lovely face. "Let me start at the beginning so you can understand how I got into cleaning. After my pathetic ten-month marriage, I divorced my husband."

"You said it was over fast."

"I should never have married him. We met while we were both in a play in high school for our drama class. It was a watered-down version of *Le Vicomte de Bragelonne*, better known as *The Man in the Iron Mask*. I played a maid and Christophe took the role of a groom of one of the Musketeers."

"The Dumas tales are some of my favorites," Raoul interjected.

"Mine too. We had a lot of fun and performed for four nights. Between the costumes and all the makeup, it was very exciting. He was cute and loaded with personality. Everyone liked him, especially the girls.

"After it was over, we started seeing each other until we became inseparable. He brought excitement into my life and I was convinced I'd fallen in love. We wanted to get married." She flicked Raoul a glance. "Big mistake."

Raoul eyed her intently. "Why didn't it work?"

"Naively, I thought he wanted a real marriage. I intended to be the best wife possible. We got married midsummer and moved in with his parents. He had a Vespa and we got around on that until we could afford to buy a car. He was an only child. They had room at their house and insisted we live with them until we got on our feet."

"You liked them?"

"Yes, but by the end of our first month I was unhappy."

He squinted. "Only a month?"

She nodded. "By then I knew our marriage was never meant to be. He'd lost his job at a car body shop. I found out later he'd been going in late and not finishing his work. He was a child who liked to play too much. Christophe wanted things, but he didn't have the money to pay for them."

"How did you manage?"

"I got a job at a *librairie* and sold books."

His brows went up. "So it was *you* who brought home the paycheck."

"Yes, and his parents provided a home for us. He applied for another job at an *epicier* and kept it for a while. But one night he came home drunk, and confessed he'd lost that job. I found out later he'd gotten involved with a girl who worked there."

Her story was a terribly sad one. "I'm *desolé* for you, Cami."

"Things went from bad to worse. When I found out he'd been with another girl and couldn't hold on to his next job, that was it. We weren't going to make it. Thankfully I hadn't gotten pregnant and couldn't believe I'd gotten myself into such a bad situation. He had no desire to go to college or learn a trade. I told him I wanted a divorce."

"How did that go over?"

"He took off. That was his way when he couldn't cope. Of course he always came back to his parents when he ran out of money. At that point I didn't care and went to court to obtain a divorce with the money I'd earned at the bookstore. Then I moved back in with Maman."

"How could he have let you go? I can't comprehend it." Raoul couldn't imagine it. "Didn't he try to fight you on it?"

"Not Christophe." She started to say something else, then held back. There was still something she wasn't telling him. He had an idea it was important. Cami had sounded far away from him just now. Raoul knew a serious issue of some kind was going on inside of her that had nothing to do with her disastrous marriage seven years ago.

"We've talked about your divorce, but I didn't ask if there's someone else in your life now." He didn't really believe it, not after the way she'd returned his kisses, but he had to ask.

"More like some*thing* else."

"You mean your new job."

After a slight hesitation he heard her say, "Yes. I intend to succeed."

Again Raoul had the impression there was more she wasn't telling him. Before long he intended to find out what it was.

"As we both found out, not all marriages are happy ones, Cami."

"You're right. I quit my job and started going to work with Maman cleaning houses. That's how my cleaning career got started. The pay was so much better and paid the insurance. When I'd saved enough money to pay for the first semester, I enrolled in business and finance at Sophie Antipolis University in Nice."

His thoughts reeled. "That means you had to be a top student in high school."

"My high school English teacher encouraged me to work hard and apply for a scholarship."

"And you got it."

She nodded. Cami's modesty was another quality he admired about her. After their first meeting, she hadn't come on to him at all, or try to impress him. Nothing flirtatious. Just the opposite in fact. That quality made him want her more and intrigued him.

"I told you my father was a taxi driver. He suffered from the fact that neither he nor my mother ever went to college. Both of them impressed upon me the need to get good grades and attend university since neither of their families had ever gone for higher education."

"Your mother must be so proud, but I'm sorry your father still isn't alive to see what you've accomplished."

"Me too. Anyway, I matriculated and commuted by bus. I'd work with Maman for one semester to earn money, then attend the university for one semester. I told you our boss at NI was terrific. She let me work when I could. After seven years, I've taken my last exams and graduated mid-November."

Raoul sat there in shock. The patience and determination she'd displayed to get to this point made her outstanding in his eyes. "You didn't just get a job there. It means you must have graduated with highest honors."

She brushed it off. "What matters now is to prove myself. I was an intern there for the last semester and will be working in the same accounting department as before."

"Even those intern jobs are handpicked." He shook his head. "The way I've seen you work around here has been a revelation. I have no doubts they'll be thankful they hired you."

"Thank you, Raoul. Give me ten years and we'll see if all that schooling was worth it. Now I'm afraid I really have to go." She got up from the table. "Thank you for everything."

"I don't want you to leave." Raoul followed her out to the car. "You look so beautiful out here with the light shining from the window." He kissed her hungrily and heard her moan of desire, igniting his passion. "I don't know how I'm going to let you drive away, but I realize I have to."

"The last thing I want to do is leave, Raoul." They kissed again, both of them breathless before she got in the car.

"Your presence in the pool made a difference with Alain."

"It was so much fun with him."

"I know he enjoyed you. We'll do it again soon. As for tomorrow evening, will you let me pick you up around five thirty or six? We'll have dinner and drive around to see the sound and light show in Vence. The car will keep us warm."

"That sounds fabulous."

He kissed her once more and shut the door before waving her off.

Raoul was in a daze when he walked in the villa. She was a college graduate with honors and would be starting to work at Gaillard's in January. She'd worked so hard for everything all her life. What an incredible woman. Tomorrow night he wanted to do something special to surprise and honor her. For that to happen, he needed to make a certain phone call.

On Thursday evening Cami and her mom returned to the apartment after work and she got ready to go out with Raoul. Her thoughts were focused on his life that had been so different than she had imagined.

Being with him made her long to be with him all the time, which was an impossibility if she didn't have a clean bill of health. That's what was troubling about daring to dream.

"*Non*, Maman," she said before her mother could ask her if she'd told the truth to Raoul. "But I'll tell him soon." With that promise, she hurried to shower and get ready.

She knew her mom was right, especially after the scare she'd had last evening when Raoul had asked her about continuing with her cleaning career. For a moment she'd feared he'd somehow figured out something was wrong with her physically.

Cami couldn't put it off any longer, but wondered if her parent was being too optimistic about the success of the operation. Cami might not have a good recovery and wouldn't be able to take the position at Gaillard's after all.

She might turn into an invalid with a shorter life span. How would Raoul feel about that? What if Cami was one of the small percentage that died during the procedure? Not everyone survived a heart operation, even if they'd been in excellent health otherwise.

She'd read stories on the internet that had frightened her. In the dark hours of the night she'd sometimes wake up in a cold sweat worrying that something could go wrong. The doctor had advised her not to dwell on the negative, but he wasn't the one who'd been living with this threat for the last five years.

When Raoul came to the apartment to pick her up, he was wearing a dark brown suit and lighter brown shirt without a tie. She had to discipline herself not to stare at him. "Are you ready?"

"Yes." Beneath her coat she wore a silky soft orange blouse and navy skirt. Before they reached the car he started kissing her. They must have been out there five minutes trying to become one before someone pulled in to the parking lot and he let her go.

"We're eating at Le Petit Auberge. Have you been there before?"

"No." She'd heard of it, but her budget couldn't have afforded to dine there.

"They serve the best beef kebabs. Another favorite of mine is chicken stuffed with veal and served with vegetables from their hothouse garden."

"Already my mouth is watering."

Cami felt like she was in a fantastic dream as he drove them up the mountain road. He took several winding roads that eventually brought them to the *auberge* hidden in the trees. Such an idyllic setting.

There weren't many cars, but of course the hour was early for most people to go to dinner. He parked the car and shut off the motor. "I know you're going to like this place."

"I have no doubt of it."

After helping her out, they walked inside. He cupped her elbow. He would never know how much she craved the contact. The need to touch him was growing into an ache that refused to go away.

This was no bistro. Raoul was greeted like royalty and they were shown a table, the only one with a centerpiece of pink roses. She marveled that he'd gone to all this trouble for her.

Once seated, a waiter arrived to pour the wine while another waiter brought menus and took their orders.

Raoul's eyes roamed over her, sending her heart into thud speed. "You look ravishing tonight. I decided we need to celebrate your new position at Gaillard's."

Heat filled her cheeks. "You're the most thoughtful person I've ever known."

He shook his head. "You deserve honoring. I don't think you have any idea of how phenomenal that is."

She sipped the wine. "Why do you say that?"

"Because the CEO is a close friend of my father's."

"You're kidding—"

"I happen to know that you had to pass a stringent series of tests to be hired there. They don't let just anyone work for them."

"Naturally I never met the CEO. What's he like?"

"In truth, he's ruthless like my father, and scary to approach. If he agreed to hire you, then he was impressed by your performance more than you know. Otherwise you wouldn't be working for the company." He sounded far away just then.

"I guess it's nice to hear I was offered a position there." But what he'd said about his own father and his childhood sent a shiver down Cami's spine and brought forcefully to mind his troubled relationship with the men in his family. Now that she knew so much more about his unhappy past, she could understand why he was breaking with them.

"I told you this to pay you a compliment, not to worry you."

"At least I've been forewarned."

Cami was glad the waiter came with their dinner. She'd chosen the chicken and veal. "This food is absolutely delicious. I haven't tasted anything this good in ages."

"Neither have I," he confessed.

Her thoughts raced ahead. "Have you found a new housekeeper yet?"

"No."

"Will you ask this one to cook for you?"

"Only a few meals."

"Then you'll cook the rest of the time?"

"Yes, especially when I go out on the sailboat. It's moored in Nice."

Of course he had a sailboat. While she was imagining it, he called the waiter over and ordered some takeout for her mother, then turned to her.

"Would you like dessert?"

"No, thank you. I couldn't."

Their meal was coming to an end. The drive was coming up. That's when she planned to tell him about her heart condition, but she was nervous.

"Before we leave, I have a little gift for you." He pulled it out of his breast pocket and put it on the table above her plate.

She shook her head. "No more. You've done too much already. I couldn't accept it."

"Not even to commemorate you're being taken on at Gaillard's?"

Cami took a deep breath. She assumed it was chocolate and was so small it couldn't be too expensive. She didn't want to appear impolite so she picked it up and unwrapped it. To her surprise it was a weightless, three-by-four-inch black box with a lovely purple violet on the lid and the name Gaillard printed below it. Not understanding, she lifted it.

Inside the tissue she counted twelve exquisite, individual violet heads of petals that glistened with sugar crystals. She shot him a questioning glance.

"Today Gaillard's is famous for its chocolate. What few people know is that five hundred years ago the first Gaillard concocted a recipe for sugared violets that eventually grew to other kinds of sugared flowers. They became the first candy company in Provence enjoyed by kings and queens from all over Europe before the product was discontinued and chocolate took over."

Cami was astounded.

"Since you're going to be working for them, I thought you might like to taste the first product they ever made. Your coworkers will be impressed that you have knowledge of something that isn't generally known.

"In fact, I venture to guess that no one working there today has ever eaten one. Other companies make them, but they came later and never could replicate the original. I had this especially ordered for you because it's a secret recipe and no longer available except for a select few clients who have an in with the man at the top."

Meaning Raoul himself.

Cami looked down, aware of tears stinging her eyelids. She loved him so terribly, and had already found out Raoul was an amazingly generous man. But for him to do this expressly for her in honor of her new job left her touched...speechless.

"Thank you. I—I can't wait to try one," she stammered. But the whole time that her gaze was fastened on the box of sugared violets, she was thinking about all he'd done for her and knew she'd fallen madly in love with him. But it frightened her.

Suddenly Cami couldn't handle this any longer.

"Raoul—why have you done all this for me? I don't mean just the violets. I'm talking about everything since the day I came to clean for you—the flowers, the dinners out, your kindness to my mother. You must know I'm overwhelmed by all you've done."

CHAPTER SEVEN

"THEN LET ME EXPLAIN," he said in a thick-toned voice. "I'd been in hell for a long time before I found out I had a son. I've wanted to make everything perfect for him. When I saw an attractive woman up on the ladder cleaning my son's room with such care, I didn't realize I'd startled you. It would have been my fault if you'd had a bad accident.

"After you fell in my arms, I found myself staring into a pair of incredible eyes. Blame their color. You had me mesmerized. The truth is, I found myself wanting to get to know you better."

"I still don't understand why."

"I guess you'd have to be a man to understand."

"Please tell me the real truth." She refused to be put off.

One black brow lifted. "That *is* the real truth," he came back with force.

Cami sat back in the chair, appearing haunted by his remark. "How often does this kind of thing happen to you? Everything that's happening seems too good to be true."

He finished the rest of his coffee. "That's a fair question. You have every right to ask it. The answer is, it has only happened to me one other time in my life. In truth it was on the night I met Alain's mother at a bistro near the vineyard three years ago.

"She taught elementary school and had come in with friends one night. I had been checking the wine inventory and was so drawn to her from that first moment, I approached her to have a drink with me. We fell in love that night."

"But then you stopped seeing her and got married. Do I have that right?"

Raoul nodded. "Before I ever met Antoinette, my parents gave a lavish party where I was introduced to Sabine Murat. I soon discovered that her parents and mine had been plotting to arrange a marriage between us for a long time. I admit I found her attractive and intelligent, but the more I spent time with her, the more I realized the essential ingredient I needed to feel was missing."

Cami nodded. "As I told you, after a month of marriage I felt the same way, Raoul. Only I'd already taken vows."

"Understood," Raoul murmured. "Like a fool, I slept with her once. It was wrong, but I thought maybe that would change the way I felt about her. But it didn't. I wasn't in love and I broke it off with her because it wasn't fair to either of us. I'd had relationships with several women over the years, but I'd never been in love. I began to believe love was out of my reach.

"Then I met Antoinette. We spent every possible moment together and I knew I wanted to marry her as soon as we could. Before we could let her parents know, I received a call from Sabine whom I hadn't seen for over a month." He grimaced. "To my horror she told me she was expecting our baby. I couldn't believe it, knowing I'd taken precautions. But the doctor confirmed it."

"You had a *baby* with her?" A groan escaped her lips. He knew he'd shocked her. "I had no idea and can't imagine what a nightmare that must have been."

"You'll never know. I had to give up the only love of my life and marry Sabine who moved in my apartment at the château. I never saw Antoinette again, though I tried calling her to talk. She refused, knowing we couldn't have a future. It was agony.

"From that point on I concentrated on the pregnancy and birth of our little girl, Celine. She brought me my only happiness, but she was born early and died of a bad heart within the month."

"What?" The shock of hearing Raoul had a baby with Sabine was one thing, but the revelation that it had died of heart problems was almost too much for Cami to bear.

Raoul eyed her soulfully with those black eyes. "I was in despair over losing her. When I asked the doctor if the baby's heart condition was the reason for her being premature, he shook his head and said Celine had been full-term."

"I don't understand. You didn't know that?"

He took a deep breath. "I'm afraid not. Those words meant the baby *wasn't* mine."

"No—" Cami blurted as the truth of it sank in. "She lied to you?" He nodded. "I can't imagine it." Tears filled her eyes. "The pain you must have suffered."

"Celine was someone else's," his voice grated, "though at the time it never occurred to me she wasn't mine. Worse, I suffered horribly to realize no surgical procedure could save the baby. Her heart was too damaged."

A shudder ran through Cami. Her greatest fear was that the surgeon would find that her own heart was too damaged to fix. Throughout their dinner she'd been on the verge of telling Raoul the truth about the operation coming up, but she couldn't do that now. He'd been through too much. It would be better to go through the surgery without him knowing anything in order to spare him.

"I'm so desperately sorry for you, Raoul. I don't know how you've lived through all this."

"It wasn't the best of times. Sabine pretended the baby was mine so I'd marry her. She didn't love the man who'd made her pregnant."

"I don't know how she could have done that to you."

"She'd been determined to marry me from the beginning and hold on to me. I wanted to divorce her, but the psychiatrist Sabine's family had brought in told me to put it off. He explained she was so grief-stricken over the loss and burial, he advised me to wait until she'd recovered enough to deal with the breakup of our marriage.

"I waited as long as I could stand before filing. We'd lived apart for over two months. During that time I visited Celine's grave several times, but I only became a free man the day before my grandfather died."

While he'd been telling his tragic story, Cami's mind reeled. Not only had the baby been born with a heart problem like hers, Raoul wasn't the man she'd believed went through women like water whenever he needed a diversion. He hadn't had an affair on Sabine. Cami had judged him without knowing the truth.

"It was during that waiting period Sabine's family wanted us to go in for marriage counseling. She demanded more money from me if I refused, but I couldn't do it. Nothing could fix what was wrong between us when I wasn't in love with her."

"I hear what you're saying," Cami murmured. "When love dies, that's it."

"Amen," he said in a gravelly tone.

"Raoul? How did you and Alain find each other?"

He finished his coffee. "During that desolate time, Nathalie came to the vineyard looking for the stranger who had impregnated her deceased stepsister Antoinette. She posed as a grape picker and met my cousin Dominic. They fell in love, which is an amazing story in itself."

"You mean she actually helped with the harvest?"

"Yes, for several weeks. They became enamored right away. In time he found out her real reason for coming to the vineyard. It turned out she thought Dominic or his brother Etienne might be Alain's father because they all look so much alike. But neither one claimed to know Antoinette.

"Then she met me and wondered if *I* could be the one because of the strong family resemblance."

"You and Alain are clones of each other," she cried.

"Don't I know it. We looked so much alike I was in shock. When she showed me Antoinette's picture, the puzzle was solved and I was united with the son I'd had no knowledge of. The whole thing was miraculous."

"I'll say it was," Cami murmured in amazement. "Antoinette never told her family your name?"

"No. We'd wanted to keep everything quiet until our announcement. When I had to tell her about Sabine's pregnancy, she didn't want her parents to know anything."

A groan escaped Cami's lips. "How impossible and heartbreaking for both of you."

"I'm still suffering from guilt over hurting her the way I did."

Cami's heart was pained for him. "You should let it go. Alain's grandmother seems to love you very much."

"I'm still in awe over her kindness to me."

"She has to be thrilled you're her grandson's father."

"I'm thrilled too. One look at him and I saw Antoinette in his features. It was like getting part of her back. The joy of knowing I had a son brought me alive again and I determined to be the best father possible."

"I can tell you already are," she said softly.

"Time will tell. Dominic married Nathalie and we both bought villas near each other. My life took on new meaning to plan a future around my son. Getting the villa ready, finding housecleaners so I could furnish everything meant the world to me. Now you've come into my life, I'm happier than I've ever been."

She felt the same way, but couldn't say it back. Not now. He didn't need to hear about the state of her health. In a few more days she'd be away from his world, dealing with the crisis she'd been dreading.

He wouldn't be there with her...

By now the waiter brought a bag with the food, which Raoul took. It was time to go. Cami got up and the two of them walked outside to his car. He put the bag of food in back before helping her. Again she felt his hand on her elbow. Before they got in his car, he pulled her against him and lowered his mouth to hers, kissing her possessively.

Cami moaned, relishing the taste and feel of him. She couldn't get close enough. Every touch of his hands and lips electrified her. The sensual tension between them was so strong, she knew he felt the same way.

"I was dying to kiss you like this the whole time we were inside," he admitted, then let her go because people were arriving, but there was a marked change in their relationship because she was totally in love with him.

They drove into town and looked at the illuminated buildings. At one point, he parked the car. "Shall we have our dessert now?" Raoul lifted the lid on the violets and put the box in front of her. "Are you ready to enjoy the favorite treat of royalty that kept the dentists of the time busy?"

Cami broke into laughter. She couldn't help it. "Have you ever tried one?"

"No. This will be my first time too."

He reached for one and put it in his mouth.

She followed suit and sucked on it before chewing it. "Um. It tastes like a violet smells."

"Agreed. I think I prefer chocolate." His grin delighted her.

"I can't wait to show these to Maman. I have to admit I'm curious to see if she'll try eating one. It's so odd to think of eating flowers."

"Many violets are edible and can be sautéed or steamed. Some cooks stir them into soups as a thickener."

"I had no idea." His knowledge astounded her.

"Do you know our company makes a yellow-green liqueur called Fontesquieu Chartreuse? The secret ingredient includes carnation petals among the other herbs and plants distilled."

"You're kidding—"

"Not at all. Jerome originated the recipe. It's in one of the journals and I have to get them back. One day I'll take you to the winery again and you can test it out for yourself."

"That would really be something. Imagine drinking carnations and eating violet soup. I feel like I've entered a world full of magic."

"It was Olivarri who said, 'Wine is the only art-work you can drink.'"

More laughter escaped as she studied him. "It's so much fun spending time with you, I've lost all sense of my surroundings."

"You're not the only one," he whispered and kissed her. They both tasted of violets. This evening had been heavenly, but there wouldn't be many more of them. Though she was dying inside of love for him and wanted to pour out her love, she couldn't do it. Until the operation was over, he was better off not knowing anything.

After they reached the apartment and he'd parked, she turned to him. "Thank you for tonight. I'll re-member it forever."

"So will I, but it's only the beginning for us, Cami." His eyes burned like dark fires as they stud-ied her features. Then he reached for the food and came around to her side of the car to open her door.

When they reached the apartment door, he rocked her back and forth in his arms, hugging her for a long time. She wanted to invite him in and never let him go, but she couldn't. The man had suffered too much to go through any more trauma in his life.

"Before I go, let's make plans for tomorrow eve-ning. Alain has his checkup at the doctor's tomorrow afternoon. After we get back, I'll cook dinner for the three of us and we'll have a fun evening at home."

She eased away from him. "I have an even better idea. Tomorrow afternoon Maman and I are taking the afternoon off. I'll bring the groceries and cook dinner. It's my turn to wait on you." Cami wanted to do something special for him after all he'd done for her.

"If you mean that, nothing could make me happier," he murmured against her lips. "I'll leave the back door open for you. *À bientôt, ma belle.*"

Cami's body hummed as she entered the apartment. He'd set her on fire and she was burning up with desire. Once inside the apartment, the first thing she saw were the fabulous lavender roses, a reminder of Raoul, a man who was larger than life. She'd never forget this day for as long as she lived.

"Maman? I've brought you dinner, compliments of Le Petit Auberge."

Her mother emerged from the other room. "You mean Raoul Fontesquieu. How did he handle what you had to tell him?"

"I didn't say anything, but there's a reason. Sit down and I'll explain why."

By the time she'd explained everything about Sabine's lie, including the fact that the little baby he'd loved had died of a bad heart, her mother looked shocked and saddened.

"What a shame when you're both in love with each other. Anyone can see that. Doesn't he deserve to know what's going to happen, no matter how painful it might be for him?"

"I don't want to talk about it." She was still struggling with the pain of what the result could be following the operation. The worst result was too excruciating to contemplate. On her way to bed, she took the roses with her.

* * *

Friday morning Nathalie came to the villa to help Raoul interview a woman for the nanny position. The trim brunette Parisian widow had no children and was in her early fifties.

For three years she'd been a nanny for a diplomat's family in Paris following the death of her husband. The family no longer needed her. Since her married sister lived in Vence, she'd decided to apply for a nanny's job here to be near her only living family.

She reminded Raoul a little of Minerve, very down to earth and came with impeccable credentials. Nathalie appeared to like her too. Alain moved back and forth and played with his blocks. He didn't seem to mind a stranger being there and responded favorably to some of the things she said to him.

Raoul gave her a brief background on Alain so she'd understand this would be hard for his son to get used to a new nanny. Following a tour of the villa and an inspection of the nursery, she indicated she'd like to take care of Alain. The decision was made to hire her temporarily and see how things went. She could move into the guest room in the upstairs hall next to the nursery at any time.

Alain scuttled off Nathalie's lap and ran to him. It caught at his heart that he and his son had a special bond already. He lifted him and hugged him hard.

"He's a precious boy, Monsieur Fontesquieu."

"He is. Please call me Raoul."

"And the two of you call me Delphine." She got to her feet. "I'll leave now, and be back tomorrow."

Raoul kept Alain in his arms while he saw Delphine to the front door. "From now on, plan to park in the back. Here's the key to the back door."

"*Très bien. Au revoir*, Alain." She touched his son's cheek before leaving.

He shut the door, feeling an enormous weight lift from his heart that he'd found a woman he could work with. Though there were no guarantees, hopefully Alain would learn to like her, but it would take time.

His son squirmed to get down. Raoul lowered him to the floor and they walked back to the sitting room to find Nathalie.

She smiled at him. "I like her, Raoul. She's solid and very cute with Alain."

"I agree with you. I think it'll work with Delphine."

"I couldn't be happier for you. After you've taken Alain to the doctor, why don't you drive him to La Gaude? Mom and I will tend him. Later Dom and I will bring him back in time for bed. You don't know how much I miss him."

His sister-in-law knew he was dying to be alone with Cami. There were no secrets at this point. "You're sure?"

"Don't be an idiot. It's long past time you found someone." She gave Alain a kiss.

"Thanks, Nathalie."

"I owe you big-time after the way you helped me get back with Dominic. We're so happy it's ridiculous, and we want you to know that same feeling again." She kissed Raoul's cheek and left.

Raoul wasn't far behind with Alain to take him to the doctor. So far his son seemed perfectly healthy, but Raoul was a bit nervous. This was all part of being a new parent as Arlette had reminded him earlier. The knowledge that Cami would be arriving at the villa later to fix their dinner filled him with excitement and helped him deal with his worry over being a dad.

When Cami arrived at the villa at three, it was clear that Raoul hadn't returned from the doctor yet. He'd left the back door unlocked and she was able to walk in and get busy cooking her specialty of *escalope de veau* and roast potatoes.

She was still smiling over her mother's surprised reaction to the candied violets she ate and loved when she heard the doorbell ring. It was probably a delivery of some kind for Raoul. She wiped her hands on a towel and walked through the villa to answer the door.

A stunning auburn-haired woman probably late twenties, dressed in a designer suit stood there scrutinizing Cami who was wearing jeans and a pale yellow crewneck pullover. The woman carried two wrapped packages hanging at her sides.

"May I help you?"

"I'm here to see Raoul Fontesquieu."

"I'm afraid he's not here, but I expect him later."

"Will you see he gets these as soon as possible?"

"Of course."

She handed her the packages and left before Cami

could ask the woman's name. Cami suspected she'd just met Sabine.

After she disappeared down the steps, Cami shut the door and carried them to the kitchen where she placed them on the counter. No sooner had she put their dinner in the oven than the phone rang.

It was Raoul. Her pulse raced as she clicked on. "Hi!"

"Hi, yourself. I dropped off Alain at his grandmother's and I'm driving home from La Gaude, but there's been a traffic accident. I may not be there for another ten minutes."

"That's no problem. As I've got you on the phone, you should know a woman came to the door and left two packages for you."

"Interesting. Will you do me a favor and open them?"

"All right." She walked over and undid the paper on both of them. "They're framed oil paintings of a vineyard. Oh! Your great uncle Jerome's signature is in the lower right-hand corner of both. I didn't know he was an artist too!"

"He was a Renaissance man and did them when he was in Bordeaux. I thought I'd seen the last of them. They're one of my treasures. I can't wait to see them and will be home soon."

They hung up and Cami set the table. Before long Raoul walked in the kitchen. His dark gleaming eyes found hers. He kissed her long and hard. "Something smells wonderful, *ma belle*. You didn't have to do all this."

"I wanted to, and I have to tell you how impressed I am by the way you've put your kitchen together. No more boxes."

"Nope. Alain helped."

"That I would have loved to see. Which brings me to the burning question. What's the verdict from the doctor?"

He washed his hands. "My son is in perfect condition and is taller on the chart than most children his age." She noticed him examine the paintings.

"It would be a shock if he weren't," she quipped. "Come sit down and I'll serve you." As she put a plate of food in front of him, she said, "You seem particularly happy. What else is going on?"

"A lot of things. When I was out of town before, I made my cousin Jean-Pierre the official head of Sales and Marketing at a meeting. It's an enormous relief, but more importantly, I've found a nanny for Alain."

"Really?" She served herself some food and sat down, looking excited for him. "What's she like?"

"Delphine LaVaux is older and solid as Natalie said. She was a nanny in Paris for three years. Best of all, Alain didn't act shy around her or fuss like he did with the other women."

"Sounds like a good sign. You must be ecstatic."

"It's a start. She'll be over tomorrow to spend the day with him. Things are slowly falling into place. By the way, I love this veal dinner. You're a wonderful cook."

"Thank you. It was fun to prepare with all the new kitchen equipment."

"Since Nathalie will be bringing Alain home in a few hours, I thought we'd sit in front of the fire."

"I'll do the dishes first."

"Leave everything. I'll take care of things after you go home." But while they were talking, his phone rang. He glanced at the caller ID and flashed her a frustrated look. "I have to take this call. Excuse me for a minute."

After he left the kitchen, Cami had time to clear the table and start to load the dishwasher. When he returned, he looked preoccupied. The happy expression he'd brought in to the villa was no longer in sight.

"I have to go to the office and meet Jean-Pierre. It's an emergency."

Cami's heart sank. "I totally understand."

"There's no one like you." He brushed his mouth against hers. "I'll walk you out to your car. You have no idea how sorry I am, but I'll make it up to you. Since tomorrow is Saturday, I want to spend the whole day with you. I'll call you later tonight to make plans."

A whole day with Raoul? Nothing could sound more divine, but it disturbed Cami to see he was upset right now though he tried to hide it. He helped her on with her coat and walked her out to the Citroën.

"Drive home safely, *mon amour*. I couldn't bear it if anything happened to you."

His words and endearment haunted her all the way home.

It had never occurred to Cami that in cleaning other people's houses, she'd meet Raoul Fontesquieu, a man who had the power to make all other men melt into insignificance.

The results of her heart operation would determine if she ever saw him again. It frightened her that she could finally count in hours how long it would be before she checked into the hospital. Right now she couldn't comprehend life without him.

CHAPTER EIGHT

ON HIS WAY to the office at the vineyard, the conversation with Jean-Pierre went through Raoul's mind. Something was wrong. His cousin wanted help dealing with the Frères Oliviers in Aix, but that didn't make sense. They'd come to the meeting in Fréjus and there'd been no trouble. To Raoul's dismay he heard a trace of panic in his cousin's voice and knew he needed to get to the bottom of it.

The call couldn't have come at a worse moment. He'd needed time with Cami tonight, but it would have to wait until tomorrow. To walk out on her after the marvelous dinner she'd made crushed him, but it couldn't be helped.

When he arrived at his old office and walked inside, it was his graying father who was waiting for him. Heavy lines marked his face.

Today had been full of surprises! First Sabine. Now his father.

There was no sign of Jean-Pierre, which meant this meeting had been concocted to force the inevitable confrontation. Poor Jean-Pierre who now had to function under Raoul's father.

At last the moment had come Raoul had been waiting for. He was ready.

His tall, thin parent stood there on the verge of exploding. "What do you mean putting Jean-Pierre officially in charge?"

"My cousin is perfect for the position and has earned it. I told you the day Gran'pere died that I didn't want the CEO position, nor would I continue to be the head of Marketing and Sales. I've quit."

For once Raoul knew he'd shocked him, and took advantage of the silence.

"Since I've developed my own company, I've resigned my position and have separated myself completely from our family business.

"By now you should have received my official resignation in an email. I sent it before I left for Fréjus. I expect you to correct the announcement you made to the media. If you don't, it will bring you more headaches, not me."

His father's cheeks went a ruddy color. "Sabine told me she met your illicit lover earlier today. I'd hoped that news was a piece of fiction."

Raoul knew it. Sabine's visit to the villa where she'd met Cami had ignited his father's wrath to the exploding point. It made sense this was confrontation was happening now.

"Knowing how you feel about me, let's agree it's much better I've separated myself from the company and will follow my own path from now on."

Lines broke out on his austere features. "What about Sabine and the child you lost?"

Raoul refused to go there or expose her lie. "Celine will always have a place in my heart, but my divorce is past history. We were never suited. It's another fact you need to make clear to the media. I'm building a new life."

"With your mistress and bastard son?"

Raoul wasn't surprised his father knew about Alain, but he wasn't going to explain about Antoinette or Cami.

"You mean Alain Fontesquieu? Has your source also learned that Alain's other grandfather died several years ago? But Alain still has a living grandfather in his *gran'pere* Matthieu Fontesquieu. If you ever want to visit and get to know your grandson, you're welcome at the villa. Is there anything else? If not, I'm leaving."

He started for the door but his father followed him. His hands had formed fists at his side. "You're going to give up everything?" he bit out incredulously.

"If you mean money, I already have, and never took a sou of Sabine's. But I *am* a Fontesquieu. You don't give up your heritage, and I've had a good life to this point, but times are changing. I'm embracing those changes to make new memories and would hope you and Maman are a part of them. That's up to you."

With nothing more to say, Raoul turned on his heel and walked out of the office, leaving his stunned father to his own devices. For the first time in his life, Raoul actually sensed a crack in his papa's demeanor.

After getting in the car, he was so relieved to have thrown off the yoke that had bound him, he felt liberated and wanted to be with Cami. Unfortunately she wasn't available, so he hurried home. Nathalie would be arriving with Alain. Raoul wanted to put him to bed. Then he'd phone the woman he adored.

After Cami got back to the apartment, she found her mom talking to her aunt and uncle on the speaker-phone. They were making plans for next week after Cami's operation was over.

Not wanting to think about it, she hurried into the bedroom and got ready for bed. While she was brush-ing her teeth, her cell rang. She jumped and picked up after the first ring.

"Raoul?"

"I'm glad you answered so fast. I've needed to hear your voice."

"Are you all right?"

"I'm fine, but I have news we need to talk about. Tonight it was my father, not Jean-Pierre, who was waiting for me. We had the confrontation predes-tined for a lifetime, and I officially resigned from the company."

A gasp escaped. "Was it terrible?"

"No. I'm rid of a great burden, but I won't bother you about it right now. What I'm asking is that you go sailing with me tomorrow. We'll have the whole Saturday to ourselves."

Thrilled, she clutched the counter with one hand. "What about Alain?"

"Delphine will be here. They need time together and I have to get away. Please come. There's a lot I want to talk to you about. By tomorrow the whole family will have heard this news. The reaction will be ugly. Sabine told my father about her visit and seeing you at the door. He was upset by that news.

"I'm hoping this doesn't touch you in any way, but I can't promise that it won't, or show up in the news. We need to discuss it, but not here. I'll pick you up at eight if that's all right."

"Eight is fine. *Bonne nuit*, Raoul."

Saturday turned out to be cold, but not freezing. An hour after leaving Vence, Cami and Raoul reached the port in Nice beneath a semisunny sky. They bought some food at a Chinese bistro, then Raoul drove them to the dock where they boarded his thirty-eight-foot state-of-the-art sailboat.

He helped Cami on board and handed her a life jacket to put on. Soon they went downstairs to the living area that included the captain's console. Above and below it was luxury personified. Within a few minutes the air was toasty and comfortable.

Raoul had given her startling news over the phone last night. He'd hinted at repercussions that could reach the media. Since his divorce she knew he didn't put anything past his family.

No one was kidding anybody. A new nightmare could be starting. She didn't want to be any part of it, but recognized she'd needed to come with him today so they could talk.

Raoul undid the ropes and started the motor to edge them out to the bay beyond the buoys. Through the windows belowdecks she had a spectacular view of the Mediterranean. A few boats skimmed the calm, dark blue water.

He drove ten minutes, then lowered the anchor. Once he'd pulled some drinks from the mini fridge, he walked over to the sculptured couch that ran the length of one side of the room to join her. He handed her a can of soda and sat on a chair opposite her.

"Thank you for coming with me. I wanted you to hear the whole truth from me in case something comes up during the days ahead that could worry you while you're on vacation."

Cami couldn't stand it any longer. "Was it hard telling your father?" Heavens—how could it not be? Her heart ached for him. Though he and his parent had never gotten along, there had to be love deep down.

"Your compassion is extraordinary, but the truth is, I've wanted to break with my father since my pre-teens."

She winced. "You're serious."

"Afraid so. I fought his demands for as long as I can remember. There's no flexibility in him, no room for another avenue of thought. He was a virtual task-master who expected total obedience.

"When I was ten, he did something I couldn't for-give. I kept a hamster in my bedroom. Jerome secretly bought it for me and taught me how to take care of it. My father didn't allow animals of any kind. One day after school I found it dead and asked the maid what she knew about it. She was on my side and said my father had been in there earlier. From that day on I made preparations to run away from home."

Cami couldn't prevent tears trickling out of her eyes. His father's cruelty shook her to the foundations. "Where did you go?"

"I borrowed a friend's sleeping bag and stashed a lot of food on the top floor of the Tour de l'Est."

She leaned forward. "What is that?"

"A massive round tower on the property I've been wanting to show you. Alain would love it. The land itself was deeded to our family and contains battlements from the fifteenth century.

"Years ago someone cleared out the old weapons and munitions from the east tower. Now its eight-foot-thick walls with rooms on four floors are used to store wine. During those days I was in hiding, I'd fill my thermos with water from the main floor sink when the guard did rounds outside."

"I can't believe it. How long were you gone?"

"Ten days."

"Oh, Raoul. Your parents must have been terrified something horrible had happened to you."

"They called the police who looked for me, but they didn't find me. It was Jerome who figured out where I might be hiding. He was the one who'd shown me around the Tour when I was younger. Sure enough he came one night when the guard was patrolling the perimeter and called out to me. He talked me into going back to the château with him. Of course, it wasn't hard to coax me."

She smiled. "You ran out of food, right?"

He chuckled. "That, plus I admit I was happy to see him. He was always kind and told me I had to let my parents know I was safe. He backed me up and talked my father out of punishing me. Jerome knew what had happened to the hamster and understood how I felt. He counseled me that when I turned eighteen, I could go away legally if that was what I wanted."

Cami stirred in place. "Why didn't you take his advice?"

"I wanted to. In fact I would have joined Dominic in Paris. He broke with his father when he turned eighteen. I was a year younger and would have gone to Paris after my eighteenth birthday. But by then Jerome was diagnosed with lung cancer."

"Oh, no—"

"He swore me to secrecy and didn't even tell his wife. Because he was a scientist, he handled his health care in his own way and turned to alternative medicine."

She couldn't believe what she was hearing. "What did he do exactly?"

"Jerome used holistic interventions of supplements, herbs, enzymes. He changed his diet and he prayed. Knowing he would eventually die, I couldn't leave him because I loved him too much. Unfortunately I couldn't even tell Dominic until the other day when we went shopping."

She let out a moan. "So you're saying your cousin had struggles with *his* father too. How heartbreaking."

Raoul nodded. "Our fathers are clones of each

other and pretty impossible. The reason Dominic took off to Paris was because his relationship with his father was so toxic. He worked at different jobs and put himself through college. Afterward he got in with a prestigious investment firm and became wealthy in his own right."

"That's incredible. You and your cousin are both alike."

"Hardly. He stayed in Paris until last year."

"That long?"

"Yes. Of course he came home for major events and vacations, but never to live. Then my aunt begged him to return because my uncle was ill with pneumonia and they thought he might die. So Dominic took over the funds department in the family until my uncle recovered and was made vice president of the company. I begged Dominic to stay on, which he did."

She pressed a hand to her throat. "And *you* remained all these years because of Jerome."

"Yes. After he died, I vowed to leave the family business altogether, but I had to make sure I could support myself when the time came. Jerome had talked to me about his many business ideas and what he'd do if he were only forty years younger. His ideas became mine and I began to see light at the end of the tunnel. But by then my life had turned upside down."

"Because of the phone call from Sabine," she murmured.

Raoul suddenly stood up. "That's all in the past. Last night I told my father I was building a new life and memories. If he wants to be a part of Alain's life, he's welcome at the villa."

Cami stared at the wonderful man who could still find forgiveness inside his soul. She adored Raoul. "What did your father say?"

"It stunned him when I told him I'd resigned. There was nothing more to say and I left the office."

"I take it he didn't run after you."

"That'll be the day."

Cami might have lost her father early, but she'd always known she was loved to death. She hurt for Raoul who would never know that feeling. His father didn't deserve him. "I'm glad you've told me what happened. It's better to be forewarned."

She didn't know what the future would hold, but at least she knew he'd be happy at home with his son and running his new business. No one could have fought harder through his agony for what he wanted. If his father did anything to bring him more pain, she couldn't bear it.

For once in her life, she couldn't follow her mother's advice. There was no way she could tell him about her heart condition now. He was building a new life and didn't need anything else to worry about. As she'd once told her mother, his life was full of heartbreaks. The last thing she'd want to do was add to them.

Raoul glanced at the woman he loved. It always helped when he talked to her. Cami looked beautiful in a soft peach-toned sweater and jeans. Today she'd worn her hair back with a clip. It made him want to undo it and run his fingers through its glossy blackness again. But he'd do it later after they'd talked.

Raoul walked over to the open kitchen area and made coffee before putting it on the table. "I hope you're hungry because I am. Shall we eat?"

"That sounds good."

After pouring the steaming brew into mugs, he put out the cartons of Chinese food. They started eating before he handed her a fortune cookie, which she opened.

"A big event is going to change your life," she read aloud. "What does yours say?"

He smiled at her before opening his. "First comes the rain before you can expect sunshine. I don't know if I like the sound of that."

"I agree neither fortune is very reassuring."

"Let's forget them. I want to talk about a week from Saturday."

Her gaze flew to his. "What's so important about it?"

His black eyes impaled her. "Dominic and Nathalie have invited us to a party. They want us to spend an evening with them."

She bit her lip. "That's sounds lovely, but by then I'll be on vacation with my mother."

He stopped chewing. "I realize that, but you won't be away from Vence, will you?"

"No, but I'll be busy."

"The whole time?"

"Yes."

Raoul put down his fork and reached for her hand.

"What's going on with you, Cami? Don't tell me it's nothing. I've been around you long enough to know something is wrong. Why are you putting me off when you know I'm dying to be with you day and night?

"The only reason I haven't tried to make love to you is because you've been in my employ. But that's over and now that you're going to be on vacation, there's no reason why we can't be together all the time. I know in my heart you wouldn't be with me if you didn't feel the same way I do. Surely you realize by now that I want to marry you."

She eased her hand away, refusing to look at him. "You couldn't possibly mean that."

"You think I don't? Trust me. I fell for you the first day we met. Don't tell me it's too soon. I know what I feel. Sometimes love happens at first sight and it happened to us. You can't deny it."

"There is no us. There *can't be*." She jumped up from the table and moved over to the couch.

He followed and sank down, sliding his arm around her shoulders. "What do you mean there *can't be*? There's something you're not telling me. You've been elusive from that first amazing day. I've been waiting for you to tell me how you feel, but you've held back. I've spilled my guts to you, but maybe that isn't enough. Is it because I have a son?"

"How can you ask me that?" she cried out. Her cheeks had gone hot with color. "I've loved every minute he's been with us. He's the most precious thing on earth!"

"Then what am I missing here?"

She lowered her head. "You and I come from different worlds. You're the son of a duke and a duchess. I'm the daughter of a taxi driver and a cleaning lady."

"Come on, Cami," he bit out. "Don't pull that nonsense on me. The ridiculous business about people being born on the wrong side of the tracks has always been absurd, and I don't buy it for a second. That's not honest. I want the truth from you. If you only knew how I felt about you."

Without conscious thought he put his hands on her upper arms and heard a cry escape her lips. She fought him, but he refused to let her go and pulled her against his chest.

"I've been desperate to get close to you. That first week I used work as the only ploy I could think of to keep us together. It couldn't be any surprise that I've fallen deeply in love with you."

Her body was trembling. "You don't know what you're saying."

"Then why have I been in agony every time you've had to leave and go home? You have no idea what I went through when I had to leave town. It was pure torture for me not to be able to see your exquisite face and hold you in my arms."

"Don't say anything else."

"I can't help it." He turned her so she would look at him. "You're all I can think about, and I know you have the same problem. When I caught you in my arms that first day, we both recognized something glorious had happened. After Antoinette, the last thing I ever expected was to fall in love again, but I did."

"Y-You don't know what you're talking about." The words came out halted.

"Oh, but I do." He slid his hands to her flaming cheeks. "Before we do anything else, I'm dying to kiss you. Don't deny me what I've longed for."

He lowered his head, needing her kiss like he needed air to breathe. After moaning in protest, the mouth he'd been craving to taste again finally opened to the pressure of his. Her response electrified him and they clung to each other. He'd been wanting this for so long.

No kiss could satisfy him. It wasn't long enough or deep enough. Raoul never wanted it to end. Their hunger for each other caused him to lose track of everything but loving this divine woman who'd come into his life. He hadn't expected to feel love like this again, not after what he'd been through.

"You're so beautiful, and I love you so much. Marry me, Cami, just as soon as it's possible," he whispered, covering her face and throat with kisses. "We belong together and need each other desperately."

"Raoul—" she cried, but he smothered the sound and pulled her down on top of him.

"Let me love you, *mon tresor*. I almost died when I had to leave you last night to go to the office. Don't put me off now."

For a while longer they tried to appease their longing for each other. But far too soon his ecstasy was cut off when she pulled away from him and raced to the kitchen area.

He hurried after her, but she'd backed up against the counter. "Please don't touch me again. We can't do this, Raoul. *I* can't. I stopped believing in love a long time ago. Let's agree that we've found ourselves attracted and vulnerable, nothing more, but it mustn't go on."

"Cami—" He was frustrated out of his mind.

"I mean it, Raoul. I treasure the time I've spent with you and Alain and all the wonderful things you've done for me, but it has to be over."

"*Has* to be over? *Can't? Mustn't?* You're not making sense!"

"Please will you take us back," she begged him. Tears poured from her eyes. He'd never seen her like this before. Something was terrifying her, but he couldn't get answers from her right now. She'd closed up on him for the time being.

"I'll take us back, but you have to promise me you'll come to the villa tomorrow. It's a special day, Jerome's birthday in fact. I want to honor his memory at the cemetery and would like to take you and Alain with me. If you'll come at noon, I'll fix lunch and we'll leave."

She swallowed hard. "If I come, will you promise not to press me about marriage?"

"I didn't realize how much your divorce still pains you," his voice grated. Why hadn't she told him everything? "But yes, I promise."

In deep pain, he reluctantly let her go and walked

forward to the console. After raising the anchor, he drove the boat back to port. When he pulled in the slip, he turned to see her tear-splotched face. "This isn't the end, Cami. I can promise you that."

She refused to look at him while she removed her life jacket.

Raoul would give it through tomorrow. After that, he'd do whatever it took to break her down, even talk to her mother.

Cami arrived at the villa at noon on Sunday looking gorgeous in a red sweater and black skirt. He'd left the back door open for her. Today she'd worn her hair tied back with a black-and-red print scarf. She was stunning. A flowery fragrance clung to her.

She was a vision, but Raoul didn't try to kiss her. "I hope you like steak for lunch." They were sizzling on the grill.

Cami flashed him one of those sunny smiles, but he knew she was hiding a secret from him. He had a hard time believing she hadn't recovered from her divorce. What else it could be he had no idea.

"First an Olympic swimming champion, now a *cordon bleu* chef!"

Laughter burst out of him. "Anything to impress you."

"Cam—" Alain called out pointing to her.

"Bonjour, Alain!" She hurried over to kiss him.

Raoul had put his son in the high chair by the table and had wrapped a bib around his neck.

She sat down next to him. "Um. Junior chicken

and noodles in the jar and a banana." Cami looked up at Raoul. "Can I feed him?"

"He's waiting for you."

He watched her get busy cutting the banana into bite-size pieces. "Do you want some bananas too?" she asked Raoul.

He chuckled and watched her find ingenious ways to feed him his chicken.

"Bana—"

"Yes. You want more of those, don't you?"

While she fed him, Raoul put the salad and brioches on the table with their plates of steak. Lunch was an incredibly happy affair. When it was time to leave, she wiped Alain's hands and mouth with a moist cloth.

"Lunch was delicious, Raoul. Thank you."

He had to get a grip on his emotions that were bursting inside of him. After finding his son's little coat, he put it on him and they walked out to the car. Alain was making happy noises as he fastened him in his car seat in back. Then he drove them down the drive to the main street. Cami talked to his son while Raoul took them to the estate and wound around to the cemetery.

The headstone for his grandfather hadn't been placed yet. Raoul kept going until he came to Jerome's grave and stopped the car.

"Will you come with us?"

"Of course."

She got out while he opened the back door and pulled Alain from his car seat. Holding him in one arm, he reached for the tin of flowers on the floor and carried everything to the site.

"Cam—" Alain called out and reached for her. To Raoul's delight she pulled him into her arms. He played with the ends of her scarf. Raoul put the daisies at the base of the monument.

"Aren't the flowers pretty?" She let Alain get down but held on to his hand. "Those are marguerites. Can you say *mar-guer-ites?*"

He listened, then said, *"Marg—"* emphasizing the hard *g*. It made her chuckle.

"That's right. Your papa sent my mother marguerites. She loved them. I think they must be his favorite *fleur.*"

"Fleur."

"Yes!" Cami cried excitedly. "You know that word and are so smart." She leaned over to give him a hug. Though Raoul's thoughts were on Jerome, he watched her take Alain on a little walk, talking to him the whole time. Her tenderness with his son touched him to the core.

In a few minutes they walked back to the car and got settled. He turned to Cami. "Let's take him home and start a fire."

"I won't be able to stay. Maman and I have an early cleaning job." She was trying to act unaffected, but he saw the little nerve throbbing in her throat.

"How about my coming by for you tomorrow at five thirty? I won't press you about getting married, but I'd like an explanation of why you can't even talk about it. If you're no longer interested in me, I have to know the truth, whatever it is."

"I have a better idea. I'll come to the villa so you don't have to leave Alain. We can talk, but I won't be able to stay long."

"Thank you for that."

When they reached his house, she got out first. Maybe it was a trick of light, but he thought she'd lost some coloring. *"Au revoir, petit,"* she called out to Alain before shutting the door.

CHAPTER NINE

THIS AFTERNOON CAMI'S world had been completely transformed. She'd been with Raoul and Alain. It had felt like they were a family. He made her want things that were impossible, increasing her pain. She was in turmoil by the time she entered the apartment Sunday evening.

"There you are. I wondered when you'd get home."

"I went to the cemetery with Raoul and Alain. He wanted to put flowers on his great uncle's grave. I had the time of my life, and no, I still haven't told him about my heart condition. Please don't remind me it was a mistake."

"I wasn't going to say anything."

"I keep making them. Tomorrow I'm going to make one more and see him after work." He worried that she wasn't attracted to him anymore. If he only knew the truth.

All she could do was tell him she wasn't ready to talk about marriage. She had to be sure before she could make a commitment like that, and hoped he could deal with it. "But it will definitely be for the last time." At least until the operation was over and she knew anything concrete.

"Since you're getting so attached to the boy, it's probably better for him that you won't be there after tomorrow."

For him and for me.

Her mom knew she'd fallen fathoms deep in love with Raoul and his son, but she'd chosen the right words to bring her back to earth in a hurry.

"That's what I've been telling myself." Cami poured herself a drink of water. "How was your day?"

"We cleaned a house that had been damaged by a flood."

"We've done ones like that before. I hope it didn't hurt your shoulders too much."

"I'm fine. It's you I'm worried about. I'm not going to let you go to work on Tuesday. You need a day's rest before you go into the hospital."

Her love for Raoul wouldn't let her rest, but the surgery wouldn't be long now. Then what. *Oblivion?*

When Raoul saw Cami's car out in back, he got up from the table to open the back door for her. She'd come in jeans and a tan sweater, this time with her hair put back in a chignon. She was gorgeous no matter how she did it.

Alain called out to her from his high chair when she walked in the kitchen. Cami hurried over to the table and sat down by him.

"There's my boy," she said, giving him a kiss. "It looks like you've eaten all your dinner."

Just then an older woman came in the kitchen. She looked at Cami. "You must be *la fameuse Cam*."

"Delphine LaVaux?" Raoul spoke up. "Let me introduce you to Cami Delon."

Cami chuckled, enjoying the woman's sense of humor. "It's very nice to meet you, Delphine. You have charge of a very precious little boy."

"You're right," the Parisian woman smiled. "We're slowly getting acquainted."

She liked the other woman on the spot.

"I've come in time to put you down for the night and read you a brand-new story I know you're going to like."

Raoul nodded. "He's all fed and ready."

Cami got up to undo the tray and pick him up. But when she went to hand Alain to the nanny, he let out a loud *"Non—Non—Cam—"* and hugged her around the neck.

Raoul came closer to intervene. He pulled his son out of Cami's arms and handed him to Delphine. "It's time for bed, *mon fils*."

"Come on, Alain," the older woman coaxed him. But he didn't like it and protested. Cami could hear him crying all the way through the house and up the stairs.

She glanced at Raoul. "Oh, dear."

"He'll get over it," Raoul reminded her. "These are early days."

"He's adorable."

"I'm biased and agree." He sat down. His penetrating black eyes studied her for a long moment. "You said you'd tell me the truth. I want to hear it."

Unbelievably his cell phone rang, interrupting them. This time he let out what sounded like a curse before he checked the caller ID. In an instant his brows furrowed and he clicked on, then jumped to his feet. After a short conversation, he hung up.

"That was Dominic. He says there's trouble at the winery and wants to pick me up. He swears it won't take long. I pray not because I need to talk to you before the night is out. Will you wait for me? Please?"

The urgency in his voice kept her planted there. "Of course. I hope it's not serious."

"You never know, but I'll be back as soon as I can." He raced through the villa and left out the front door.

A few minutes later the doorbell rang. Was it Raoul? Had he forgotten his key?

Cami hurried to the foyer. When she opened the door, she came face-to-face with a dark-haired attractive woman who had to be Raoul's mother. She was shorter than Cami would have supposed, but she and her son shared certain facial features around the nose and mouth you couldn't mistake.

Had she come because of the trouble and wanted Raoul's help? She'd come with a package she held in her arm.

"May I help you? I'm Cami Delon."

"How do you do. I'm Madame Fontesquieu and I've come to see my son."

A second visitor. "I'm sorry, madame, but he isn't here. You just missed him. I don't believe he'll be long. Would you like to come in and wait for him?"

"I would. Thank you."

She'd dressed in a three-piece light green wool suit, the epitome of high fashion, and wore her hair in a becoming short style that revealed streaks of silver near the temples.

Cami showed her into the sitting room off the foyer. "May I bring you coffee while you wait?"

"That would be fine."

"I'll be right back." She hurried to the kitchen and poured her a cup, which she brought back to the sitting room. His mother was wandering around examining everything.

"Here you are."

The older woman turned around and sat down on the love seat to drink it. "Who are you exactly?"

"I'm a friend of Raoul's. We met while I was helping clean the villa. I work for Nettoyage Internationale here in Vence with my mother. We've been cleaning houses for seven years." His mother deserved to know the truth.

Her brown eyes narrowed on Cami. "Do you live here?"

That said it all. Raoul had warned her about the talk surrounding him. Sabine must have added her own assumption after coming to the villa. "*Non*, madame. I live with my mother."

"Who takes care of his son?"

So his mother *did* know about Alain. "His nanny, Delphine LaVaux."

"Is she here?"

"Yes."

"I would like to meet her."

"Excuse me. I'll go upstairs and tell her."

Cami hurried up to the next floor and found Delphine playing blocks with Alain in his bedroom. He called out her name when she walked in.

"*Bonsoir*, Alain." She gave him a peck on the cheek and looked at Delphine. "Excuse me, but Raoul's mother is here and wants to talk to you. She's in the sitting room, waiting."

The two women eyed each other before Delphine got up from the rocking chair and lifted Alain in her arms. "Come on, *mon petit*. Let's go see your *gran'mere*. It will be a first for both of us."

By that remark Cami deduced that Raoul had explained his family dynamics enough to Delphine that she understood certain facts. Cami could only admire her calm and maturity. She decided Raoul had hired an exceptional woman.

Delphine carried Alain downstairs. Cami followed. They found Raoul's mother on the phone. The minute they entered the sitting room, she put her cell phone in her purse and stood up.

Cami heard her sharp intake of breath as her brown eyes filled with tears the second they fastened on Alain. The likeness of him to her son had to have shocked the daylights out of her.

"Madame Fontesquieu, this is Delphine LaVaux."

"How do you do," Delphine spoke right up. "It's lovely to meet you, madame. You have a wonderful grandson. Come on, Alain." She tried to turn him so he'd look at Raoul's mother, but he fought her and kept his arms around her neck. "Say bonsoir to your *gran'mere*."

Alain started crying and wasn't having any of it.

"Let me take him in the kitchen for a snack," Delphine offered. "It will calm him down. We'll be right back."

Again Cami marveled over Delphine's handling of a very difficult situation. Her composure was worth its weight in gold and Raoul needed to know.

His mother reached for the package she'd put on an end table with the coffee cup and handed it to Cami. "Since you don't know how long he'll be gone, I've decided to leave. Please will you see that Raoul gets this?"

"*Très bien*, madame."

Cami followed her to the door and opened it for her. "He'll be sorry he missed you."

Her expression appeared haunted before she walked out on the porch and disappeared down the steps.

After closing it, she carried the package to the kitchen. Delphine had put Alain in the high chair and was feeding him some strawberries.

"She's gone, Delphine."

"Raoul warned me his mother might come by one day. Can you imagine seeing your own grandchild for the first time? I think it went well enough. Who couldn't love this little angel?"

"Especially his *gran'mere*. He's absolutely angelic. Since it's getting late, I'm not sure when Raoul will be back. He had to leave on an emergency. I'll stay awhile longer, but then I must go. Please see that Raoul gets this package she brought him."

"Bien sûr."

"I'll go get the coffee cup left in the sitting room." Cami started through the house and walked right into Raoul's arms. He'd just come in and gripped her arms so she wouldn't fall.

"I'm so sorry," she blurted. "I didn't see you and now you've saved me from another fall."

"Where do you think you're going so fast?"

She eased away from his hard body. "I need to get the coffee cup in the sitting room. Your mother came while you were gone. She brought you a gift. It's on the table in the kitchen."

Raoul hurried through the villa where he found Alain finishing off another strawberry. He kissed the top of his son's head. "Thank you for everything, Delphine. If you'll take him up to bed now, I need to talk to Cami."

"Of course."

"Bonne nuit, mon petit." He gave Alain another kiss before they left the kitchen.

Cami sank down on a chair while he opened the package.

"This is incredible," he murmured. "My mother has retrieved these without my having to resort to a court order to get them. I'm pleased beyond words."

"What are those?"

"The journals Jerome willed to me."

"Oh. That's wonderful!"

"Nothing could make me happier. I need them for

the new business I've started. My mother knew how important they are to me and must have prevailed on Sabine to let me have them and the paintings."

"It sounds like your mother loves you very much."

"Mother hasn't known what to make of me for years."

"Why is that?"

"My father has never approved of my way of thinking about life and we've never seen eye to eye. Unfortunately he has intimidated her for years. I've rarely heard her express her true thoughts. She's afraid to say or do anything that will upset him. It took a great deal of daring for her to bring me those journals."

"But they belong to you!"

"True, but my father didn't want to lose Sabine. She fought the divorce, and held those journals and paintings back to use for leverage. My father loves the prestige of the Murat money and influence. He tried to make me hold on to Sabine at all costs. He even had my *gran'pere* declare me the CEO so I wouldn't divorce her. He held out against hope. That's the reason he refused to tell the truth to the media."

Finally Cami had the answer to that question. "According to the newscast, she brought millions to your marriage."

He nodded. "My father can't bear to see me part with all her money. One day she'll be an heiress. Her parents feel the same way about the Fontesquieu fortune. Being married to me, she had access to some of it."

"Does your father know about Sabine's lie to you?"

His dark head reared. "No one knows except Sabine, the doctor, Dominic and Nathalie, Arlette and now you." And Cami's mother. "That's the way it's going to stay. The ugliness over money and power in this family has gone on long enough. My father, along with Sabine and her parents, have done everything in their power to keep us together, but it's far too late."

"I love your mother for doing that for you."

Their gazes met. "It's a miracle she was able to convince Sabine to return the paintings and the journals to me. Naturally the news will get back to my father, and Maman will pay a price for it. That's what concerns me."

"It's obvious she was willing to take the risk. That's because you're her only son and she has never stopped loving you. You have to know the truth of that deep down."

"I do. I think this was her way of giving me a peace offering. I told her recently that I would be leaving the business soon."

"I don't know how your father ever let you go."

"He had no choice."

"You know what I mean."

"I've told you about him. There's no hope where he's concerned. I've refused the CEO position. That, plus my divorce, has hardened his heart. When I said goodbye, he didn't try to stop me."

"How tragic for him, but I know your mother couldn't feel the same way. Oh, Raoul—you should have seen her eyes when she glimpsed Alain for the first time. They were flooded with tears. I had the distinct impression she was seeing you when you were his age. You both look so much alike."

"That's the reason Nathalie had such a hard time trying to figure out which Fontesquieu was Alain's father."

Cami smiled. "Delphine brought him downstairs and I introduced them to your mother who was speechless. I have to tell you that Delphine is the perfect person to be his nanny. She handled those first silent moments with your mother with such grace and respect, I was stunned."

"What about you? How did she treat you?"

"Your mother was civil."

Raoul stopped pacing. "That's what I was afraid of."

"Please don't misunderstand. The second she saw Alain, everything changed for her."

Raoul loved this woman who was trying her best to defend his mother. He moved closer. Using his free hand, he traced her beautiful features with his index finger. "Do you have any idea how wonderful you are?"

She averted her eyes. "Y-You're not listening to me," her voice faltered. "When I saw her to the door, I could tell she'd undergone a shock and I felt sorry for her. Alain is so adorable and she's missed out on the joy of watching her only grandson grow to this point. No doubt she has suffered over the loss of Celine, just as you have."

He loved the depths of this woman. "When I call

to thank her for the gift, I'll tell her she can see him whenever she wants. We'll see if she can talk my father into coming around. But it's *you* I need to thank for being you and knowing how to deal with this whole ugly situation."

She was trembling. "Don't forget Delphine was a saint."

"In my opinion you're both candidates for the title. This news has made my day.

"Are you really all right, Raoul?"

He nodded. "The trouble at the winery was easily solved. Word still hasn't reached some of the workers that I'm no longer associated with the business. They insisted on an explanation."

"It's hard for people to let go."

"That's true for me too. What is the one thing you haven't told me? I'm still waiting for that answer."

"I'll give you one, but I didn't expect to stay this long."

"That's my fault."

"I promise we'll talk again, but not tonight. Suffice it to say I'm not ready to talk about marriage yet. It's too soon."

"So are you saying you need more time?"

"Yes, now I have to go." She got up from the table.

"Cami—"

"Please—it's all I can tell you right now."

It was pure torture to watch her leave. He waited until he saw her headlights and she'd gone. If she needed time, he'd give it to her.

The first thing he did after getting in bed later was

phone his mother. Cami's explanation over what had happened earlier went a long way to help him find the right words.

"Maman?"

"Raoul... Thank heaven you called."

There was new warmth in her voice. "As if I wouldn't. I'd planned to invite you over next week to meet Alain."

"I...decided I didn't want to wait. He's wonderful and looks so much like you, I—I couldn't believe it," her voice faltered.

"So are you for coming on your own and bringing the journals. How did you manage it?"

"I reminded Sabine that those were your private possessions and she had no right to them. She hasn't been kind about a lot of things for a long time. She was especially negative about Camille Delon. I'm afraid I wasn't friendly to her when she answered the door. She said she was a friend and that she'd helped clean your house."

"Maman, Camille Delon is the love of my life and the woman I'm going to marry," Raoul declared. It was a relief to say it out loud.

"Married? I guess that doesn't surprise me. I'm very much aware you love that little boy's mother and no one else. How soon are you planning the wedding?"

"I hope to have that answer soon, but I need to tell you the truth of things. Cami's not his mother."

"What do you mean?"

"Alain's birth mother died ten days after he was born."

The silence was deafening. "She's dead?"

"That's right. Over eighteen months ago. Her name was Antoinette Fournier. She's buried in La Gaude. I'd planned to marry her. Instead I had to give her up. Her wonderful mother, Arlette, and her stepsister, Nathalie, raised him until a few months ago when Nathalie traced him to me."

"Dominic's wife?" Too many shocks in one day, but his mother needed to know the truth. Of necessity there'd been too much secrecy.

"Yes. She was looking for me when she met Dominic and they fell in love. She is Alain's adored aunt. Now I'd like him to get to know and love you. You're his *gran'mere*. I've already told his nanny that you don't need an invitation to know you're welcome at the villa anytime. Cami knows it too."

"When did you meet Cami?"

"The day after *gran'pere* passed away."

"And you're in love this fast?"

"Madly, desperately. I didn't think it could happen again in this life, but it did and I wanted you to know before anyone else." He told her about Cami's story and her trips to the vineyard with her father and mother. "She used to dream she was the princess in the château."

"She sounds very sweet and was very polite to me. Why don't you plan to marry her in the château chapel? It would thrill me to know you're going to marry the woman of your heart there, even if you have moved out."

Raoul couldn't believe what he was hearing. "What about Papa?"

"Leave him to me. He's suffering over you. A marriage at the château might be just what he needs to feel better about everything."

That had to be a first. "I'll think about it."

"I can see there's a lot we have to discuss. *Je t'aime, mon fils*," her voice trembled. "I'll visit soon to get acquainted with her and my grandson."

Those were brave words considering she had to deal with his father. "Can you come over tomorrow? No one else will be around. Alain will love it."

"I'll work something out and let you know."

His throat swelled with emotion. "*Je t'aime*, Maman."

Raoul couldn't sleep all night and finally got up to shower and shave. At seven the next morning he hurried to the nursery. Alain was standing up in his crib waiting for him. The sight thrilled him every time. He put him in some rompers and carried him down to the kitchen where they both ate breakfast.

Cami had gone home last night and there'd been nothing he could do about it. The second Alain had discovered she'd gone, he'd started to cry. It had taken Raoul quite a while to console him before he fell asleep in his crib.

If his mother could come over later, she'd phone him first, but he worried his father might have other plans. Raoul decided to take Alain to Arlette's for the day. He needed to have that serious talk with Cami, and didn't believe she wasn't ready for marriage. She was holding a secret he needed to get out of her.

A part of him had hoped she might try to reach him last night, but it hadn't happened. All morning he waited for a phone call, then he phoned her. To his chagrin, the call went through to her voice mail. Worse, he couldn't leave a message because the box was full.

He hung up in frustration. Toward the end of the day he walked into the kitchen where Arlette was feeding Alain. "I'm leaving for a while, but I'll stay in touch with you."

"Go for as long as you want, or overnight. We'll have great fun here, won't we, Alain?"

"Thanks, Arlette. I couldn't do without you."

Raoul kissed his son and left the house. He assumed Cami and her mom were at the apartment in Vence and had decided not to take calls. They'd be home from work by now. He would drive by to see if their Citroën 2CV was parked there. If so, he'd knock on the door and surprise her.

A half hour later more disappointment met him when there was no sign of the black car around the eight-plex. Still, he got out and knocked on their door in case one of them was home. When that didn't work, he walked to the next apartment and knocked, hoping to get some information. Unfortunately no one was home there either.

As a last resort, he went back to his car and called NI. He had to leave a message and asked the manager to phone him back ASAP.

Madame Biel called him ten minutes later.

"Monsieur Fontesquieu? I just saw the message that you'd phoned in. I have found a woman whom I believe would make an excellent housekeeper. Her name is Charisse Verot. Shall I make an appointment for her to come to the villa?"

That had been the last thing on his mind, but he might as well deal with it now. "Could she come next Monday? Say 10:00 a.m.?"

"She'll be there."

"Thank you, but before we hang up, I need to ask you a question. Did the Delon family work today?"

"Actually no. They've gone on vacation."

A day earlier than planned? "Do you have Juliette's phone number?"

"Of course. Here it is."

Raoul put it in his phone. "I'd like to get in touch with her and find out what their plans might be. I've tried phoning Camille several times, but her voice mail is full."

"I'm sorry about that, monsieur. They didn't share any of their plans with me."

"I understand. Thank you for returning my call."

"Of course. I hope Madame Verot works out well for you."

"We'll see."

Right now he couldn't concentrate on anything. At this point Raoul was convinced that Cami was deliberately hiding from him. He phoned both numbers. Even Juliette's message box was full.

Grimacing, Raoul went back to his villa and spent the night. In the morning he drove to a café for a quick breakfast and went back to the Delon apartment once more. By now he knew in his gut something was terribly wrong.

Their black car still wasn't there, but that didn't matter. He pulled into the parking area at the side of the building and got out to investigate. There was no answer after he knocked and rang the doorbell. For the next little while he knocked on the other apartment doors of the eight-plex to see if anyone was home and knew anything about the Delon family.

Unbelievably no one answered. He went back to the car and sat there to wait. Someone had to come home eventually. He'd stay there all day if he had to and phoned Dominic to tell him what was going on.

"I know she's avoiding me, Dom."

"Then stick to your plan and find out what you can from the neighbors. If you need more help, I'll be available after work to help."

"No one ever had a better friend."

They hung up. Around four thirty a woman probably close to Juliette's age, pulled into the parking and got out.

Raoul called to her from his car window so he wouldn't alarm her. "Excuse me, madame. Do you live here? I'm looking for Cami and Juliette Delon. Do you know them?"

The woman smiled. "Yes. They live in the apartment next to mine."

His heart pounded fiercely. Maybe this waiting had produced results after all. "My name is Raoul Fontesquieu. I've been trying to reach Cami. She and her mother were on the team that cleaned my villa two weeks ago."

"I remember Juliette telling me they had a big job. You're the one who sent the flowers!"

"That's right."

"How can I help you?"

"Did you see either of them today?" She shook her head. "Do you know their plans now that they're on vacation?"

"I believe they were intending to be with family in Nice like they always do."

Nice? Cami had never mentioned extended family living there. Why had she lied to him that she wouldn't be leaving Vence? What kind of a secret had she been keeping from him? "Do you have a name or an address where I can contact her there?"

"I'm sorry. All I know is they always spend time with her father's family."

Her *father's* family with a last name *Delon*? "Thank you. You've been very helpful."

After she walked off, he phoned Delphine and told her he might not be home all night. She assured him she could stay indefinitely.

With that resolved, he drove to the office on the estate to see Dominic and eat dinner with him. Between the two of them they could get on the phone and try to track down Cami's family.

CHAPTER TEN

CAMI'S MOTHER DECIDED to go on vacation a day early. They left town on Monday and drove to Nice with their suitcases. They spent the next two nights there with family and got everything ready so that when they returned after the operation, they'd have what they needed.

Those were difficult nights to get through for Cami. On Wednesday they drove back to Vence and checked into the hospital. That evening the technician doing Cami's labs had finished drawing blood for a second time. After he left the hospital room, house-keeping came in and set up a cot where her mother would sleep for the night.

Now that they were alone, Cami eyed her ever faithful mom who stood at the side of her bed.

"Well, Maman, this is it. By tomorrow morning at nine o'clock, Dr. Molette explained that the keyhole surgery will be over."

"That's right. He said you would have smaller scars and get out of the hospital quicker. Better yet you'll have less pain while the scars heal and will get back to normal activities sooner."

"That's an impossible dream, Maman."

"Nothing's impossible, Cami."

She sat up straighter in the bed. "You also heard him say that if it doesn't work, I'll have to come in again for open-heart surgery after he returns from vacation."

Her mom reached for her hand. "It'll be a success. Your uncle Emil and aunt Liliane have planned for us to come to their house while you recover. Everyone is anxious to wait on you."

Cami loved her father's older brother and his wife. He ran a small trucking company in Nice. They lived in a charming home where she'd spent many hours over the years, especially during the semesters while she'd been attending the university.

"That would be wonderful, but I don't have your faith about the outcome of the operation. We might not be going anywhere."

I might not make it out of the hospital.

"Nonsense. You've always been so brave about this, and I'm so happy it's finally here I could cry."

"You and me both."

"It hasn't been fair to you all these years, waiting and waiting."

Cami squeezed her mom's fingers gently. "Nor to you. Have I told you how much I love you? When I was with Raoul on his sailboat, he told me a story about his tragic relationship with his father. It made me appreciate even more being born to the best parents in the world."

Her mom's eyes watered. "Thank you, darling. Certainly you know how much joy you bring to mine. But let's change the subject because I know how deeply in love you are with Raoul. Why not tell me what else happened while you were out there with him?"

"H-He wanted me to go to a party at his cousin's place in a couple of weeks." She stumbled over her words. "But I told him I'd be on vacation. After we got back to the villa, I thanked him for a lovely time, said goodbye and left."

"And he let you go, just like that?" Her mom was going to keep this up until she'd wrung the truth from her.

Cami hugged the pillow against her. "No," came her muffled response, but the tears falling down her cheeks betrayed her. "He asked me to marry him."

"That doesn't surprise me a bit, but you obviously said no or he'd be here at your side this very minute."

"I couldn't put him through this."

"Why not?"

"Because I haven't told you everything about his life. While he was married, his wife had a baby girl."

"He had a baby with his wife?"

Cami stared at her mom. "But he found after the birth that his little daughter, Celine, wasn't *his*!"

A frown broke out on her mother's face. "His wife *lied* to him about that?"

Cami nodded. "She tricked him so he would marry her."

"Ah. That explains why he had to let Alain's mother go and he never got to see his own boy."

"There's more, Maman. He adored that baby in spite of the lie, but suffered grief when the doctor told them the little girl had such a damaged heart, she wouldn't survive. They buried her on the Fontesquieu estate a month after she was born."

Cami watched her mother pace for a moment before she came to a halt. "I finally have my answer why you never told him about tomorrow's surgery."

"How could I after all he's been through? He loved that baby and it killed him she died of a bad heart!" Cami cried. At this point she broke down sobbing. "He's so remarkable, so wonderful and doesn't deserve to go through any more pain or suffering."

"That's because you're convinced that you're not going to make it."

"I don't know what to believe," she bit out. "Can you guarantee I *won't* die?"

Silence reigned for a moment. "No, my darling girl, but I know God is watching over you and He's not going to let that happen. Excuse me while I freshen up in your bathroom, then I'll come in and lie down on that cot by you. I want to hear more about this incredible man who's going to become my son-in-law one day."

"Don't joke with me about this."

"Who's joking?" she asked from the bathroom door.

"I'm afraid you're not going to get much sleep."

Cami wiped her eyes. "The nurse will be in and out during the night."

"It'll be worth it when morning comes and I find out my daughter came through her surgery perfectly and will be free of worry for the rest of her life about her heart."

Free of worry.

Incredibly, for the first time in years, Cami had something else on her mind besides the outcome of the surgery. She was still so shaken by the feel of being in Raoul's arms, let alone his marriage proposal, she couldn't think straight.

Raoul had been right about one thing. She'd fallen crazy in love with him and his son. The way she'd returned his soul-searching kisses told him everything she hadn't been able to say in words.

Cami had escaped his world just in time. He deserved to find a woman of his own class who would love Alain and make a wonderful home for him. She would have to be a woman of whom his parents could approve of. Cami didn't care how much Raoul denied it, his father's opinion had to mean something to him. She could never be his parent's choice of daughter-in-law.

Of course, Cami's mother didn't have the same problem when it came to Raoul. She'd approved of him from the beginning.

But the only matter of importance was tomorrow, the most important day of her life. Until the operation was over, she had no idea what her life would be like. No one could predict the future.

Antoinette had died of infection ten days after giving birth to Alain. Within a month of being born, Sabine's baby had died of a bad heart, adding to Raoul's grief over the lie she'd told him.

Maybe Cami wouldn't come out of the anesthetic. Thank heaven her mother had family to turn to if the worst happened and Cami's heart stopped beating altogether.

Anything could happen. Thankfully her beloved Raoul would know nothing about it. That was the way it had to be.

The next morning, her operation was scheduled early. Before going to sleep the night before, they'd given her a medication to make her less anxious. When morning came she was administered the anesthetic. When Cami awakened in the recovery room later on, she saw her doctor smiling at her.

"Welcome to the world, Cami. Your mother told me how frightened you've been, but you don't have to be any longer. Your operation was a complete success. You're going to live a long, full life. For now you must rest. You'll be taken to your room in a little while. Tomorrow I'll release you."

Cami couldn't believe it. Tears spurted from her eyes. "You mean I'm not dreaming? I'm really going to have a normal life?"

"Yes." He patted her arm. "I understand there's a wonderful man out there somewhere who'll rejoice when he hears this news. But for the time being you need to stay quiet and rest."

Raoul.

More tears streamed from her eyes. She was alive! The operation was over and she was going to live a full life. She couldn't wait to tell Raoul everything!

Two days later Cami and her mom drove to Nice to be with the family while she recovered. Cami half lay on the bed in her robe watching the 5:00 p.m. news, but one announcement caused her to sit up straight.

"More news from Provence. Matthieu Fontesquieu has been named CEO of the Fontesquieu empire in Vence due to his son, Raoul Fontesquieu, stepping down after his divorce from Sabine Murat. More on this story is forthcoming."

"Raoul, darling," she whispered to herself. His father had finally accepted what had happened. Now Raoul had gotten his wish and was now truly on his own.

She gotten her wish too.

The operation had made her well! Joy, joy! Since the doctor had talked to her in the recovery room, she'd wanted to phone Raoul and tell him everything, but had needed to wait a few days until her strength had returned.

Her mom had gone to the beauty parlor to get her hair done and hadn't returned yet. That's what Cami needed to do. Hers needed to be cut. It had grown too long to manage.

"Cami?"

"Come in."

Her sandy-haired aunt Liliane peeked inside. "I have a message for you from Emil."

She couldn't imagine. "What is it?" They'd been so wonderful to her.

"Raoul Fontesquieu would like you to call him as soon as you can. Apparently your message box is full and he hasn't been able to get through. Emil said he sounded pretty desperate on the phone."

"Raoul talked to Emil? But how could he?"

"I don't know." Her aunt smiled.

"No one knows where I've been recuperating!"

"Why don't you call him and find out?"

Cami couldn't believe it. No one at NI, or at the hospital had any idea where she'd been. Had he hired someone to find her? Would he actually do that? This wasn't supposed to have happened. She'd planned to call him tomorrow.

Too many emotions had converged at once, but the one that overpowered her most was a joy beyond bearing. According to the doctor, the keyhole surgery had fixed her heart. She wouldn't have to worry about it ever again. But right this second it was beating so hard, she feared there could be real damage.

Her aunt was still standing there. "Did he tell Raoul I've had heart surgery?"

"No. He feels it's your place to do that."

"Tell him thank you for that. I promise to get hold of Raoul tomorrow."

"I think that would be a good idea."

From that point on Cami was an excited, nervous wreck. She kept going through her mind how she would approach him and what she would say. Finally she got on her laptop and sent an email to the Degardelle Company.

Dear Sir

My name is Edouard Sorel. I'm from Marseilles and read your ad in La Provence. I've been in Nice and would like to meet you in person.

I realize it's quick notice, but I'm afraid to get into something and fill out forms without meeting the head man first.

Would it be possible to come to your office in Vence? I only have a small amount of money to purchase land for a future vineyard and have several spots in mind. Perhaps none of them will do, but I'd like to hear what an expert like you has to say.

I could be there by tomorrow evening at seven if that works for you. Otherwise I'll have to wait a month before I can come back to Vence.

I await your response.

Sick with nerves and excitement over what she'd done, she hurried to the salon to tell the family her plans. They all had dinner, then she hurried back to the bedroom to see if he'd answered. She trembled with happiness to read his response.

Monsieur Sorel.

I'll meet you at seven.

I'm afraid it will have to be a short meeting because I have another engagement.

Just follow the map and knock at the outside door with the sign on it.

Cami answered.

Merci mille fois, monsieur. I'll be there on time.

She closed the lid of the laptop. "Raoul Fontesquieu? Get ready for a big surprise, my love."

The next day Cami and her mom drove back to their apartment in Vence. The doctor cautioned her to be careful. She had to take it easy, but it was good for her to be up and around. Depending on how things went, her mom might return to Nice the next day. As for Cami, anything could happen.

She took a shower and washed her hair. This time she would wear it long again and brushed it from a side part until it gleamed. The last time they'd been together, he'd revealed how much he loved it loose.

She pulled her dressiest dress out of the closet. A sleeveless, filmy black affair with a round neck. Cami had only worn it one time to a party with her friends after they'd graduated in November. The operation had transformed her into a new woman.

After putting on her lavender-blue earrings and slipping on her black high-heeled sandals, she was ready. It was time to knock the socks off her prince. Before leaving the apartment, she changed handbags to the silky black one. Then she gathered the shopping bag holding some gifts for him and Alain.

One more item to go. A stylish, waist-length black

coat she'd spent some money on when she'd bought the dress. Cami was so glad she'd purchased it. There'd be no sign of the cleaning lady tonight.

Giving her mother a kiss, she left the apartment and got in the car. Despite the fact that she was still recuperating from the operation, her body was so alive, she could be a rocket getting ready to fly into space.

Raoul kissed his son who was still in his high chair. "Be good for Delphine." He eyed the nanny who was turning out to be a treasure. She'd had a lot to put up with since he'd returned from Nice so devastated he was barely functioning. So far no return call from Cami. "I'll look in on him later. I have a client coming to the office."

"This late?"

"It's all right. What else do I have to do but try to make more money?" He heard her chuckle before he left the kitchen and went upstairs to shower and shave. In a few minutes he put on dark trousers and a dark blue long-sleeved sport shirt. When he was ready, he headed for his office.

Dominic's brother Etienne had invited him over to the château for dinner. He loved him, but didn't want to go near the place. They settled on meeting at Le Petit Auberge at nine.

As soon as he entered his office, he heard the knock on the door. He walked over, but when he opened it, he was surprised to smell the delicious flower fragrance Cami wore.

"*Bonsoir*, Monsieur Fontesquieu." When she walked in looking a heavenly vision in black, he thought he was hallucinating.

"*Cami*—"

"I'm afraid Monsieur Sorel couldn't make it because he doesn't exist. I made him up and hope you're not angry with me. The thing is, I had to see you or die in the attempt. I can't live without you, Raoul. That's why I'm here." Her eyes dazzled like rare amethysts. "I love you more than life itself, but you better not touch me until I can explain."

"What do you mean?"

"I'm recovering from a heart operation I underwent on the eighteenth."

"A heart operation?" He looked staggered by the information.

"I know it's a shock for you to hear that. Like your Celine, I was born with a heart murmur, but by some miracle the surgeon was able to fix it. In another two weeks I'll have recovered enough to get back to normal living. I'm afraid for you to hold me too tightly."

One look at Raoul's chiseled features while he stood there with a more princely aura than any royal and Cami almost passed out. His blazing black eyes played over every inch of her, missing absolutely nothing. The intensity of his gaze robbed her of breath. She walked to the love seat and sat down so she wouldn't sink to the floor.

"Are you still in a lot of pain?"

"No. The cuts are healing and I no longer have to take painkillers."

"Dieu merci," Raoul muttered.

"I've been waiting five years for the keyhole surgery to be performed. It's a good thing I did because the new technology fixed everything."

His eyes moistened. "When I think of all your hard work, I—"

"My heart condition didn't stop me from doing normal activity," she broke in on him. "I was glad for all the tasks. They helped me from thinking too much."

"But if I'd known the trial you were facing, I would have come to the hospital and stayed with you. I can't believe you went through that experience without me."

"Raoul, you've gone through enough suffering, especially over Celine. I didn't want to add to it until I knew the outcome."

He closed his eyes for a moment. "You've been a hard person to find," he spoke in his deep voice that set every cell of her body on fire. "I tried to call, but your message box has been full."

She swallowed hard. "I know. I left it that way on purpose. How did you know where to find me?"

"Your next-door neighbor at the apartment."

"I don't understand. She wouldn't have known anything."

"When I asked her if she knew your plans, she said you always went on vacation with your father's family in Nice. It only took me and Dominic six hours to eliminate every Delon who lives there until I found your uncle Emil at his trucking company.

"When I explained I needed to talk to you, he phoned your aunt. But he didn't tell me about your heart."

"I didn't want you to know about it until I could tell you in person. But I wasn't sure I'd be able to tell you anything if I didn't make it out of the operating room. I had fears about dying. That probably sounds hysterical to you."

"No it doesn't. What hurts me is that you've kept all those fears to yourself." He sounded more emotionally upset than she'd ever heard him.

"You didn't need to hear about my condition, which would be a reminder of all you've suffered. When I told you about my bad marriage, I never told you that my ex couldn't cope with my condition. He freaked out when I told him I couldn't run in a marathon he wanted to do. I guess he thought I might die. I don't know what he thought. He wouldn't talk to me about it."

"So you thought I wouldn't be able to handle it either."

"I didn't know, darling."

He raked a hand through his black hair in what she knew reflected pain and frustration. "You remained silent for *my* sake."

"Because I loved you so much."

"Thank heaven you came into my life. We felt an instant attraction and were thrown together long enough to realize we want to spend the rest of our lives together.

"Now that you've been told you'll never have heart

trouble again, there's nothing to stop us from being together forever. Let's get married before you have to start work. I've already talked to my mother about it. She wants us to get married in the chapel at the château. She was very impressed with you and wants us to be happy."

Cami was overcome. "She really wants us to be married at your old home?"

"Yes. She thinks it might even soften my father."

"Is that what you would want?"

"I can't think of anything more wonderful than marrying my long-haired princess in the château she loved as a child."

"With Alain as our witness?" she cried with happiness."

"Absolutely."

"What's he going to say when he grows older and finds out I was your cleaning lady?"

"By that time he'll discover his brilliant mother is a Renaissance woman who's part of the vital financial team at Gaillard's."

"Now I know I'm dreaming. Oh, Raoul—" Cami's throat swelled. "I want so much to be the perfect wife and mother."

"My mother already likes you."

"Mine adores you. She's not going to believe it when I tell her where we're going to be married."

"Maman is sorry she wasn't kinder to you that day and is looking forward to getting to know you."

"Thank you for telling me that. I want so much to

be the perfect mother and wife. But I know your father won't be happy."

"Not at first, but hopefully in time he'll come around. Just remember that part of life is getting hurt and we'll deal with it if and when it happens."

He reached out and drew her into his arms. "You and I have both found that out in the past. But instead of dwelling on the dark side of everything, why don't you start chasing after the sunshine? I think my fortune cookie was meant for you," he whispered against her lips.

"Raoul."

"*Mon amour.* It's been too long. Kiss me so I can believe you're back in my arms, alive and well." He ran his fingers through her shoulder-length hair. "You don't know long I've wanted to do this. You're so breathtaking I'm never going to be the same again."

Raoul clasped her gently, but her shopping bag and purse fell to the floor. "I can't believe it's you. You're the most beautiful sight this man has ever seen," he cried before covering her mouth with his own. In a heartbeat they were devouring each other.

When he couldn't get close enough, he removed her coat, then carried her back to the love seat and caught her against him. They clung, trying to show each other how they felt. "I love you so desperately, Cami."

She kissed every inch of his face. "I wanted to come the day I woke up in recovery, but had to wait a few days."

"If you only knew what I've been through since you said goodbye to me."

"I'm so sorry, darling." Tears poured down her flushed cheeks. "You know I didn't mean it. In the beginning I was just so afraid I couldn't be the wife you wanted, or the mother Alain needs. I was afraid to let things go further, but somehow they did."

Raoul groaned. "You think I don't know that?" He started kissing her again until neither of them could stop. "Are you ready to marry me now?"

"You know I am or I wouldn't be here. The doctor told me I could get back to real normal in another two weeks."

"Then that settles it. Stay right there. I've got something for you." He kissed her long and hard before hurrying over to his desk. After reaching for something inside the top drawer, he rushed back to her and got down on one knee.

"Camille Delon, will you do me the honor of marrying me?"

"Oh, Raoul, yes!" she cried. More tears ran from her eyes. He caught hold of her left hand and pushed a gold ring with a large violet-blue stone onto her ring finger.

"You've just made me the happiest man alive." He pulled her down gently and they ended up entwined on the floor. "I love you, I love you."

"Darling—"

The world reeled away as they got lost in each other's arms. So deep was their rapture, Raoul didn't realize there was a knock on the door.

"What is it, Delphine?"

"Your son wants to say good night."

"Come in."

She opened the door. Alain stood there clinging to her hand. Raoul didn't know which of the four of them was the most surprised.

"Cam!" It took his son a few seconds to recognize her with flowing hair.

Cami sat up looking gloriously disheveled and held out her arms. He came running into them. "Oh, my darling, darling boy. You really are going to be *my* boy!"

Raoul looked up at Delphine with moist eyes. She stood in the entry. He got to his feet. "You're the first to know that Cami and I are getting married."

The nanny was all smiles. "I've been hoping for this. Congratulations. Unless you need me, I'll be upstairs."

"Thank you, Delphine." He turned to Cami. She was entertaining Alain. He watched her hand him a present from the shopping bag lying on the floor.

Alain tore at the wrapping and unveiled a red toy Jaguar that looked just like Raoul's car. He couldn't believe it. Suddenly she looked up at him and handed him a package. "This is for you, *mon amour.*"

In a daze, Raoul took it from her. After undoing the wrapping, he came face-to-face with an eight-by-ten framed photograph of a young, handsome Jerome. "Where in heaven's name did you find this? I've never seen this one." Raoul was stunned.

"I searched the internet and found a story about

him when he lived in Bordeaux. There was an article about the vineyard and pictures. This one brought him to life for me. He loved you so much and it spoke to my heart. I forwarded it to a shop that made up this picture for me. They're doing another one of Danie I'll pick up in a few days."

Raoul got back on the floor where his son was moving the car around. He reached for Cami and pulled her down to him. "You couldn't have given me anything I'd treasure more. I'm so in love with you I think I'm the one with the heart condition now."

They began kissing again, but his phone rang. He ignored it the first time, but when the caller didn't give up, he let her go long enough to pull the cell out of his pocket.

"*Zut.* It's Etienne. I agreed to meet him for dinner at nine."

She grinned. "It's kind of late, like ten o'clock. Why don't you call him back and invite him to come over. In fact why don't you invite Dominic and Nathalie too. I'd like to meet them all."

"You mean it?" He was on the verge of exploding from joy.

"*Bien sûr, mon cheri.* It's going to be so exciting for me to have cousins. We can announce our engagement to them. Alain will love having everyone here. I'll go out to the kitchen and cook up some appetizers. I know you have a stock of your best wine in the cupboard. We'll party for as long as we want. What do you say?"

"I say I've died and gone to heaven with the two people I love most in this world."

"That's exactly how I feel. But I'd like to stay on the earth long enough to have your baby. Alain is going to need a brother or sister."

"Speaking of brother or sister, Dom and Nathalie just found out they're expecting."

"That's fantastic."

"Like I said, we need to get married immediately. Dominic knows a judge who'll waive all the rules for us."

"I have to admit I don't mind marrying into your aristocratic family after all. A perk like that I can live with. But the greatest one of all is that I'm actually going to marry the prince I once dreamed about. Dreams like that just don't come true in real life."

"Kiss me again before I call my cousins. They'll be in shock when they find out I'm marrying the most gorgeous woman in all Provence."

Alain came running over and clasped them both around the legs. He looked up with those shiny black eyes so much like Raoul's, Cami melted.

"Papa—Cam—"

"Oh, darling—" Her heart was bursting with happiness.

Raoul pulled her closer. "This is heaven."

* * * * *

BETTING ON A FORTUNE

NANCY ROBARDS THOMPSON

This book is dedicated to Susan Litman and Marcia Book Adirim, our fearless Fortune leaders.

Also, to my sprinting buddies, Cindy Kirk, Katherine Garbera and Renee Ryan. You're wonder women. Together, we can achieve mind-boggling feats of prose. Or at least get those books done. I don't know what I'd do without you.

Chapter One

"I'm here to see the owners." The deep, masculine voice was attached to an equally sexy guy in a sport coat. "Ashley, Nicole and Megan Fortune? I have a ten o'clock appointment."

Ashley let go of the high-top table she'd been moving and shoved a strand of blond hair out of her eyes. She hadn't scheduled an appointment for this morning. She'd set aside the entire day to stage the dining room.

The soft opening of Provisions, the restaurant she owned with her triplet sisters, was set for next week. She was in the weeds. The furniture had arrived yesterday morning—two days late. After she'd spent several hours unwrapping and checking it in, she'd discovered they'd shorted her a table and four chairs. She had lost more valuable time resolving that problem, but by the end of the day, after a lot of sweet-talking, the owner of the Houston-based restaurant furnishings company had delivered the missing items himself.

She'd hired some of the staff to come in today to help her set up everything. They would be here within the half hour. It was the final step toward transforming the place from an old feed and grain mill to the restaurant of her dreams.

It was imperative that she work with the staff, showing them how she wanted everything arranged. She couldn't be holed up in an office in appointments...even if the guy was tall, dark and jaw-droppingly handsome.

"I'm Ashley Fortune," she said, offering him her hand.

He smiled and accepted it. "Rodrigo Mendoza."

That smile. Those perfect white teeth. Ashley melted a little inside. Okay, maybe she could spare ten minutes—fifteen tops—for Mr. Perfect. Besides, she needed a break.

"Nice to meet you, Rodrigo. How may I help you?"

His smile faltered. "We have an appointment? I'm the restaurant consultant you hired."

"Excuse me?"

For an awkward moment, they stood looking at each other—him in that expensive-looking sport coat, Ashley realizing she looked far too casual in her gray T-shirt and shorts. Even if they were 7 For All Mankind and they'd cost her an entire day's pay, they suddenly felt a little ratty.

"Rodrigo Mendoza," he repeated. "Vines Consulting Group? Ring a bell?"

Ring a bell? She narrowed her eyes at him. She and her sisters did not forget business appointments.

"No, I'm sorry, it doesn't. Are you sure you're in the right place?"

Maybe one of the nearby establishments had hired a consultant to help up its game since Provisions was sure to take a bite out of business. Granted, Rambling Rose wasn't exactly known for its restaurant scene. They had a café-diner, Mexican and Italian restaurants and the food truck convoy stationed at Mariana's Marketplace.

The lack of culinary offerings was one of the aspects that her brother Callum had recognized and labeled as untapped potential in Rambling Rose. The sleepy Texas town was a diamond in the rough. He and her brothers, Steven and Dillon, who made up Fortune Brothers Construction, had jumped at the chance to purchase the old downtown property. Callum was such a great big brother. He knew how much his baby sisters wanted to realize their dream of opening a restaurant and he'd found them the perfect location.

"You're Ashley Fortune, right?" Rodrigo asked.

"And this is Provisions? In Rambling Rose, Texas, right?"

"Yes to all three questions."

"Then I'm in the right place." He flashed that smile at her. *Ooh, the guy is cuu-ute.* For a split second, she felt herself slip under his spell.

Until she forced herself to snap out of it.

She was too busy for this nonsense.

Squaring her shoulders and pretending her hair and makeup were perfect, she channeled the power she'd feel if she were wearing that sleek, black double-breasted Alexander McQueen suit she'd spied at Neiman Marcus before she'd left Fort Lauderdale for Texas.

"I'm sorry, Mr. Mendoza." Why did that name sound so familiar? "There has be some kind of mix-up. We didn't hire a restaurant consultant. We have everything perfectly under control. Thanks for thinking of us, though."

Suddenly it hit her. This could be a scam. Or a new tactic for securing business. A consultant on the lookout for potential new clients reads the business pages and then walks into a place acting like their working relationship is already a done deal. While he's there, he uses his million-dollar smile and smooth-operator tactics to seduce the woman setting up tables and *pow*! He's in like Flynn.

Whoever Flynn is.

Maybe *in like sin* would be more apropos.

Rodrigo looked perplexed and she was tempted

to say *Sorry, dude, you're not fooling me.* Before she could, he said, "Excuse me. I'll be right back."

She watched him walk out the door, pausing a moment to appreciate the rear view, imagining that his backside, which was covered by the expensive jacket, was just as nice as the rest of him.

Ashley couldn't blame him for being ambitious. In that regard, they spoke the same language. Who knew, maybe this Vines Consulting Group was legit, despite his dubious method of procuring new business.

The restaurant business wasn't an easy game to win.

Her sister Megan was the financial brains of their operation. She had scrutinized every single expenditure, making sure they stayed on budget and set aside an emergency fund.

No matter how smooth and tempting Rodrigo Mendoza might be, he did not qualify as an emergency.

What a shame.

Right now, Ashley needed to give Provisions her complete and undivided focus. It was her and her sisters' one shot at making their collective dream come true. They had invested every penny they'd been able to scrape together, adding it to the generous cash infusion their father had gifted them upon turning twenty-one—as he did for all of his children. If the restaurant tanked, they would lose everything.

But it wasn't going to tank.

At twenty-three years old, she and her sisters might be young, but they had years of experience in the restaurant industry. Among the three of them, they'd worked in every role—from cleaning bathrooms and washing dishes to setting tables, pouring water and taking reservations to planning menus and cooking food. Granted, their experience wasn't in fine dining, but their tastes were.

They'd been at this since they were sixteen years old. Not only were they good at what they did, they were hard workers.

There was still a lot to learn, but they had a solid handle on the industry, which was why her brothers and their father believed in them.

With one last wistful glance at the front door, Ashley figured that was the last she'd see of Rodrigo Mendoza.

He wasn't coming back. When he'd realized he wasn't fooling her, he'd known he needed an exit strategy. The guy was long gone.

Ashley turned her attention back to moving the high-top table.

She ran her hand over the glazed concrete tabletop. Everything about the furnishings was perfect—all copper-patinaed metal and neutral-toned upholstery. It flawlessly complemented the industrial décor of the converted warehouse, but still offered an inviting, come-hang-out vibe.

Ashley was proud of her findings. She and her sisters had chosen to furnish the place without the help of a commercial interior designer. It was one way to cut costs without having to scrimp on the quality of the furniture. They had worked together, choosing the color palate and furniture, but as front-of-the-house manager, Ashley had taken on the lion's share of the decorating and sourcing.

Megan was busy with the budget. Nicole, who was Provisions' sous chef, had been too busy working with the executive chef they'd hired, dreaming up potential menus and whipping up dishes for the staff to try.

Ashley was pushing the table into position when the door opened again. "Let me help you with that."

Rodrigo Mendoza was back.

Really?

"No, I'm fine," she said through gritted teeth. "But thanks."

"Be careful," he said as he lifted the opposite end of the table. "This is too heavy to move by yourself. Lift with your knees, not your back, or you'll hurt yourself. Why isn't anyone helping you with this?"

Was he trying to figure out if she was alone?

"My sisters are in the kitchen with some of the staff. I have people coming in to help. They'll be here any minute."

Why was she explaining?

"Mr. Mendoza, is there something I can help you with? If not, now really isn't a good time. However, I'd like to invite you back to dine with us after we officially open."

No sense in putting off a potential customer.

"Please, call me Rodrigo." He set down the table and opened his folio. After thumbing through a stack of papers, he selected one.

"Do you know David Fortune?"

Ashley nodded. "I do." He was her father.

And he will not be pleased when he finds out that you're trying to worm your way into our business with sneaky tactics.

"Is he available?"

Ashley put her hands on her hips and frowned. "No. He's in Fort Lauderdale."

"Hey, Ash," Megan called as she came into the dining room by way of the office, which was near the kitchen. She was carrying a stack of papers and catalogs. "Do you have the invoice for the throw pillows for the lounge sofas? Remember, we ordered them separately and I—"

She stopped and blinked as she looked at Rodrigo Mendoza, who was looking back and forth between Megan and Ashley, a bemused smile on his face.

"You two are twins?" he asked.

"No, we're not twins," Megan said. "Who are you?"

"I'm Rodrigo Mendoza of Vines Consulting Group. I'm here for our ten o'clock appointment."

"Did you set this appointment?" Ashley asked her sister. "Because I didn't."

"Your father, David Fortune, is the one who hired me and scheduled the appointment," Rodrigo interjected. "I have the contract right here. Did he not tell you?"

Ashley and Megan looked at each other.

"Contract?" Ashley said. "Did Dad say anything about this to you?"

Megan shook her head.

"May I see that piece of paper, please?" Ashley held out her hand and Rodrigo complied.

She glanced at the contract. It looked legitimate. And it was her father's signature.

"I know how to get to the bottom of this." She pulled her cell phone out of her back pocket. "I'm calling my father."

Luckily, David Fortune answered on the second ring. "Hello, sweetheart. How are you? Is everything coming together with the restaurant?"

"I'm fine, Dad. But I'm a little confused. Do you know a guy named Rodrigo Mendoza?"

"Of course," he said as if Ashley had just asked him if he knew the sum of one plus one.

"Um—okay. Did you hire him as a consultant for Provisions?"

"I did. Hold on a second, sweetheart. I'm on the golf course. It's my turn and I don't want to hold up play."

Ashley looked at Megan, shook her head and shrugged.

"What's he saying?" Megan asked.

"He's golfing. He's taking his turn."

Ashley felt Rodrigo watching her and she wondered if she and her sister should move the conversation into the office where they had more privacy. Because right now, being caught unaware and waiting for her father to play golf made her feel about as professional as she did when she and her sisters used to play restaurant with their Fisher Price appliances in the playroom of their parents' Fort Lauderdale home.

"I'm back," said David. "Are you there, Ashley?"

"I am. What's going on, Dad? Did you hire a restaurant consultant without discussing it with us?"

"I did hire Mendoza."

Wonderful. There goes the budget.

Ashley opened her mouth to object, but she realized Rodrigo was watching her. She and Megan really should finish the call privately. "Hold on a moment, Dad. Meg and I need to take the call in the office."

She motioned with her head, indicating that her sister should follow her, but Megan wasn't paying attention. She was chatting with Rodrigo Mendoza. The smile on her face hinted that she didn't find him as off-putting as Ashley did.

"Megan," Ashley commanded, "let's go into the office, please."

"Can y'all come in here and taste something?" Nicole walked out of the kitchen wearing an apron, wiping her hands on a white towel. "I can't decide if I like the broccoli slaw with or without dill. I'm doing a taste test and— Oh!"

In much the same fashion as Megan, Nicole stopped when she saw Rodrigo standing in the dining room.

"All three of you look exactly alike." Smiling as if he was the butt of a joke, Rodrigo looked back and forth between the trio.

"We're triplets," Megan said.

"Come on, let's go into the office, please." There was an edge to her voice. As she watched Megan flirt with him, pinpricks of irritation pierced her patience.

"I can't say I've met a set of triplets before." He smiled at Megan before turning to Nicole and offering his hand. He introduced himself again. Nicole hooked the towel she was carrying into the waistband of her apron.

"Nice to meet you," she said as she shook his hand.

"Wow! It's uncanny how much you look alike."

"I know, right?" Ashley said. "And we have a situation. Nicole, please come into the office with Megan and me. We need to talk to Dad."

"We'll be right back," Megan said. "Feel free to make yourself at home, Rodrigo. Sit wherever you'd like."

Inwardly, Ashley rolled her eyes at her sister's solicitous comment. Megan would change her tune as soon as she realized the hot guy in the suit had blown their budget. She started walking and her sisters followed, each of them casting a backward glance at Mendoza, as if to make sure he was really there and not just an apparition.

Oh, yes he was. Not only was his muscled bulk taking up space, but also the sheer beauty and presence of him seemed to be sucking all the air out of the room.

At least, that was the excuse Ashley made for the way her heart was thudding and why she found it increasingly difficult to take full, deep breaths.

That and the blown budget.

She had never been so happy in her life to shut herself inside her office.

"Okay, Dad, we're back. What is going on here?"

She put the phone on speaker so her sisters could hear, too.

"Are you not familiar with the Mendozas?" David asked.

"Should we be?" Ashley's tone was flat. She looked at her sisters and shrugged.

"Hold on," Nicole said. "Are you taking about the same Mendozas who have the winery and restaurant just outside of Austin? I was reading about them the other night."

"Then you should know the family has a long history of success in the restaurant business, going all the way back to Red and other establishments in Red Rock, Texas," their father said.

Wonderful. If they were super successful, it probably meant Rodrigo Mendoza's services were super expensive. It took every ounce of Ashley's self-control to keep from stamping her foot, which would do no good because their father couldn't see her.

He had to learn that he couldn't do things like this. Not only would this move wreck their budget, it meant he didn't believe they could handle the business without his help.

"I'm happy for the Mendozas and all their success," Ashley said, "but we can't afford to hire a restaurant consultant, much less someone like Rodrigo Mendoza."

"Ashley—"

"Dad, it's not in our budget. I wish you had asked us before you'd taken it upon yourself to hire him and—"

"Ashley, take a breath. I'm paying for this. Think of it as a business-warming present."

He just didn't get it, did he? "So, you think we can't do this on our own?"

"That's not what I think. Not at all. It's just that—"

"We may be twenty-three years old, but we've been working in restaurants since we were teenagers. That's a collective twenty-one years of experience among the three of us. Besides, Dad, we're Fortunes. If you don't think we're capable of running a restaurant, we'll prove you wrong."

He was quiet for a long moment. Ashley's ire stoked once more as she wondered if he'd put down the phone again so he could take his turn at golfing, but then he said, "I don't know if I'd fly the Fortune flag so proudly. They're not exactly role models."

Her father had only recently discovered that he was related to the Texas Fortunes. Along with that birthright came a rich and complicated history. Thanks to patriarch Julius Fortune's numerous affairs, the Fortunes were an ever-expanding family. Each year they seemed to grow even larger. Branches of the Fortunes family tree had sprouted in Houston, Austin, and Horseback Hollow, Texas; Atlanta; New Orleans; New York; Ft. Lauderdale; among other places. They'd even discovered a royal branch in England.

Her father had recently learned that Julius Fortune, his biological father, had refused to acknowledge him. His mother, Penny, had gone to great lengths to protect David from that rejection.

But that didn't matter. David was very proud to be a self-made man. He'd said time and again that he didn't need or want the Fortunes' money and all the baggage that came with it.

However, Ashley and her siblings thought discovering new and vast branches of their family tree was kind of cool.

In the past, before it was confirmed that they were indeed related to the infamous Fortunes, people would ask if they were related to *those* Fortunes, as if they were American royalty. Until just recently, when they'd learned the truth, they'd had to say no, no relation. It was disheartening to see the way some people dismissed them, as if they were less-thans or somehow didn't measure up. Even though their father had made a name for himself—and his own fortune—in the gaming industry. People, especially Texans, seemed to revere the Texas Fortunes as celebrities.

Now it was fun using their birthright to their advantage. It wasn't hurting anyone or costing anyone anything. So why not use the name to its fullest advantage?

After all, they were legitimate Fortunes, even if ol' Julius had rejected their father.

Ashley knew better than to rehash that argument with her dad. It was one area where they would have to agree to disagree. Besides, her father was still talking.

"The first step in operating a successful business is to be open to help, girls. The fact that you're balking at listening to Mendoza shows your inexperience and naïveté."

Ashley gave an incredulous snort. Her face went hot. She looked at Nicole and Megan, silently telegraphing that they were free to jump in at any time. Nicole was staring at her with her mouth agape. Megan had crossed her arms and was frowning.

"Our father is calling us inexperienced and naïve," she said, fully intending for David to hear the hurt in her voice. "And I thought he believed in us."

"I do believe in you," David said. "I also want to equip you with every possible tool for success.

We've already talked about the restaurant failure rate. I want Provisions to be a success story and I know you can do it. But you don't have to learn lessons through the school of hard knocks. Learn from someone who has been there. Getting help is simply smart business."

As much as his interfering went against her grain, their father was a smart, creative, self-made businessman. He'd taken his love of video games and parlayed it into a multibillion-dollar business. He had a proven business track record. She and her sisters hadn't even gotten out of the starting gate yet.

It rankled her, but he might have a point—even if she didn't agree with the way he'd gone about hiring Rodrigo.

"Dad, we appreciate your concern," Megan said. "And we do appreciate your help."

Nicole wasn't so quick to see his point. She huffed and rolled her eyes as she mumbled something under her breath that sounded like, "Mendoza had better not think he can step one foot in my kitchen and tell us how to run it. Nuh-uh. He's got another thing coming."

Megan swatted away Nicole's words.

"Listen, girls, don't mistake my intentions. I guess it's the father in me coming out. I know the three of you are smart, strong, talented young women who are perfectly capable of handling whatever challenge is thrown at you. But you'll always be my little girls. My babies. You can't blame a dad for that. Ash, you there? Do you forgive me?"

"Oh, Dad. Of course, I do. Actually, there's nothing to forgive. I'm just stressed. I have a million things to do and the soft opening is next week. I guess my gut reaction was fear that Rodrigo Mendoza would try to undo everything we've already done. But you know what? I'll consider his suggestions and if he makes some good ones, I'll take them into consideration."

"That's my girl," David said. "Look, it's my turn and I'm holding up play. The foursome behind us is shooting daggers at us, so I'm going to run. Let me know how things go with Mendoza after you've worked with him awhile."

Ashley's stomach did an unexpected twist at the thought of working with Rodrigo Mendoza.

Why was she suddenly all jumpy at the mention of the guy's name? Because Rodrigo Mendoza and his handsome face with that million-dollar smile was a distraction she didn't need.

Even so, she'd be lying to herself if she didn't admit that she felt a little breathy at the thought of working closely with him, but she'd get ahold of herself.

"All right, I've got to run. It's my turn to putt again."

"'Bye, Dad," they said in unison.

Trying to quell the sensation of butterflies, Ashley placed her free hand over her abdomen as her father disconnected the call.

"Well, the upside is that Rodrigo Mendoza is hot," said Nicole, as if reading Ashley's mind. "It could be much worse."

"I know, right?" said Megan.

"Yeah, he's definitely a good-looking guy, and I'm pretty sure he knows it. But we need to focus here." Ashley clapped her hands. Right now, focus was more important than ever. In a sense, the restaurant was an extension of them. Since they were each in charge of a very specific cog of the business, if one of them stopped turning—because she'd gotten tangled up in a hot dude—then they were destined to fail.

"We need to keep our eyes on the prize, which is making Provisions successful. Are we all on the same page?" Ashley held out her hand, palm up.

Without hesitation, Megan and Nicole put their hands in, too.

"Sisters before misters," they said in unison.

That had always been their mantra and Ashley intended to show this mister—and her father, for that matter—that she and her sisters knew their stuff.

Chapter Two

As Rodrigo sat at one of the tables waiting for the sisters to finish their conference call, he surveyed the restaurant. Granted, everything was in a state of disarray, but he could see the vision.

He had to give the Fortune triplets credit. They had done an admirable job with the renovation and the décor looked top-of-the-line.

Someone had good taste.

Of course, it was easier to have good taste when you had a lot of cash to spend.

Based on the research Rodrigo had done before making the trip to Rambling Rose, the triplets were from yet another branch of the extended Fortune family tree. They'd never opened a restaurant, but they had a lot of cash, compliments of their father.

Rodrigo tilted his head back and took in the restaurant's slanted corrugated-metal roof with its exposed beams and ductwork. In between the beams, skylights gave the place a light and airy atmosphere. The polished concrete of the high-top tables in the bar area complemented the metal-and-blond-wood stools. A grouping of couches, love seats and overstuffed chairs commandeered the center of the room. Cocktail and end tables completed the grouping. A set of glazed concrete steps led to a second level, which, he imagined, was the dining room.

It looked cohesive, but it didn't look too matchy-matchy—as if they'd ordered the furniture from one of those stores that marketed predesigned rooms.

If the upstairs dining area was even half as inviting as the lower level bar area, he could see this as a place where he would meet up with friends. They could grab a cocktail and catch up while they waited to move upstairs for dinner.

The triplets were definitely on the right track. With his guidance, they could make this place a success. But it would take some finessing.

His research had told him there wasn't anything like Provisions in Rambling Rose. No fine dining establishments. Only casual places to eat: La Ventana, a Mexican restaurant located on Main Street down the street from Provisions, and Osteria Oliva, a new Italian restaurant that local Carla Vicente had opened at The Shoppes, the new shopping center in Rambling Rose that Callum and his brothers had developed.

There was also the Crockett Café, a casual place where people could get inexpensive comfort food like eggs and pancakes, grilled-cheese sandwiches, burgers, fries and milkshakes. Also, there was a fleet of food trucks parked at Mariana's Marketplace. While they were the most casual of all the offerings, they provided variety and were still an option that would compete for the locals' food budget. He made a mental note to check them out some time next week.

The one challenge Provisions faced was making sure the locals bought into the upscale casual farm-to-table concept and the slightly higher price point that came with it.

To make Provisions Rambling Rose's new hot spot, the Fortune sisters had certainly nailed the ambience. However, once patrons got past the wow factor, would the restaurant's menu deliver on its promise? He had yet to find that out.

He regretted that he hadn't gotten off to a smoother start with the sisters, no doubt due to the confusion about his arrival. He'd never had someone set an appointment and not tell everyone involved about it. But his motto—especially in this business—was Expect the Unexpected. When you owned a winery, you never knew what each new season would bring. The best way to not only survive, but to flourish, was to learn how to navigate the twists and turns along the way.

The Fortune triplets were young. He'd venture to guess that they hadn't been out of college very long. All three of them were invested in the restaurant but there was something about Ashley...

In many ways, she reminded him of his sister-in-law, Schuyler, who had married his brother Carlo. Both women were forces to be reckoned with.

Maybe it was because Rodrigo had interacted with Ashley the most, but he could already discern differences between Ashley and her sisters. She was feisty and smart, as well as being gorgeous. But something else beyond her beauty and her quick wit drew his gaze to her over her sisters. It was something he couldn't quite define—yet.

Rodrigo smiled at the thought.

Then he reminded himself that now was the time for business, not for pursuing this infatuation.

After he'd taken the job, Schuyler had mentioned that the bunch in Rambling Rose were newfound cousins of hers. These days, the Fortune family seemed to be expanding exponentially, especially in Texas. He wasn't surprised that a branch had taken root in the up-and-coming community of Rambling Rose.

Carlo and Schuyler had met David Fortune and his son Callum last year in Paseo at the wedding of David's half-brother Gerald Robinson, who was also known as Jerome Fortune. Learning about Callum's and Fortune Brothers Construction's plans to develop Rambling Rose, Carlo had given David his card and told him to call if he needed help. When David had called asking about restaurant advice, Carlo had referred him to Rodrigo, who had a restaurant consulting business.

Though David was himself an astute businessman, his roots were in the gaming and technology industry. Without any experience in restaurants, he'd been wise to seek the help of Vines Consulting Group. And Rodrigo was eager to provide his assistance to Ashley and her sisters.

"We're sorry to keep you waiting, Mr. Mendoza."

As if his thoughts of the women had conjured them, he looked up.

Ashley shot him a dazzling smile. "I apologize for the confusion," she added.

He stood. "Please call me Rodrigo. I insist. Did you get everything straightened out?"

"We did, Rod," Ashley said. "My father does love to surprise us."

"Actually, it's not Rod. It's Rodrigo." He smiled to soften the words. He hated to correct her, but better now than letting it go on too long. "The mix-up was a surprise for both of us. Why don't we start over and reintroduce ourselves?"

"Well, you just told us your name is Not Rod," Ashley said. "It's nice to meet you, Not Rod Mendoza."

Not Rod?

He frowned, not quite understanding what she meant.

After a couple of beats of awkward silence, Ashley said, "I was joking. And obviously very badly since it fell flat on its face. You said, I'm not Rod... So, I said, It's nice to meet you, Not Rod. Okay, never mind. That's why I chose the restaurant business and not standup comedy."

"No, I get it." Rodrigo laughed, feeling like a dolt and hating the way she could throw him off his game. "I do. It just took me a minute. I guess it's a day of misunderstandings. But you're funny. You are."

As they laughed together, Rodrigo felt something electric zing between them, an invisible connection that felt both thrilling and completely off limits.

"Anyway, we were starting over?" Ashley stuck out her hand. "I'm Ashley Fortune."

Rodrigo accepted it and there it was again. That zip of electricity that confirmed that he needed to watch himself or— Or what?

Yeah, he wasn't exploring the *or-whats* right now.

Instead he withdrew his hand and reclaimed his personal space.

"I'm Rodrigo Mendoza. I started at the Mendoza Winery and La Viña Restaurant. I helped my family open the place and mold it into what it is today. After working there for a couple of years, I decided to venture out on my own and help other restaurants achieve the success and buzz we've built at La Viña.

Since then, I've been booked solid and I'm happy to have built a good portfolio of success stories. I'm excited to look over your business plan and lend my expertise to Provisions. You won't have to make the mistakes some new restaurants make learning by trial and error. So think of me as your knight in shining armor, here to save you."

He was trying to be funny, match her joke for joke—bad joke for bad joke.

"For the record, we're not damsels in distress," Ashley said. "We don't need to be saved, but thanks anyway."

Somehow, he'd known Ashley was going to say that as soon as the words had fallen out of his mouth.

He figured the Fortune sisters had probably heard their share of quips about them being Daddy's little princesses. Even if they were, it wasn't his place to judge. Everyone's circumstances were different.

He had his brothers and cousins. They had worked hard, saving and pooling their resources to make Mendoza Winery and La Viña a success. Would they have liked family money to get them off the ground? Certainly. They wouldn't have turned it down. But a cash infusion wasn't an option.

If not for the winery and La Viña, he might not be in the position he was in right now. Was that not family help of a different kind? It had given him the option to break away from the confines of the family business, which had started to feel claustrophobic. He needed something that was all his. Hence, Vines Consulting Group.

Now the Fortunes were his clients. That meant no matter where or how the triplets got their money for the restaurant, he would treat them with the same respect he afforded all his clients. He would help them turn Provisions into a successful moneymaker.

"Of course you don't need saving," he told her. "I'm not Rod and you're not damsels in distress. We're off to a brilliant start."

She nodded, as if saying she was accepting his unspoken apology, then continued introducing herself, finishing with her role in Provisions. "I handle the front of the house, social media and publicity."

Rodrigo's brows shot up. "You have your hands full, Ashley Fortune."

She gave a one-shoulder shrug. "I'm not afraid of hard work."

"Then you're in the right business."

"Yes," Ashley said. "My sisters and I have a lot of experience in the restaurant industry. We didn't just decide to open this place on a whim."

"Good. I'm glad you know what you're getting yourselves into. That's half the battle. A lot of people think owning a restaurant means it'll be a party every night. They don't realize they're going to work harder than they've ever worked in their lives. You'll be working when everyone else is playing, celebrating and relaxing."

Ashley met his gaze with an indulgent smile.

"Been there. Done that. And our father already grilled us on the ins and outs of owning a business."

"I didn't mean to lecture. I'm just telling you how it is."

She said, "Okay," but the implied meaning seemed to be *Tell me something I don't know.*

Rodrigo hoped he wouldn't be met with resistance the entire month he was scheduled to be there. His consulting services didn't come cheap and the people on the receiving end had to be open to constructive criticism and willing to make changes. Otherwise it was a waste of money.

Megan explained her duties as chief of finances and how she was keeping them on budget.

"Hi, Rodrigo. I'm Nicole. I cook."

"Nice to meet you, chef," he said.

A sheepish smile turned up the corners of Nicole's mouth. "Actually, I'm the sous chef. Rosemary Allen is our executive chef."

Hiring Rosemary Allen was a good move. She was making a name for herself in the industry after winning a prestigious award for young chefs.

It was curious that he hadn't heard the news that Rosemary had agreed to run their kitchen.

"She's a good addition to the Provisions' family," Rodrigo said. "Have you sent out a press release about her joining the staff?"

The sisters looked at each other.

"Not yet," said Ashley. "But I'll handle it."

She pulled out her phone and began typing what he presumed was a reminder.

She was organized.

Of the triplets, Ashley seemed to be the queen bee, which made her a natural to handle the front of the house. She ran the show, but her sisters didn't seem to mind. She was assertive, but she wasn't bossy. And she had tact. Even though she hadn't been expecting him, she'd managed to recover and invite him back when the restaurant opened rather than just turn him away.

"I'm happy to help you with that," said Rodrigo.

Ashley smiled. "Thanks. I'll take you up on that offer."

Their gazes lingered and, again, he felt that zing hit him in the gut.

Come on, man. This is business. Get your act together,

It would be a challenge, but Rodrigo was going to enjoy this change of pace, this fresh challenge that Ashley Fortune promised to be. She was gorgeous and sassy and everything he didn't need in his life right now. Not only was she was too young for him, there was the lingering Bonniefactor.

A few years ago, Rodrigo had ended a relationship he'd thought might be the real deal. He had even been looking at rings and getting ready to propose. Thank God, he'd found out Bonnie wasn't who she'd claimed to be before he'd irretrievably linked his life to hers. It was the first time he had even considered marriage.

Even though he'd been single for a while, and the pain had dulled to a blunt ache, not a day went by that he didn't remind himself that ending the relationship had been the best thing that could've happened to him.

He'd dodged a bullet.

He certainly wasn't going to open himself up for that kind of hurt again.

"Thanks for coming in today, everyone," Ashley said to the seven workers who had arrived to help her wrangle the bar furniture into place. "Hang out for a minute. I just need to take care of something and then we'll roll up our sleeves and get to work."

She made her way back to Rodrigo, who was still seated at the high-top table with Nicole and Megan. "As soon as I get the dining room set up, we can work on the Rosemary Allen press release."

"I'm happy to do it for you," he said. "It would be one more thing to check off your list."

"No. I'm good. Thank you."

There was no way she was going to let him do it when she should've sent it out the minute Rosemary had agreed to come on board at Provisions. She'd meant to. In fact, it was even on her extended to-do list. She had to fight the urge to pull it up and show it to Rodrigo. But with all the other things that had come up since then, the press release had gotten pushed farther and farther down her list.

The truth was she hadn't written many press releases. Okay, she'd never written one, but he didn't need to know that. She was a quick study, and how hard could it be?

If he knew she'd never written one, it would make her look like an amateur. She would prove she wasn't, but right now she needed to put the waitstaff to work and get the furniture in place. By doing this now, she would have time to correct any potential mishaps before opening night.

Her stomach jumped in anticipation. This was really real. For so long Provisions had been just a dream. Something she and her sisters had talked about and longed for. A *someday* that at one point seemed as if it would never arrive. Now, it was about to become a reality.

Press release aside, she was willing to bet that Rodrigo would be very pleased with how well she had everything under control. Even though she didn't really care what he thought.

She was just about ready to instruct the workers when Rodrigo said, "I think the best way to start is for me to tour the place. Which one of you would like to do the honors?"

Nicole frowned. "I have to get back to the kitchen. I'm up to my elbows in coleslaw."

Megan was just opening her mouth to volunteer—Ashley could read her sister like a book—when Ashley cut her off at the pass.

"Actually, if you want to make yourself useful, I could use some extra help arranging the lounge and bar furniture. I'm sure you'll have plenty of opinions on how we should do it. You might as well help us with the grunt work rather than just bossing us around." She showed him she was kidding—sort of—by flashing her most dazzling smile.

Megan shot her a strange, almost wounded look.

"Meg, I know you're busy. After we're done, I'll give him a tour. By the way, the pillow invoices you asked about are in the folder on my desk. Feel free to get them. I know you need them. While you're at it, would you tell me how much money we have left in the budget for furnishings? I'm still debating whether we should get those blown-glass salt and pepper shakers for the bar tables."

Maybe this was case in point of how she was the bossy, micromanager to Megan's quieter, more laid-back personality and Nicole's creative, bohemian vibe, which could fluctuate between moody and dreamy.

Still, she couldn't ignore the weird feeling that had been hanging over her like a storm cloud since Rodrigo Mendoza had walked in the door. For some reason even she didn't understand, she did not want Megan to be the one to show Rodrigo around the place. She wanted to do the honors. Really, it was just as much Megan's place as it was hers, but Megan owned the budget and Nicole had made it clear that she and Rosemary owned the kitchen, so that made Ashley take even more ownership of the front of the house.

If anyone was best equipped to make sure Rodrigo didn't step over the line, it was she. Maybe a tiny part of her didn't want Megan to be alone with him but, really, this was about business.

It was only logical that she should be the one to conduct Rodrigo's tour.

But first, furniture.

Ashley clapped her hands. "Good morning, everyone. Thanks again for coming in to help. Did everyone clock in?"

There was murmur and a couple of people raised their hands to indicate they hadn't.

"Okay, go do it. You know where the time clock is. This is good practice. If you don't clock in, you won't get paid. After you're done, come back. In the meantime, I'll talk about the master plan I've created."

She held up the floor plan that she'd hand drawn on graph paper. As soon as she set the drawing down on the high-top, Rodrigo picked it up.

She'd expected as much.

"Donny and Sam, will you please start moving the four-top tables over along the wall? There are six of them. They should be equally spaced and have four of the barrel chairs at each table. While they're doing that—"

"Actually, have you thought about arranging them in two rows of three?" Rodrigo asked.

Ashley gave him the side-eye but didn't answer. "As I was saying, while Donny and Sam are arranging the four-tops along the wall as I have laid out here on the chart—" she plucked the paper out of Rodrigo's hand— "Mike, Tom, Doug and Bobby, will you please move the couches and love seats up here?"

After the crew started moving furniture, Rodrigo said, "I didn't mean to interrupt you."

"Yes, that was rude," Ashley said.

"But think about it," he continued as if he hadn't heard her. "If you put the tables in a row down the wall, the last two are going to be off in a corner by themselves and there won't be much room for the chairs. People are going to be on top of each other. You won't be able to scoot the chairs in and out without bumping the person behind you."

"Have you ever considered that maybe some people might like the thought of having an intimate table in a corner by themselves? Not everyone needs to be the center of attention."

Rodrigo shrugged. "Fine. Do it however you want, but I'm speaking from experience when I say that most people who come to the lounge are either waiting for their tables and want to be within eye-shot of the hostess or they're meeting people for drinks and they want to be in the center of the action. If people want a quiet, intimate table, they'll get that with the dining experience. But we can do it your way."

"Of course we will do it my way." Ashley smiled. "You're a smart man, Not Rod."

She winked at him.

"Look, if you don't want my help, I can go." His voice was low and his gaze held hers, but he didn't seem amused by her nickname. She made a snap decision to retire the endearment.

"Your dad has already paid me," Rodrigo said as he began to turn to leave. "It's a shame that you're not willing to at least keep an open mind. This is a tough business. But you seem to know what you're doing."

"What? You're just going to walk away because I'm not jumping at your every directive?"

"I have other things I could be doing rather than standing around watching you."

Ashley's stomach performed the oddest little two-step at the thought of him watching her. She knew he didn't mean anything by it. He meant he didn't want to waste his time standing around waiting for her to finish what she was doing. But even rationalizing it like that didn't slow her pounding heart or make her feel any less…less what?

Like she and all of her decisions were under a microscope.

"Did you stop to consider it from my perspective?" she said. "Until about twenty minutes ago, I had no idea that my father had hired a consultant. Had hired...*you*." She thrust a finger at him. She hadn't meant to touch him, but she accidentally poked him in the pec, and damn, if it wasn't rock-hard. It made her traitorous mind start wondering if there was an equally rock-hard six-pack a little bit lower. She reined in that thought and continued. "Then you waltz in here and expect me to rearrange my floor plan because you say so?"

Rodrigo blinked then he held up his hands. He cleared his throat before he said, "We've gotten off to a bad start today. I apologize for that. I didn't know your father would forget to tell you about our appointment. This has never happened before. I think it threw everything off. Would it work better for you if I came back another time?" He paused, his look suggesting he expected her to acquiesce.

"I think that would be for the best. I'm sorry, I've got the guys here this morning to help me and I've spent a lot of time laying out that floorplan and I want to see how it looks."

"Okay, and I'm happy to roll up my sleeves and pitch in," he said.

"As long as we do things your way, right?"

A smile tipped up the corners of his mouth. She couldn't help but notice his strong jawline and perfectly formed lips, which were on the generous side but not so full that they looked feminine. No, they looked perfect. Perfectly kissable. She blinked away the thought.

"Since you feel so strongly about it, we'll do it

your way," he said. "It's easy to change if discover another way."

"Hey, Ashley," one of the guys called from the far corner of the bar. "Can you come and look at this? There's not room to fit four chairs around this last table, and even with two, it's almost jammed up against the table next to it."

Ashley craned her neck to look at what Sam was talking about. Then she grabbed her diagram off the high-top.

Had she miscalculated? The reason she'd used graph paper was to draw the furniture to scale. One square equaled one foot... Maybe she'd measured wrong?

"Did you allow room for the chairs and room for the people to scoot back?" Rodrigo asked, looking over her shoulder at the plan. He was standing so close she could smell his cologne. Something grassy and masculine.

She felt her face heat. That's exactly what she hadn't done. She'd measured for the tables and chairs, but she hadn't allowed for adequate clearance.

"You're right," she said, bracing herself for the inevitable *I told you so.*

But Rodrigo didn't say anything. He just stood there smelling good.

She swallowed hard. "Go ahead and say it. I know you want to."

"Say what?" he asked.

She steeled herself and finally met his gaze. But

instead of the smugness she'd expected, his look was direct but neutral.

"I told you so," she said.

"You told me what?" he asked.

She blinked. Coming from most people, those words would've sounded like he was being a smart-ass. But he didn't seem that way.

"You were right about the table placement. Aren't you just dying to say, 'I told you so'?"

"No, I'm not. Ashley, I'm on your side. I didn't come here to tear down everything you've worked so hard to set up. I'm just offering suggestions to make Provisions as successful as it can be," He said. "You and I are a team. I want you to start thinking of us that way, okay?"

A team.

It was not hard at all for her to think of them that way. The only problem, she wasn't thinking of *team* in the platonic sense of the word. Rodrigo Mendoza had already proven he could get under her skin, in the steamiest sense.

Yeah, that was more like it. Instead of *team* it was more like *steam*, because he had her so hot and bothered. And she didn't quite know what to do about it.

Chapter Three

"It says right here that Rodrigo Mendoza is one of five sons of Esteban Mendoza." Megan was reading from the magazine article she'd found online. "Oh, and get this—he was born and raised in Miami, but he moved to Texas a few years ago to be closer to family and to help them get their winery and restaurant off the ground. OMG, we were practically neighbors. We grew up in Fort Lauderdale and he was right there in Miami the whole time. Where was I when he was out and about?"

"You were probably in middle school," Ashley quipped, still feeling a little bruised from what she now called "the table-gate incident." Rodrigo had been right and she had embarrassed herself. She should've been more careful when she'd laid out her floor plan. It probably made him wonder what other mistakes she'd made.

Gaaa!

Now even she was wondering what other mistakes were lurking around the corners. At least Not Rod Mendoza had chosen to take the high road and not rub her nose in it.

Joining Megan, she sat at her desk and started her own Rodrigo Mendoza internet search.

"This article says he's thirty years old, which means he's seven years older than us," she said. "Which means you were probably in elementary school when he was out and about."

"You're acting like he could be our grandfather, Ash," Megan said. "What's wrong with you? Why are you in such a bad mood?"

"Am I the only one who's irritated that our father took it upon himself to hire this guy without even consulting us first? I mean, I know the guy is hot, but come on. That doesn't matter right now."

Nicole and Megan looked at each other, threw their heads back and laughed.

"Forget Not Rod," Megan said. "His name should be Hot Rod. Hot Rod Mendoza."

"Really?" Ashley said, trying her hardest not to crack a smile because her sister's play on words was undoubtedly clever. "Are we fifteen years old? Come on, be serious. We need to talk about Dad. It really bothers me that he would do this."

"Doesn't bother me," said Nicole. "As far as I'm concerned, the more help we can get from Hot Rod, the better."

Megan laughed. "It definitely doesn't bother me. I mean what's not to like? Come on, Ash. Don't you think the name Hot Rod is totally appropriate?"

Nicole and Megan laughed and high-fived each other.

Ashley rolled her eyes, but she couldn't help herself. Her serious expression gave way and she joined her sisters and laughed at the oh-so-apt wordplay. The guy was not just hot. He was scorching.

Exactly the kind of smug, I'm-sexy-and-I-know-it guy who would burn every woman he touched. *Steam.* As soon as the thought formed in her head, her stomach fluttered.

She didn't know Rodrigo Mendoza, but she knew guys like him. She'd been burned by guys like him too many times. Guys who were either interested in her family money or getting an in with her cool video-game-developing father. Like the last guy who had asked her out. He hadn't wanted to date her as much as he'd wanted her to set up an appointment with her father so David could look at the video game he'd developed and set him on the path toward making a gazillion dollars.

It wasn't that Ashley minded helping people by putting them in touch with her father. Everyone deserved a chance at success. She just didn't want to feel used.

"Okay, Meggie, you've made it perfectly clear how you feel about Rodrigo Mendoza," Ashley said.

Megan's mouth fell open and she shot daggers at her sister. "What that's supposed to mean?"

Ashley snorted. "Since he walked in this morning, your tongue has all but been hanging out of your mouth. Now you come out with the Hot Rod name."

Megan blanched.

"Ash, that's a little harsh," said Nicole. "He's hot. Did you not notice?"

Ashley blinked at the reprimand.

"It is harsh," said Megan. "I'm just having fun. I mean even you have to admit he's gorgeous. In addition to the knowledge he has about the restaurant industry, I think he'll do us some good simply by lightening the mood."

This time, Nicole snorted. "Yes, because someone definitely needs to lighten up."

Ashley frowned and crossed her arms. "I don't know where your heads are right now, but to me, Provisions isn't a game. I don't intend to lighten up, as you say, until the place is up and running and successful. If that's wrong, then I don't want to be right."

"And in the meantime, we need to make sure we don't have one second of fun, Meg," Nicole said. "Got that?"

"Got it," Megan said. "Thanks for the warning."

Her sisters were joking, of course, but there was a grain of truth in their sarcasm.

Ashley took a deep breath. The dynamic of three meant sometimes one of them felt like the odd woman out. She wouldn't go so far as to say they ganged up on each other, but that was part of life as a triplet. When push came to shove, she wouldn't trade being a triplet for the world.

"I know this is supposed to be fun, you guys. But sometimes I feel like I'm the only one who is taking it seriously—or at least I'm the only one who is stressing over it. And when I stress, I can't have fun. But it doesn't mean I don't want you to have fun."

The other thing about her sisters was that they could be real with each other—more than anyone else in the world. Because another perk of being a triplet was that it came with the gift of unconditional love.

So she had to admit the truth: she was so stressed, she wasn't having fun.

"Just take a deep breath." Nicole's tone was soothing. "Everything will be okay."

"And maybe be a little more open to what Rodrigo Mendoza has to say," Megan offered. "It sort of feels like you've been on the defensive since he walked in the door."

Ashley shrugged. "I guess I have, haven't I? It's not him. It's me. I hate surprises like this."

"Consider this…" said Nicole. "The surprise wasn't his. It was Dad's."

"I know Dad says he's just trying to help," Ashley said. "But why does he think we need help? You don't see him sending in a consultant to check up on our brothers' construction business, do you? He'd never admit this, but I get the feeling that he doesn't believe we're capable of pulling this off ourselves, either because we're too young or because we're women."

Megan and Nicole glanced at each other as if assessing the validity of her words.

"I don't know," Nicole said. "It's depends on how you look at it. Either way, since we've got Rodrigo, we may as well hear what he has to say."

"That's easy for you to say. Because of Rosemary, Rodrigo is not going to wade too deeply into your kitchen, which means he'll be channeling all of his prescriptive energy into the front of the house. With me."

There was that freaky butterflies-in-the-stomach feeling again. She tried her best to ignore it and keep her focus on her argument.

"What do we know about this Rodrigo Mendoza?" She turned back to her computer and typed in his name again. "I mean aside from his family's winery and restaurant, what else has Rodrigo done? What makes him such an expert? He's only thirty years old. And yes, he's older than we are, but that's not a lot of years to set the world on fire."

"Dad wouldn't have hired him if he didn't bring some legit creds to the table," Megan said.

"Isn't it interesting that Rodrigo didn't even offer

his credentials to us?" Ashley said. "He just arrived and expected us to receive him."

"That's not entirely true," Nicole said. "In all fairness, he thought he had an appointment with us. Also, he said Vines Consulting has been stolidly booked and he has a portfolio of success stories to prove it. We didn't ask him for specifics."

Ashley didn't totally buy it. She continued her search till she found the web site she was looking for and opened it.

She hated that her sisters felt like she was sucking all the fun out of their dream. They could open a successful restaurant and still enjoy themselves in the process. But why had their father dumped Mendoza into the equation?

Her gaze found the photo of Rodrigo on his bio page on the Vines Consulting Group web site. "It says here, he's the president of the company. They promise to take our business to the next level while staying true to what makes us unique."

She paused to let that sink in. Nicole's eyebrows rose. Then she tapped away at her own computer keyboard. Megan was staring off into space, still wearing that dangerous, dreamy, Rodrigo-Mendoza-inspired look on her face.

"I guess I'm jaded, but I'm automatically suspicious of people who claim to possess all the secrets," Ashley said. "If he's so good at making restaurants profitable, why isn't he running a restaurant himself?"

"It says right here that he helped get La Viña off the ground," Nicole noted.

Ashley smirked. "And one family-owned restaurant makes him an expert?"

"La Viña is doing very well," Nicole said as she typed. "It's sort of the same vibe as Provisions."

"We don't have a vineyard," Ashley quipped.

"Right, but the restaurant is in the middle of nowhere. Sort of like Rambling Rose. They took what they had and established a nice place that people are willing to come to the middle of nowhere to experience. That's how we're similar."

"But he's not actively involved in the day-to-day running of the place," Ashley said.

"He used to be," Nicole pointed out.

"Maybe he doesn't like the day-to-day grind of working in a restaurant," said Megan. "It's not an easy business. It kind of owns you. It doesn't leave you a whole lot of time for a personal life. So unless you've been bitten by the bug like we have, then it's hard to get excited about it."

"Speaking of personal lives, does it say anything about his?" Nicole asked.

"No, the bio page is all business," Ashley said.

That was a good sign. His personal life shouldn't matter.

"Is there anything else on the internet about him?" Nicole asked.

"Let's look," Megan said. "We know he's thirty and he wasn't wearing a wedding ring. Yes, I looked and I'm not ashamed to admit it. Don't pretend like you two weren't curious."

"I didn't look," Ashley said. Only because she hadn't thought of it.

"I'd love to know if he has a girlfriend," Megan said. "See if you can find his social media pages."

Ashley clicked back to the main search page. The third article listed below the Vines Consulting Group web site was a three-year-old post from a Miami-based glossy magazine. She clicked on the link.

"*Ooh*, here's something," she said. "Three years ago, *Lux Miami* magazine named Rodrigo Mendoza one of Miami's most eligible bachelors."

Her sisters got up from their desks and gathered around. Ashley frowned at the accompanying photo that showed him looking gorgeous as ever, standing behind a South Beach bar.

Ashley glanced at her sisters who were reading over her shoulder. "Looks like Miami's Mr. Most Eligible is a player when he isn't out saving the restaurant world."

"Yeah, but this was three years ago," Megan said. "I'd bet the photo is even older than that. Now that he's thirty, he's probably all grown up and settled down."

Ashley and Nicole laughed.

"I'm willing to bet once a player always a player," Ashley said. "Especially because it appears that all of his social media is locked, except for his Twitter account. On there, he's just retweeting a bunch of restaurant business articles and stats."

Nicole and Megan went back to their desks and started typing. It was a silent contest to see who could unearth something more current—and more exciting.

Then Megan gasped.

"What?" Nicole asked.

"What?" Ashley echoed.

Megan bit her bottom lip.

"I know that look," Nicole said. "You're up to no good."

Megan raised both hands in surrender. "I am not. Clearly, I'm sitting right here with you acting like the perfect angel. I just came across several different articles about Mendoza weddings. Apparently, their family is nearly as vast as the Fortunes.

"It says here Matteo Mendoza married Rachel Fortune Robinson. Cisco Mendoza married Delaney Fortune Jones. Joaquin Mendoza married Zoe Fortune Robinson. Alejandro Mendoza married Olivia Fortune Robinson. And I'm only scratching the surface. Would you like me to continue? It appears that the Mendozas have a long tradition of hooking up with and marrying Fortunes. And now, lucky for us, a Mendoza has presented himself to us."

Megan's eyes danced.

"I know what you're thinking," Nicole said. "In our situation, there's only one Mendoza and three Fortunes."

Megan laughed. "I would share almost anything with my sisters, but I draw the line when it comes to sharing a man."

Nicole winced. "The question is, which one of us will land him?"

"Guys!" Ashley said. "Seriously? I think we have much bigger fish to fry right now. Let's not get distracted by a good-looking guy."

"Oh, don't play innocent, Ash," Nicole said. "I saw the way you were looking at him."

Ashley's eyes widened and she did her best to feign innocence. But there was no denying the way her stomach kept jumping at the thought of *landing* Rodrigo Mendoza.

Nicole had her number. It was uncanny how at least one of her sisters always seemed to be able to read her mind. It was a strange kind of triplet telepathy.

It was true.

No matter how loudly she cried "business," she wasn't immune to the charms of Rodrigo Mendoza. Her fluttery stomach wouldn't let her forget it.

"And while I know I shouldn't encourage you," Ashley said, "all I have to say is…may the best Fortune win."

"No, you shouldn't encourage us," Megan said.

"I think Ashley should go for him," Nicole said. "It might help her lighten up a little bit."

"Come on, ladies," Megan protested. "I saw him first."

"No. You did not see him first, Meg," Ashley said. "I did. So, if you want to play it that way, he's mine."

Meg gave Ashley the side-eye then rolled her eyes. "Whatever. He's yours. At least act professional. No hanky-panky in the pantry."

"For that matter, no hanky-panky anywhere in my kitchen," said Nicole. "That sounds unsanitary."

"For the record, there won't be any hanky-panky anywhere in the restaurant," said Ashley."

"Yeah, we'll see about that," Megan muttered under her breath.

"Meg," Ashley said. "Are you okay?"

"Why wouldn't I be okay?"

"Are you jealous?" Ashley asked. "It seems like this is bothering you. I mean…if you're interested in him, I'll back off."

"I'm not interested in him. You saw him first. Knock yourself out."

"If you are upset, it's important for you to say so now," Ashley said. "We've always promised ourselves we would never let a guy come between us."

"And we won't start now," Megan said. "I'm fine. I'll admit, he's a good-looking guy. Maybe if the circumstances were different, I might be interested. But I'm not. Besides, of the three of us, I think I sensed a spark between the two of you. There. That's the tiebreaker. He's officially yours."

"It wasn't a spark," Ashley said. "It was banter. I was simply me keeping him in line and him trying to justify himself. And to be perfectly honest, I'm talking a big game about hooking up with him. My sisters and Provisions come first. I'm not going to put that in jeopardy over some guy."

"Not even Hot Rod Mendoza?" Nicole asked.

"No," Ashley protested. "Not even Hot Rod Mendoza."

She put her hand over her stomach to quiet the butterflies, whose presence were indicating an entirely different story.

The next morning, Rodrigo arrived at Provisions promptly at eight. It was unfortunate that he and the triplets—well, he and Ashley, actually—had gotten off to a rocky start, but now that the Fortune sisters were expecting him, he intended to make everything right.

"I think the first order of business should be me shadowing one of you," he said to the sisters. "If that works for you."

His suggestion was met with three nearly identical faces wearing questioning expressions. He hadn't been around the triplets very long, but already he was beginning to notice subtle differences among them. First off was their vastly different styles of dressing. Nicole was wearing jean shorts and a T-shirt; Megan was dressed for business in a conservative skirt, jacket and heels; and Ashley was wearing a boho-looking floral dress with wedge sandals that made her taller than her sisters.

One of the things that made him good at his job was his ability to read people. Body language, facial expressions, moods. Everyone had tells, and part of his job was interpreting them. He had to listen to and understand his clients before he could figure out how to make the most of their business. His wasn't a one-size-fits-all industry.

Nicole seemed to be a little more straightforward and her expressions seemed to show that she tended to march to her own tune. No surprise since the kitchen was her domain. Megan was a little shyer, which made her a little more reserved and a little harder to read. He attributed that to her accounting work. She seemed to defer to Ashley, who was the tough nut to crack. She seemed to be the gatekeeper for the trio, the one he would probably have the most challenging time convincing to change things. For that reason alone, Rodrigo decided to start with her.

"What I mean is that I want you to go about your job doing what you would do in a typical day," he said. "Act as if I'm not even here. If you all don't object, I think I'll shadow Ashley first."

Ashley folded her arms and frowned. "What good will that do?"

He smiled, expecting this response from her. "We have to start somewhere. One thing I want you to understand is that I'm not here to force a program on you. I need to know how you work and what makes you happy. Does that make sense?"

"Makes perfect sense to me." Nicole stood and

started edging toward the office door. "Since this round obviously doesn't involve me, I'm going to duck out. But just so y'all know, Rosemary and I would like to have another tasting today. Plan on that for lunch. Today we're working on different brisket sandwiches. We're using all locally sourced ingredients. Come hungry. I promise you won't regret it."

"Sounds like a plan," Rodrigo said.

With a quick wave of her hand, she was out the door, leaving him with just Ashley and Megan.

"Since you're working with Ash today," Megan said, "I'm going to duck out, too. Be good, you two. Don't do anything I wouldn't do."

Immediately, Megan bit her bottom lip and her cheeks turned a bright shade of pink.

"I mean— Well, you know what I mean," she said before she exited, leaving him and Ashley alone in the room with the weighted suggestion hanging in the air.

Unlike Megan, Ashley didn't blush. Instead she wore an inscrutable look and cleared her throat. "Okay, then. What do you want me to do?"

"Whatever you'd be doing if I wasn't here. Just pretend like I'm not here."

She knit her brow and laughed, but it wasn't a humorous sound. "That's absurd. You are here and, from the sound of it, you will be lurking over my shoulder, judging my every move. How could anyone pretend like you're not invading their space?"

Some people could. This evaluation was how he

began most of his consulting jobs. But he wasn't going to waste time arguing his point.

"Right now, I'll bet you're thinking that you're not going to waste time arguing with me," Ashley said.

Rodrigo flinched. "Do you list mind reading as one of your marketable skills on your résumé?"

"So, you were thinking that?" she said.

His gaze landed on her lips, which were slightly fuller than her sisters'. Another subtle difference that set her apart from the other triplets. And she had the most delicate mole at the base of her left eye.

He'd noticed that yesterday, and this morning, his eyes had been drawn to it.

He forced his gaze back to her eyes and saw that she was staring at him with a raised brow. Always the left brow. Another Ashley tick.

He couldn't figure out if somehow she had read his thoughts again. He made a mental note to watch himself and to keep everything—including his thoughts—professional.

"Why don't we start by taking a look at your plans for the soft opening."

She nodded. "Okay. I can handle that. As long as you don't try to change everything."

He held up his hands. "Can we come to an understanding?"

It was meant as a rhetorical question, but she said, "That would be nice."

"Ashley, I'm not here to undo all your hard work.

I know you, Nicole and Megan have put your heart and soul into Provisions. There's nothing more frustrating than to feel like someone is following behind you and judging everything. Here's what I want you to know... Any suggestion I make is meant for the good of Provisions."

He thought that was a given, but now that he considered it, before this point, all of his clients had hired him. Before he'd even walked into their restaurants, they had bought into what he was selling. Ashley, however, hadn't even had a chance to digest his being here.

"Okay." Her voice was flat and she stood there frowning at him with her arms crossed. Closed-off body language.

As far as Ashley was concerned, he was an intruder, an interloper. If this was going to work, he needed to win her over.

"What would it take for you to trust me?" he asked.

"Normally, the people I trust don't have to ask me to trust them. You know that old saying, trust is earned. Maybe we should start with why should I trust you?"

He nodded. "That's a good question. Why should you trust me? To start with, if the suggestions I offer you fail, it's not going to do my business any favors. So, you lose, I lose." He punctuated the sentence with a shrug.

She looked unmoved.

Okay. Clearly he was going about this the wrong way.

"Look, if you don't want my help, I'm happy to refund your father's money and we can call it good. It's up to you. Just say the word."

"My father's money." Her voice was flat.

He nodded. "I'll give him a refund."

"That's what it always comes down to—my father's money."

Rodrigo blinked, unsure of what to say. He felt the swagger drain from his step. Her father's money seemed to be a hot button and he'd pressed it.

"It's always about my father's money. It's not about the fact that my sisters and I have worked hard to get to this point. How am I supposed to trust you when you obviously don't know anything about us and I don't know anything about you?"

"That's why I want to see what you do in a typical day," he said. "But if that bothers you, why don't we start over and you can tell me more about yourself and a more detailed account of your vision for Provisions. After that, I'm happy to answer any questions you have for me."

Now it was her turn to blink at him. She bit her bottom lip and he could see the virtual wheels turning in her head. Then something shifted.

"I can work with that," she said.

She went into greater depth about her past jobs and how she and her sisters had been saving for years to make this happen because owning a restaurant was a dream come true for all of them.

After they'd spent the better part of an hour talking, she said, "Why don't I give you a tour?"

Already he'd learned something very important that he suspected went to the heart of what made Ashley Fortune tick. She may have had the benefit of the Fortune name and her father's money, but he could sense that she wasn't a spoiled little rich girl. He had to hand it to her for setting him straight.

She showed him around the bar area, with the furniture neatly configured as he had suggested yesterday, though he wasn't about to gloat over it. She introduced him to the bartending staff, who were busy stocking the mirrored shelves behind the bar.

"Rodrigo, this is Byron Biggs, our bar manager. Byron, this is Rodrigo Mendoza. His family owns the Mendoza Winery and La Viña Restaurant in Austin."

"I've been there," Byron said, offering his hand. Rodrigo shook it. "To both the restaurant and the vineyard. Great places."

"Thanks, man," Rodrigo said. "I'm glad you enjoyed them."

"Rodrigo is here to see the place and offer us some words of wisdom before we open," she said.

Words of wisdom. Okay. If that's what she wanted to call it.

"I'm happy to help any way I can," he said.

Ashley answered a few questions Byron threw

at her and Rodrigo noted that she had an easygoing way with the staff. Open, accessible, but professional. It was obvious that they respected her.

"I created a series of cocktails for the restaurant," said Byron, a wiry guy who looked like he was in his late twenties. "Do you want a taste test before the soft opening?"

"Absolutely," Ashley said. "How about today around five thirty? Does that work for you?"

"Works for me," Byron said.

Next, she showed Rodrigo to an arched wooden door at the far end of the bar. After selecting a key from the crowded fob she carried, she unlocked the dead bolt and motioned for him to follow.

"This is our wine cellar." She flipped a light switch, which ignited several sconces fitted with flickering bulbs meant to imitate a gas flame.

As they headed down the narrow flight of stairs, holding on to a wrought-iron railing attached to the stone wall, Ashley said, "This was one of the most amazing transformations of the whole place. See all this stone?" She ran her hand over it as if she were admiring it. "It wasn't here before. The walls were plain concrete. This used to be a dank, damp basement where they stored feed. Wait until you see the transformation. The builder covered the walls with curated stones and turned the place into an authentic-looking French wine cellar."

Although the passageway looked ancient, once they cleared the steps, the room itself was full of top-of-the-line modern conveniences. The space was large enough to use for tastings and special events. It could even be used as a private dining room.

Ashley crossed her arms and rubbed them. "The room is temperature controlled, set at a steady fifty-five degrees, which I'm sure you know is optimum for wine storage."

She was right. Heat was enemy number one for wine.

The tasting room was finished with reclaimed brick on the floors and the walls. There were floor-to-ceiling wine racks for horizontal racking of the bottles.

In the middle of the room was an expensive-looking Persian rug. On top of it sat a large trestle table with sixteen chairs for serious tastings, and there were three smaller, more intimate seat group-ings all consisting of luxurious cognac-colored leather that looked butter-soft.

"Impressive," said Rodrigo as he followed her up the stairs after the tour. "I'm sure you have all kinds of ideas on how to utilize that space."

"Yes, we have big plans for the wine cellar," she said.

If a community like Rambling Rose was open to embracing such a sophisticated space.

The newcomers who were moving into Rambling Rose Estates, the exclusive gated community on the outskirts of town, were more of a demographic that would feel comfortable in the cellar. Whether or not the locals who lived closer to the quaint downtown area and the restaurant would be as excited about it remained to be seen.

Rodrigo decided to save his comments and observations for the end of the tour.

Next, they peeked inside the kitchen. The first thing he noticed were the side-eyed scowls from Nicole and Rosemary, clearly communicating that he wasn't welcome.

After Ashley introduced Rodrigo to Rosemary, she said, "Don't worry, we wouldn't dream of disturbing your kitchen kingdom. But I'm giving Rodrigo a tour of the land. He needs to know where the kitchen is so that he can understand the boundaries you've set. You do understand boundaries, don't you, Rodrigo?"

He nodded, even though he would get into that kitchen sometime. But that was a battle for another day.

"Good. Wave at the nice chefs and let's be on our way. The brisket smells delish. Can't wait for lunch."

Rodrigo's stomach growled. "Amen to that." He waved and followed Ashley away from the kitchen door.

"How many servers have you hired?" he asked.

She told him.

"Have you held an orientation yet?" he asked.

"Last week."

"If you'll allow me, I'd like to speak with them before the soft opening."

"Why?"

"To see who you've hired and to make sure everyone is up to snuff."

"I vetted everyone before I hired them, Rodrigo. Of course they're up to snuff."

"Remember what I said about not talking things personally?"

"Vaguely."

"This is one of those times."

"Let's go upstairs," she said, changing the subject. "I'm sure you want to see the dining room."

He followed her up the stained concrete steps that led to a loft dining room that was an equal balance of upscale and comfortable casual. The loft ran in a U shape above the lower level. Ashley took pride in pointing out the kitchen alcove with its heated dumbwaiters where the kitchen expeditor would send up food to the dining room waitstaff.

Too bad they couldn't have built the kitchen upstairs, but it was too late for that now.

The décor echoed the earth tones used downstairs, but white tablecloths lent an elegant touch.

"Starting out, we're only serving dinner," she said. "Once we've mastered that and we see that we've built a steady clientele, the next phase will be Sunday brunch and then we will phase in lunch."

"What have you been doing to reach out to locals?"

"Do you mean advertising?" Ashley asked.

"Yes, but I'm also talking about community outreach. How have you been getting the community excited about Provisions?"

"My brother Callum, who has been in Rambling Rose longer than my sisters and I have, has been helping us with that. But we've been giving tours. The locals know this place as the old feed and grain warehouse. They've been amazed by how we've transformed it. Any kind of gentrification helps everyone's property values.

"In addition, we're buying local as much as we can. That, in itself, has helped generate excitement. If Bob Smith has sold his tomatoes to us then he's going to be eager to not only come in and see how we prepare them, he's going to tell others, too. Which reminds me, did you see the giant chalkboard downstairs just inside the door?"

Rodrigo shook his head. "I didn't. What's it for?"

Ashley smiled. "I'm glad you asked. We're going to keep a running list of all the farmers and vendors from whom we source our food. Not only will the locals be proud to share the word, they will also be listed on our 'Locally Fresh' board. For instance, I believe we got the brisket that Nic and Rosemary are cooking from the Happy C Farm, over in Centerville. So, if we were serving their brisket, we would list them on the board. It's a friendly shout-out."

"That's a great idea," Rodrigo said.

"But?"

"But what? I didn't have a *but*. Do you?"

"I thought I heard one in your voice. I was just preparing myself."

"No buts from me," he said. "I think you're doing a great job. We might want to beef up special incentives for other non-farmer, non-grower locals. Maybe offer trivia nights in the lounge area or beer specials. But we can talk about that after the soft opening."

Ashley's left brows quirked. "You're staying through the soft opening?"

"I'd planned on being here for a month. That way we can trouble shoot any problems that might arise during the grand opening. If I'm welcome, that is."

"Of course, you're welcome," she said. For the first time, she was actually looking him in the eyes and he noticed the absence of challenge. He also noticed that her eyes were the exact color of the Mediterranean Sea, a particular shade of azure that gave him pause so he could drink them in.

He cleared his throat, forcing his mind back on the restaurant. "Is there anything else you'd like to show me?"

"There's a private room for small special occasions. It holds about fifty people. It's downstairs off the bar area. With the wine cellar and that area, we have ample space for private dining."

She led the way. He followed, thinking that he had to hand it to her. She was poised and professional, and seemed to know her stuff, especially for someone so young.

With the uncanny way she seemed to be able to read his mind, he braced himself for her to turn around and set him straight on the age-related thought. She didn't, of course, but it did make him pause and consider age. She wasn't that much younger than he was—just seven years. She certainly had her life much more together than he'd had at that age.

Seven years ago, he'd been a punk tending bar at a South Beach club. He'd had no idea of what he wanted to do with himself. He'd been making just enough money to get by. Enough to allow him to coast along, working nights, part of the South Beach party scene, but in his mind, since he was "working," he had a legitimate reason for being there.

That's when he'd met Bonnie. Sweet Bonnie, or so she'd led him to believe. Her father owned the club where he bartended and she used to come in and sit at the bar where he'd pour her drinks.

She'd led him on one hell of a merry chase.

But he didn't need to be cluttering his brain with thoughts of her. He'd stopped letting her live rent-free in his head a long time ago. Why was he thinking of her now?

He tried to shake thoughts of her from his head, but not before a stabbing mental jab reminded him that he knew a thing or two about rich girls whose daddies catered to their every whim.

Ashley Fortune was not Bonnie. But he was not

interested in Ashley. Not on a personal level. So that meant there was no reason for comparison.

He was here because David Fortune had hired him to ensure Provisions' restaurant was as strong as it could possibly be when they opened their doors to the public.

When Ashley stepped off the last step as they returned to the first floor, she turned around and smiled at him. He refused to let himself notice her cheekbones and the way her cheeks formed dimples when she smiled. So very blond, blue-eyed and beachy all-American, as opposed to Bonnie, who had been dark and sexy and exotic and into all kinds of things she shouldn't have been into. She'd showed him one beautiful face, while the other side, the side she'd hidden from him, was ugly and sordid and heartbreaking.

Bonnie had made him doubt his judgment. After they'd broken up, he'd vowed that it would be a long time before he trusted his heart again.

But Bonnie was personal. Ashley Fortune was business.

He smiled back at the woman in front of him, who decidedly was not Bonnie Rivera.

"Hey, Ash. There you are. I was looking for you." The sound of a male voice landed Rodrigo firmly in the present. A tall, guy with dark hair was walking out of the offices.

"Oh, Adam. Hi," Ashley said. "I'm so glad you're here. I want you to meet Rodrigo Mendoza.

"Rodrigo, this is my cousin, Adam Fortune." Ashley giggled. The sound was contagious and made Rodrigo smile.

"What's so funny?" he asked.

Ashley shook her head. "Oh, it's nothing. It's just that I'm still getting used to the fact that Adam and I are cousins. His father, Gary, is my dad's half-brother. Our families just found each other a short while ago. We're both from the newfound branches of the illustrious Fortune family."

The Fortunes went way back. They had recently discovered so many new branches—compliments of patriarch Julius Fortune's many extramarital dalliances—that he was having a hard time keeping track. All he knew was even the newer branches seemed to have a lot of money.

Creating wealth must be in the Fortune DNA.

"Until we discovered Adam and the other Fortunes, we didn't have any extended family. It's still sort of a novelty."

The way Ashley wrinkled her nose when she smiled warmed Rodrigo's heart. It was so sweet and innocent. So was the fact that finding a long-lost cousin made her giddy.

He couldn't help but recall how, toward the end of their relationship, Bonnie had been so jaded and cold.

And that was enough Bonnie comparisons, he told himself. They'd ended things more than two years ago. In many ways, he had her to thank for where he was now.

Again, he thought about how a better comparison was how much Ashley reminded him of his sister-in-law, Schuyler.

She was the best thing that had ever happened to his brother Carlo. She worked alongside Carlo at the winery and restaurant back in Austin. Rodrigo would've been lying if he didn't admit that sometimes he envied Carlo and Schuyler's relationship. It was a good one and it was great to see his brother so happy and settled.

After going through the ringer with Bonnie, being happy and settled with a woman was the last thing on his mind. He had enough on his plate traveling around the country and doing his job.

Rodrigo held out his hand to Adam. "Nice to meet you."

"Adam and I are sharing restaurant management duties," Ashley told him. "That will make the job easier to handle for both of us and we will be able to cover the restaurant's needs more efficiently."

But what did that do to the budget? Restaurant managers didn't come cheap, and if they were doling out a double salary...

"Good to meet you," Adam said. "Yeah, Ash, when you get a minute, I need to go over the front-of-the-house staff schedule for the soft opening."

"Why don't we do that now?" she said. "Rodrigo can join us. He is a restaurant consultant. My father hired him to give us some helpful hints before the opening."

Adam cast him a wary glance, as if he wasn't sure whether or not he was dealing with the enemy. He exchanged a look with Ashley and Rodrigo noticed that her smile was a little too bright, a little too wide. She held it a little too long, as if she had plastered it in place. And he'd thought she had gotten past her resentment. Well, as long as she was pretending, he would pretend he didn't notice.

"I'd love to take a look," he said. "Ashley was just showing me around the place. You've all done a great job getting it to this point. She was telling me about some of the plans you have for attracting the locals. I think you're on the right track."

Out of the corner of his eye, he saw Ashley do a double-take, looking at him as if she hadn't expected him to be so complimentary.

He was being sincere.

Despite how hard he was trying to focus on business, he couldn't help but think that there were a lot of other compliments he'd love to offer Ashley Fortune.

Chapter Four

The big night had arrived: the soft opening.

Ashley had completed every task on her to-do list and checked each item twice. Megan said they had stayed within budget, and after tasting upon tasting, Nicole and Rosemary had perfected the menu. She and her sisters were ready.

She glanced at herself in the mirror of the restaurant bathroom, blotted her lipstick and then turned this way and that to make sure everything was just so. Every hair was in place. The little black dress she'd purchased especially for tonight looked fabulous with her Louboutin stilettos—professional with an edge of sexy. Just sexy enough to make a certain restaurant consultant sit up and take notice?

Possibly.

She'd have to wait and see.

As if on cue, the Peggy Lee song *I'm a Woman* began playing through the sound system. It was one of the selection of upbeat jazzy, bluesy standards they'd chosen for the restaurant.

Ashley smiled at the poetic irony of the song. If Hot Rod Mendoza would give her the chance, she would never let him forget he was a man.

With a bounce in her step, she left the bathroom and returned to the dining room where she did one last sweeping check. They would open the doors in ten minutes and seat the first parties in their brand-new restaurant.

Her parents had flown in for the occasion. So had her brother Wiley, who had joined the rest of her siblings who lived locally. Also on the guest list, along with a select roster of local VIPs and influencers, were some of the other branches of her new Fortune family. Her father hadn't been thrilled that she had included them, but they were family. She needed some friendly faces tonight.

She knew that they would still have to work through some kinks before they opened for real. Who better to be real with you without breaking your spirit than family?

"Hey, Ash," Adam said. "I just checked the men's room. It might be a good idea to put some extra paper towels under the sink to make it easier to re-

stock. Who did you assign to bathroom duty tonight?"

"Ron Turner volunteered. He's right over there."

Ashley and Adam turned to see Ron walking toward them carrying a bundle of paper towels.

"I thought we could use some backups just in
case," he said.

"Well, there you go," Ashley said to Adam. She
turned to Ron. "Keep up the good work and we'll
be forced to give you a raise."

Ron smiled. "Sounds good to me." Then he continued on his trek to the men's room.

"Ron," Ashley called. "When you're finished,
please join us in the bar area for a quick meeting
before we open the doors. Okay?"

"Be right there."

Ashley walked over to the hostess stand one more
time and looked at the electronic reservations moni-
tor. She'd printed out a hard copy just in case. Everyone was still getting used to the new machine.
She didn't want to keep the customers waiting on
the off chance there was a glitch.

In all likelihood, there wouldn't be, but Ashley
wanted to be prepared for everything.

Just to be on the safe side, she called up tonight's
reservations list again for at least the fifth time in
the past two hours and scrolled through. The machine worked perfectly and showed a full slate of
reservations.

She put her hand on her thudding heart and took

a slow, deep breath. All their hard work would pay off tonight.

When she walked into the bar area, the first person she saw was Rodrigo talking to Adam. Rodrigo was dressed in a black suit with a black shirt. His olive skin, with its perpetual tan, made him look quintessentially South Beach. He'd said he lived in Austin now, but she wondered if he went back to Florida often. And whether he missed Miami's international pizzazz since it seemed to be imbued in him.

Watching him standing at the bar, Ashley realized there were so many things she didn't know about him. So many things she wanted to know. They just had to get through tonight and she would make a point to create some opportunities for them to talk. Because the clock was ticking. After they got Provisions up and running, Rodrigo Mendoza would be going back to his life in Austin or South Beach or wherever it was he kept his gorgeous self.

As if he felt her vibe, he turned and caught her watching him. The smile that spread over his handsome face reached all the way to his dark eyes and made them crinkle at the corners. It took her breath away for a couple of seconds.

She resisted the urge to put her hand on her stomach to quiet the butterflies. Instead she held his gaze and smiled as she drew in a deep breath through her nose and parted her lips so she could gently let the breath escape.

Their gazes held for a few beats longer than was strictly professional. Not that it was unprofessional to look your colleague in the eyes. But what passed between them was a little more electric than she'd like to admit. The spark flared in a place that was quite personal, igniting a fire that spread upward and outward, making her belly tingle and her face go hot.

"Ashley, there you are." Megan's voice broke the spell and, for a moment, Ashley wondered if her sister had done it on purpose. She tore her gaze away, telling herself it was a ridiculous thought because… well, because even if it was true, Megan was doing her a favor. Tonight the restaurant needed her attention. She needed to focus and make sure she didn't blow all their hard work on a flight of good-looking Mendoza fancy.

"Hey, Meg. What's up?"

"Didn't you want to say a few words before we open the doors? Do you want me to gather the staff?" Megan was talking to Ashley, but she was looking at Rodrigo, who had resumed talking to Adam.

"I was coming in here to do just that," Ashley said.

Between the two of them, they gathered the front-house staff and Ashley called the huddle to order.

"First, I want to let you know how much we appreciate everyone's hard work," Ashley said. "We couldn't do this without a dedicated team. You are all so important to us. Tonight, as you serve our friends, family and neighbors, please know that you are family."

Her speech was interrupted by a spontaneous round of applause. She smiled. Once it died down, she continued. "As soon as everyone is in place, I'll open the doors. Let's go out there and show them what we've got. Thanks in advance for a great first night."

Amid the whoops and yeas, the staff high-fived, fist-bumped and pumped each other up. And on that wave of positivity, Ashley walked toward the doors.

Rodrigo fell into step beside her. "Would it be wildly inappropriate if I told you that you look nice?" he asked.

It was the first time he'd gotten even remotely personal. The heat from earlier returned. "Not as long as I can return the compliment. You clean up nicely, Mendoza."

"Yeah?" There was that smile again. It, too, seemed more personal than the multitude of pleasant expressions he'd showed since he'd arrived. "I try."

This was a guy who could wear anything—or nothing, she imagined—and look great. Suddenly, it was the *nothing* that she was curious about.

"You don't have to try very hard," she said. "You always look good."

"Really? You noticed?"

He seemed a little taken aback, but he was the one who'd started it. And oh, how she would like to finish it. Well, maybe *finish* wasn't the right word.

Because they had to *start* first. Then something told her that once they did, the last thing she'd want to do was finish it.

"Yeah, that's right. I've noticed."

He'd presented the opening for this conversation and Ashley figured she might as well run with it because if she didn't, his guard might go back up and she might not get another chance.

"Right now, we need to open the doors. But I'd love to continue this conversation later." Her heart was racing as fast as the words left her mouth.

He didn't say anything, just smiled that sexy Hot Rod smile.

After she unlocked the door and turned around, he was gone.

Had her forwardness scared him away?

Even before he'd complimented Ashley, Rodrigo knew he was playing with fire. But he couldn't help himself. That dress…the way it hugged her curves, letting just a hint of cleavage peek through, was about to drive him crazy. And those heels…the minute he'd seen her, a mental picture of Ashley back in his room at the inn wearing nothing but those heels had flashed in his head.

He knew it was wrong because she was a client and beyond that, he was still concentrating on building his business. He didn't have time to get involved. And he still questioned his heart's judgment. Especially, when his libido talking so loud sometimes he couldn't even hear himself think.

Her father, David Fortune, the person who had hired him, the man who had signed his check and could blackball him and his business with a single decisive word, had just walked in the door surrounded by an entourage.

If seeing her father wasn't a sobering reality check, Rodrigo was hopeless.

While he hadn't met David in person, he'd looked up the successful video-game developer after their first phone conversation. Rodrigo researched all his potential clients. He always did his homework because he prided himself on being prepared. Preparedness was what won him jobs. But all the research in the world hadn't prepared him for Ashley Fortune. Everything about her spoke to his basest nature. She was a force of nature that could so very easily take him under.

He waited for the hostess to seat David and his party, which included Steven Fortune and his pregnant wife, Ellie, who was the mayor of Rambling Rose; Acton Donovan and his fiancée, Stephanie Fortune, who was sporting the barest hint of a baby bump; Callum Fortune and his wife, Becky, a nurse at the Rambling Rose Pediatric Center; and Dillon Fortune and his fiancée, Hailey Miller, who was the assistant manager of the Paz Spa. Then he went over to the huge table for ten.

"Mr. Fortune?" Rodrigo stuck out his hand to the

tall, thin man with salt-and-pepper hair and blue eyes that were the same shade as Ashley's. "Rodrigo Mendoza, Vines Consulting Group. It's nice to finally meet you in person."

David Fortune stood and accepted the handshake. "Good to meet you, Rodrigo. How's everything going?" He didn't give Rodrigo a chance to answer. "I guess tonight I'll see for myself how everything is shaping up."

"I'll let you be the judge, but I think you'll be pleased."

David nodded. "I'm counting on it. Sounds like you have everything under control."

Ha! Rodrigo laughed inwardly at the thought of controlling Ashley. The woman had a mind of her own. "Provisions is a great place and your daughters have done a commendable job. All we needed to do was to fine-tune a few things."

"I take it that means they're cooperating with you? Sometimes they can be a little strong-willed. They get it from their father."

David Fortune chuckled and glanced at the beautiful woman sitting in the chair next to his.

"I'll say," she echoed. The woman, whom Rodrigo presumed was David Fortune's wife, Marci, was well dressed in a cognac-colored linen sundress that complimented her tan. Blond and blue-eyed, she looked exactly how he imagined Ashley and her sisters would look when they reached their mid-fifties. This woman had to be their mother.

David smiled lovingly at her and affectionately put his hand on her shoulder. "Marci, this is Rodrigo Mendoza. He's the restaurant consultant I hired to help the girls get Provisions off the ground. Rodrigo, this is my beautiful wife, Marci."

"Aren't you a handsome guy," she said, offering a hand, which Rodrigo shook. Her voice dripped with Southern charm, but not in an overly flirty way. "It's nice to meet you, Rodrigo. We're excited to see what you've helped the girls do. David and I are just thrilled for them and we're so grateful that you agreed to work with them."

Marci's blue eyes sparkled with obvious pride for her three daughters. Rodrigo found this touching. His own mother, Ginger, hadn't been part of his and his four brothers' lives after growing weary of his father's womanizing and drinking. She'd mostly washed her hands of the Mendoza lot.

"Mom! Daddy! You're here! I'm so happy you could make it." Ashley's voice sounded from behind Rodrigo. Before he could turn around, Ashley rushed by him on those stiletto heels and threw her arms around her mother. "I've missed you both so much. Look at what Nic, Meg and I have done. Isn't it wonderful?"

She threw her arms out wide, gesturing toward nothing in particular and everything in general.

"It was nice to meet you both," Rodrigo said, intending to leave so Ashley could have time with her family. "Enjoy your dinner."

"No, Rodrigo, don't go." Ashley placed her hand on his arm. Even through the layers of jacket and shirt, his arm felt hot where her hand touched him. "Why don't you stay and we can tell my father about our plans for Provisions?"

She smiled up at him. She was standing so close to him, he could smell her perfume—something floral with notes of spice and citrus. Just like her personality—feminine laced with spice and zest.

Watching Ashley with her family made him realize this was a different side to her than he'd seen before.

"Rodrigo has offered some good ideas, Daddy," she said, sliding her arm through his. "Meg, Nic and I know a lot about the business, but Rodrigo has helped us take what we thought was good and make it even better."

Ashley beamed up at him and Rodrigo tried not to think about the way she had complimented him before they opened the doors. His will was strong, but being this close to her made it difficult to remember why he was trying to resist her.

His stomach tightened and bunched at the thought.

Rodrigo remembered quickly when he saw David frown and his gaze fall to their arms, which were now entwined because Ashley had wrapped her left arm around his and had pulled him closer and placed her right hand on his bicep. It looked much more intimate than it probably should.

David's frown seemed to deepen with every second that Rodrigo's body was touching his daughter's. His gaze was pointed.

Rodrigo looked at his watch. "Look at the time." He did a quick sidestep away from Ashley. "I need to check in with the kitchen to make sure everything is going well. It was nice to meet you all. Enjoy tonight's celebration and please let me know if you need anything."

He made his way through the dining room, noting that there wasn't an empty table in the place. They were holding two seatings tonight to get used to turning over tables for later reservations. Everything else would run the same as if it were a regular night at the restaurant. People would order from the menu and bar. The waitstaff would serve the dinners and drinks. Rodrigo would stand back—as far away from Ashley as he could professionally manage while her father was there—and make sure everything was running as it should. Including the kitchen. Yes, that's right. He'd said he was going to check on things in the kitchen.

It would give him a chance to regroup and refocus.

As Ashley made her way across the dining room, she waved at Adam and his brother, Kane Fortune, who were dining with three locals in the second seating. They looked like they were enjoying the appetizers.

Seated at the other tables was a cross section of people from Rambling Rose: shopkeepers, teachers, farmers, ranchers. She waved at Frances Elliot, who made hand-knit scarves and sweaters, and Alice McKinley, who sewed beautiful quilts, all for sale at Mariana's Market.

Mariana herself, one of the grand dames of Rambling Rose, was front and center, presiding over her table of six like the queen bee she was.

These people were the heart and soul of Rambling Rose and it was important to win them over. Provisions was a different kind of place than what they were used to. Ashley pushed aside the worry that maybe there was a reason for that. Maybe this town just didn't support a higher-end establishment. Without their support, Provisions was doomed to fail.

With that in mind, they'd taken care to not make the place too fancy-schmancy. The restaurant's concept was farm to table fresh. There wasn't a dress code, though Ashley secretly hoped that the ambience would inspire people to dress up—even a little. Frances and Alice had certainly made an effort. The two seemed dressed in their Sunday best.

Ashley and her sisters had done extensive market research on pricing. While they were decidedly more expensive than La Ventana, Osteria Oliva and the Crockett Café, they took pride in offering a dining experience that the people of Rambling Rose wouldn't get anywhere else within a twenty-five mile radius. But the challenge was to not make it too inaccessible.

Of course, the menu would change often, depending on what was fresh and to keep things interesting, but there would be regular items, too. Such as ribeye steaks and Nic's famous fried chicken, made from a closely guarded recipe.

It was food that would appeal to the locals, only elevated to make them feel good about turning out and spending the evening with the new kids on the block.

Her brothers Stephen, Dillon and Callum had made a lot of headway in earning the locals' trust. Now it was Ashley and her sisters' mission to win over their taste buds.

"Did you fill out the comment card?" Ashley asked two hours later as she walked Frances Elliot and Alice McKinley to the door. They were the last of the guests to leave.

"Mine is right here," Frances said, waving it in the air. "Oh, but this was supposed to be anonymous. If I hand it to you, you'll know what we said."

"Frances, don't scare the poor dear," said Alice. "Besides, it won't be anonymous because we both signed our names. We wrote down our email addresses, too. Will we both get that coupon you're offering?"

To build their mailing list, the sisters had offered their guests the option of providing an email address on the comment card. If they did, the reward was a ten percent off coupon emailed to them to use the next time they dined at Provisions.

"Of course you will," Ashley said.

"Oh, good! Because we will definitely be back. We loved it, and we only had good things to say about our experience tonight. Here, let me read it to you."

Alice held her card out in front of her and cleared her throat.

"'Thank you for dining with us tonight. Provisions is excited to be part of the Rambling Rose community. We want to make sure every visit is the best it can be. Your feedback will help us improve your experience—'"

"Alice, she knows what the card says," Frances interjected. "Cut to the chase."

"I was just putting it all in context, Frances. Take a chill pill."

One thing Ashley had quickly learned was that the pace in Rambling Rose was a lot slower than in Fort Lauderdale. In Fort Lauderdale, people were always in a hurry. People honked even before the light turned green. In Rambling Rose, when you stepped outside, you'd better be prepared to spend a good ten minutes chatting with every person you ran into, otherwise they'd think you unneighborly.

The thing was, they were all genuinely interested to know how you were doing, what was new. They'd ask about your family even if they'd never met them.

Ashley and her sisters had taken to calling it "Rambling Rose time."

So Ashley did her best to smile and nod and listen, even as Alice read the instructions on the comment card that Ashley had written herself.

"'Question 1. How was the food?'" Alice read. "We both checked the first box that said, 'very good.' See, here's mine." Alice turned the card toward Ashley so she could see. She also saw that the woman had given them all highest marks for service and atmosphere, but she had only given a middle-of-the-road score for menu variety.

Alice must've seen Ashley looking because she said, "As you can see, I loved everything, but we both agreed that the menu was a little...limited. You asked us to be honest, dear, and we were."

"We were very lucky because we loved the offerings," Frances interjected. "But if you get a picky eater, you might run into some problems with the limited menu."

Ashley smiled. "Since this is a farm-to-table restaurant, the menu will change daily."

Frances and Alice both pulled faces.

"A farm to what?" Frances asked.

"Farm-to-table," Ashley repeated. "As much as possible, we buy our food locally so it's always fresh, and it supports local growers and artisans. But that means we are at the mercy of what's available and, except for the handful of items that will be permanent offerings, the menu could be different every time you come in."

Alice blinked. "Isn't that going to be a lot of work? I mean it sounds like a lot of trouble, and expensive, too. You have to print new menus every day."

Ashley laughed. "It's no trouble at all. We just type up the day's menu and print off the copies on our office printer. It's what we do, and that means you get the very best, freshest food every day. Plus, the menu will be a surprise every time you come in. Doesn't that sound like fun?"

Frances frowned and shook her head.

"No. I don't think I like that at all," the older woman finally said. "What if I fall in love with a dish and have cravings for it and then you never serve it again? Or what if you do and I can't make it on the day you're serving it? That would be frustrating."

She paused to take a breath before explaining.

"People in Rambling Rose know what they like and, when they like something, they can't get enough of it. Like that bread pudding. Nope. I think you're setting yourselves up for a big fall with this ever-changing menu idea. In fact, maybe I should write that down on my comment card."

Frances reached for the comment card that Alice had been using to fan herself.

"We would be delighted if you fell in love with something on the menu," Ashley said. "If so, all you have to do is let us know you'll be coming in and, if we can get the ingredients, we will make it for you special."

Rodrigo put his hand on Ashley's back and gave a light tap. Her head jerked to look at him and he did an ever so slight shake of his head.

Was he telling her not to do that? What in the world?

Frances and Alice were bent over the hostess stand, their heads together, amending their comment cards.

"What?" Ashley whispered.

Rodrigo turned and walked a few paces away from the women. Ashley followed.

"Rule number one. Don't promise things you may not be able to deliver," he said in a low voice.

"Excuse me?" Ashley said.

"You just told Frances she could make requests."

Ashley nodded and shrugged. "And?"

"Have you talked to Rosemary and Nicole about that?"

"Well, no. Not yet. But I will."

"What if they can't get fresh blackberries when Frances calls and especially requests blackberry cobbler for dessert? For that matter, what if the kitchen painstakingly plans out a menu and the entire town calls in special orders? Where will you draw the line? Because you won't be able to do that for everyone."

Ashley rolled her eyes. "If the whole town is calling, we'll be in a very good place."

"Yoo-hoo," Alice called. "Here's the card. We added a comment, but we didn't change any of our scores because it was a lovely night. Simply lovely."

"Thank you for including us, dear," Frances added and handed the card to Ashley. "When is the official opening date?"

"One week from today," Ashley said.

"Good to know," Alice said. "We'll definitely be back."

Ashley smiled and the two women waved goodnight.

Alice paused at the door.

"You know, you two make a very handsome couple." She winked and let the door close behind her, but her parting words seemed to hang in the air.

Ashley felt her face heat. It started at her neck and slowly burned its way up to her forehead. She was sure she must have turned a color close to the raspberry coulis they'd served tonight, as she stood there like a deer caught in headlights. She waited for Rodrigo to say something that would alleviate the awkward tension. But he was silent.

Strains of Patsy Cline's *Crazy* mixed with the clinks and clatters of bussers clearing the tables and the soft *woosh-woosh* of one of the crew running a Hoky sweeper over the wooden floor. A mélange of delicious smells from tonight's menu lingered in the air.

Ashley didn't think she could be any more morti-
fied, then her stomach made a sound like an angry
bull walrus.

And that did the trick.

At first, it was obvious that Rodrigo had been
trying to keep a straight face, but then his staid expression gave way to a smile and the smile turned
into a laugh.

"Hungry?" he asked.

She was famished. "I just realized I was so nervous about tonight that I hardly ate anything today.
But it went well, didn't it? I really think it did."

"It felt good," Rodrigo said. "The staff is almost
done with cleanup. Why don't we raid the kitchen
for leftovers, get the comment cards and read them?"

"That sounds like a great idea, but first I think
we need to gather the staff and have a toast to all
their hard work. After all, this was a very special
day. The start of something big."

"That's a great idea," he said. "Why don't you
gather everyone and I'll ask Byron to open some
bubbly."

Ten minutes later, the staff had gathered in the
bar and Rodrigo had begun handing out glasses of
champagne. When everyone had a glass in hand,
Ashley raised hers. "Tonight was a success because
of you. My sisters, Chef Rosemary and I want to
thank you for all your hard work and dedication.
And special thanks to Rodrigo Mendoza, who was

an unexpected but much appreciated addition to the team."

She lifted her glass. "Here's to you all. Now, we just have to do it all over again on opening night, but I know you're up for it."

Her gaze snared Rodrigo's and she lifted her glass in a special, private toast.

After the front-of-the-house cleanup was done, Ashley pointed to a bottle of champagne that was almost full.

"No sense in letting it go to waste," she said to Rodrigo. "Want to help me finish it?"

Of course, he wanted to. But champagne...the high of a perfect soft opening...the chemistry between them—they were all ingredients to a recipe for disaster. Albeit of the most enjoyable kind.

"Shouldn't we put a champagne stopper in it and save it for the paying guests?" he suggested. He knew what she'd say before she said it.

"Provisions won't see paying guests for another week and the champagne will go flat by then. I certainly can't have that on my conscience."

She grabbed two fresh glasses and the bottle off the bar and stated walking toward the office.

"Can you bring that stack of comment cards?" She stopped to smile at him over her shoulder. "We're working here."

Against his better judgment, he did exactly as

she asked, as if he was following the pied piper into the office.

They *were* working. She'd said it herself. After all, they needed to read the comment cards to see what areas they could improve upon before next week at the grand opening. Besides, he told himself, this was the restaurant business. Most people who worked in restaurants ended the night by sharing a drink. This wasn't a big deal.

His better judgment chimed in. *You've already shared a toast with the staff. Now you're drinking champagne alone in an office with a client. A very attractive, very tempting client.*

After he entered the office, Ashley shut the door.

"Maybe we should keep the door open?" he said.

"Why? Are you afraid I'm going to get you drunk and take advantage of you?"

Yes.

"I don't want anyone to get the wrong idea."

They heard a loud crash coming from the kitchen, followed by a string of curse words and then a chorus of laughter. Then someone switched the music from the bluesy standard that had been playing to the Talking Heads, cranking up the volume so that *Burning Down the House* nearly shook the walls.

"Don't worry," Ashley said. "Your virtue is safe with me. But I do need to be able to hear myself think. They may not be burning down the house, but they sound like they're wrecking it."

The office hadn't been wired with speakers for the stereo, so it was markedly quieter with the door shut.

Self-control, Mendoza. You're a grown man, not a teenage boy.

Though she did make him feel hormone-controlled too often.

The sisters shared an office. There were three workspaces set against three different walls.

She pointed to the chair where Megan usually sat. "Pull that over here, please." She indicated the space next to her desk.

Again, he did as she asked.

As he arranged his chair, she poured two glasses of Veuve Clicquot, handed him one of the flutes and raised her glass to his.

"I'm thrilled with the way things turned out tonight, Rodrigo. I was totally serious when I said we couldn't have done it without you. Thank you."

His gaze searched her beautiful heart-shaped face, landing on her blue eyes and full lips that were tilted into a sincere smile that coaxed out the dimples in her cheeks. Tonight, dressed up for the soft opening, she was wearing a little more makeup than she usually wore, but it worked. Paired with that black dress, she looked polished and professional, even at this late hour of the evening.

He cleared his throat. "That's what I'm here for. Are you ready to see what everyone had to say?"

Ashley let out a little squeal and clapped her hands. "Let's do this."

Her enthusiasm was contagious and it made him smile.

As the focus shifted back to business, Rodrigo breathed a silent sigh of relief and gratitude.

One by one, they went through the cards, taking turns reading the glowing comments.

"'I could subsist on your blackberry cobbler.'"

"'Can I come back tomorrow?'"

"'How in the world did you infuse that scrumptious smoky flavor into the brisket? It was heaven on a plate.'"

"'Quite simply some of the best food I've ever eaten in my life.'"

"'I'd like to make reservations for the grand opening. How soon can I reserve a table for four?'"

All in all, seventy-eight people signed up for Provisions' electronic mailing list and the only bit of constructive criticism was what they'd already heard from Frances and Alice.

"We should address Frances and Alice's concern about the changing menu," Rodrigo said. "One of the most important things I've learned over the years is you have to listen to your customers."

"Even if it's just two people taking issue with the changing menu?"

He nodded. "How would you feel about having a few more items that are always on the menu, rain or shine? Such as a good chocolate cake and house-made ice cream? It would be easy enough to get a reliable source for those ingredients and you can always have them available."

"You have a point. However, this is really an issue we should take up with Nicole and Rosemary at our morning meeting. Right now, I'm low on champagne." She topped off their glasses. "Plus, I'd like to take a few minutes to bask in the glow of tonight's success, if you don't mind."

She held his gaze for a moment, then closed her eyes and sipped her champagne, turning her face upward. She looked the picture of someone savoring the moment.

Rodrigo took advantage of the time to drink in her fine bones, her smooth skin, her perfect features. When she opened her eyes and caught him staring, it seemed like the most natural thing in the world.

She leaned in and her knee pressed into his. Neither of them moved away.

"I was thinking…" she said. "Other than possibly adjusting the menu, I don't think we need to do much differently for the grand opening. Don't you agree? I mean, if it's not broken, don't fix it."

"How are the reservations looking?" Rodrigo asked.

Ashley gave a one-shoulder shrug. "Last time I looked, we were about fifty percent booked, but after tonight's response, I think we'll fill up. Word of mouth is a powerful influencer."

"It is, but we need to go over your advertising

and social media plan to see if there is anything more we can do."

Ashley leaned forward and reached past him to grab her phone off her desk. In the process, her hair brushed his cheek. He could smell her shampoo and the way it mingled with the delicate floral scent of her perfume. It was subtle, but it was sexy...and personal.

It tempted him to lean in closer, to breathe in deeper.

It didn't get any less tempting when she settled back into her chair, allowing him to reclaim his personal space...for a moment.

"Look at this." She had called up the Provisions' Instagram page. "I think we need to do more posts like this."

The only way for him to see what she meant was to lean in so he could see the picture of the menu she'd posted.

"We could post a photo of the provisions board that lists all the locally sourced ingredients. See what I did there? The restaurant is Provisions and I'm calling it our provisions board."

"I noticed that. You're clever." He looked up to smile at her and their lips were a breath apart. All he had to do was lean in a fraction of an inch and he would be able to taste her...

Chapter Five

Ashley had never seen a man move away from her as fast as Rodrigo did. One minute, she was sure he was going to kiss her. Their lips had been *that* close. Then he was acting as if it was the most unnerving prospect in the world. He leaned back so fast, she was afraid his chair would topple over backward.

She should've taken the matter into her own hands.

She should've leaned in and kissed him and not given him that split second to change his mind.

After his feat of near gymnastics, he was sitting there looking at his phone. For a moment, she contemplated leaning in and finishing the job, but he was angled away from her. It would be an awkward climb.

If he thought she was so repugnant, he could've gotten up and left. No one was making him stay. Yet here he was. That's why his resistance almost seemed like a personal challenge. It was obvious that he was attracted to her. She had a sixth sense for that.

So what was wrong?

"Um…what was that about?" she asked.

"What was what about?"

Did he know how bad an actor he was?

She *tsked*.

"Rodrigo, we almost kissed."

He opened his mouth then shut it. Blew out a breath.

"I'm sorry about that," he said. "It won't happen again. That's why I stopped it."

"You big dummy, I wanted it to happen."

He sat there staring at her, his brow wrinkled in apparent consternation.

"If I'm not being clear, I want you to kiss me."

She leaned in to close the deal.

This time, he stood and she nearly fell forward, but he caught her arm and righted her before she could.

"I'm sorry," he said. "Are you okay?"

Her mouth fell open but all that came out was a sputtering sound. "No, I'm not okay. What's wrong with you? Or maybe I should ask what it is that you find so unappealing about me."

He laughed, but it was a miserable sound and it

only confused matters. So did the way he so deeply exhaled that it seemed like it was meant to help him cool off.

"There is not a thing in the world wrong with you, Ashley. You're gorgeous. You're smart. You're funny and creative, but you're also my client. And that's why our relationship has to remain strictly business."

"I'm the client and I am telling you it's okay. I want this, Rodrigo. I mean…if you're worried about me coming back and falsely calling harassment, I'm more than willing to sign a statement, but that wouldn't be very romantic—"

"Look, you are a hell of a woman, Ashley. Under any other circumstance, things would be very different right now…maybe. I mean, I'm way too old for you—"

"Okay, grandpa, I don't know who taught you how to count, but seven years is not a far stretch. I mean, we're basically the same generation. Are you just not interested?"

"I'm not interested in dating anyone right now, Ashley. I travel a lot for work and I can't do it."

"Is this about my dad?" she asked. "I know he's the one who hired you, but this is my restaurant. Mine and my sisters. He's not an investor or a partner. He has no part of it. So, if that's what's stopping you, don't let it."

She knew damn good and well when a guy was attracted to her. Rodrigo showed all the signs. But once again, as with every relationship she'd had in the past, her father managed to come between her and the guy. Because David Fortune was rich and famous and too cool for school, he ran the show. This time, instead of the guy wanting to be with her to get close to him, Rodrigo *didn't* want to get close to her because he was more concerned about how it would affect his business relationship with her father.

It was ridiculous.

"That's partially the problem," he said. "My business is young. I can't afford to alienate people like your father."

"I am a grown woman, Rodrigo. My father does not get to dictate who I get involved with—"

He was shaking his head and it stopped her mid-sentence better than if he'd reached out and put his hand over her mouth.

"Fine." Her voice was cool and calm. She picked up her purse and her phone. "If you're more interested in getting in good with my dad than getting to know me, knock yourself out. Mendoza. It's your loss. Please make sure the doors are locked when you leave."

She was so furious she wanted to kick something. But she made herself remain calm and walked out of the office with as much dignity as she could salvage.

She was so tired of her father getting in the way of her relationships.

Then she remembered what Rodrigo had said about not wanting to date anyone right now.

That was interesting. It sounded like he really didn't know what he wanted.

After she got into her car, she sat there for a moment as a plan began to take shape.

If Rodrigo Mendoza didn't know what he wanted, maybe she needed to help him figure it out.

As Rodrigo drove toward Rosebud House, the bed and breakfast where he was staying, he was warring with two separate but equal emotions, both inspired by Ashley Fortune. She was captivating. But she was too damn young. Not to mention, she was a client, which was a fact, not an emotion, he reminded himself.

Shouldn't that fact alone tip the scales toward the side of reason and help him do the sane, professional thing and keep his distance?

It seemed like a no-brainer.

Even so, Ashley tempted him to break all the rules.

Since her sisters had elected her to be his go-to person for the restaurant, it wasn't as if he could avoid her.

Given he had no choice but to work with her, he needed to step back and listen to the voice of reason. Either that or he needed to get out of his own head.

Sure, he'd almost kissed her. He'd wanted to kiss her. And it had taken every bit of moral fiber he had to resist her, but he had stuck to his guns.

This time.

Recognizing that his will was weak was a positive step toward staying on the straight and narrow. Still, it would benefit him if he could come up with a way to remind himself not to do anything stupid in the future.

As he steered the rental car into an empty parking space at Rosebud House, it hit him. All he needed to do was to make sure he was never alone with her. He wouldn't be inspired to kiss her in front of a crowd.

Since David Fortune wasn't in town on a regular basis, he needed to somehow involve the family that was here—the siblings, the cousins and any others who would provide cover to ensure he would not be alone with Ashley.

Removing the temptation would remove any future problems.

It was that simple.

Of course, given the way Ashley had a stormed out of the office tonight, the need to keep his distance might be a moot point. Ashley Fortune was a woman who was used to getting what she wanted. Obviously, she wasn't used to hearing the word no.

As he sat in the parked car contemplating Ashley, another woman who had been used to getting what she wanted elbowed her way into the forefront of his mind.

Bonnie.

His heart tugged at the memory.

He'd once made the mistake of getting involved with a woman like this. He'd made excuses for her behavior much the same way he was making excuses for Ashley. He'd played the fool for her.

He'd been young and foolish. He'd even been ready to propose. Then he'd learned the ugly truth. He'd put everything he'd had into that relationship, but when all was said and done, his best hadn't been good enough for Bonnie.

Looking back now, he'd dodged a bullet.

"If you play with fire again, you'll get burned." He said the words aloud, hoping they would sink in. That they would stick.

The front porch lights of the B&B, the only one in Rambling Rose, glowed with welcoming warmth. This town and its people had a way of getting to you, he realized. Had a way of making you forget yourself and why you'd worked so darn hard to get to where you were.

In Miami, in the early days, he'd been a hardworking nobody. He'd known he was destined for so much more than the hand he'd been dealt at birth. Now, here in Rambling Rose, he knew exactly what he had and how hard he'd worked to get it.

He and his brothers hadn't succeeded by sitting back and letting things happen to them. They'd been proactive and now they actively protected the businesses they'd built.

He wouldn't repeat the mistakes he'd made in the past. Even if he'd temporarily lost his senses tonight, he reminded himself again what happened when he forgot himself with Bonnie—where he'd come from and the life he'd worked so hard to build.

Rodrigo knew what he needed to do to protect himself now.

"Callum, thanks for coming over on such short notice," Rodrigo said as Ashley's brother walked into the Provisions' dining room, joining his siblings Steven and Dillon, who were already there, along with Adam and his brother Kane.

"Glad to be here." Callum accepted Rodrigo's outstretched hand. "It was good timing. I've been wanting to talk to you to see if you could give me some pointers about the hotel we want to open. Do you do that kind of consulting?"

"Sure, let's talk about it today after the Provisions' meeting," Rodrigo said.

"And what exactly is this Provisions' meeting about?" Ashley stood at the top of the stairs with her hands on her hips and a scowl on her pretty face. Despite her obvious annoyance, she looked fresh and rested.

At least one of them had gotten some sleep after last night's awkward exchange.

She was wearing a pretty blue dress and those wedge sandals. They tied at the ankle and tempted his eyes upward. But he wasn't looking. She'd swept her hair off her face into a ponytail. Her makeup was minimal, proving she didn't need it—

He shouldn't be noticing things like that.

"I thought your brothers and Adam should join us for the meeting this morning," Rodrigo said. "We can get their input about what worked last night and what didn't." He motioned her over.

Her brow creased. "Okay. I guess. I thought you and I were meeting to discuss everything first. If you want to involve my entire family, maybe we should get my parents on the phone?"

She was prickly today, but he was going to ignore her mood.

"Probably not." Rodrigo kept his tone light. "I think your brothers and Adam will be sufficient."

She squinted at him then glanced at her watch. "Why didn't you tell me about the change in the guest list?"

"I figured you would be here soon enough," Rodrigo said, hoping like hell she wouldn't see through his plan and know that he needed chaperones more than opinions.

"As I was driving home last night," he said, "I got the idea to talk to a panel of people who had attended the soft opening and also understood the mind-set of the locals. Because you're right—Frances and Alice are just two people. I want to get more opinions and I wanted to bring in everyone while their minds are still fresh."

"Well, Nic and Rosemary aren't scheduled to come in until noon and Megan has an appointment off site this morning. Shouldn't we wait to include them?"

"We'll have another meeting with them," Rodrigo said, that would give him more cover later. "Since this is mostly front-of-the-house business, I thought it would be easier to keep it small."

"Small? There are seven people here," she said. "That's not my idea of a small meeting. Small would be just you and me."

He could read the disappointment in her eyes. He looked away and reminded himself that was the reason he couldn't be alone with her.

"I think this is a smart idea, Mendoza," said Callum. "Ash, you did a great job with the soft opening, but there's always room for improvement and I think we need to talk about things while they're still fresh."

"Maybe," she said. Her voice still had an edge, but he sensed her mood was lightening. "I can't take complete credit for last night. Nicole was responsible for the food that came out of the kitchen, and Meg has been brilliant at keeping us on budget. Rodrigo has given us wonderful guidance, but what you saw in the dining room was me. Forgive me for tooting my own horn, but it's the truth."

"Of course it was," Callum said. "I always knew you could do this. You're a natural at this business. You've worked hard to get to this point and I know Provisions will succeed, but there's always room for improvement. Right, Mendoza?"

"Absolutely," he said. "Your sister has an innate

ability to anticipate a customer's needs. That is half the battle."

And to drive me to the brink of insanity...

He shoved the thought out of his head, but he couldn't ignore the heat of Ashley's gaze on him.

"Overall, the takeaway from last night was positive," he said.

"It was extremely positive," Ashley interjected. "I don't know how the message could've been any clearer."

She looked him squarely in the eyes, and he knew she wasn't talking about the feedback from the comment cards.

"But there are still some major concerns," he said. Before the others at the table caught on that Ashley's comments were personal, he launched into Frances's and Alice's points about the changing menu.

"Of course, this thing we have here… It shouldn't be thought of as something bad," Ashley said. "I mean, if we were creative, we would look at it as an opportunity or a challenge."

"Right," Rodrigo said, too quickly. "I mean—I mean no. We have to be careful." She had him so flustered he was stumbling over his words. "What I'm trying to say is the customer is always right. That's what we're talking about here."

He felt himself start to sweat. He had to stop feeding into the subtext that she was speaking.

He had no idea if what they were doing was making any sense to the others. Or if they were being completely transparent.

And unprofessional.

He prided himself on being professional.

That reminder was all it took for him to rein himself in and refocus on business.

But the only way to remain focused was not to look at Ashley.

"It will be fun for the locals to see their names and the names of their neighbors on the Provisions' menu board. It should make them buy in to the place. It's a great celebration of everything that makes this community what it is. Does that make sense?"

They batted around a few more ideas, such as trying to squeeze a couple of extra tables into the dining room to accommodate more reservations without making the place feel overcrowded and discussing with Rosemary and Nicole the possibility of expanding the offerings on the permanent menu.

As Rodrigo wrote down the suggestions, he realized Ashley had been quiet for a while. Damned if he didn't give into the urge to look at her. Her gaze lingered a few beats longer than was strictly platonic. It touched the most primal part of him and his body responded.

It was a very good thing the others were present, because who knew what would happen if they were alone? God, he hoped they hadn't noticed the heated exchanges.

Callum was taking notes and seemed oblivious

to everything but what he was committing to paper. The others were chatting among themselves.

It was painfully clear that rather than ignoring what happened last night, they needed to talk about it. This wouldn't be a problem if they didn't work together. For a fleeting moment, he considered suggesting that they see each other after he'd fulfilled his contractual obligations... But why? She lived in Rambling Rose. He would return to Austin. While it wasn't an impossible commute—

No. He wasn't opening Pandora's Box.

He wasn't in a place in his life to get involved. Especially when the woman who was singing the siren's song was so eerily similar to the woman who had taught him his first and final hard lesson about not wading into waters where he didn't belong.

"This all sounds good," Callum said, closing the cover on his digital tablet. "Ash, I'm proud of you. I think you're on the right track. I'm in awe of all your hard work."

Ashley smiled. "You know me. When something is important to me, I don't stop until I make it happen."

She pinned Rodrigo with a gaze that he couldn't believe no one else was seeing. He nodded and looked back at his notes and tried to act nonchalant.

"That's true," Callum said. "My sister is a determined one. She's wanted this restaurant for a long time. I'm glad we have Mendoza here to help you.

The soft opening was perfect, but in a sense, we were preaching to the choir.

"We need the rollout to the community to go well so that we strike a good note with the locals. If we get everything right, we stand a better chance of growing the business in a positive direction. Speaking of…" he turned to Rodrigo. "I'm eager to hear your thoughts about the hotel concept. With Provisions getting off to such a great start, I think it bodes well for the hotel, don't you?"

Rodrigo sensed Callum was expecting positive words about the future prospects, but it was too early to know. One thing he prided himself on was keeping it real. Under promise and over deliver, he always said.

Every eye in the room was watching him, waiting for his verdict, but all he could see was Ashley.

"It's a little early to tell," Rodrigo said. "But one thing holds true in most ventures. Don't expand too fast. If it were me, I'd hold off on the hotel until Provisions got off the ground."

His advice was met with silence—all the way around the table.

Clearly, not the answer anyone was hoping to hear.

"Is there anything you can do to get more of the neighbors on your side?" he asked. "We need to figure out a way to understand what makes Rambling Rose tick?"

"I picked up a scrapbook at Mariana's a couple of months ago," said Steven. "I grabbed it because it had all kinds of interesting pictures of Rambling Rose. Maybe it can help give us some insight into the town."

"That's sounds interesting," said Ashley.

"Yeah, I'd like to see it," Rodrigo said. "Would you mind if we borrowed it? Maybe something in it will spark some ideas."

"We met with the mayor and some of the locals a few months ago," Steven added. "We let them know a new hotel would provide a lot of new jobs for Rambling Rose. It took a little convincing, but now they're interested."

"More than interested," said Callum. "They're on board with the idea. Of course, it doesn't hurt that Steven is married to the mayor."

"If you open the hotel, have you considered holding job fairs to see who's interested?" Rodrigo asked.

"We hadn't considered it, because it's a little early," said Steven. "We just assumed that people would submit applications if they were interested." He shrugged.

"I know you've been working hard to let the townspeople know how dedicated you are to investing in the betterment of the town. What if you took it a step further and found a way to make it more personal? Just like we've done with the menu board. You know, show them what's in it for them?"

Everyone in the room exchanged glances as if they were looking for clarification from each other.

"How would we do that?" Ashley finally asked.

"What's in it for them?" Rodrigo said. "Jobs. Make it clear to the town's influencers that you want to hire local talent. It might mean hiring someone with less experience, but you could establish your own training program. For that matter, why not consider starting a hospitality apprenticeship program? That way you can train your own workers."

"That's a good idea, but it's a lot to think about," said Callum. His elbow was on the table and he was leaning on his hand. He didn't look convinced.

"I know it's a lot to absorb," said Rodrigo. "But you asked for my thoughts and that's what I'd recommend."

Again, his words were met with silence. In cases like this, silence usually signaled dissent. Silence was a challenge that Rodrigo could never resist.

"Look, I have to be honest," Rodrigo said. "I wouldn't be serving you well if I didn't point out that Rosebud House has vacancies. It's the only lodging in town, right?"

Callum nodded. "However, I think it might be a fluke that the B&B isn't full. You might have hit it on an off week. Tourism is beginning to pick up in town with the opening of the Shoppes and the Paz Spa. The locals I've spoken to have mentioned that they've been doing more business than ever, which translates to people from outside the community visiting the local ranches and farms."

"This is good to know," Rodrigo said. "We need to factor it into Provisions' business plan.

"Everything I've said to you today about the hotel has been off the cuff. To give you a fair assessment, I'd need to do more research. The bottom line is you need to consider the location and who your prospective guests will be. You need to make your place different. What if you created a first-class resort, then it could be a destination in itself? Offer great service and world-class amenities—a place where people wanted to go to get away from it all—then it might draw people in. But if you're just building another hotel…" Rodrigo shrugged.

Ashley mirrored his gesture. "But don't we want the most skilled employees we can find? If we want to offer this first-class service you're talking about, aren't we better off bringing in people from Houston or San Antonio or even Austin?"

"I am living proof that sometimes all a person needs is a break," Rodrigo said. "Not everyone has a family to fall back on." He realized it sounded like a dig. The words had come out a little sharper than he had intended.

At least he'd stopped himself before he said, *Not everyone has a rich father to help them achieve their dreams.*

Still, he wished he could take back the words. Sort of. There had been so many times in the past when he hadn't gotten a job because of his lack of experience and, more profoundly, because of his lack of connections. What he would've given for an apprenticeship program like he'd mentioned. A chance for a leg up because he'd never wanted a handout—like Bonnie had accused him in the end.

He and his brothers and cousins came from a solid middle-class upbringing. While they hadn't wanted for the basics of life, there hadn't been money for extras—like hotels and restaurants. Even so, he and his brothers had done well for themselves. Their success was a direct result of hard work, and yes, some lucky breaks combined with good timing. His mantra had always been "When preparedness meets opportunity, it coalesces into success."

Basically, he and his family had never had anything handed to them.

Ashley was shooting daggers at him with her eyes. She seemed to be mentally telegraphing her thoughts.

So what are you saying that the only reason my family and I are in this position is because of our father or our name?

Now all eyes were on him. The funny thing was that the Fortune brothers were watching him but they didn't look as offended as Ashley seemed. In fact, they almost looked fascinated by the back-and-forth, as if they were watching a sport.

Maybe they hadn't been as oblivious to their earlier exchanges as he's thought.

He resisted the urge to swallow hard. Last night he'd vowed to stay away from Ashley, but by playing into her banter this morning he'd put himself right in her path.

Ashley was determined to not take what Rodrigo said personally. She changed the subject.

"It wouldn't just be another hotel, just like Provisions won't be another restaurant," Ashley said. "Rambling Rose is an untapped gold mine. Right, Callum? You said so yourself."

She didn't wait for her brother to answer.

"It is an up-and-coming destination. Look at how the families are moving into Rambling Rose Estates in droves. Granted the locals who live in the town proper are one set of clientele, but we're well on our way to winning them over with Provisions. The residents of Rambling Rose Estates are upscale. They will have equally upscale guests visiting them who will be an entirely different market than the locals."

"Right, but the average house in Rambling Rose Estates is huge," Rodrigo countered. "Wouldn't they have plenty of room to house their guests rather than farming them out to a hotel?"

"I have no idea," said Ashley. "All I know is what

my gut is telling me. And it's screaming that if we don't act now, someone else will move in and do it. You snooze, you lose, Mendoza."

She hoped he'd picked up on the double meaning.

Chapter Six

For the rest of the week between the meeting and the grand opening, Rodrigo seemed to cut Ashley a wide berth. She did the same for him, too. There was no denying the guy was hot, but hot seemed to become combustible when they were together. That was the last thing she needed right now. She didn't need distractions. She needed this grand opening to go off without a hitch.

That's why she'd been just as happy when Rodrigo had spent most of his time working with Nicole and Rosemary in the kitchen, helping them hone and perfect the menu.

Frankly, Ashley found it annoying the way they seemed to hang on his every word and suggestion.

Please.

When she had suggested they come up with a couple more specialties that could be available most of the time, they had both balked, saying, "I don't know Ashley. The concept is farm-to-table, which means seasonal."

Then when Hot Rod had suggested it, they'd acted like he had just invented sliced bread.

For God's sake.

Sure, she might have rolled her eyes. And who wouldn't when these two grown women were acting like total nincompoops? Like they'd never seen a pretty face. But she refused to dignify their behavior with her energy.

Instead she'd focused on her mile-long to-do list, and now, finally, the big night was upon her.

After the soft opening, they had been inundated with requests for reservations for the grand opening. In addition to the couple of tables they had decided to add upstairs, they'd decided to squeeze in a few more. They hated to turn away anyone who was interested. Since word of mouth was good, they wanted to keep up the excitement around town.

They would just have to work a little bit harder.

"We're opening the doors in fifteen minutes," Ashley called out. "May I have everybody who works front of the house in the bar for a quick word, please?"

Fresh from the family dinner, which was a chance for all the servers and other employees to have a bite to eat together and taste the menu offerings to familiarize themselves with the night's fair, it took everyone a minute. But soon they had gathered in the bar area.

"We have all worked so hard for this night," Ashley said. "And it's finally here. We're ready. I want you to know how much I appreciate all your hard work getting to this point and I want to thank you in advance for making tonight a success. I know we added a few tables in everybody's sections, but I have faith in you. I know you can handle it. So give yourselves a round of applause. Tonight is going to rock."

Ashley lead the applause and smiled as she watched the servers high-five and fist bump each other. She loved this energy. Besides the food, the energy was one of the things she loved the most about this business.

She took a moment to take it all in, savoring the sweetness of it, loving the way her heart was pounding and her passion was coursing through her veins.

She looked over to see Rodrigo standing in the corner, watching everyone. In a show of goodwill, she nodded to him. He nodded back. It was confirmation that she had this. Tonight was going to be a glorious success. The official start of something great. She could feel it in her bones.

She and Rodrigo had mostly avoided each other this week, but they had butted heads a couple of days ago when he was looking over the reservations list. He seemed to think that they were overbooked. She reminded him that they had added more tables and the servers were more than willing to stretch a little and take on an extra table or two in their sections. She was beginning to wonder what kind of a consultant would turn away money. Because, after all, reservations translated into food sales, which translated into money.

But she wasn't holding it against him. He would see that she was right. That this wasn't her first restaurant rodeo. Granted, it wasn't his, either, but they needed to agree to disagree on this issue.

They simply had different styles. Even so, she was glad to see that he was being a good sport about her making an executive decision.

"It's just about six o'clock," Megan said. "Is everyone ready? It looks like people are lined up outside the door. We shouldn't be late letting them in."

Butterflies swarmed in Ashley's stomach. With adrenaline pumping, she called, "Places, everyone! We are opening the doors now."

Meg was right. People were waiting outside. And while it wasn't quite a Black Friday type frenzy, when the first customers stepped up to the hostess stand, a respectable line formed behind them.

Ashley discreetly slipped a card into the hostess's hand. It was a free drink card to celebrate Provisions' first official customers. Sarah would give it to the server, who would congratulate his table for being their first official diners and, therefore, receive a complimentary first round of drinks or a bottle of wine.

Ashley didn't take a breath until the first set of reservations was seated. Then she and Megan went around to each table to greet the customers.

"I'm excited to finally have a fancy restaurant in town," said Jeremiah Middleton, one of the city council members, when she stopped at his table.

"Frankly, Provisions is a much-needed perk for Rambling Rose. Nothing against our existing establishments, mind you."

"Mr. Middleton, we are so grateful to have you with us tonight and so appreciative of your enthusiasm. We need positive word of mouth from people like you to help break the ice for us."

He laughed a hearty laugh. "Oh, I think you just need to take a good look around to realize you don't need me to tell people that this place is fabulous. The food will do the talking." He gestured to the juicy steak before him.

"Um, Ash, may I steal you away for a second, please?" Ashley turned around to see Megan standing behind her wringing her hands. All she had to do was to take one look at her sister's face to know something was wrong.

"Excuse me, Mr. Middleton. My sister needs me. Please enjoy your evening."

Jeremiah Middleton turned back to his table of four and seemed blessedly oblivious to Megan's distress.

Ashley started to lead her sister over to an alcove that housed the beverage station, so they could talk privately. But Megan grabbed Ashley's wrist and gestured toward the stairs.

"I need you to come to the kitchen with me." Her wide eyes told Ashley something was terribly wrong. Megan never set foot in the kitchen during business hours. Nicole wouldn't stand for it.

"What's going on?" Ashley asked as they descended the stairs, away from the diners' ears.

"Oh, there's just been a little incident in the kitchen."

"What's happened?" Ashley said. "Is everything okay?"

"Well, yes. Mostly. But you know that expensive fire-suppression system we invested in? Something set it off and not only did it spray that white powder all over everything, but it, um, sort of summoned the fire department."

"Are you kidding me? Did you call them and tell them to stand down, that everything is fine?"

Megan's face crumbled. "I tried, but the dispatcher told me that Rambling Rose regulations dictate that when a system like that goes off in a commercial building, the fire department has to come and sign off that the structure is safe. Plus, we're going to have to call the company that services the system and have them come in and reset it. Until then, we can't use the kitchen."

They had just entered the kitchen, which was covered in a fine white powder that looked like baking soda, when firemen clad in yellow jackets and safety helmets stormed in.

"Where's the fire?" the guy in front asked.

"There is no fire," Ashley said. "Everything is fine. Really. Something set off our fire-suppression system. I don't know what happened."

"Until we can ascertain what happened, we need everyone to clear the premises."

"You mean the kitchen?" Ashley asked.

"No, I mean the entire restaurant. Everyone out."

"Go ahead and say it," Ashley said.

"Say what?" Rodrigo said as he looked up from the opening night profit-and-loss statement he had been reviewing.

Just as the fire chief had said, they'd had to evacuate the building. Those diners who had gotten their food had been forced to leave it on the table and exit the premises. Though little damage had been done to the kitchen itself, all the food had been rendered inedible. The worst part was, the catastrophe had destroyed their opening night because they'd had to close for the rest of the evening.

Ashley and her sisters had made a spur-of-the-moment decision to offer everyone a free meal if they returned once Provisions reopened. So not only had they lost the profits from a fully booked evening, they would have to subtract a whole bunch of comps.

That was the cost of doing business, Rodrigo had reminded her.

"I know you're dying to say, 'I told you so,'" said Ashley.

"No I'm not." Rodrigo returned his gaze to the profit-and-loss statement, simply because he did not want Ashley to see that he was enjoying this moment a little more than he should.

He had warned her that taking on too much too soon was the wrong thing to do. The cooks had been in a hurry and tried to squeeze too much into the stove. From what he could gather, someone had bumped into someone who'd upended a pan of duck fat into the gas flame. Because one of the line cooks had neglected to turn on the vent system, the flare-up activated the kitchen's fire-suppression system. Would it have happened if they hadn't tried to cram more people than Rodrigo had recommended into that first sitting?

Who knew?

He had already decided he was going to take the high road and not gloat.

"What good would saying 'I told you so' do?" he asked.

"It would probably make you feel very satisfied," she said.

He smiled, but he kept his gaze on the report in front of him.

"See, you know you want to say it. Go ahead. Do

it. Get it out of your system—" Her voice broke on the last word.

When he looked up, he saw a tear slide down her cheek.

"Ashley, don't cry. Please." Before he knew what he was doing, he had bolted from his chair, rounded the desk and was pulling her into his arms. She clung to him like he was a lifeline.

As she sobbed on his shoulder, he held her as if his arms could keep her from falling apart.

Even though he tried not to make it personal, he could smell her shampoo. The way it mingled with her perfume was just short of intoxicating. It was enough to make a man lose control of his senses and tip up her head and kiss those delicious lips.

He wanted to. He wanted to hold her and kiss her and finish what they'd started the other night when common sense had ruled and he'd walked out of the office. But right now his common sense seemed to have gone the way of last night's food—right into the garbage.

And everything would be ruined if he gave in to his weakness and kissed her.

She slid her arms around his neck and tilted up her head and looked at him. An unspoken invitation. An invitation that he longed to accept. Her eyes looked turquoise through the tears and her pretty face wore the most heart-wrenchingly vulnerable expression.

He couldn't.

But he felt himself leaning in. Succumbing to the silent siren song of her essence.

No! Stop it. You know better than this, man.

It was awkward, but he took a step back and grabbed a tissue from the box on the desk. When he offered it to her, she looked at him as if he was trying to pawn off a used paper towel he'd plucked from the kitchen floor.

"Look, what happened last night was just one of those things. It happens. I really believe it wasn't catastrophic. Sure, it wasn't how we had hoped things would go, but we will survive this."

Clearly, she wasn't listening to him. "That's fine, but I need to know what is it about me that you find so repelling, Rodrigo."

He blinked at her non sequitur.

"Ashley, this isn't about you. Believe me. Please."

He took another step backward and sat on the edge of the desk because he had no other place to go.

"Yet, you can't seem to put enough space between us."

The emotion in her eyes was gut-wrenching.

"Ashley—" He reached out and touched her cheek. The look on her pretty face was heartbreaking and he felt his resolve start to crumble.

"There is absolutely nothing about you that I find repelling. Nothing. In fact, it's quite the contrary. I am very attracted to you. It's all I can do to keep my hands off you. But I can't act on my feelings because it violates my professional code of ethics."

And there were other, more personal reasons he didn't want to get into, even thought she was looking at him as if she was weighing the BS factor.

"I swear to you, if things were different, we would be having a completely different conversation right now. You know what I'm saying?"

She pinned him with her most seductive look. "I take it there wouldn't be a whole lot of conversation."

He closed his eyes and laughed, ran a hand through his hair, trying to regroup, trying to ignore the way her comment had zinged right to his most primal places, stirring things up. "Right now we need to focus on getting the kitchen reopened and rebooking the reservations we lost."

She crossed her arms and rolled her eyes, obviously not happy with the way he'd changed the subject.

"Come on, it's not the end of the world." he said, pretending she was still upset over the kitchen incident. "What's that saying? Fall down seven times get up eight?"

"God, I hope we don't have six more incidents like this," she said, finally coming around.

He shrugged. "It's the nature of the business. Things happen. You have to put them in the past and go on."

He was tempted to ask if the previous restaurants she had worked in had had their own sets of trials and tribulations. But that would not help things.

This was different. It was more personal when the place was yours.

"Well, if you are not going to say, 'I told you so,' I guess I have to admit that I have a lot more to learn than I thought I did. Owning a restaurant and working in them are two different things."

"Welcome to the big time, Ashley Fortune."

She laughed, but the sound wasn't humorous.

Then their gazes locked and Rodrigo felt that old familiar zing.

Ashley Fortune, what am I going to do with you?

All the way back to Rosebud House, Rodrigo couldn't get Ashley out of his mind. He knew she had worked hard to get to this point. He'd gleaned that the reason she and her sisters had held jobs since high school was because of her father's values. She'd chosen the restaurant business because she had a passion for it, despite the food industry being renowned for hard work.

Their common interest in food, though, didn't erase the fact that they were from two different worlds. While Rodrigo had had to work to support himself, he knew she'd worked because she'd wanted to, not because she'd had to earn a living.

David Fortune could easily provide her anything she wanted. And from the looks of things, she didn't want for anything. She was driving a high-end luxury car and, even though Rodrigo didn't know much about fashion, her clothes were obviously expensive.

She'd worn a different pair of designer sunglasses every day this week. You couldn't live in Miami Beach all the years he had without becoming familiar with some of the most popular designer brands—and the fact that they came with a hefty price tag.

As Rodrigo entered his room at Rosebud House, his cell phone rang.

He set down the to-go order he'd picked up at La Ventana—two beef tacos and a chicken burrito—and glanced at the phone screen.

It was David Fortune.

"Rodrigo Mendoza," he said into the receiver.

"Mendoza, David Fortune here. I'm calling to see how things are going."

That was a loaded question.

Especially considering the fact he had neglected to tell his daughters he had hired Vines Consulting Group and they felt like he was there to change everything they'd worked so hard to accomplish. And that Rodrigo was fighting a spark of attraction with one of his daughters.

"Things are going great. Couldn't be better."

"I'm glad to hear that," David said. "I was a little concerned, but I should've known you could handle it. I'm glad to know you have everything under control. My daughters are strong-minded young women and it's not that I doubt them as much as I just want to make sure they don't get sidetracked by the minutia. Nicole is a whiz in the kitchen and Megan is basically a bottom line kind of gal—numbers don't lie.

"Just between me and you, it's Ashley I'm worried about. I love her passion and drive. But I'm afraid that occasionally that enthusiasm can be self-sabotaging. Sometimes her passion causes her to have tunnel vision."

What was he supposed to say to that? *Yeah, I caught a glimpse of that passion and I'd love to explore it?* He blinked away the thought, replacing it with another. *Ashley sure is strong-willed. A woman who knows what she wants and isn't easily talked out of it.*

He shook off that thought, too, and fashioned a professional response.

"From the moment I first talked to Ashley, I could see her commitment to Provisions. I had a chance to shadow her today and she knows what she's doing. She's got a good handle on the business."

"If she's so perfect, then what the hell am I paying you for?" David Fortune barked.

A string of curse words darted through Rodrigo's mind before Fortune laughed.

"I'm messing with you, Mendoza," he said. "I know my daughters and I can tell you're being professional by not detailing their shortcomings to me. I trust that you will keep them on track and rein them in when they need to be reined in. I'm also counting on you to keep me posted on your end. I know it's not practical to have daily phone calls, but why don't you email me a daily recap of the progress you make."

It wasn't a question. It was a command. It wasn't unheard of for off-site clients to want daily updates, but this felt different. After all, Ashley, Nicole and Megan owned the restaurant.

"I want to know everything," Fortune said. "Even though it was ostensibly the girls' money, I gave it to them. It's nearly half a million dollars. That's not chump change."

"I'll see what I can do," Rodrigo said.

"Don't see what you can do," David said. "Just do it. And a little piece of advice—you might want to keep our communications between us. It will make your job easier if my daughters don't know that we're talking behind the scenes."

They had to close Provisions for two days as they waited for the company to come in and reset to the fire-suppression equipment. While Ashley didn't want to lock their doors for that long, she knew it was the best thing.

The last thing they needed was a replay of the other night.

With cleanup done and everything else mostly in place—except for the equipment that needed to be reset—she and her sisters were enjoying a rare relaxing night at home.

Home was their suite of rooms at the expansive Fame and Fortune Ranch, a compound that she, Megan and Nicole shared with her brothers Callum and Dillon.

After their older sister Stephanie had gotten engaged to Acton Donovan, she had moved out of the ranch and onto Acton's grandparents' ranch in Rambling Rose.

Ashley was bone-tired, but not sleepy because she couldn't get Rodrigo's words out of her mind.

I swear to you if things were different, we would be having a completely different conversation right now. You know what I'm saying?

Heart thudding, she'd gone out on a limb and said, "I take it there wouldn't be a whole lot of conversation."

The way he'd looked at her had started a fire of a different sort, one that began in her belly and spread to very personal parts of her body.

Rodrigo Mendoza was a man of principle. She had to appreciate that about him. On one hand, it made him even sexier. But on the other, it was so darn frustrating. He had admitted that he was attracted to her. They had almost kissed the night of the soft opening.

It wasn't just that he was a challenge...was it? Maybe she wanted to prove that this time the guy she was attracted to wasn't just interested in getting to know her because of what her father could do for him.

It was such a dilemma because her father had hired him, but despite that and their mutual attraction, he kept pushing her away.

That's where this glimmer of hope that Rodrigo might be different came from.

As she sipped her mug of bedtime tea, she made herself examine the situation honestly.

Was she just attracted to Rodrigo because he was emotionally unavailable?

After thorough contemplation, she could say without hesitation that her attraction to Rodrigo went much deeper than the sheer thrill of the chase. She wanted him. She had wanted him from the first moment she'd set eyes on him. He had admitted he wanted her, too.

And now, she decided, it was up to her to fix this problem.

"I'll have what she's having," said Nicole as she sat on the sofa adjacent to the love seat where Ashley was curled up with a cozy blanket.

Ashley held up her mug. "The water in the kettle is still warm. If you turn on the burner, it won't take long for it to come to a boil. Help yourself to some tea."

Nicole quirked a brow at her. "I'm not talking about the tea you're drinking. More like what's going on in that head of yours... Or what's happening when you think you're behind closed doors."

Ashley drew in a sharp breath and in the process almost sloshed some of the hot liquid out of her mug. To cover it up, she held the mug away from her body and drew her blanket-covered knees up to her chest.

In the seconds it took her to perform the action,

she contemplated whether it would be better to ignore what her sister had said or ask her what she meant. One look at the expression on Nicole's face and Ashley knew her sister, who was the youngest of the triplets by mere minutes, wasn't about to let it go that easily. Had Nicole seen something?

"What are you talking about?" Ashley sipped her tea and tried to act as casual as she could.

"I'm talking about you and Hot Rod."

Ashley knew that pretending to not understand what she was talking about wouldn't fly. However, it was never a good thing to give away more than the other person needed to know.

"What exactly do you mean?" Ashley said, readjusting her grip on her mug.

"Come on, Ash. I saw the two of you in the office last night."

Ashley blinked and took another long sip of her tea, buying herself some time.

When Nicole didn't continue, Ashley said, "And?"

Nicole laughed. "And the two of you looked awfully cozy in each other's arms."

Ashley waved away her sister's comment and rolled her eyes. "It was a bad night, Nic. I'm sure I don't have to remind you. I was upset. He was comforting me."

"Mmm...okay. I was upset, too, and nobody comforted me like that." Nicole's smile was a little too sweet.

Damn her. She was like a pit bull with a bone and she wasn't going to let this go. And why, Ashley wondered, was she feeling the need to keep this from her sister? It wasn't as if Nicole was her boss and could bust her for fraternizing.

Good grief, Rodrigo Mendoza wasn't even an official employee. Their father had hired him. If she wasn't so attracted to him, and if she was inclined to play games, it would serve her father right if Ashley had a little fling with Hot Rod Mendoza. That would show her father what happened when he meddled.

Her stomach twisted at the thought. In her twenty-three years, she hadn't had that much experience with men. She had always played it cautious because the men she had encountered had only been interested in her proximity to her father.

Now that she'd had a chance to mull it over, beyond his obvious tall, dark and handsome good looks and charm, her attraction to Rodrigo did seem to stem from the fact that he didn't seem interested in using her to get to her dad.

Yes, that made him unspeakably attractive, but there was more to it than that. It was something she couldn't explain. Something she'd never felt before in her life.

"Okay. Nic, I like him. I like him a lot."

Nicole's mouth fell open and she leaned forward. "I knew it. I knew there was something going on between the two of you. Does he feel the same way?"

And this was where it got complicated. "Yes and no. But mostly yes. I don't know how to explain it."

"Just start from the beginning."

"The beginning of what?" Meg came in fresh from the shower wearing her bathrobe. Her long blond hair was twisted up into a soft white bath towel. "What am I missing here? It sounds serious."

"It is serious." Ashley set her mug on a coaster on the wooden coffee table. She squeezed her eyes shut and fisted her hands into her hair.

"Oh my gosh." Meg perched next to Nicole on the sofa. "Tell me what's going on. Is everyone okay?"

"Do you want to tell her or should I?" Nicole's eyes sparkled.

When Ashley hesitated, Nicole blurted, "Ashley has a thing for Hot Rod Mendoza."

"Oh, that's all?" Megan looked disappointed. "That's old news."

"Meg, this is a big deal." Ashley's voice sounded small even to her own ears.

Meg's face softened and she reached out and took Ashley's hand. "I know it is, honey. But why do you look so forlorn? You should be happy."

Ashley knew that in the beginning, Meg had been interested in Rodrigo, too. But Ashley was sure her sister's interest had been all about his looks. All on the surface. Simple lust.

For Ashley, it had been different. The first time she'd seen Rodrigo Mendoza, the feeling had hit her like the proverbial bolt of lightning. If the tables had been turned and it had been that way for Megan, Ashley would have gladly stepped aside. Just as Meg was stepping aside for her.

Just as Meg was doing for her.

"This is where it gets complicated, Meg. He has feelings for me, but I'm his client. We are his clients. Dad is his client. Rodrigo is a man of principle and right now he has decided we need to keep our business and personal lives separate."

"So what's going to happen after he fulfills his consulting contract with us?" Meg asked.

"I don't know. Again, it's complicated. He lives in Austin. I live in Rambling Rose." She refused to let herself doubt what she felt in her heart. Because it felt right.

"You need a plan," said Nicole. Her eyes shone with determination. One of the things Ashley loved the most about her sisters was that when one of them faced a challenge, they all got on board to find a solution. "You need a Land Your Man plan."

"A Land Your Man plan?" Ashley laughed. "I love it! Right now, I have two goals in my life. Number one is to make the restaurant a success. And despite what happened opening night, I really think we're on our way. Number two is to make Rodrigo realize he can't live without me."

"Hence the Land Your Man plan," said Nic.

Ashley could tell by the determined look in her sisters' eyes that they were both already on board.

Meg laughed out loud. "I love it. It sounds like a book title. Nic, you should write a book."

Nicole looked a little sheepish. "Actually, it is a book. *Seven Days to Land Your Man*. I found it in the bookstore and I couldn't resist. I bought it."

"And you've been holding out on us?" said Ashley.

"Well, it's a little bit embarrassing," Nicole confessed.

"Yeah, until you need it," said Meg.

"Oh, great, it's a book for the desperate and lovelorn, and it's the perfect read for me." Ashley groaned.

"Come on, you know you want to see it," Nicole said.

"Of course, I do. Go get it."

Nicole left them and quickly returned with a slim paperback. She handed it to Ashley. "Good luck."

"I don't know if it's luck I need as much as a solid strategy."

Ashley cracked open the book and perused the contents.

It listed a seven-day plan to make him fall head-over-heels. Judging by a quick glance at the advice, she was well into day three. Ha! Almost halfway there. That boded well. She'd already made him notice her. In fact, he'd confessed that he was attracted to her.

All that was left was to get him to seal the deal. Her stomach fluttered at the double entendre. Of course, she needed to get him to kiss her again before they could seal anything else.

Patience, Grasshopper.

"What does it say?" Meg asked, wedging her way in next to Ashley on the love seat so she could see the book.

"'Ask his advice—men like to feel needed,'" Ashley read. "Well, that one is built in since he's helping with the restaurant. It's also sort of a Catch-22 because that's what's keeping us apart."

"But it does give you a proximity to him and we need to make him feel needed," Nicole said.

Ashley frowned. "I am not going to sacrifice myself and my own integrity to land a guy. Anyone who is worth my time will respect my opinions and realize that I have a brain and I intend to use it."

"Ash, you're missing the point," said Nicole. "Of course, you don't want to compromise anything. Especially if it has to do with the restaurant. But you could seek his opinion on things."

"I don't know," Ashley said, closing the book. "This feels a lot like playing games."

"Isn't love one big game?" said Meg, who had taken the book from Ashley and opened it to the page where they had left off.

Meg continued. "It also says here 'make eye contact.'"

Ashley groaned. "If I made any more eye contact with him, my eyes would be physically glued to him."

Meg ignored her. "It's suggests that you get out of town. Go on a vacation together."

"It's all I can do to get him to be alone with me in the same room."

Meg looked up from the book. "So he does everything he can to avoid being alone with you and you think he's into you because…?"

"Because he told me he was, Meg," Ashley said. "Pay attention."

Meg gave her a dirty look. She put down the book and took her time taking her hair out of the towel and tussling the wet locks. When she was finished, she picked up the book again and looked at Ashley.

"Okay, it says you should celebrate the little things."

"Like him confessing he was attracted to you." As soon as the words left her mouth, Nicole pursed her lips. "Well, maybe celebrate that one privately or with us. But there's lots to celebrate about the restaurant. Or at least, there will be."

"Okay, next it says, 'give him his space.'"

Ashley shrugged. "Yeah, well, he's making sure he has plenty of that."

Meg shot Ashley another look. "Sounds very romantic."

"He is a man of integrity, Megan. Wouldn't it be a little skeezy if he wanted to jump me in the office?"

"I'm confused," Meg said. "I thought that's what you wanted."

"Well, yeah, I do, but not like that." Ashley bit her bottom lip at the thought. "What else does it say?"

"Next on the list is '*plan a date.*'"

Meg and Nicole looked at each other with wide eyes.

"That could work," Nic said.

Ashley started to say, *Hello? Remember the part where I said you should listen?*

Meg held up her finger and silenced her. "No, really, that could work," she said. "He doesn't need to know it's a date. Think about it. Remember how you told us during that meeting he had suggested a good way to help the success of the restaurant was to get out into the community and get to know the town better? Well, that's the perfect opportunity to ask him to go with you on a fact-gathering field trip. You know it's a date. But he doesn't have to know it's a date. As far as he's concerned, it's strictly business."

"Yes. That's perfect," said Nicole.

Ashley's stomach fluttered at the brilliant suggestion. "Actually, I think you might be onto something."

Chapter Seven

Rodrigo was pleasantly surprised when Ashley was all smiles and warmth the next day at work. Appropriate warmth. No innuendoes or too personal questions about the two of them.

Her about-face was confusing. At one point, he even silently questioned whether one of her identical sisters might have stepped in to cover for her. But not only were Megan and Nicole present and accounted for, he was beginning to be able to tell the triplets apart.

He knew the subtle nuances of Ashley that set her apart from her sisters. The distinctions that made her unique, such as the way she moved, which was completely different from Nicole and Megan. The way she lifted her chin when she laughed, and that tiny mole at the base of her left eye that was so maddingly sexy. Her sisters didn't have that or the undefinable something that attracted him to Ashley.

To the uninformed, the Fortune triplets might seem identical and interchangeable. But not to him. Rodrigo was beginning to understand why Ashley seemed so determined to prove herself. All novelties aside, being a triplet probably presented challenges when it came to standing out from the pack.

Still, even though he could pick Ashley out, he could only tell Megan and Nicole apart by the way they dressed. Nicole's standard uniform was a chef's coat and cotton pants. Megan stuck to a more tailored, business-like uniform. Neither had that certain something that made him aware Ashley had entered the room even before he saw her.

This morning, Ashley had come to work all brightness and enthusiasm, insisting that she'd had a breakthrough. "Rodrigo, we need to get out of the office and into the community. We need to talk to people. We need to get out there and subtly sell Provisions by letting the community know that we care."

It was a brilliant idea. It went hand-in-hand with Steven's scrapbook, which Ashley was casually thumbing through as she told him about her plan.

"Also, I was thinking about holding a recipe contest, where members of the Rambling Rose community submit their favorite, tried-and-true recipe and the winning recipe is featured on the Provisions' menu as a standard always-available item. Don't you think that would make people buy in? It would make them care...

"Of course, we could offer prizes like Provisions' gift certificates to the honorable mentions and runners-up. We could have the community join us in judging the entries. Don't you think that's exciting, Rodrigo? I think it will rally the town and make them care because it shows them that we care about them."

"You know what I like about you?" he asked.

She blinked as if he'd caught her off guard.

"Um...no, what?"

"I love your enthusiasm. I love that rather than taking the lumps of the setback, you've come up with a terrific way to turn it around in our favor."

"Well, thank you," she said, smiling and lifting her chin a notch.

Something stirred in his stomach. A forbidden heat that made him want to reach out and pull her into his arms. It would be the most idiotic thing he could do because it had taken until this point to make her understand that they could be nothing but friends. Right about now, he was questioning his own wisdom. Then again, if she could get over him that fast, maybe the just-friends policy was for the best. She obviously didn't seem to be suffering very much. But that was good, he reminded himself. There was no need for anyone to suffer. If that was the truth, what the hell was wrong with him?

"You're very welcome," he said. "When do you want to take this field trip around town?"

Ashley swept her long blond hair off her face and pulled it into a ponytail, securing it with an elastic band in what seemed like a one swift move.

"I'd say the sooner the better. When are you free?"

"I'm mostly free today. I had planned on doing some catch-up work and I wanted to be around when the company came to reset the fire-suppression system in the kitchen, but that's something Rosemary and Nicole should be able to handle themselves. If there's a problem, they can always call me."

"No offense, but they would probably prefer it that way," Ashley said with a mischievous smile that had him nodding his agreement.

It was things like that—the slight tilt to her head and the way her left cheek gave way to a dimple when she smiled. Those things set her apart from her sisters.

"You're probably right."

"Then what are we waiting for?" she asked. "Let's go out and walk around and see what we can see."

She grabbed her purse, a small expensive-looking number that she could casually swing across her body, keeping her hands free. She tucked her cell phone inside the purse and was ready to go. That was another thing about Ashley. For all her designer sunglasses and manicured nails and polished way she presented herself, she seemed fairly low maintenance when it came to things like this. One small bag and she was ready to walk out the door before he could grab his jacket and his cell phone.

She was wearing a black skirt with white polka dots and a white blouse. Her manicured feet were clad in flat sandals. She looked both polished and professional. Casual enough to be approachable but still taken seriously. Perfect and appropriate in every way.

"Let me tell Nicole and Rosemary that we're going out."

Her left eyebrow shot up and she smiled at him as she pulled her phone out of her purse. Her thumbs flew as she typed a text and sent it.

"Done," she said.

Before he could protest, her phone dinged. "Nicole says, 'Have fun.'"

"Well, okay then," he said. "What are we waiting for?"

He held the front door for her as they left the restaurant and followed her lead as she turned left and walked along the sidewalk of downtown Rambling Rose.

"I've been thinking about Steven's scrapbook," he said. "What if we chose some photos from it, had them enlarged and hung them in the bar area? Some of the people in those pictures are relatives of current residents. Wouldn't it be fun for them to see their relatives living on the walls of Provisions?"

"I love that. Do you think we could do it life-size? I know of a company that might be able to blow up the photos into a collage on wallpaper. I'll look into that as soon as we get back. It would be like people were visiting their relatives when they came to Provisions.

"First, let's go into the grocery store and have a look around," she said. "I figured we could browse the aisles and see who we can see. It seems like a good, nonthreatening place to strike up conversations, don't you think?"

Haynes grocery store was about a quarter-mile down the road from Provisions.

"It's probably a good place to start since the other shops don't open until ten o'clock," he said.

Inside the little mom-and-pop shop, a group of men stopped talking and turned to look at them when the bell chimed, announcing their entry.

"How dee do, Miss Ashley?" said Curtis Haynes.

Rodrigo recognized the man from the soft opening. He also recognized the way the older man's face softened when he looked at Ashley. It was pure appreciation.

"Mr. Mendoza," the grocer added.

Rodrigo shook his outstretched hand.

"How can I help y'all today?"

"It's good to see you, Curtis," Ashley said. "We're

just out and about, and thought we'd stop in to say hello. And I wanted to run something by you."

She told him about the recipe contest and asked if he would allow them to put up a poster.

"I think that sounds like a good idea," he said. "I'd be delighted to help you out in any way I can. That's the thing about Rambling Rose. The neighbors stick together. Just like we did for that little baby Linus. Sure is a shame that he's so sick. But did you see the way the town turned out? Everyone was willing to be tested for the poor little guy. I can guarantee that whoever is a match will step up and give whatever is needed."

In January, the baby's mother, Laurel, went into labor at the new Rambling Rose Pediatric Center, but they sent her to a hospital in San Antonio with a NICU for the birth. Afterward, Laurel, had left newborn Linus at the Fortune's Foundling Hospital, with a note saying that she believed her child would find his rightful home through the hospital.

Ashley's older sister Stephanie had served as the baby's foster mother until someone claiming to be his biological father had learned of his birth and come to town to claim the child. However, a few weeks later, Eric Johnson had returned with baby Linus, because he feared the boy was sick. Sadly, his suspicions were right.

Since then, the authorities had been looking for Laurel, but had not yet been able to find her.

The entire town of Rambling Rose had rallied

around Linus and had organized a blood marrow donor drive to see who would be the best match.

"What a wonderful community," Ashley said. "Any word on the test results?"

"Nah," said Curtis. "Not that I've heard. I reckon it will be big news once the results are in."

As they left the grocery, Ashley and Rodrigo walked side by side in silence for a few moments. She stole a glance at him and wondered if he was thinking of baby Linus and how their problems seemed to pale by comparison.

At least, her own problems seemed unimportant. She realized that she didn't know much about Rodrigo beyond what she'd read about him.

What did he harbor underneath that perfect exterior? Had he known disappointment? Had anyone ever broken his heart?

The thought of a woman falling out of love with him seemed almost beyond belief.

What would it be like to have Rodrigo Mendoza's love, to wake up every morning and see his handsome face?

Her stomach did a little cha-cha at the thought.

There was no denying that he was a good-looking guy, though from this angle, his profile was not model perfect. His nose was a little too big. The vaguest hint of crow's-feet were forming at the corners of his eyes, no doubt from soaking up that South Beach sunshine. And she knew without seeing it that his front tooth was just a hair crooked. The sum of those perfectly imperfect parts made him even better looking than any of the guys in the magazines.

Then he turned his head and caught her staring at him. His grin brought out his dimples and those creases at the corners of his eyes. Ashley believed she had never seen a more perfect face. Her heart flipped in her chest.

"What?" he asked.

"Oh, umm… I was just thinking about the recipe contest…"

Liar.

The way he was looking at her, she was sure he knew she hadn't been thinking about work.

She cleared her throat.

"What if we gave people the option of either downloading a copy of an application from the restaurant's web site—I can draft one and post it by tomorrow afternoon. Or, if they don't have access to a computer and printer, they can drop by the restaurant and pick up a copy. It's a win-win, either way. If they print one themselves, they will go to our web site and, hopefully, will browse around. Or, if they drop by, it gets them in the door and they'll have to return to drop off completed applications. See what I'm doing there? One way or another, I'm getting them inside the restaurant where they will see how nice it is and maybe they'll even stay for dinner. Especially once we get those photos up."

She was rambling, but his gaze lingered and that smile didn't falter.

"Has anyone ever told you you're a born marketer?" Rodrigo said.

She looked up at him and batted her eyelashes in an exaggerated manner. "Why, thank you, kind sir." She put her hand on her throat and cocked her head to the side. "I do believe that's one of the nicest things anyone has ever said to me."

They shared the laugh and as soon as they quieted down, the feeling seemed to morph into something else that pulsed between them like a living thing that wouldn't be ignored.

She was fighting the urge to slip her hand into his and lace his fingers through hers as they walked.

He was keeping a respectable distance between them and she knew that pushing the boundaries would ruin the moment.

They walked in amiable silence toward the entrance to The Shoppes at Rambling Rose. The former five-and-dime had been vacant for more than twenty years, but Callum had redeveloped it into a glamorous building that housed a series of upscale boutiques.

Rodrigo put his hand on the door but paused before opening it. "You ready for this?"

His gaze seemed to smolder and she felt the intimate tug that preceded the inevitable melting sensation.

"Rodrigo Mendoza, I was born ready."

* * *

Over the days leading up to the recipe contest judging, there came a point when Ashley questioned her tendency to be a masochist.

As if re-launching Provisions after the fire system mishap hadn't been enough of a challenge, she'd focused on the recipe project, which had been met with more enthusiasm than she could have imagined.

It gave her the opportunity to work very closely with Rodrigo. That brought its own particular brand of frustration to the table, but she had decided to file it under *hurts so good* because the only other option was to distance herself from him completely and why would she want to do that? Not when her Land Your Man plan was in full swing. She'd already resigned herself to the fact that nothing was going to happen between them until his contract was up, in another two weeks.

She had decided to think of this as extended foreplay.

Or masochism.

Her cheeks heated at the thought and she had to bite her bottom lip and take a good long, deep breath to get her hormones under control.

That man... Oh, that man and the things he did to her.

But today she had to channel her hunger into something more...tangible...and get in the mindset of local recipes and food, because there would be a lot of it in every shape and form. Today they'd pick the winner of the contest. Open to any Rambling Rose resident, the recipe contest had drawn more entries than she'd ever imagined.

The judging panel consisted of Rodrigo, Ashley and her sisters, Rosemary, Ellie Hernandez Fortune, the mayor of Rambling Rose, and three townspeople. They had been chosen from a random drawing of people who hadn't entered the recipe contest.

The Rambling Rose representatives were treated as special guests of honor.

The judging table was set up on the Provisions' patio and the event was open to anyone who wanted to stop by.

The prepared recipes had been arriving since noon, with the judging set to start promptly at 2:30 p.m. When Ashley set out the judges' name tags, she'd taken special care to seat herself next to Rodrigo.

They had Provisions' staff members on duty to man stations where drinks and light hors d'oeuvres were for sale. They also had other waitstaff to serve each of the judges portions of the prepared recipes in the designated order they appeared on the master list.

In the three categories they'd arranged, there were fifteen appetizers, twenty-two entrées, and thirty-four dessert offerings. In a blind tasting, the judges would assign scores for taste, presentation and how easily the recipe could be adapted to fit Provisions' menu.

Rodrigo sighed and closed his eyes as he tasted the banana split pie. "This is delicious."

When he opened his eyes again, he had a small spot of whipped cream on the top of his lip. Without even thinking about it, Ashley reached out and wiped it away with the pad of her thumb.

His gaze snared hers and before she could second-guess herself, she licked the whip cream off her thumb. When Rodrigo didn't look away—and oh how she loved the way he looked at her—she bit her bottom lip and let her knee fall to the side until it touched his. Then she turned her focus back to the pie in front of her.

Rodrigo didn't break the contact until they had to get up from the table to deliberate about the dishes that had made it to the final round.

In the end, Nalria Gaddy's spicy zucchini bread won first prize and the honor of being one of the few permanent desserts on Provisions' menu.

Provisions seemed to be back on track. Reservations were rolling in and there seemed to be a general air of goodwill among the Fortunes and the community. Rambling Rose residents as a whole were starting to indicate that they would embrace the Fortunes' gentrification plans for the town. There was still some winning over to be done, but they were moving in the right direction.

Rodrigo had done his job and helped get the restaurant off to a good start. He had equipped Ashley, Megan and Nicole with the tools they'd needed to be successful.

Ashley had already proved she had the instincts and stamina to weather any possible storm the restaurant might encounter.

In fact, all three of the Fortune triplets were strong, smart women who were fully capable of standing on their own feet. He had to admit, now that they had reopened and things were up and running, he had been looking for projects and reasons to prolong his stay, but it was time to start wrapping up this job.

It had never been like this with a project before. He had never felt such an emotional connection to a client, which was all the more reason he needed to get the hell out of town and back to business in Austin.

Rodrigo let himself in the front door of Provisions and locked it behind him. He made his way to the office, which was right off the kitchen.

Before he entered, he could hear voices. It sounded like...children?

"I am so excited that you are interested in food," said Ashley.

He heard little girl voices talking at the same time, all excitement and enthusiasm.

He paused when he got to the office door.

Five girls, who looked to be about ten or twelve years old—he wasn't good with age, but they looked like they weren't quite in their teenage years—were sitting in chairs in front of Ashley's desk.

"I got interested in cooking when I was about your age," Ashley said. "I remember how badly I wanted to learn how to cook. Even if you don't end up going into the restaurant business, being a good cook is something you will be able to use all your life. Plus, it's fun."

Rodrigo shifted his weight from one foot to another. Ashley must've caught the motion out of the corner of her eye because she turned and smiled when she saw him standing there.

"Rodrigo, good morning," she said. "Please come in and meet Provisions' first junior cooking class or summer camp. We're not quite sure what we're calling ourselves just yet, but we'll figure it out. Right, girls?"

The small group nodded in unison.

"This is Mr. Mendoza. He has been helping us open the restaurant. Mr. Mendoza, this is Callie, Audrey, Lucy, Taylor and Daisy."

A cooking class? This was the first he'd heard of it.

Ashley must have read the confusion on his face because she said, "You've been so busy the last couple of days with the changes to the menu, I didn't have a chance to tell you that Daisy Miner and her friend Callie Davis approached me at the recipe contest event and asked me how I learned how to cook. They told me they were interested in learning and then as we were talking, I realized it would be a great community outreach project if we started a summer camp here at the restaurant. It'll be an opportunity for kids to learn all about nutrition, cooking and the restaurant business. Doesn't that sound like fun?"

Actually, it was. Not only would it give kids something active to do over the summer, it would teach them a valuable lesson about work ethics.

"We have a few weeks before the kids get out of school and these girls have volunteered to help me put the program in place. I thought it could be part of our apprenticeship program that Megan and I are working on."

Though it was another good way to involve the community, Rodrigo had to admit he was a little perplexed that she hadn't talked to him about it. Since their second close call on the night of the grand opening, she had been giving him a lot of breathing room.

It was strange. She was as nice and cordial as ever, but there was an undeniable distance.

Of course, it was for the best... But why did it not feel that way?

If he wanted to border on melodramatic, he might go as far as saying it sounded as if she had already moved on. Again, that was for the best, but...

"This is very cool," he said, mostly addressing the girls.

The girls looked at each other and giggled in that way that kids did.

"I wish I could've done something like that when I was your age."

"Will you be one of our teachers?" a small girl with dark hair asked.

"I wish I could, but I don't live in Rambling Rose. I'm from Austin, and I'm going back there in the next couple of days."

He felt Ashley's reaction before he saw her gorgeous blue eyes darken a couple of shades.

"But I'll check in to see how the camp goes."

He shouldn't check in. They both knew that.

If Ashley or one of her sisters or David Fortune called on him, of course he would be there to help them, but really he shouldn't initiate future contact. He should make a clean break because this thing between them wasn't going to work. They were just too different. He'd learned his lesson the hard way when he was with Bonnie. He'd fooled himself into believing the chasm between them, the fact that they came from two different worlds, didn't matter, but it did.

Even though his head was telling him to do what was right—make a clean break. His heart was singing an entirely different tune that sounded more like the blues.

"So tell me about this camp. What are you going to learn?" he asked.

All five girls looked to Ashley with bright, adoring faces. He had been around boys most of his life, but he remembered what it was like to be young and impressionable and stumble upon somebody who was a role model. The girls definitely looked at Ashley with a glint of hero worship in their eyes. And Ashley seemed to take it in stride.

There was a fine line between patronizing and galvanizing impressionable, enthusiastic spirits, and she seemed to strike just the right note. She looked at the girls and said, "Okay, committee, that's a good question. What do you want to learn in the summer camp?"

"I want to learn how to make French fries," said the little redhead who had a spray of freckles across her nose.

"I want to learn how to make grilled cheese and mac and cheese," said the girl sitting next to her.

"No, those are too carby. We need to learn how to make healthy food," said another.

Ashley's brow furrowed. "I think it's important for us to learn about healthy eating, but it's also important to learn about enjoying things in moderation. I have always embraced the principle of enjoying food and not necessarily thinking of foods as too carby or too fatty.

"I like to think of good food as delicious and nutritious. You can have grilled cheese or mac and cheese and French fries one day, but then balance it with fruits and vegetables and other things that are lighter and good for you another day. The most important thing is to remember that each and every one of you is beautiful just the way you are—no matter what size you wear or how tall you are or what color your hair is."

"John Crintenton told me I was fat," said the girl who had objected to the grilled cheese and mac and cheese. "He said I needed to go on a diet."

Ashley's mouth fell open. "Oh, honey. Oh, Callie. That wasn't very nice of him. You look absolutely perfect to me. Doesn't she, girls?"

The others nodded and murmured their agreement.

"Don't ever *ever* let anyone make you feel bad about yourself," she said. "Boys sometimes show attention in the weirdest ways."

The girls voiced their collective support of Callie.

This was a testament to what a good person Ashley was. Here she was, new to town, trying to get a new restaurant off the ground, battling her own set of obstacles, but she was making time to take in this group of impressionable girls and make them feel valued and valuable.

"Boys are dumb," said the redhead.

"Yes, they can be." Ashley's lips tilted upward into a smile. "Someday they'll get their act together and realize what they're missing and stop acting like such dummies."

"And if not, it's their loss," said Callie.

"You're absolutely right," said Ashley.

"Miss Ashley, do you have a husband?" asked one of the brunettes.

"No, I'm not married."

"Do you have a boyfriend?"

The little girls giggled.

Ashley slanted a glance toward Rodrigo.

"No, I don't." She raised a brow and leaned in. The girls mirrored her movement. "But I do have a big crush on a boy who I think likes me, but he can't seem to make up his mind whether he wants me to be his girlfriend or not."

The girls giggled and gasped and *oohed*.

"Well, he's a dummy if he doesn't like you. You're so pretty. Isn't she, Mr. Mendoza?"

Rodrigo smiled. "Not only is she beautiful, but she's a good person. Any guy would be lucky to call her his girlfriend."

"It will be his loss if he's too dumb to realize it," said the redhead.

"Yes, it will," Ashley said. "But I'm not giving up hope just yet. I don't think he's a totally dumb boy. But you know what? If he turns out to be that way, I know that there will be someone else who is better for me. In the meantime, I'm perfectly okay not having a boyfriend. I have a restaurant to run and a group of very smart, nice, beautiful girls to work with to get the first annual Provisions' summer camp, which they were calling, Young Chefs In Training, off the ground."

The girls cheered, but Rodrigo was still stuck on

the part about someone else out there being better for Ashley than he was.

He couldn't stand the thought of her in someone else's arms.

Chapter Eight

Maybe she should've been an actress, Ashley thought as she congratulated herself for the way she had kept her distance from Rodrigo over the past few days. It had been no easy task, but it might just be the most important tool of her Land Your Man plan.

Though she had not meant for the summer camp girls to be part of her plan, she couldn't discount how perfect the timing was that Rodrigo had overheard their "dumb boy" conversation. She would never purposely use the girls to further her own agenda, but the conversation had been beneficial to them.

She couldn't help it if it sent a message to Rodrigo in the process.

He had said any guy would be lucky to call her

his girlfriend. At face value, she could overthink it and worry that was his way of being polite, but there had been something about the look on his face that made her sure his feelings ran deeper than that.

Her plan had involved a delicate two-step of long periods of time spent ignoring him and then "dates"—even though she was the only one who was aware that they were on a date—such as their walk around Rambling Rose and the strategic seating at the recipe judging event.

The whipped cream incident had been on him—literally—and he certainly hadn't recoiled when she had tidied him up and rested her knee against his.

This evening, a trip to the wine cellar was on the agenda. A moment ago she had texted him to ask if he could help her inventory the wine. The restaurant was closed on Mondays and even though there had been people in and out of the restaurant all day, she was sure they would have relative privacy down in the cellar this evening. She smiled to herself because it would appear to be strictly work related.

"You rang, my queen?" he said as he entered the office.

His voice startled her out of her reverie and she felt her cheeks warm as a byproduct of what she had been thinking about before he'd arrived.

"I love a man who knows how to address a lady," she said. "Maybe I should have you give my sisters lessons in due respect before you leave."

They laughed.

"No, seriously," she said. "I know it's late, but would you have just an hour or so to help me out with a project?"

"Of course," he said. "You'd mentioned needing help inventorying in the wine cellar. I never met a wine-related task I didn't like."

"A man after my own heart. You're the best. I know it's late to spring this on you. Megan was going to do it, but she got called away on business, and Nicole is menu planning with Rosemary."

Her sisters had helped her come up with this "date night" by volunteering to be too busy to deal with the wine.

"The computer inventory system got messed up after we gave away so many bottles the night of the grand opening. I need to do a quick inventory so we can update it before we open tomorrow."

Not really, but it sounded like a valid excuse.

She needed to stop talking. It looked as if she was protesting too much. Rodrigo was a sharp guy. If she didn't watch it, he might see through her plan.

"When did you want to get started?"

She had considered suggesting they get a bite to eat, but that would involve venturing out into public where they would have no privacy.

So she had put together cheese and charcuterie boards and put them in the cellar refrigerator. If all went according to plan, they would count some wine bottles and then relax with a bottle of champagne that also just happened to be chilling in the same fridge. She would tell him it was a way to show her appreciation.

Because when it came to Rodrigo, she was very, very appreciative.

She chuckled to herself as she got up from her desk and walked toward the door.

"Don't we need a clipboard or a legal pad or something?" he said.

Ugh. Amateur mistake.

Okay, girl, get your head in the game. Don't blow it now.

She pointed at him. "It's been a long day. See, that's why I need you, Rodrigo. You help me keep my head on straight. Would you grab that legal pad on my desk?"

"Why don't we plug into the system through a tablet?"

No! If they used the computer, this process would go much too fast. She wanted to *do it the old fashioned way.*

She bit her bottom lip to suppress a smile.

"And while you're at it, grab a couple of pens, if you would, please."

She winked at him and it seemed to throw him off balance.

He cleared his throat. "Of course."

Whoa, girl. Calm down. You don't want to frighten the poor guy.

The near flub and subsequent overcompensation had knocked Ashley off her game. She was quiet as they walked through the bar to the arched plank door with its wrought-iron hinges and handle that led to the basement they had converted into a wine cellar.

She flipped the switch to illuminate the antique-looking sconces that lit the stairway. As they headed down the narrow passage, the door closed behind them with a click that reverberated off the stone walls.

Standing in the room with Rodrigo—alone for the first time in days—she couldn't remember feeling cozier anywhere.

"I've never really done inventory before," she said, turning in a slow circle, surveying the bottles. "I guess we just need to write down the name of the wine so we can see what we have. I'll enter it into the system later and Adam can re-order what we need."

The night of the botched grand opening, when things went south, they'd ended up comping all the drinks and food that had been served. The comps would be a write-off, of course. So this *date* disguised as an inventory was legit. Sort of. Because at one point they had been grabbing bottles and drinks to pacify the customers while they assessed the kitchen situation. Not everything had been re-corded.

Tonight, Ashley needed to make sure she stayed on course long enough to not blow her cover.

"I guess the best way to start is from the first

rack and work our way around?" she said. "Unless you have a better idea?"

Rodrigo shrugged. "That sounds like a plan. Actually, though, when I was working with Megan, I thought I saw a preprinted wine inventory list. Something that lists the staples. In fact, shouldn't the system automatically subtract whatever the staff goes through and automatically deduct it?"

Yes, but that would mean we would have no reason to be down here right now.

"I don't know, Rodrigo. Maybe there's a discrepancy with it because Megan asked me to do a hand inventory."

Standing there with his arms crossed and his brows knitted, Rodrigo looked dubious.

"If there is a glitch, we need to get that fixed right away. The main feature of that system is inventory control."

The only glitch is you not cooperating with my plan.

Why did he have to make this so difficult? She wished she could tell him the truth. She wanted to be alone with him to show him how good they could be together. Because one minute he was sending her mixed signals and the next he wanted nothing to do with her.

"I'll tell you what," he said. "Let's go up to the office and see if we can pull the report from the system. If not, then we can come back down and do it by hand."

Great. There goes our night.

The goal was not inventory. The goal was to kiss him.

After that, she'd planned on confessing her scheme. They would laugh and toast each other and make love.

It was a simple plan. Why was he making it so hard?

Reluctantly, she followed him, feeling a little foolish. As a general rule, she did not chase men who had no interest in her. But she'd never felt this way for anyone.

Suddenly, she felt very small and exposed and vulnerable. Rodrigo was a smart guy. He could probably see through her plan. That wouldn't have been so bad if the plan had shaken loose his last bit of hesitation.

She had made it perfectly clear how she felt about him. Despite what he'd said about keeping things strictly business, he had been sending her mixed signals.

As she followed him up the stairs, doubt began to set in.

Maybe what she was reading as mixed signals was simply his way of not hurting her feelings? Even so, he had been leading her on.

But bottom line, something she hadn't let herself even consider, what if he really wasn't interested? Because even if there was an automated inventory system, if he was interested, this inventory-by-hand ruse was the perfect way for them to be alone—the perfect romantic atmosphere to be together and let nature take its course. But he couldn't get out of that wine cellar fast enough. The thought hit her like a cold splash of wine in the face.

Her stomach dropped to her knees.

She was either going to look completely stupid for *forgetting* about the auto inventory function, or she was going to look like a fool for chasing a man who had absolutely no interest in her.

Her mind raced, formulating a plan for damage control.

Of course, Rodrigo would be leaving soon and she could get back to work. Burying herself in the restaurant would be the best cure for a broken heart.

She swallowed a sob that was working its way up through her windpipe.

Get hold of yourself. You've already made a big fool of yourself over this guy.

Rodrigo put his hand on the antique doorknob, but he didn't open the door.

What now?

Was he one of those guys who always wanted to be the one in charge? He didn't seem that way. But every time she had been the aggressor, he had backed way off. She wanted a guy—she needed a guy—who accepted her as an equal. Even though she had done her share of acting to give them an opportunity where this feeling she sensed between them could grow, she couldn't stand idly by and play the helpless female. That wasn't who she was.

"Um, is there a secret to opening this door?" Rodrigo asked.

Oh, for God's sake. "Here, Let me do it."

They did an awkward shuffle in the narrow stairwell so that she could move to the top step and he could move behind her. Their bodies did a full court press, which she did not even allow herself to enjoy.

On the contrary, it was just maddening, feeling his large, toned body pressed against her frame, breast to chest.

She'd had to grab on to his bicep to keep from losing her balance. She just had to forget how the muscles felt flexing and bunching under her palm.

Once the electrically charged do-si-do was complete, Ashley stood on the top step and gave the doorknob a smart turn and a push that contained all of her repressed feelings.

The door didn't budge.

She did it again.

Same. It didn't give.

She rattled the knob. Nothing.

"This is weird. I don't know why it won't open," she said. But then something dawned on her. Her sisters were the only ones who knew of her plan for the wine cellar "inventory."

She hadn't thought to mention it to Byron, the bar manager. It was his job to make sure the wine cellar was locked tight every night before he left.

Ashley laughed. It was a nervous, uncomfortable sound. "You're not going to believe this," she said. "I think the bar manager may have inadvertently locked us in."

Rodrigo leveled her with a knowing look. "Is that so?"

Before Ashley could answer, Rodrigo pulled his phone from his back pocket and handed it to her. "We can call someone to come and let us out."

Ashley's mind raced.

Given that Rodrigo had already backed down a couple of steps away from her, it was obvious he wanted no part of this cozy wine cellar evening— and for the record, the locked door had not been part of the plan. She wasn't a psycho. And that definitely had psycho written all over it. She had no choice but to call someone to get them out. For that matter, the wine cellar date had completely lost its appeal.

She sat on the top step.

Rodrigo sucked in a breath and squeezed his eyes shut. He raked his hands through his dark hair before he turned his attention to his phone.

"I know this sounds really weak, but I'm a little claustrophobic," he said. "I really need to get out of here. No offense, I mean. I just don't do well in tight spaces."

Oh, no. She had no idea,

"I'm sorry," she said. "Why don't you sit down and call the restaurant's main number? Maybe somebody is still here and they can get the master key out of the office and let us out."

For a split second she fought the urge to tell him the locked door was not part of her plan. But that wouldn't help matters and she knew it.

"That's a good idea." He exhaled an audible, slow, measured breath.

Oh, man, this really was bothering him.

"Come on," he muttered holding the phone up.

"What's wrong?" she asked.

"I don't have a signal."

He moved the phone around, to no avail.

Ashley held out her hand. "Here, let me try."

He handed her the phone and watched she could feel him watching her as she tried to work her magic on the uncooperative cell.

"I hate to tell you this, but I'm not getting a cell signal down here at all," she said.

"Are you kidding?" He muttered a choice word that seemed completely out of character for him.

"Here, let me see it," he finally said. "Maybe if I get closer to the door, I'll be able to get a couple of bars."

As they switched places so that he could be on the top step next to the door, Ashley noticed the fine bead of sweat that had broken out on Rodrigo's forehead. Since the temperature was a chilly fifty-five degrees, she knew he wasn't kidding about the claustrophobia issue.

She felt bad for him. It didn't make him look

weak, it made him human. Until now, Rodrigo Mendoza seemed like a man who had a common-sense handle on the world—the kind of man who couldn't be shaken by anything—not kitchen disasters, not business challenges, and certainly not sexual attraction.

But he was panicked by close spaces.

He sat on the top step and held the phone flush against the door.

"Come on," he muttered under his breath, moving the phone around, first holding it high and then gradually lowering it.

"What the hell is this door made of?" he said. "Wood-covered steel?"

Ashley shrugged, unsure what to say. Clearly, it was a rhetorical question. So there was no need to say anything.

She opted for the banal. "No luck?"

"No." He banged on the door. "Anyone out there?"

His query was met with silence.

Still, he tried again. *Bang, bang, bang, bang.* "Hello?"

Nothing.

Again, Ashley fought the urge to apologize. This was not part of the plan. In fact, it was starting to freak her out a little, too.

She borrowed a page from Rodrigo and took some slow, steady breaths.

In through the nose. Hold...hold...hold...hold. Out through the mouth.

She exhaled in a steady whoosh.

"Nobody is out there right now," she said. "Let's go back downstairs where we have more room."

"But if someone comes in while we're down there, we won't hear them." His voice sounded panicked.

"Rodrigo, at the very worst, Byron will unlock the door tomorrow morning when he comes in. It's not like you're stuck in here with me forever."

She turned and headed downstairs without waiting for him to answer.

When she got to the cellar, the first thing her gaze landed on was the yellow legal pad.

She picked up the pen and wrote "Locked in wine cellar! Please unlock the door!" in large block letters.

The plan was to see if she could slide it under the door. That way, if anyone came in before the morning shift, they might see the note and set them free.

Paper in hand, she climbed the stairs.

Rodrigo was still standing on the top step, moving his phone around.

"Any luck?" she asked.

"Not yet."

"There's always this." She held out the yellow paper.

"What's that?" His voice was low and serious.

"It's a secret map of how to dig ourselves out of here." She smiled.

He took the paper and squinted at it.

"It's a note to slide under the door, silly," she said.

"That way you can come downstairs, have a glass of wine and relax, and if someone comes into the restaurant, they'll know we're down here and can unlock the door. Come on, you'll feel a lot better if you get out of this narrow stairway."

It took a moment to work the paper through the rubber climate-control stripping at the base of the door, but Rodrigo managed to slide it through. Then he followed Ashley down to the tasting room.

Ashley tried to keep her face neutral as it dawned on her that this little mishap might be a blessing in disguise. Because neither of them were going anywhere for the time being. Except, maybe, into each other's arms if the cellar got too chilly.

She was already in need of some warming up.

Chapter Nine

Rodrigo watched as Ashley selected a bottle of champagne from the refrigerator.

"I have a hankering for some bubbly," she said. "If you'd prefer something else, we can open another bottle."

"That's fine."

She took two flutes from the glass rack next to the fridge.

He took a deep breath and felt some of the earlier tension release.

Joining the effervescent Ashley Fortune for a glass of bubbly was probably exactly what he needed right now…or possibly, the last thing he should be doing. But he didn't have a whole lot of choices right now. He might as well go with the flow and make the best of it.

She removed the foil and the wire hood that kept the cork secured. Holding the cork, she twisted the bottle and coaxed it loose with precision. It disengaged with a satisfying *puft*.

"Nice technique," he said with approval. "A lot of people would've just let 'er rip." He made a flicking motion with his thumbs as if he were popping the cork from a bottle.

Her left brow arched and she looked vaguely insulted.

"I'm hardly a rookie, Rodrigo. I took Champagne 101." Then, realizing he'd meant it as a compliment, she added, "I actually took some mixology and wine service classes once we decided to open the restaurant. You know, to make sure I could cover front-of-house-service end to end."

She filled their glasses but left them on the cocktail table. Returning to the small refrigerator, she pulled out cheese and charcuterie boards and walked them over to the cocktail table.

"I don't know about you, but I'm starving," she said.

"Hmm," he said.

"Hmm, what?" She opened a cupboard, took out a slim baguette and began slicing it into rounds.

"Why are there fresh bread and meat and cheese

boards down here? I wasn't aware of an event. That's not exactly something that would keep."

Had she planned for them to get locked in down here?

As if she read his mind, she said, "Don't, Rodrigo. Just don't, okay? I did not mean for us to be locked in down here. So don't even go there. I don't want to be here under these circumstances any more than you do. I think I've made it perfectly clear how I feel about you, but I want to set one thing straight. I wouldn't lock you in a wine cellar against your will.

"Fine, I admit it. I set up the food so that we'd have it after we finished the wine inventory, which, yes, I know could easily be done by computer. But was it so bad that I wanted to spend time with you?"

She held up her hand before he could say anything.

"You know what? Don't answer that. It was my bad. If I hadn't asked you to help me, we wouldn't be stuck in here. But I can assure you that after we get out of here, I won't bother you again. Just so we're clear, I don't make a habit of chasing guys who aren't interested in me. Clearly, you're not. But, hey, thanks to my planning ahead at least we won't go hungry while we're down here."

She sat on one of the chairs and curved her legs to the side.

This was a different side of Ashley, one he'd not seen until now. Her voice was calm and matter-of-fact. Despite what she said, her demeanor did not suggest that she was pitching a fit because she wasn't getting what she wanted. Despite her earlier intent to bring them together, he sensed this was her way of signaling the white flag. She was giving up on him. He should be happy about it, but the thought left him feeling a little hollow.

Now that he was down here with room to breathe, if he didn't think too hard about the fact that they were trapped underground without a way out beyond the locked door at the top of the stairs, it wasn't such a bad thing to be spending the evening with a beautiful woman.

And yes, he believed her when she said she had not meant for them to get locked in.

She took a sip of champagne and licked her lips. Though he found it inherently sexy, it seemed more of a contemplative move, not a flirty one.

"Can I ask you a question?" she said.

He nodded as he settled into the chair next to hers.

"Why do you always seem to think the worst of me?"

He nearly choked on his sip. "Are you kidding me? What are you even talking about? You are so far ahead of where I was when I was at your age."

He shook his head because the question was almost too absurd to comprehend.

"When you were my age?" She scoffed. "Rodrigo, you're only seven years older than me. You talk like there are decades between us."

He shrugged. "I don't mean to talk down to you. If it ever seems like I have, I'm sorry. I didn't mean it that way. At first, it was a little hard to reconcile that someone so young has her act together like you do. But you do, Ashley."

"Why do you keep harping on age?"

"I know you're not going to like this, but the difference between a twenty-three-year-old and a thirty-year-old is more of a stretch than, say, a twenty-seven-year-old and a thirty-four-year-old. It's life experience. It's not personal. It's just reality."

They sat in silence for a moment, each in their own heads.

"At least you don't have claustrophobia," he said. "You helped me settle down. I'd say you were more the adult in that situation than I was."

"I'm not judging you," Ashley said. "We all have our Achilles' heels."

"What's yours?" Rodrigo asked.

He prepared himself for her to spout off some kind of innuendo, but as soon as the thought went through his head, he realized that was pretty pompous because he wanted the innuendo to be about him. He knew he couldn't have it both ways. He shouldn't hope for her to keep flirting with him after he kept insisting they needed to keep it professional.

"I guess I'd have to say my Achilles' heel is fear of failure. Opening this restaurant isn't just a privileged girls' whim. My sisters and I have worked hard to get to this place. Because we are only twenty-three years old, we have a lot of eyes on us. And, I would imagine, a few haters who would love to see us fail. Because they think that we're spoiled rich girls using our daddy's money. Provisions blowing up in our faces is my worst nightmare. I don't know that we would get another chance because we would lose our investment."

"You'd get another chance. I mean, I don't think you're going to fail. But let's just say worst-case scenario happened. You're good at what you do, Ashley. Any restaurant out there would be lucky to have you as their front-of-the-house manager."

"Thanks, but I don't want to work for someone else. My sisters and I have scrimped and saved and sacrificed to get where we are. I'm not asking for sympathy, but I would like some respect. I'd like for you to forget that I'm twenty-three years old. Age is a number. And I'm not talking about anything personal...

"I'm talking about in the arena of business. I want you and everyone else not to see me as Ashley Fortune, the privileged daughter of David Fortune. I want to be respected for my hard work and innovation. I mean, how would you feel if people in the industry couldn't see beyond the fact that you're connected to Mendoza Winery and your family's restaurant? If they didn't give you credit for bringing your insights and creativity, if they just scoffed and said, 'Oh, he's only there because of his family.'"

"I hear you. I guess we're not so dissimilar after

all. We both got a boost because of our families. We've taken that boost and made it our own."

Ashley met his words with a one-shoulder shrug.

"I'm glad you can see that. Rodrigo, I'm not asking you to feel sorry for me. I don't want you to think *Oh, poor little rich girl*. All I ask is that the rest of the time that you're here, you forget that I'm twenty-three years old and forget that David Fortune is my father."

"If I'm being too nosey, just tell me to back off, but I can't help but feel that there's more to this than you not wanting to be reduced to being David Fortune's daughter. You could do a lot worse."

She bit her bottom lip and looked at him as if she was considering the question, maybe considering whether or not she was going to share the reason with him. He knew it had to be deeply personal. And he wanted to know.

This was the first time since he'd met her that Ashley seemed to be willing to let down her guard.

It wasn't a matter of being disingenuous. He'd never thought of her as disingenuous or shallow or fake. But he sensed that she had a tendency to be a little theatrical, to put on a show. Since being locked in the wine cellar, he sensed he was seeing the real and genuine Ashley Fortune. He'd caught glimpses of the real her when she'd talked to the girls on the committee for the summer camp. He'd seen her big heart and her patience.

The rest of the time, it was as if she was protecting herself.

"Why do I have a hard time being reduced to being David Fortune's daughter? I mean, beyond the obvious of wanting to be my own person and not live in the shadow of my dad? I know all of my siblings and I feel that way. It's a double-edged sword. A curse and a blessing. Ninety-nine percent blessing. I love my dad and wouldn't trade him for anyone. But there is a downside that comes with having a cool, rich, creative father."

She exhaled audibly and then drew her lips in between her teeth so that they made a thin line in the middle of her pretty face. "So, it's like this. In the end, it's turned out that almost every guy I've dated has been more interested in getting to know my dad than in being with me. They used me to get to him because they thought he could do something for them. Like he was the key to selling or producing their own video game concepts. Or there were the ones who might not have started dating me because of my dad, but they would go all fan boy when they found out who he was. It's like a cult."

Rodrigo wrinkled his nose. "What kind of guys have you been dating?"

Ashley laughed. "Obviously the wrong ones. What is it about guys and video games?"

"Don't ask me. I've never been a gamer."

She pursed her lips and her eyes went soft. She looked at him almost reverently.

"What?" he asked.

She shook her head. "Nope. I'm not going to say it. You don't want to hear it and I told you I was done with you."

"Technically, you said you were done after we got out of this place."

She tilted her head to one side and the look on her face was heartbreaking. "Why do you do that?"

"Do what?"

He knew exactly what she was talking about. He was baiting her. He knew he needed to stop and he would once they got out of there, if that's what she wanted. He hadn't meant to mess with her. He was feeling the chemistry and, despite how much he wanted to remain professional, sometimes—like now—it was too much to fight.

Plus, right now, he was finding this down-to-earth, *real* version of Ashley Fortune much too interesting and enticing to ignore.

Maybe it was his turn to be real.

As he weighed his words, she set down her empty champagne flute on the cocktail table, crossed her arms and rubbed them briskly.

He picked up the bottle and refilled their glasses.

"Are you cold?" he asked. She was wearing a light summer dress. The light pink color looked fabulous and fresh on her, but the thin fabric probably wasn't doing much to keep her warm.

"Come here." He got up, moved to the leather couch and patted the place beside him.

She eyed him dubiously. "Why?"

"I'll keep you warm." He smiled. "Body heat."

She placed her palms on the seat cushion of her chair and leaned forward. "See, there you go again. Why do you keep sending me mixed signals, Rodrigo?"

"Why? Because I like you. That's why. I'm interested in you, but I can't get involved with the daughter of a client—"

She snorted. "See? That's exactly what I'm talking about. Good ol' David Fortune strikes again. Somehow, he always manages to elbow his way between me and the guy I'm interested in. Only you're more confusing because you don't want anything from my dad, but it's because of him that you don't want anything to do with me. Or are you just trying to let me down easy? Because if I take off my blinders, it looks like you're really not interested. You're not, are you?"

Rodrigo raked his fingers through his hair, fisting them at the nape of his neck. He stared at the floor for a moment, weighing his words.

She thought he wasn't into her and that the "keeping it professional" line was just a way of sparing her feelings.

"You really think I'm not into you?"

She nodded.

"I must be a better actor than I realized because that couldn't be farther from the truth. In fact, it's the exact opposite of the truth."

So there it was. The truth was out.

As Ashley got up from her seat and sat next to him in the space where he'd invited her, he had to wonder if the truth really would set them free or further complicate an already complex situation.

But the doubt began to melt away after he put his arms around her...tentatively, at first. Testing the waters.

Gently, he stroked her arms, trying to help her warm up. The goose bumps that had been present when she'd sat down multiplied as he touched her. He wasn't sure if he was helping. But it felt so good to hold her.

Then, as she melted into him, all of his senses heightened. The feel of her body next to his, the way she seemed to fit so perfectly. The way she smelled of floral and spice, a scent that was so her and was becoming so familiar.

Lines blurred and Rodrigo's focus narrowed until all he knew was that he felt like he would die if he didn't taste those lips that had been beckoning him since the first moment he'd set eyes on her.

When Ashley turned her head ever so slightly toward him and her cheek brushed his, he met her the rest of the way. His lips found hers in that first, cautious joining. It was a soft kiss, but it made his blood surge and his primal need hungrier than ever. Those lips that he had been longing to devour tasted like champagne and...something sweet and female.

He didn't stop, despite good sense warning him that he should, even if she was inviting him in.

Maybe he should stop.

No. He wasn't going to.

Ashley had longed for this moment, but she'd wondered if a man who prided himself on playing by the rules the way Rodrigo did would ultimately take such a bold chance.

She was beyond happy that he had and she slid her arms around his neck. The feel of his lips on hers set her soul reeling and cartwheeling as if it had been set free.

The perfect kiss had started slow and soft, lips exploring lips with playful nips and hints of tongue, and then it had ignited, exploding into something ravenous that had them parting their lips and inviting each other in. She fisted her fingers into the cotton of his shirt, leaning into the kiss as if her next breath would come from him.

He answered her by pulling her even tighter, staking his claim with unspoken confessions they hadn't dared utter pouring out in this wordless acknowledgment of how deeply their feelings ran.

She couldn't remember the last time she'd felt so alive, felt so much need, so much want.

The whole world disappeared. Until the kiss broke naturally. They sat there blinking, both a little dazed and disoriented. Ashley was searching for something to say. But Rodrigo found his voice first.

"I've wanted that for a long time."

"We both have," Ashley answered. "I mean… I have, too. I didn't want to stop. Why did you stop?"

She leaned in and planted a soft kiss on his mouth, gently nipping his bottom lip.

He smiled, but he didn't take it any further. Instead he took her hand, lacing his fingers through hers. "We have to, because if we don't, we're heading for something else—"

"I want to be with you, Rodrigo. And I know you want to be with me, too. I think if we don't, I am going to explode. I mean literally blow the roof off this place."

"That would be a feat since we're at least twenty feet underground."

"That's what I'm talking about." They chuckled together, but when the laughter faded, a certain look on his face told her it wasn't going to happen.

Here we go again, she thought. Rodrigo Mendoza, the consummate study in contradiction.

"Why, Rodrigo? Why don't you want me?" Her voice sounded small and fragile.

He lifted her hand to her lips and kissed her knuckles. The gesture was so sweet, so tender, her eyes misted and she closed them until she could swallow the lump in her throat.

She leaned away from him, needing her space so she could think straight.

"Ashley." His voice was low and rich and sounded

a little tortured. "It's taking every ounce of me to not make love to you right now..."

"Why?" she asked.

"Why? Because we're in the wine cellar of the restaurant I was hired to help you launch."

"I know. And my dad hired you." She crossed her arms over chest. "Oh, hey, Dad. Come on in and have a seat on the couch, right here between Rodrigo and me. I should've been expecting you." She scooted over and patted the space she vacated. "You're a tease, Rodrigo Mendoza."

"I'm not. I don't have any protection on me, do you?"

Her eyes widened.

"Sorry, I don't know how to put it any more delicately than that." He shrugged.

"You're right. I don't." She would sound like an idiot admitting she hadn't even thought about it. "I had hoped we could share some wine and a light bite to eat, but as much as I wanted this, I guess I hadn't thought the opportunity would present itself. Not tonight."

She shrugged. "Believe me, if I'd had the slightest inkling, I would've been prepared."

He nodded.

"So that should show you that I didn't plan on us being locked in together tonight."

"I believe you," he said.

She leaned in so that her shoulder touched his, and he put his arm around her, holding her as she marveled at what an honorable man he was. She had been ripe for the picking. He could've had her, contraception be damned.

She lowered her head to his shoulder. She was smarter than that. When it came to her track record with men, she was usually on her guard. Granted, she hadn't been with many men, and she'd never slept with any of them without protection being at the forefront of her mind. She'd never gotten so caught up in the moment that she'd...forgotten.

Until now.

What was it about this man that made her lose her mind? She'd never felt this way before. Never experienced this before. She had it bad for him, and as she melted a little more into his arms, she knew she was leaving herself open for heartbreak of the worst kind.

But it was a risk she was willing to take, because she was in love with Rodrigo Mendoza.

Oh, my God. I'm in love with Rodrigo Mendoza.

The sudden realization knocked the wind out of her, but in its place was the best feeling she'd ever experienced.

So, this is what love feels like.

Her heart pounded. It was as if she'd been floating along and had finally touched down on the most perfect golden cloud.

This man was exactly who she had been waiting for all these years. He was exactly what she needed.

And she was beginning to believe that he just might need her, too.

They held each other without talking for so long, she lost track of time and her eyes grew heavy.

In her sleepy haze, she found herself on the beach. Was it Fort Lauderdale or Miami? She couldn't tell. Maybe somewhere between his home and hers. They sky was an inky wash, dotted with a million twinkling stars—the stars of a thousand moonless nights under which she'd been searching, one star for each reason she needed him.

But tonight, there was a full, silver moon and it smiled down on them, approving. Ashley thought she could hear it say, "You were brought together for a reason."

Yes, they were.

Her heart joined a chorus of the souls of the generations of lovers who had first discovered each other in this magical place, with coarse sand beneath their feet.

She tilted her face up so that she was gazing right into Rodrigo's eyes. She let herself look at him in the light of the moon. She'd never seen him so clearly, the smooth, tanned vee of his throat visible at the open collar of his shirt. The dark hair that had just the right amount of curl to it. The way he was gazing down at her with an intensity that reflected the desire shimmering through her.

The desire was palpable and it left their bodies, mingled and merged.

They were one.

In those seconds before their lips met, in the anticipation of what was certain to come next, she knew this was right.

She leaned in and whispered, "I want you."

The look on his face was pure love. He didn't have to say a word. But he nodded.

As he took her hand, her heart was pounding and her knees felt a little wobbly, but holding his hand, she managed to walk to the water. The full moon made the crashing waves look like diamonds. With the quicksilver water lapping at their ankles, she put her arms around him. As he ravaged her mouth, she tugged him down into the water, letting the goddess of love baptize their union.

Her arms were around his neck and he slid both hands down her waist and hips, sliding them under her to cup her bottom and pull her to him. She let him do as he pleased with those glorious hands, loving the feel of his rough fingers on her skin, arching under him, demanding more.

Demanding everything.

Because he was everything.

He pulled back a little. "Are you sure about this?"

She answered by reaching for his belt buckle. Her fingers worked his zipper, but he pulled back again.

"Wait a minute." He was breathless. "Stop."

She pressed her mouth to his. "No, Rodrigo, I don't want to stop."

Then a wave crashed over them and he was gone.

She was alone.

The night was suddenly cold and dark. A chill grabbed hold of her and she started shaking.

"Ashley?"

The voice echoed like the sound of footsteps on a stone floor, but there were no stone floors at the beach.

Where was the water and sand? The moonlight?

She opened her eyes and woke soundly back in reality. She was still in Rodrigo's arms, but they were fully clothed because he had been the strong one of sound reason, not making love to her without protection.

But in her dream they had come so close.

"Are you cold?" he whispered.

She nodded.

"I'll keep you warm." He pulled her closer and held her like he would never let her go.

Chapter Ten

In the hazy twilight of slumber, Rodrigo thought he heard voices. He bolted upright, holding on to Ashley so she didn't topple off the couch.

"Hello!" called a female voice. "Anyone down here? Ashley? Rodrigo? Are you here?"

The light flicked on, and he and Ashley both jumped apart, blinking at the sudden brightness with sleepy eyes.

"We're down here," Ashley said.

The patter of feet on the stone steps sped up.

"Oh my gosh," Megan and Nicole said, speaking on top of each other as they appeared in the archway that separated the stairs from the tasting room. "You're okay! We were so worried."

Rodrigo glanced at his watch as Ashley met her sisters halfway and they knotted into a three-way hug.

It was four o'clock in the morning.

"We knew you two were doing inventory, but when you didn't come home and you weren't answering your phone, we panicked," said Nicole.

"Ashley always answers her phone," Megan said to Rodrigo. "When she didn't return our texts and calls, we got worried. You can never be too careful these days."

Her gaze swept over the empty champagne bottle and glasses and the leftover cheese and charcuterie boards.

He got the feeling she had put one and one together and it had added up to the fact that her sister had been locked in a wine cellar all night with a guy.

It certainly didn't look like they'd been working.

At least they were fully clothed. If not, there would've been nowhere to hide and there wouldn't have been time to get dressed between the sisters announcing themselves and rushing down the steps.

"When you didn't answer, we texted Rodrigo and then called his room at the B&B. Call it triplet telepathy, but when neither of you answered, we had a weird feeling something was wrong. Then when we saw both of your cars parked out front, we came inside and found the note outside the wine cellar. That was a good idea."

Nicole hugged Ashley again and then held her at arm's length.

"My phone is in my purse in the office," Ashley said. "Rodrigo had his, but we couldn't get reception down here."

"How in the world did you two get locked in down here?" Megan asked.

"That's a good question," Ashley said. "You know we were going to do a quick *inventory* by hand," she said. "I think someone in the bar must've locked the door before they left for the night. It's part of their closing procedure."

"We're glad both of you are okay," Nicole said. "We need to make sure that everyone knows to give a shout downstairs before they lock up at night."

"Or maybe we should keep a key to the dead bolt down here just in case," Megan said. "We wouldn't want this to happen again."

As they discussed stashing a key in the cellar, Rodrigo forced himself not to look at Ashley. Because if he did, he was certain he would give himself away and Nicole and Megan would be able to read his feelings on his face. Nothing had happened and yet *everything* had happened last night. Even though they hadn't made love, what had happened was much deeper, much more significant. It was tender and passionate and personal.

They had crossed a line.

He couldn't deny that he had feelings for Ashley

and the biggest part of him was happy he might be able to explore them.

However, he still had some doubts that he couldn't get around. First, there was the fact that they came from different backgrounds. While their worlds did intersect at points, the age difference worried him. Seven years wasn't wildly inappropriate, but Ashley was so young in that she had lived a relatively sheltered life compared to him. He worried that she might be prone to flights of fancy, such as falling in love with the idea of a challenge…wanting what she thought she couldn't have and abandoning it once the challenge had lost its shine.

Which brought him full circle. If he was completely honest with himself, the *Bonnie factor* still lingered beneath the surface and reared its ugly head, even after he thought he'd exorcised the demon.

When it breathed fire at him, his natural instinct was to run and protect himself.

He had to be careful. He and Ashley were treading a fine line. There was no taking back what happened tonight, but for the sake of professionalism—and his own sanity—it might be a good idea to keep things on the down low until his work at Provisions was finished. That would give him and Ashley a chance to see how they felt after this glow had dimmed in the shade of real life.

It never hurt to err on the side of caution.

David Fortune and Ashley's brothers might not

take kindly to the idea of him hooking up with Ashley while on the job. Could he blame them? They were in the position to hire him or recommend him for future jobs. Of course, he was confident that the job he was doing and his reputation would speak for itself, but it was best to not to muddy the waters with romance while he was under contract. Especially not with the boss's daughter.

Even with all the reasons *why not* neatly outlined in his head, all it took was one look from Ashley for him to know that plan was easier in theory than in real life.

While he didn't want to be duplicitous, he was a realist. It was going to be very difficult to resist her.

If this thing between them wasn't going away— if it was going to keep moving toward the inevitable—at the very least, they needed to keep things quiet while they were at work.

He would insist on that, and he had enough faith in him to believe that she would see the good sense in it.

"Come on, we'll drive you home," Megan said to her sister. "You can get your car tomorrow—or should I say, later this morning."

Ashley slanted a glance at Rodrigo then gestured at the mess on the cocktail table.

"No, you two go ahead," Ashley said. "I want to clean up before I leave. The last thing I want is for someone from the bar to come down here and find it. It wouldn't set the right example."

"We can help you," said Megan. "It will make it go quicker. Besides, aren't you too tired to drive? It's almost five in the morning."

"No, believe it or not, I got sleep," Ashley said. "That couch is deceptively comfortable. You two go on. Let me do this and I'll be home within a half hour. Thank you for being there for me. I don't know what I'd do without you two."

They huddled into another group hug before Nicole and Megan ascended the stairs, leaving Rodrigo and Ashley alone, listening to their retreating footsteps.

A moment later, Rodrigo said, "What a night."

Ashley walked over and put her arms around his neck and kissed him long and slow.

"Best night ever," she said, her lips still on his. "But I think we have some unfinished business to tend to."

Heat flared in Rodrigo's gut and it was all he could do not to finish what they'd started right there. Especially when Ashley's hands slid from his neck and trailed down his back to finally cup his butt. Pulling their bodies flush, pushing the proof of his desire into the soft recess of her body.

"And I'm happy to see that you feel the same way."

He answered her with a kiss.

"I do," he said. "But we need to talk about things. What are you doing tonight?"

"I hope I'm spending the evening with you," she

said. Her tongue darted out and she licked his bottom lip. If she didn't stop that, he was not going to be responsible for what he did.

He smiled at the thought.

"What are you thinking?" she asked. "I am dying to know what inspired that gorgeous smile."

"I am thinking the sooner we get this mess cleaned up, the sooner we can get at least a couple hours of sleep and then spend some time together tonight."

"Sounds like a plan," she said as she put some space between them. "What are we going to do tonight?"

"How about if I surprise you?"

It was the longest day, waiting for her evening with Rodrigo.

He didn't have to say it, but Ashley had a feeling he was going to say he wanted to keep things strictly business while they were at work.

She expected that much from the Provisions' employees, so she would set the tone. Plus, she'd sensed a strange mood from Meg after she and Nicole had rescued them from the wine cellar.

All day, Meg had been strangely quiet, but Ashley hadn't wanted to discuss it at work. Before she and her sisters had come into the office, they had agreed they wouldn't mention anything to the staff about her and Rodrigo being locked in.

It could start gossip. The last thing she wanted

right now was for the two of them to be under the microscope.

After all, she was only human. She could busy herself to keep her hands off Rodrigo while she was in the office, but she couldn't promise what her face might do if he was nearby—the way her gaze might follow him around the room and her eyes might go all traitorous and tell-all.

Nicole had once said it was a good thing Ashley didn't want to be a professional poker player, because she had an expressive face that was bound to give her away.

A long debate ensued about whether it was triplet telepathy that allowed Nicole to know what Ashley was thinking and feeling or if Ashley really did have the worst poker face in the world. They hadn't reached a conclusion, but now wasn't the time to put the theory to the test.

On weeknights, the restaurant was open until 10:00 p.m.

By 11:10 p.m. that night, the last customer had left the dining room, the doors were locked, the dining room was clean, and the front-of-the-house employees had clocked out.

After last night's unconventional sleep, Ashley should've been bone-tired, but she wasn't. Maybe she was running on adrenaline and coffee, maybe it was sheer anticipation. Either way, her heart raced when Rodrigo stuck his head in the office.

"Are you ready to go?" he asked.

She'd told her sisters that she would be with Rodrigo tonight after work. She'd reinforced that she would get in late, but she would be home tonight.

While she hadn't gone into the details of their plans, she'd kept it neutral. Nicole and Meg hadn't asked where they were going, and Ashley hadn't offered the info, mainly because she hadn't known. She had hinted that she and Rodrigo had some work matters to discuss, but she'd left out the personal end of it.

Because they were talking about work. About how they would handle this new direction in their relationship.

This morning, the sisters hadn't had time to talk about what happened when Ashley and Rodrigo had been locked in the wine cellar because morning came early and they'd taken separate cars to work. The restaurant wasn't the place to talk about personal matters.

Honestly, Ashley had taken big strides to stay busy to avoid possible questions.

Not only did she not want to kiss and tell, but unlike times in the past when she'd shared every detail of a date with her sisters, this felt different.

She wasn't sure what was going on between her and Rodrigo. She had a good idea of where they were headed, but this felt bigger than anything she'd ever felt before. The stakes felt higher. It felt like something she needed to hold close until the two of them had it figured out.

"Ashley?" Rodrigo said. "Where'd you go?"

She shook her head, as if shaking away the thoughts and worries that had settled there in the past few minutes.

"You looked pensive," Rodrigo said. "Is everything okay?"

She forced a smile and made sure it reached her eyes. "Everything is great. Why don't we get out of here?"

Something crackled in the air between them. In his eyes, she could see the promise of everything she'd hoped for them.

"I went to the market and put together a picnic for us," Rodrigo said. "I thought we'd go out to the lake and have a midnight supper. How does that sound?"

"That sounds heavenly."

Ashley's mind flashed back to her dream last night. While they'd been at the beach in her mind, Rambling Rose was landlocked. The lake was their beach and it was one of the few places that would allow them to be alone—and under the stars.

It was as if he'd read her mind.

Her senses sang at the thought of it just being the two of them tonight.

She and Rodrigo locked up the restaurant and got into his rental car. He drove them to Rambling Lake, which was about ten miles out of town.

He parked near the water, spread a quilt on the ground and unpacked a sumptuous picnic, complete with a bottle of Côtes du Rhône.

He pulled out a waiter's corkscrew. "I borrowed this, but I will return it."

"I know the owners. I'm sure it's okay," Ashley said as she watched him unroll two wineglasses from white-linen napkins and light three votive candles.

"All of this is on loan, too," he said, handing her a glass of wine.

Her heart raced as she watched him. He looked so handsome sitting there with the full moon highlighting his features.

After they'd eaten the food that he'd spread before them, she decided she should cut to the chase.

"Rodrigo, what are we doing?"

His eyes flashed as if he was about to crack a joke, but then a serious look erased it.

"We do need to talk about that, don't we?"

She tensed, wondering if he was preparing to do another about-face.

"Surely, you didn't go to all this trouble to put together a romantic picnic only to let me down?" she said. "Because that's kind of been your pattern. Just when I think we're making progress, you pull back."

He started to say something, but she held up her hand.

"I need you to know that I want this," she said, moving her hand in a circle, a gesture that was meant to encompass everything—the two of them, the romantic night, the picnic—but mostly the two of them. "I want to finish what we started in the wine cellar. I want to give us a chance because I think this could be really good. I—I have feelings for you, Rodrigo. If you feel the same, we owe it to ourselves to see where this is going."

"I want this, too," he said. "But how are we going to handle it at the restaurant?"

"I'd like to keep it just between us until after your contract is up," she said. "Does that work for you?"

He answered her by leaning in and kissing her. It was an unhurried kiss, soft and slow. It started with a whisper of lips touching and hints of tongue. With his free hand, she felt the motion and heard the sounds of him shoving away their used plates and containers.

His hands skimmed the edges of her body and found their way to her derriere. They lingered there a moment before he pulled her closer and kissed her, turning her toward him so he could deepen the connection. She slid her arms around his neck and opened her mouth.

She reveled in how alive her body felt, at how wonderful it was to lose herself in the touch of a man and to have her body respond to that touch the way it did.

It had been so long.

So long since she'd felt like a man was interested in her—for herself.

No ulterior motives. No sneaky plan to romance her to get to her father.

She lost herself in the refuge of his arms. All the

hurt she'd suffered at the hands of careless lovers of the past drifted away as the whisper-soft connection of their kiss transported her.

Her heart pounded and her body sighed, *Ooh, yes*.

Vaguely she wondered if she'd said it out loud.

Even if she had, she didn't care, because he was sliding his arms around her waist and deftly lowering her onto the quilt. All the while not breaking the kiss.

Damn, he was a good kisser.

Then his hands were on her body. Every single sense sang, heightened by his touch. It was as if he had awakened them from a deep slumber.

She heard the ragged edge of his breath just above the sound of longing rushing through her body. She felt the heat of his hands searing through her clothes. He smelled like heaven and the way he tasted nearly pushed her over the edge. The seductive mix teased her senses, made her feel hot and sexy and more than a little bit reckless.

As he tasted and teased, she surrendered and let go. Rodrigo's touch fired her blood and made her body thrum.

His fingers found the edge of her blouse and slipped beneath it, working their magic as they lingered and traced small circles on her belly that made her stomach muscles tighten and spasm in agonizing pleasure. Then his hand dipped further still, teasing its way to her breasts and eventually finding its way down her body to a silken, hidden place that begged for his touch.

Those long, strong fingers searched, stroked, coaxed one moan after another from her until her entire body spasmed and liquefied like wax at the flame of his touch.

She ached for more.

As if answering her unspoken plea, he kissed her deeply, with an intensity and passion that she felt all the way to her toes. Then he made quick work of ridding her of all obstacles—clothes, panties, bra. She helped him out of his shirt, trousers, briefs. Then he covered her body with his. She wrapped her legs around his waist. They fit together just as perfectly as she'd known they would. As if they'd been made for each other.

It stole her breath, drove her deliciously mad. As a moan escaped his lips, his gaze locked on hers and he tucked his hands beneath her, helping her match his every smooth glide, until they exploded into a million brilliant pieces and became one with the stars and the night.

Chapter Eleven

Ashley got back to the Fame and Fortune Ranch at about three in the morning. She let herself in quietly, taking off her sandals so they wouldn't make noise on the wooden floors as she floated on the heady feeling of love for Rodrigo.

She sighed as she locked the door behind her and turned to make her way in the dark to her bedroom. She was so in love with him. She'd never felt like this for a man in her entire life. And she hadn't felt the silly thrill of sneaking in this late since she was a teenager.

Then someone turned on the hall light. A sleepy-looking Megan stood there in her nightgown, squinting at Ashley.

"Oh!" Ashley exclaimed then lowered her voice so as not to disturb Nicole. "You scared me. Sorry, I didn't mean to wake you up."

"You didn't wake me," Meg said. "I was getting up to get a drink of water. What time is it?"

Ashley felt her cheeks warm, suddenly feeling as if she had been caught doing the walk of shame.

"It's late," she said. "Go back to bed and I'll bring you some water."

Nicole's door opened.

"It's three o'clock in the morning. What are you guys doing?"

Great. Now everyone was awake and well aware of the time she was dragging in.

"We're going to bed," said Ashley. "You should do the same."

Nicole put her hands on her hips and smiled a suggestive smile. "Are you just getting home, young lady?"

Ashley nodded. Wonderful. Here came the inquisition.

Suddenly, Nicole looked wide awake. "Have you been with Rodrigo this whole time?" Nic's smile broadened.

"Have you?" Meg asked.

"I think she has, because something is different," Nicole said, her eyes sparkling. "And I don't think they discussed much business. Or at least not business that has to do with Provisions. Spill it, Ash. We want all the juicy details."

Nicole's eyes sparkled.

Her sisters had her cornered and it was clear nobody was getting any sleep until she told them what they wanted to know.

Damn that triplet telepathy.

For a moment, she debated how much she should tell them.

She and Rodrigo had agreed that they would keep their relationship on the down low for now, but she couldn't lie to her sisters. And that's what she would be doing if she said nothing had happened.

"Okay, yes, I have been with Rodrigo, and no, things weren't strictly business. We kind of have a thing going on. But, guys, I'm tired and I'm sure you are, too, after searching for me last night. Let's get some sleep and I promise I'll let you know all about it in the morning. Actually, in a few hours. After we wake up."

"Wait, you can't leave us hanging," Nicole said. "Is this *thing* serious? Is the Land Your Man Plan working? Please tell me it is."

Before she said another word, Ashley took a deep breath and gathered her thoughts.

"I guess that remains to be seen," Ashley hedged.

"I'm not buying that." Meg smiled a knowing smile. "Why are you being so cryptic about everything? Tell us."

Ashley looked down at her bare feet, at her toenails that were painted the perfect shade of red. "I don't mean to be cryptic," she said. "I'm trying to be respectful."

"Respectful?" Nicole said. "Of what?"

Ashley was unsure how to proceed. Should she be forthright and risk breaking her promise to Rodrigo? This was such a double-edged sword. On one side, she wanted to keep her word, but on the other side, these were her sisters. They weren't just anyone. She was in love with Rodrigo and, though he hadn't said the words, she could tell he felt the same way. She needed to share this momentous news with them.

Now, was she supposed to choose between the love of her life and her sisters?

If it came down to it, she would choose her sisters.

"Respectful of our business partnership," Ashley said. "Respectful of my...of Rodrigo. We promised each other we'd keep things quiet until after his work here is finished."

"It's as clear as the menu board at the restaurant, he's in love with you, Ash. We're happy for you. For both of you. So, stop dancing around the subject and give us the full report in the morning, okay?"

Sunlight streamed into his room at Rosebud House, and Rodrigo stretched and yawned as he lay in the king-size bed. He felt the best he had in a long time. After last night, things had changed in a big way. Most notably, he more than guarding his heart, he wanted to try and make things work with Ashley.

It had been a long time since he had felt this way for a woman. Since Bonnie, he had been plagued by doubt and fear of being hurt again, but now he was certain this was right. He was done living in the past and ready to move forward.

He hadn't allowed himself to believe that things could work with Ashley; he hadn't allowed himself to see what was in her heart. Until they had been locked in the wine cellar and she had opened up to him. He'd seem a different side of her.

It took a while for everything to come together. Until last night, he hadn't allowed himself to see beyond the blinders he'd been wearing. He laughed to himself as he lay in bed. But after making love to her, something had shifted and it felt like divine intervention. Something was telling him in no uncertain terms that the two of them should be together.

Now that he was committed, it was up to him to show her. Or at least to make sure she didn't have any doubts.

While they had agreed to keep their relationship on the down low at work, he thought it would be a nice gesture to stop at the Crockett Café and surprise her with breakfast. Just to be on the safe side, he'd bring enough for four, since, most likely, her sisters would be there, too. He showered and dressed, then called ahead and placed the order. It was a nice gesture to show Paul West that Provisions wasn't out to put him out of business; that the two establishments could coexist.

Plus, it would be a subtle gesture to Ashley. A way of saying that he'd wished they could've woken up together and enjoyed breakfast, but he had respected her reason for going home.

Where else would they have gone? If he'd come to her house, her sisters would've been there. If she'd come to his room, there was a chance that someone would've seen her coming or going and…well, that's how gossip started.

He felt fiercely protective of her and their fledgling relationship.

Their relationship was at such a tender, vulnerable stage, he didn't want anything to derail it.

So, if that meant they had to take care in situations like that, it was a sacrifice he was willing to make. Although, one night making love on a blanket on the shore of the lake was romantic, he definitely needed to figure out a better place for them to be alone together.

That forced another reality to the forefront of his mind. In a short while, his job here would be done. He would return to Austin and Ashley would stay here. They needed to talk about how they wanted to handle the long distance mixed with the crazy hours that she would be putting in at the restaurant.

He was willing to give it a try if she was.

He smiled to himself remembering how they'd

talked about that last night as they'd lay in each other's arms at the lake.

They'd agreed they would talk specifics later.

But first, breakfast.

Ordering food had highlighted that it was still the early days of their relationship. He had no idea what she liked to eat. He did know whether she favored tea over coffee and if she drank it with or without cream and sugar. But he figured they could each get their own drinks from the beverage stations at Provisions.

He took a leap of faith and surprised her with a variety of breakfast items—scrambled eggs, hash browns, home fries, plain and cheese grits, bacon, sausage, pancakes and French toast. He would set up the food buffet-style in the office and everyone could help themselves to what they wanted. There would be plenty even if Adam showed up.

On the surface, his food gift would simply look like the hired consultant bringing breakfast to the client. But Ashley would know that it meant so much more.

As a special secret love note, he'd taken the rose-bud that had been in the vase in his room. Since he was arriving a little earlier than the others usually did, he would leave it in her desk drawer.

She would find it, and the meaning behind it would be their secret.

It was going to be fun figuring out creative ways

to show his feelings without making a spectacle of their relationship.

When he pulled into the parking lot at the restaurant, he was surprised to see Nicole's and Megan's cars in the lot so early. Ashley's wasn't there. Not so surprising since he'd kept her out so late.

He would set aside a little bit of each food for her so she could enjoy it when she came in. In fact, as soon as he set down his load of takeaway containers, he would text her good morning and tell her to come to work hungry.

He smiled to himself. That's what a good boyfriend would do. It had been so long since he'd thought of himself as anyone's significant other that he was out of practice. But yes, gestures like that and good-morning texts were essential.

He juggled the containers as he unlocked the door and closed it behind him.

The restaurant was silent, but as he grew closer to the office, he heard the sound of voices. Megan and Nicole.

He was about to announce himself when something one of the sisters said preempted his greeting.

"I guess her Land Your Man plan worked."

He was close enough to see that it was Megan speaking, but he wasn't sure he'd heard her right. What was the "Land Your Man plan"?

"Ashley always did love a conquest," Megan continued. "Between you and me, I had my doubts that she could pull it off, but she did. If Dad doesn't like it, I guess that'll teach him not to interfere in our business."

"Yes," said Nicole. "If he gets upset that Ashley is involved with Rodrigo, basically, it's on him. He sent Mendoza right to our door."

The sisters laughed.

Rodrigo's blood ran cold.

Conquest?

Ashley *had* been the pursuer. Had it all been a plan to get back at their father for hiring him?

He turned and walked away before the women caught him listening. He hadn't intended to eavesdrop, of course. That's why he'd walked away. He needed time to think, time to process what he'd overheard.

He let himself out, locking the door, and taking the breakfast for five with him.

His first thought was to call Ashley to ask her point-blank. Had she pursued him simply to prove a point to her father?

He couldn't imagine that the woman he'd fallen in love with would do something like that, something so childish. But then again, the way her sisters had been talking, it seemed like at some point along the way, using him to get back at their father had been discussed.

He sat in his car for a moment, trying to sort out things, trying to separate his feelings from the facts.

It all came down to one truth. He loved Ashley.

Even though he didn't like the thought of being the punchline of the joke meant to tweak her father, there had to be an explanation.

He picked up his cell phone, contemplating calling her and leveling with her, asking her straight-out.

He put the phone down.

They needed to do this in person rather than hash it out over the phone.

He needed to look her in the eyes, because only then he would know whether this thing between them was real or retribution.

Ashley took her time getting ready for work. Her sisters had told her to sleep in, but her natural body clock, combined with the sheer bliss she'd experienced in Rodrigo's arms last night, had her on a high.

Someday soon she would thank her father for butting in and sending Rodrigo Mendoza to her. He had changed her life. He had sent her the gift of a soul mate.

She changed outfits three times, finally deciding on the blue shift dress because it brought out the blue in her eyes. She paired it with black strappy sandals—just sexy enough to draw attention to her legs, but not so sexy she looked unprofessional.

She grabbed her purse and a copper travel mug of English Breakfast tea and drove herself to work.

On the way, she rolled down her windows and sang along to *Summer* by Moonlight Breakfast.

After she'd said good-night to her sisters last night, the song had started playing in her head on a loop. As she lay in bed, awake for what seemed like hours, she'd thought about how the words seemed to perfectly capture the wistful, breathless giddiness she was feeling.

Right now, low on rest and high on love, the song transported her to an ethereal almost dreamlike place. If she could live on that plane with Rodrigo, life would be just about perfect.

In a matter of minutes she would see him. She needed to get herself in the right headspace so that she didn't give anything away. While she'd love nothing more than to shout from the rafters that she loved Rodrigo Mendoza, it was kind of sexy having this secret.

Well, a secret she had shared with Megan and Nicole. She couldn't lie to her sisters and, after being with Rodrigo until the wee hours of the morning, there had certainly been questions.

Her heart swelled because she knew that Rodrigo would understand. He knew her well enough to know how important her sisters were to her.

Besides, she didn't doubt they would keep their secret.

Her heart pounded in her chest as soon as the restaurant came into view. As she steered into the mostly empty parking lot, her eyes searched for

Rodrigo's rental car. Her spirits sank when she didn't see it, but disappointment quickly morphed into anticipation.

She would see him soon.

They had been out late—two nights in a row—so maybe he was sleeping in.

His not being there wasn't a commentary about his feelings for her.

Her default was to feel skittish when it came to matters of the heart. For so long, she had been forced to protect herself from people who meant to use her. Her reflex was to remove herself and not put herself out there, but Rodrigo had changed everything.

Rodrigo had set her free. It felt simply wonderful.

She thought about texting him, just to say good morning, but decided against it when she realized the text tone might wake him up.

"He'll be here soon enough," she said as she got out of the car and made her way into the building, humming *Summer* as she walked.

Nicole and Megan were already there. Nic was in the kitchen, which meant she'd have a moment alone with Meg.

"I thought you might sleep all day," Meg said, looking up from her computer.

Ashley didn't quite know how to respond. It must've showed on her face, because Meg quickly added, "And it would've been perfectly fine if you had done that. I could've covered for you."

Megan's expression was unreadable. The words

sounded warm, but she couldn't tell what her sister was really thinking. Ashley stood there clutching her mug of tea, her quilted bag with its chain strap hanging on her shoulder, unsure what to say.

"Meg, I want you to know I won't make a habit of coming in late because I've stayed out with—"

She glanced at the office door, suddenly well aware that it was wide open. Anyone could be out there listening or simply walking by and overhear them. Ashley walked over and shut it. She turned back to her sister, prepared to continue in a low, careful voice.

"I will always carry my load here at the restaurant," Ashley said. "Just because I'm in love doesn't mean I'll flake out on you."

Megan smiled "I know you well enough to know you'd never do that. I'm happy for you. I swear. Someday my prince will come and you can happily pick up the slack for me."

"Okay, Snow White. Yes, he will, and I will cover for you. Though, I'm not very good at math. So you might not want me to do anything to the budget."

They laughed.

"We're still trying to keep things quiet while Rodrigo is working with us because I want to set a professional example for the staff. But I thought I would burst if I couldn't at least confide in my sisters. I know he'll understand. I mean, I love him. What was I supposed to do, walk around and act like, *Rodrigo who?*"

* * *

Outside the Provisions' office door, Rodrigo had been poised to knock when he heard the sound of feminine voices. Then he heard Ashley say, "Rodrigo who?"

He'd blinked, hoping he'd misheard. The few words that had proceeded *Rodrigo who?* had been muffled. But Ashley's voice was louder on the final two words and there was no mistaking her tone. It sounded decidedly...mocking. No matter how he tried to justify it he'd heard what he'd heard.

Ashley had said, "Rodrigo who?" in a flippant tone of voice that caused his stomach to tighten.

Wow. Really? Was that how she felt?

First, he'd heard her sisters talking about the plan to get back at her father and then he'd heard her loud and clear.

His blood felt like it had turned to ice and he stood there a moment with that ridiculous rosebud in his hand.

Was he an idiot? Had he completely misread things?

His mind raced as he mentally perused the events that had led up to last night.

After all he went through with Bonnie, he should've known better. He should've stuck to his principles and kept strictly to business. But he hadn't.

What was done was done.

Right now, what he needed to do was to keep his

distance from Ashley while he did some preemptive damage control.

As he turned to leave, Nicole came out of the kitchen, heading toward the office.

"Hey, Rodrigo," she said then she pointed at the closed office door. "Are you all in a meeting?"

He shook his head. "I'm not sure what's going on in there. I was just leaving."

Chapter Twelve

Ashley's heart leaped at the sight of Rodrigo's text on her phone screen.

Around 9:00 a.m., she'd given in and texted him Good morning because…well…she couldn't help it. Nicole had mentioned that he'd been in the restaurant that morning, but when her sister had spoken to him, he'd been on his way out the door.

He hadn't even stopped in to say good morning to her.

And after last night, she was starting to feel uneasy.

She stewed on it for a minute, then decided that rather than sitting and worrying about something that would probably turn out to be nothing, she should just text him. Yes, they'd decided to keep things on the DL in the office, but his avoiding her was next-level deeper than down low.

Gahhh! She hated feeling this way.

She took a deep breath and reframed her thoughts. There was probably a logical explanation. Though, she couldn't imagine what.

She'd sat there waiting for him to respond, but after a few minutes passed, she started to doubt herself even more.

Did it really happen or was I dreaming?

Of course, she hadn't been dreaming. They'd had a fabulous night and now she was functioning on less than four hours' sleep. She blamed sleep deprivation for the insecurity that seemed to multiply as each minute ticked by without a word from him.

It was 9:54 a.m. when he finally responded. His message was more than a little disappointing and confusing.

I'm doing paperwork from my room at the B&B. Will be in around 11. I know it's last minute, but can we have a quick staff meeting?

Upon closer inspection, Ashley realized his message was actually a group text that had included Meg, Nicole and Adam as well as her.

She exited the group message and looked at her text inbox to see if she'd missed a more personal response from Rodrigo, but she had none.

She waited a moment, watching her phone expectantly. Maybe he was taking care of business first. That would be fine. For now, anyway.

After a long moment went by with nothing, she set her phone down. Earlier disappointment at not hearing from him morphed into a sickening feeling that something wasn't right.

Even so, she wouldn't let herself go so far as to worry that Rodrigo had changed his mind about them.

At least, not until she could see him at eleven.

Maybe her text had glitched and he hadn't received it, she rationalized.

She picked up her phone again and opened her text chain with him. Had she forgotten to press Send? It wouldn't be the first time. A quick check proved the contrary. Her text had gone through at exactly 9:01 a.m.

For a moment she considered texting him again and asking if everything was okay. But that would sound...desperate much?

Even if she had to lock her phone in her desk drawer, she wasn't going to text him again until he texted her back.

She wasn't playing games; she just didn't want to appear overeager. It would be so nice when they got to the stage of their relationship where she didn't have to worry about looking overeager or smothering him. She longed for the time when she could text him on a whim—if she saw something funny, if she had a question, if she just wanted to say "Hey, I'm thinking about you."

Even though last night had been heavenly and they had agreed that this thing between them had legs—or at least that's the way she understood it—they weren't there yet.

Tucking her phone into her middle desk drawer for safekeeping, she busied herself with work.

She needed to get next week's schedule ironed out. A couple of servers had requested time off—one had a wedding and the other had a high school reunion. Both were important and while Ashley wanted to accommodate the requests, she didn't want to shortchange the staff in the dining room, either. Determined to make it work, she did her best to put her creeping doubt about the situation with Rodrigo aside and focus on finding a scheduling solution.

As she worked on the scheduling app, she told herself it was just exhaustion clouding her brain. Once she got a good night's sleep tonight, she would wake up refreshed and she would see that there was clearly nothing to worry about.

She wished that she could convince herself of that right now because her gut was warning her about something else entirely. She had learned from experience that when she had a gut feeling like this, it was usually right.

It didn't help matters when Nicole came into the

office about ten minutes before the meeting Rodrigo had called.

"What's this meeting about?" she asked.

"I have no idea," Ashley said.

Meg stopped typing on her computer and swiveled her chair around to face her sisters.

"Why is he working at the Rosebud?" Meg asked.

Ashley shrugged. "Maybe he needed peace and quiet?" she suggested.

"Right, because were such a raucous bunch," Nicole said. "He looked a little strange this morning when I saw him. Maybe he's just tired. Maybe this 'paperwork' that he has to do is catching up on his sleep. You did keep him out awfully late last night."

"Shh!" Ashley pressed her finger to her lips and then got up and shut the office door. "Let's not talk about that here. But when did you see him? Was it this morning?"

"Yeah," said Nicole. "I'm not sure exactly what time it was, but it was early. You were already here."

"Really?" Ashley asked.

"Yeah, he didn't look like he was in a very good mood. He told me he was leaving."

Before Ashley could respond, Rodrigo walked in.

"Well, speak of the devil," she said, infusing as much enthusiasm into her voice as she could. The last thing she wanted to do was to act like a clinging vine.

All he did was nod, which was weird.

Maybe he was tired. Maybe he was the sort who didn't function well on just a few hours of sleep.

She tried to make herself feel better by thinking about how much they still had to learn about each other—all the little quirks and idiosyncrasies. The things that made each other happy, as well as the little pet peeves and buttons the other might push.

Because you had to learn what those buttons were so you knew how to avoid pressing them.

She tried to smile at Rodrigo, but he wouldn't even look at her.

Her stomach sank.

Something was definitely off.

If he was a twin or triplet, she would think that maybe one of his brothers was standing there rather than the sweet, romantic guy who had made love to her last night under the stars.

He was thumbing through some papers in his folio, so focused on them, it seemed as if he was going over his lines for an audition or a speech.

This was just an informal, impromptu meeting.

Or at least, she guessed it was since it was so spur-of-the-moment.

They still had five minutes before the meeting was supposed to start.

She got up from her desk and put her hand on his arm. He startled at her touch and pulled his arm away.

Ashley frowned. "Can you take a walk with me

to the supply closet? I need to ask you about something."

He looked at his watch. "The meeting is supposed to start in a minute. We probably shouldn't."

"The meeting starts in five minutes and Adam isn't here yet," she said through a forced smile. "We have time to take a walk."

For the first time since he'd walked in, he met her eyes. His gaze was so cold it made her recoil inwardly. For a split second, she thought he was going to refuse her again.

Instead he said, "Let's make it quick."

Make it quick?

She scoffed quietly. Her eyes widened and she opened her mouth to challenge his tone, but she thought better of it and snapped her mouth shut.

Nicole and Meg had their backs to Rodrigo and Ashley, their heads together as they looked at a spreadsheet on Meg's computer. They seemed oblivious to Rodrigo's mood and the exchange that was taking place.

Still, if Ashley questioned him in the office, they would hear.

She gave Rodrigo a pointed look and a quick jerk of her head, indicating he should follow her.

Since the restaurant was only open for dinner, it was still early for the front-house staff to start arriving. The cleaning crew had already come and gone and a skeleton crew of kitchen staff was in, prepping the mise en place for the evening's dinner.

Even though the supply closet, which was located near the restrooms, had just been a handy excuse to get him out of the office, it would be the best place for them to talk privately.

Ashley opened the door, took his hand and pulled him inside, flipping on the light and shutting the door behind them.

They stood there looking at each other for a moment. His dark eyes were hard and as cold as marbles.

"Are you okay?" she asked.

"Of course."

She waited for him to elaborate.

He didn't. He just stood there looking at her.

"You definitely don't seem okay."

He crossed his arms, looked annoyed.

"This is just how I am. I don't know what you're expecting."

"Rodrigo, something's wrong. Something's different."

She felt herself starting to shake. "Are you having second thoughts?"

His face softened and, for the first time today, she thought that maybe she was reaching him. But a split second later, his look was ambivalent.

"Oh my gosh. You are. You are having second thoughts. You regret last night, don't you?"

He moved from one foot to another and then took a step back, but his back was against the door of the closet, which barely accommodated the mops, buckets, brooms and cleaning supplies much less two adults.

Because that's what they were, weren't they?

They were two adults who just last night had admitted they had feelings for each other. Not two indecisive hormonal teenagers.

She absolutely would not cry. She wouldn't let him see how he could reduce her to tears, how he had the upper hand.

"Less than twenty-four hours ago, things seemed pretty perfect," she told him. "What changed?"

He narrowed his eyes and looked at her like he was going to say something mean or smart-assed. But then he stopped himself.

"No," Ashley said. "Say it. Whatever it was you were going to say just then, you need to say it. I need to know what changed, because just last night you said you had feelings for me. But today you're acting like you can't stand me."

"I need to know something, Ashley," he said. His voice sounded so serious, it was chilling.

What? She tried to ask the question but the word was lodged in her throat.

"Was this all a game to you?" he asked. "Did you and your sisters make a plan to get back at your dad by you sleeping with me?"

Ashley's mouth fell open. She shook her head. "No—"

"Then tell me about this Land Your Man plan," he said.

Her hand flew to her mouth and she felt her face flame. "How did you find out about that?"

"So it's true?" He shook his head. A snort of humorous laughter escaped, but she could tell he wasn't finding this amusing.

"Rodrigo, it's not what you think. How did you find out about that?" she repeated.

"That's not important, but I do have to say I thought you were better than that. Obviously, I thought you were a different person than the person I'm looking at right now."

"Rodrigo—"

He held up his hand.

"It's okay. Don't worry about it. According to the contract I have with your father, my business here should be finished by now. I typed up my final report this morning. It's time I got back to Austin."

"Rodrigo, wait, please. I don't understand why you're so upset."

"You don't understand?" He shook his head. "That's okay, pretty soon you'll be asking yourself 'Rodrigo who?' Out of sight, out of mind. No problem."

He smiled, but it felt cold.

"What are you talking about?"

He narrowed his eyes. "*Rodrigo who?* That sounds pretty self-explanatory. Are you denying you said it?"

She had said it, but what he'd heard was out of context.

"This is a big misunderstanding," she said. "I said it, but what you heard was out of context. I told Meg and Nicole about us. I know I said we'd keep our relationship between us, but they're my sisters and I had to tell them. If I didn't tell them, I was wondering if I was supposed to walk around and pretend like I was thinking, *Rodrigo who?*"

He shook his head like he didn't believe her.

"Don't you believe me?" she asked.

"I'm not sure what to believe."

He'd been so hesitant about even getting involved, maybe latching on to something that he'd taken out of context was his way of bowing out?

She was in love with him, but right now it seemed pretty clear that he didn't return her feelings. He was making such a big deal over nothing.

Maybe she'd pushed him too hard and he was realizing he didn't want this. Maybe it was just dawning on him that soon they'd have to step out of the shadows and bring their relationship into the light.

"I told you the context and I don't understand why you won't believe me. It feels to me like you're the one having second thoughts, Rodrigo."

"I guess getting burned in the past has left me with trust issues," Rodrigo said. "But I don't want to talk about it. We need to get to the meeting. I don't want to keep everyone waiting."

He turned to open the door.

"Please don't leave, Rodrigo. Let's talk this out."

He hesitated, but he didn't answer her.

"Is this about my father?" she asked.

"No, Ashley, it's not. From my perspective, *you're* the one who has made this all about your father."

Rodrigo turned to her and shook his head. "Hey, look. It's okay. For the record, I don't regret what we shared. But it's over now, Ashley. I'm sure your dad will be plenty pissed at me when he learns that I crossed the line." He shrugged. "I knew that was the chance I was taking. So, that's on me."

His tone suggested it wasn't up for debate.

He stepped through the door.

"Thanks for meeting on such short notice. I'll make this quick. I know I was scheduled to be here for the rest of the week, but Provisions is up and running. That means it's time for me to go back to Austin."

The next day, Rodrigo was gone. Ashley had called Rosebud House to see if he was still there, but he had checked out.

"Is there anything I can do to help you, dear?" said Peggy Spalding, the owner of the Rosebud B&B.

"Thanks, but no, Peggy," Ashley said. "He, uh, he forgot something back here in the office. But really, now that I think about it, since he left it behind, I'm not sure he really needs it. I just thought I'd ask."

"Men," she said. "They'd forget their heads if they weren't attached. I'd offer to call him for you, but I suspect you have his number."

"I do," Ashley said. "I just thought I'd see if I could catch him before he left."

"Oh, say, Ashley, while I have you on the phone," Peggy said, "could I trouble you to make a reservation for Saturday night? Table for four at, say, seven. The mister and I have heard so many wonderful things about Provisions, we've been dying to try it. We were so disappointed that we didn't get in for opening night. But Saturday we want to bring Marshall's parents in to celebrate his dad's ninetieth birthday."

"I'm happy to squeeze you in, Peggy," Ashley said as she called the reservations program up on her computer. "I'm thrilled you want to celebrate such a special occasion with us. I'll make a note that you're celebrating and we'll have a surprise for him."

"Good! I was hoping you'd make him wear a silly hat while you sang to him," she said. "Or something like that. I'm sure whatever you do will be just fabulous. You and your sisters are just wonderful. We are so very lucky to have you as part of our community."

Peggy's touching words made Ashley's eyes get misty.

After months of challenges from the locals, the community was beginning to embrace Provisions, and Ashley and her family were beginning to feel welcome.

Wasn't that what mattered? Home and family and being part of a good community? The restaurant was doing well. They'd even had a repeat reservation from a Jesse Marlow from San Antonio. It was the third time he—or she—or someone of that name—had dined at Provisions. Maybe the person was a critic?

She made a mental note to be on the lookout for the person when he or she came in again. She reminded herself this was a perfect moment to count her blessings rather than dwell on what was missing from her life.

Or the way Rodrigo left after he'd presented his final report at yesterday's meeting. He'd complimented them and said they were doing so many things right, to keep up the good work. He'd left them with some final suggestions in his report, which he'd said he'd emailed to their father.

Then he'd left.

He was gone before Ashley could think of a way to stop him.

Of course, she hadn't contemplated finding a way to make him stay until this morning, by then it had been too late.

Yesterday, she'd let him walk out the door because she'd made up her mind that she wasn't going to try to force him to stay against his will. Especially when he wouldn't even give her the benefit of the doubt when she couldn't explain the "Rodrigo who?" situation.

She'd been angry at him. Angry at him for making her believe that he'd wanted their relationship as much as she did. Angry at him because he'd let something he'd overheard come between them.

So she'd let him go.

Full disclosure: she hadn't thought he'd actually leave without giving them another chance to work things out, because wasn't that what people who were in love did? But he hadn't done so yesterday and today she was bereft.

When Nicole and Megan had asked her what was wrong, all she'd said was that she didn't want to talk about it. What was there to say?

She blinked back tears.

As she finished inputting Peggy's reservation, her brother Callum walked into the room.

"Where is everyone?" he asked.

Ashley shrugged, acting like she was concentrating on her computer and not really trying to blink away the unshed tears.

It might get tricky if Callum found out that she was crying over Rodrigo. If he knew Rodrigo had broken her heart, there was a good chance it would get back to her father and…well, that had the potential to turn into a mess.

Yes, he'd broken her heart, but she still wished him well.

She still loved him.

Why would she want anything other than the very best for him?

"Nicole's probably in the kitchen," Ashley said.

"Did you see her on your way in? Adam took the day off. I'm not sure where Meg is."

"I'm right here," Meg said, walking in with a cup of coffee and a delicious-looking muffin. "Rosemary made blueberry-lemonade muffins. Go get one while they're hot."

That sounded like exactly what her broken heart needed.

"You don't have to tell me twice," Ashley said.

"Ash?" Callum said. "Are you okay?"

"Sure, why?"

"Are you getting sick?" Callum asked. "It looks like that or like you've been crying. You good?"

Ashley's gaze flicked to Meg and she silently telegraphed her sister not to say a word about Rodrigo.

To Ashley's great relief, Meg complied, training her attention on the oversize muffin on her desk.

"I'm fine," Ashley said. "Just tired."

"Did Mendoza get back to Austin?" he asked.

"Apparently so." Ashley's voice caught on her words.

He narrowed his eyes. "Are you sure you're okay?"

She cleared her throat. "Yes. Absolutely."

The way Callum was looking at her made her squirm.

"I'm just tired. Tired and hungry. I'm going to get a muffin. Would you like one?"

"I do," Callum said. "Ask Nic to come in here. She'll want to hear what I have to say."

Ashley wasn't really hungry. Her stomach had been tied in knots since yesterday. But if she didn't get out of the office, Callum was likely to subject her to the third degree. She wasn't up for that right now. In fact, she would likely crumble and start bawling her eyes out if he kept pressing her for the truth.

She wondered where Rodrigo was and if he'd deigned to spare her a thought. Or if there was a chance that he was as torn up over the way they'd left things as she was.

Unlikely. The way he'd taken off made it seem pretty clear that he couldn't get out of there fast enough.

Based on that, she was probably out of sight, out of mind.

The thought made Ashley's eyes sting and threaten to tear up all over again. She tugged at the gray cotton tunic she'd paired with black pants today. The color perfectly matched her mood.

Gray and black. Just like the storm clouds that seemed to be hovering over her.

She blinked several times, but a wayward tear escaped and slid down her cheek.

"Stop it," she whispered to herself.

She couldn't walk into the kitchen like this. Everyone would see that she was upset. She needed to get hold of herself.

Taking a deep breath, she walked into the bar area. The bar and waitstaff weren't in yet, so it was a good place for her to pause to pull herself together.

Well, in theory, anyway. The pictures from Steven's Rambling Rose scrapbook stared back at her, reminding her of how it had been Rodrigo's idea to enlarge the photos and display them in the bar area to better connect to the locals.

And it had worked.

Was there any place in this restaurant that she wouldn't see Rodrigo?

She went to the bathroom, splashed cool water on her face and blew her nose.

Rodrigo Mendoza might not want her, but she sure as hell wasn't going to let him taint Provisions. It was all she had left.

Well, that and her family.

Yes, she would always have her family. Her sisters. Never in her life had she been happier about a decision than she was about the one she'd made yesterday when she'd kept Meg's confidence—and she'd lost Rodrigo.

Oh, well. Sisters before misters.

That's the way it was and would always be.

A few minutes later, Ashley returned to the office with the muffins and her sister in tow.

"Ashley said you have news," Nic said. "What's up?"

"I was about ready to send out a search party to look for you," Callum said.

"Thanks for caring." Ashley rolled her eyes at her big brother to show him that she was fine.

He watched her for a minute and she obviously

passed inspection because he took his focus off her and held up a sheet of paper. "I do have news. Big news. The results are back from the blood test to see who might be a potential bone marrow match for Linus."

Callum glanced down at the paper.

"Don't keep us waiting," Meg said.

"Yes," he said. "In fact, they found quite a few people who could be a viable match for him. The most interesting part is that most of the people on the list are Fortunes."

The sisters abandoned their blueberry-lemonade muffins and crowded around their brother to look at the list. Their names were all on it, in addition to their sister, Stephanie, Linus's foster mother.

"How could all of the Fortunes be a match?"

She let the question hang in the air. The way her brother and sisters were looking at each other, she suspected they were all pondering the same question.

"Do you think this could just be a coincidence?" Megan asked.

"Possibly," said Callum. But he shrugged and Ashley was sure her brother was as unconvinced as she was.

"Do you remember what Laurel said when she left Linus on the doorstep?" Ashley said. "She said she believed her child would find his rightful home at Fortune's Foundling Hospital. What do you think she meant by that?"

The four of them exchanged dubious glances again.

"What if Linus is somehow related to us?" Ashley asked. "I'm certainly not a medical expert, but isn't that what it means when so many Fortunes are matches? There's some kind of connection?"

"Not necessarily." Callum raked his free hand through his hair. "It just doesn't make any sense. None of us knew Laurel before she had her baby. So, how could that be?"

"That's the million-dollar question," said Ashley. "What does Dr. Green have to say about it?"

"He's very encouraged, of course," said Callum. "He wants to do further testing on those of us who came up as positive matches."

"So the bottom line is that this is really good news for that sweet baby, right?" Ashley said.

"It sure is," said Callum. "It means someone might save his life."

Ashley's heart swelled at the thought.

Even though her own problems had been weighing her heart down, the news that there were so many possibilities for Linus lifted her spirits. That poor innocent baby. To be so young and to have had such a rough start in life—being abandoned by his mother, being gravely ill.

It made her own troubles seem trivial. She had grown up with every advantage.

So what if she had a broken heart? It would mend

in due time. Now there was hope that Baby Linus would soon be on the mend, too.

In the meantime, Ashley needed to forget about Rodrigo Mendoza and focus on something that was bigger than her own problems.

Her head knew this, but it was going to take a little longer for her heart to get the message.

Rodrigo was hesitant to take the call from Callum Fortune. Hesitant because talking to him reopened the wound he was trying so desperately to heal. Talking to Callum would make him wonder about Ashley. But if he was truly going to carry on business as usual, that meant he had to put what had happened with Ashley behind him.

Even though the hurt was still very raw.

Ashley had so many things going for her. She was smart and confident and funny and beautiful. The beauty was what had snagged him. Well, actually, it was her sass that had snared him. Her beauty had made him notice her.

She was a spectacular woman and she was only going to get better as she aged...

But Rodrigo had walked away because he couldn't trust that Ashley was in the relationship for the right reasons. His instincts were screaming that she had gotten involved with him because she'd wanted to get back at her father. That proved she was too young and too immature to commit to the kind of relationship he needed if he was ever going to give his heart again.

He'd clearly heard her say *Rodrigo who?* When he'd given her the chance to explain, she'd insisted that what he'd heard was out of context.

The "Rodrigo who?" incident, coupled with what he'd heard her sisters say about Ashley loving a conquest, made it pretty clear that this had all been a game to her. A ruse to get back at her father for sticking his nose in where it didn't belong.

Or maybe he was still too skittish to fully open his heart. Because one thing had become crystal clear at that moment—if Bonnie had scarred him, Ashley Fortune had the ability to rip his heart to shreds.

Regardless, Rodrigo should have known better than to cross that line and get involved with a client. It was a hard lesson, but at least he had been smacked back into his senses before the situation had gotten any uglier.

He had been in Austin for three days and he'd be lying if he didn't say he hadn't thought of her every single day. But thinking of her with nearly one hundred miles between them and talking to her brother were two different things.

He had no idea what Callum wanted.

Maybe he was going to give him a verbal punch in the face for messing with his sister.

Frankly, he deserved it. He'd shoulder all the responsibility.

As he sat in his office with the door closed, contemplating the framed photographs of all the restaurants that had been his clients and the empty space where a picture of Provisions should go, he knew what he had to do. He had to let Callum Fortune say his piece.

Once Callum got that out of his system, maybe he would be generous enough to let bygones be bygones and they could all get on with their lives.

Once Ashley's pride healed, she would be fine. She'd said it herself, right? She'd be thinking "Rodrigo who?"

He opened his contacts, pulled up Callum's phone number and connected the call. He braced himself for the long-distance thrashing.

"Mendoza, thanks for calling me back, buddy," Callum said.

Rodrigo blanked, processing the jovial tone of Callum's voice, wondering if, like his sister, he had a tendency toward leading a person one way before going in for the kill.

"How's everything going?" Rodrigo asked.

"Good. The restaurant is holding its own. We're booking all kinds of reservations. Can't complain. But that's not why I'm calling."

Again, Rodrigo hesitated. He was still waiting to hear something—anything—about Ashley. Maybe something to the tune of how he shouldn't mess with a woman's heart. To which he would want to reply that she should be fine because what happened between them had been a game to her. Of course, if Callum did push it, Rodrigo wouldn't say that. He would just take his lumps and let Callum have his say so they could move on.

Instead, Callum said, "Are you there?"

"I'm here. Sorry. How can I help, Callum?"

"Actually, I think it's more of a matter of how I can help you. Are you interested in hearing what I have to say?"

"Talk to me," said Rodrigo.

Chapter Thirteen

"Please tell me you're kidding," Ashley said. She leaned back in her desk chair.

Actually, inside, her heart was pleading *Please tell me you're* not *kidding*. But her voice had left out the negative word, keeping it inside as if it could protect her heart.

Please tell me you're not kidding, because that means Rodrigo will come back and there might be a chance for us.

"Why would I kid about something like that?" Callum looked confused. "I mean it's not a done deal. We're still in negotiations and the town council hasn't yet approved the plans for the hotel. But I want us to have everything finalized so we're ready to go once we get the green light to build."

"I'm confident it's going to happen. Fortune Brothers Construction and Rodrigo Mendoza are going to join forces to open the Hotel Fortune in downtown Rambling Rose."

As Callum studied his smartphone, Ashley and Megan exchanged anxious glances, to which their brother seemed oblivious.

Ashley's heart thudded against her chest as her emotions warred inside her. Part of her wanted to be upset because she was hearing this news through her brother and not from Rodrigo. But this was Callum's business deal. And there was the minor detail that she and Rodrigo hadn't spoken since he'd left town.

The optimistic part of her heart, where hope lived eternal, kept reminding her that if this deal went through, Rodrigo would still be in her life. Even if it was on the periphery. The hotel would bring him to town on occasion. Maybe it would provide an opportunity for them to make amends. Not necessarily in the romantic sense, but just so they were on better terms. She wanted to make things right since there was a chance that he might be her brothers' business partner.

"But wait a minute," said Meg. "How did this even come about? I mean one minute Rodrigo Mendoza is the unwelcomed surprise that Dad was springing on us and now he's a business partner? I'm not making the leap."

"You remember that meeting he called before the grand opening?" Callum looked at Meg, but she met him with a blank stare. "Oh, that's right. Ashley was the one who was there."

"Yes, that would be me," Ashley said. "The other blond triplet in the office."

"Sorry, Ash," Callum said. "I'm a little distracted because I'm waiting for Dad's assistant to email his correspondence with Rodrigo pertaining to Provisions. I want to factor it into our business plan."

"His correspondence?" Ashley asked. "What do you mean? The pitch that made Dad hire him?"

"No, apparently there's more to it than that," Callum said. "I'm talking about the notes he was sending Dad about the progress of Provisions. I thought it would be helpful as we planned for the opening of the hotel because we want to build a restaurant in the hotel. You wouldn't know of a successful restaurateur who might be interested in partnering with us, would you?"

He waggled his eyebrows suggestively and grinned at his sisters.

It vaguely registered that the hotel restaurant was an opportunity that should make Ashley very happy.

It did and she was making all the appropriate outward noises. Inside, though, she was stuck on what Callum had said about notes that Rodrigo had been sending her father about the progress of Provisions.

Had Rodrigo been communicating with her father behind her back the whole time he'd been there?

She knew that she shouldn't jump to conclusions, that she should look at the correspondence first, but a slow burn had started inside her. It was like someone had lit a long fuse.

This was her and her sisters' restaurant. Their investment. Not their father's.

"I'd love to see those notes when you get them," Ashley said, keeping emotion out of her voice. "Will you print a copy for me?"

Since Rodrigo didn't bother to copy us on it.

"Sure," said Callum. "It will be a nice souvenir to add to the Provisions' scrapbook."

Again, Ashley and Megan exchanged a look that Callum didn't catch. Obviously their brother had no idea of what had happened between Ashley and Rodrigo. That Rodrigo had left her with a broken heart.

Ashley squeezed her eyes shut against the pain.

But this new tidbit about Rodrigo's back-channel communication with their father? Maybe it was for the best that he had walked away.

"Here it is," Callum said. "Do you mind if I use your printer to print out this file?"

"Go ahead," Ashley said. "Don't forget to print me a copy, too. For the scrapbook."

Rodrigo Mendoza was no better than all the other twits who had used her to ingratiate themselves to her father.

As she sat there a half hour later reading through

the daily briefings Rodrigo had sent her dad, Ashley's blood threatened to boil over.

This was a betrayal. Not just on Rodrigo's end. Her father obviously didn't believe that she and her sisters had what it took to make Provisions a success. It was the old standard that the helpless girls needed a big strong man to ride in and save them from themselves.

It was all there in the report, starting with the snafu with the bar furniture and detailing the kitchen debacle when the fire-suppressions system erupted and interrupted the grand opening night.

Ashley was shaking when she got to the last page, which chronicled the details of their outing when they'd ventured into the community to rub elbows with the locals.

That certainly wasn't the end of Rodrigo's time in Rambling Rose. There must be some missing pages.

She called Callum. "Hey, you know the files you printed for me? I think I'm missing some pages."

"How many pages do you have?"

She thumbed to the end and looked at the printer tally. "I have eight pages."

"Hold on. Let me check," Callum said. "Yep. That's what I have here."

"That's odd," Ashley said, her heart ached at the betrayal of Rodrigo going behind her back to report to her father, which made it all the more urgent to see what else he'd said about her and her sisters. "I thought there would be more."

In more than one way, she mused.

She had just hung up the phone with Callum and was poised to call her father to talk about the duplicity and to get the rest of the scoop when Nicole swept into the office.

"You're not going to believe this," she said, flapping a sheet of paper.

Ashley waved her away, confused by her sister's incongruent excitement. "I already know and, frankly, I think it's reprehensible."

Nicole shot her a perplexed double-take. "Excuse me? We are obviously not talking about the same thing. Unless you've let your broken heart completely color everything you see a particularly pathetic shade of blue."

It was Ashley's turn to do a double-take. "Clearly, we're not talking about the same thing."

"Well, Eeyore, feast your cynical eyes on this. I double-dog dare you not to smile after you read it."

Nicole handed over the paper with a flourish.

It was an article from *Best of Texas Food* blog.

No, scratch that. It was a review from an influential and sometimes caustic critic who called himself—or herself, since no one knew the critic's identity—the Ravenous Texan. The glowing review praised Provisions' food, the service and the ambience.

Ashley gasped. When she'd gathered her wits, she read aloud.

"Provisions, a brand-new restaurant in Rambling Rose, Texas, marries the best of the upmarket farm-to-table concept with a comfortable down-home atmosphere. Foodies and farmers alike will find common ground in this place, which boasts top-of-the-line service and delicious and creative food from James Beard Award winner Rosemary Allen and rising star chef Nicole Fortune. The establishment is the dream child of Fortune and her sisters Ashley and Megan. No, your eyes are not playing tricks on you. These talented ladies are identical triplets. Provisions is an A+++ not-to-be-missed winner in the Ravenous Texan's book.'"

A picture of the sisters, which Rodrigo at the time had insisted on and taken himself, was next to a photo of Rosemary and various interior, exterior building shots he had included in the online press kit—another one of Rodrigo's ideas.

Even if he had broken her heart, at least he'd done right by Provisions.

Her first impulse was to call him to tell him the good news, but why would she do that when he'd probably hear about it soon enough from her father.

Rodrigo reached the bottom of the Hotel Fortune partnership proposal and realized he hadn't comprehended a single word of what he'd read.

He scrubbed his eyes with his palms and gave his head a smart shake.

Come on, man. Get your head in the game.

It was no time to be distracted over something—or someone—who...

He wanted to say someone who didn't matter, but that wasn't true.

Ashley Fortune did matter. Despite her games and manipulations, she mattered.

Here he was contemplating a business partnership with her brothers' construction company, one that would involve a huge investment and require him to venture into a business in which he wasn't one-hundred-percent versed, and all he could do was think about Ashley.

That wasn't a good thing. He'd let down his guard, let his professional rules slip, and he'd gotten kicked in the teeth because of it.

He couldn't shake the way Ashley had looked standing there asking him in so many words to play the fool and not take to heart the very words he'd heard her say. When the words had been as clear as day.

He had been a fool.

Once again, he had been ready to give his heart to a woman who had been careless with it.

His heart tugged at the thought.

When he'd asked her to explain, she couldn't—or wouldn't—do it. Maybe she had gotten scared at that crucial do-or-die moment—the day after they'd laid their hearts bare. Maybe she'd changed her mind and hadn't known how to say it. That was her way out…

Still, it didn't add up. But right now he needed to put her out of his mind. She was in Rambling Rose and he was in Austin—a safe one-hundred-mile distance.

He needed to get through this report and decide if the hotel was an investment he wanted to make.

First, coffee. He needed coffee. Maybe that would help clear his head.

He pushed away from his desk, which was in a small closet-size office off the Mendoza Winery tasting room, and went to the Keurig. Since he was on the road so much, he only needed a desk to call home base, a place to touch down and regroup between consulting jobs. It was a rare occasion that he had a few days between jobs. But he'd blocked off time to consider the Hotel Fortune partnership.

The Fortune sisters knew what they were doing. They didn't need him standing around looking over their shoulders.

His gut bunched at the thought. He let out a heavy sigh and scrubbed his eyes again.

"What's wrong with you?"

He jumped at the sound of the voice because he thought he was the only one in the winery. They were closed on Mondays through the month of May and he hadn't expected anyone to be in today.

When he opened his eyes, his sister-in-law,

Schuyler Fortune Mendoza, was standing there clutching an empty coffee cup and staring at him.

"Nothing is wrong." His tone—an irritable bark—belied his words. "What are you doing here?"

"I work here, grumpy. You look like you've lost your best friend."

That's exactly how he felt. But he'd get over it.

"I'm just...you know...jet-lagged." He ran his hands through his hair.

That was a lame excuse and he could tell by the way Schuyler was giving him the side-eye, complete with frown and flaring nostrils, that she wasn't buying it. He took his coffee cup from the Keurig machine and blew on the steaming coffee.

"Really? I didn't realize one could get jet lag from driving a car a hundred miles," she said as she set about brewing her own cup.

The machine wheezed and bellowed a sound that resonated in his aching heart before it began spitting coffee into her cup.

"I'm just out of sorts." He shrugged and chanced a sip, which burned his lips.

He uttered a string of curse words under his breath.

It certainly didn't help matters that there were so many similarities between Schuyler and Ashley—it went beyond their beautiful faces and their long blond hair and the fact that they were cousins. They both had smart mouths and an uncanny ability to pull out of him what he didn't necessarily want to share.

He didn't have romantic feelings for his brother's wife, of course, but there was no getting around the fact that he envied Carlo's happy marriage. Schuyler reminded him of Ashley. He hadn't realized how hard it would be to be reminded of what he didn't have.

"If I didn't know better, I'd think you were mooning over a woman," Schuyler said as she emptied two packets of sugar into her coffee and stirred in some cream.

"Don't be ridiculous," he said.

"Am I being ridiculous, Rodrigo? Because my sixth sense tells me I'm not."

Just like with Ashley, he found himself opening up to Schuyler and everything he'd been bottling up inside came spilling out.

"Bottom line is I think maybe she got scared and this was her way of backing out. I don't understand why she wouldn't just level with me and tell me she'd had a change of heart. Why can't women just be straightforward? It's making me have second thoughts about the hotel investment."

Schuyler stood there silently watching him for a moment.

"What?" he said.

She opened her mouth to say something but stopped. She seemed to be weighing her words. Then she finally said, "Have you considered that maybe you're the one who got scared and is using this as a way out?"

"That's— No. Why would I do that?"

"Why would she do that? That's a rhetorical question, but just think about it. You're the one who wouldn't listen to her. You're the one who is contemplating walking away from a business deal with the Fortunes because of the situation. I love you like a brother, Rodrigo, and that's why I have to be truthful with you. I think you're letting Bonnie ruin something good."

He shook his head, raked his hand through his hair again. "No. That's not it."

"Are you still in love with Bonnie?"

"No, of course not." That was the first crystal-clear, true feeling he'd experienced since returning to Austin. "It's been more than two years since Bonnie and I broke up, and I can say beyond the shadow of a doubt that I am not in love with her anymore."

The words hung in the air.

He realized he hadn't been consciously thinking of Bonnie for a while. "Actually, I don't feel anything for her anymore. Not animosity. Not love. It's just sort of a neutral feeling." He shrugged and realized he felt somehow lighter.

"So you don't feel anything, yet you're still letting what Bonnie did, how she treated you, get in the way of other relationships. You've got to let that go, Rodrigo. Otherwise, you really haven't moved on. You have to ask yourself whether you're going to let her cost you your future happiness."

Schuyler looked at her watch. "Oh! I have to run. I have a conference call in, like, five minutes."

As she turned to go, Rodrigo said, "How do you do that, Sky?"

"Do what?" she asked.

"That thing you do where you always seem to know what's really up when sometimes we don't even know ourselves."

She smiled. "I think it's a Fortune thing. You know how we Fortune women love our Mendoza men..."

Chapter Fourteen

"So, did you hear who's in town today?" Megan asked Ashley as she entered the Provisions' office they shared. Her words were gentle. They did not sound like she had intended to poke the beast.

"Yep."

Callum had told her Rodrigo was in town to discuss the hotel partnership. All morning she'd been battling a jumpy, uneasy feeling that had her looking up every time she sensed someone walking by the office door.

If she'd known what was good for her, she would've just taken the day off and steered clear of Provisions today.

However, she had work to do in the office, and

there was always the chance that Callum would bring Rodrigo to the ranch. It would've been almost worse to be caught hiding in her suite on a business day.

As for going anywhere else? In a small town like Rambling Rose there really was no place to hide.

Unwittingly, Ashley's mind shot back to the night they'd stolen out to the shores of Rambling Lake for their midnight picnic. It seemed like the only private place in this small town that was now her home.

She'd considered taking a few days off and going to Fort Lauderdale. However, she'd nixed that idea because it meant she would come face-to-face with her father, whom she had studiously managed to avoid after learning about his secret communications with Rodrigo.

She was so angry at both of them. She knew she'd eventually have to talk to her father about it, because he was family. And even though she didn't appreciate the way he'd treated her and sisters like they were twelve years old, she wasn't about to let it come between them forever.

But right now, she was still hot. She needed to cool her jets for a while.

"Are you going to see Rodrigo?" Meg asked.

"Not if I can help it." Ashley kept her gaze trained on her computer screen. If she focused on the numbers, she stood a better chance of keeping the tears that were stinging her eyes in check.

"Ash, what happened?" Meg asked.

Ashley didn't answer because a huge lump in her throat was blocking the words.

Meg got up, walked over to her sister's desk and leaned a hip on the corner.

"Talk to me," she said. "It might make you feel better. The last I knew, you were in love. Then you weren't. What happened? What did he do to you?"

Ashley tried to clear her throat, but it came out as a strangled sob.

It was ridiculous. She needed to get hold of herself. The last thing she needed was for Rodrigo to walk by and see her reduced to tears. He'd already taken too much from her. She wouldn't give him the satisfaction of knowing just how badly his betrayal had broken her heart.

Ashley took a deep breath. "The other day, when we were talking about your crush on Rodrigo... Well, he overheard me say, 'Rodrigo who?'"

Megs brows shut up.

"When I wouldn't tell him what we were talking about, he got upset with me. He thought I was playing some kind of game, because earlier he'd heard you and Nic saying something about me loving a conquest."

Megan frowned. "And he's that thin-skinned that he would just walk away?" She seemed to contemplate something for a few seconds, then looked at Ashley again.

"Oh, honey," Megan said as she pulled Ashley

from her chair and into a hug. "I'm so sorry. I'll never forgive myself if we ruined this for you."

"You didn't, and it doesn't matter now anyway," Ashley said. "He couldn't get away from here fast enough."

Ashley's heart constricted as she remembered the final blow—the secret communications with their father. There was no sense in opening that can of worms right now. She'd tell Meg and Nic soon. Just not right now.

The last thing she needed was for Rodrigo to show up and overhear them talking about him again. He might think they didn't have anything else to talk about but him—that he was that important.

She hugged Meg one more time and whispered, "I need to get my act together."

Megan nodded, obviously knowing exactly what she was talking about. She walked back to her desk, leaving Ashley to focus on her work on her computer screen.

After the lunch hour passed and the hotel contingency hadn't come into Provisions looking for food, Ashley started to breathe a sigh of relief. Nicole hadn't mentioned anything about Callum making arrangements for the group to lunch at Provisions, and Ashley wasn't about to ask. Instead, she hunkered down in her office, startling every time someone walked by.

What a productive day.

Was it possible that this visit would come and go and she wouldn't even see him?

He had been plenty angry at her when he'd left town. Maybe he was trying to avoid her just as hard as she was trying not to see him?

The hollow thought echoed in the pit of her aching stomach.

Rodrigo was now a partner of the Hotel Fortune. He would be around. Maybe time would make that reality easier. But not right now? *Ugh. Just ugh.*

And then it happened.

She'd finally found her concentration and was finishing up an order of paper products when her phone rang.

She grabbed her cell without taking her eyes off the screen so she wouldn't lose her place.

"Hello?" she said, cradling the phone between her neck and her shoulder so she could keep typing.

There was a beat of hesitation on the other end of the line.

Just as she thought that maybe the call had been disconnected, the familiar voice said, "Hi, Ashley. It's Rodrigo. Do you have a moment? I was hoping I could see you."

Her traitorous heart actually skipped a beat then fluttered at the sound of his voice. Until she remembered how he knew this business belonged to her and her sisters, yet he'd chosen to disrespect them and communicate secretly with her father.

She sure knew how to pick them, didn't she?

Why was it that she kept zeroing in on guys who were more concerned about getting in good—or in this case, keeping things good—with her father, even if it meant violating her own wishes?

"Hi, Rodrigo," she said, modulating her voice. "Congratulations on the hotel partnership. I'm happy for you and my brothers. But I really think you and I don't have anything to talk about. Take care."

She felt a tear slip down her cheek as she disconnected the call.

Movement out of the corner of her eye made her look toward the door.

Rodrigo was standing there, still holding his phone.

He remained in the doorway. "Ashley, you may not have anything to say to me—and you don't have to say a word—but I have some things I need to say to you that I should've said a long time ago. Will you please hear me out?"

"What is there left to say, Rodrigo?" Ashley asked. "I don't need a laundry list of reasons why you left. I've seen the writing on the wall."

Rodrigo watched her stand, smooth the skirt of her red dress and edge past him through the office door.

"Ashley, don't go."

She whirled around to face him. "Why? So you can make yourself feel better? You left when you weren't happy with the way the conversation was going. Now I'm choosing to walk away."

"I talked to Meg," he called after her.

A line cook, who was entering the kitchen and got caught in the verbal cross fire, paused and did a double-take.

Rodrigo smiled at the guy and kept walking.

Ashley had stopped by the hostess stand, her back to him.

"She told me what the 'Rodrigo who?' conversation was about. And she told me that you cared for me so much that they had helped you put together a plan. I think it's fabulous how loyal you are to your sisters."

"That's the way people *should* be, Rodrigo. When you love someone, you protect them. You don't walk away from them and you don't betray them."

"I understand that and I'm sorry I walked away."

"Okay," Ashley said, but her voice and her eyes were stone cold. Certainly not as warm and forgiving as he had hoped. But if he had to work harder to get her back, he would.

"Can we go somewhere to talk?" he said. "Somewhere a little more private? Although I don't know where that would be around here. Maybe we could get coffee from the Crockett Café and take it to the lake?"

He smiled and hoped memories of their night together would make her more open to hearing what he had to say.

"Why, Rodrigo? Are you going to include that in your daily back-channel reports to my father? I only saw eight pages. Did you include our evening in the wine cellar and our midnight picnic by the lake?"

Rodrigo flinched. "Those nights were personal."

"This restaurant is personal, too, Rodrigo. Very personal to my sisters and me. It belongs to us. Not our father. I thought you understood that. You had no business reporting to him behind our backs. Yet, I guess you saw it as a way to ingratiate yourself to him. You're no better than any of the other schlubs who used me to get to my father. I thought you were different."

Ouch. That wasn't entirely true.

She turned and walked toward the door.

"Ashley," he said. "Please hear me out."

Again, she stopped. She squeezed her eyes shut for a moment, but when she opened them, she stayed put.

"I'll admit, when your father first hired me, it was just a job. My task was to come in and help you make Provisions as good as it could be. He asked me to keep him apprised of what was going on, but when I realized how good you and your sisters were at this—and it was your place—I stopped the communication. I even told him I would refund the consulting fee if it came down to that. He didn't like it, but he understood."

Ashley stood with her hand on the door. Her

frown had softened into somewhat of a squint as if she was trying to process everything.

"I think I sent him two days' worth of reports. If you want, I'm happy to pull up our email exchanges so you can see. Better yet, I'm fine if you ask him for the records. After all, it is your restaurant."

She stood there, uncharacteristically silent, and he kept talking. Because as long as he was talking and she was listening, there was a chance that they were making progress—privacy be dammed. This might be his only chance.

"I learned that I misunderstood the conversation I overheard and I shouldn't have been so quick to jump to conclusions. I also realize I haven't been very forthcoming about my past. I'm a little damaged and that's why I'm so fast to pull away. But I came back. I hope that's something."

"What happened to you, Rodrigo?" she asked. "Who hurt you?"

Before he could answer, she said, "Wait, let's get out of here. Let's walk."

As they made their way down Main Street, passing all the businesses that were so familiar they were starting to feel comforting, like friends standing up for him and showing support, making him feel like he was home, he told her about Bonnie.

He told her how he had been ready to propose, but her father had never approved because he was convinced that Rodrigo would never be anything more than an opportunistic bar rat. He told her how

Bonnie had cheated and told him to his face that she felt the same way her father felt. He would never be good enough.

In retrospect, Bonnie was responsible for him being the self-made man he was today. It went beyond wanting to prove to her that he was more; he had to prove it to himself. The downside was that he had kept his head down for so long and had been so immersed in making his business successful that he'd forgotten to live.

Before he knew it, they had reached Mariana's Flea Market.

"You have made me remember what it feels like to be alive again." They stopped walking once inside the marketplace. He turned to her and took both of her hands in his. "Ashley, I love you and I don't want to spend another day without you."

Her hand fluttered to her throat and he could see the storm of emotions in her eyes before she answered him with a kiss that was sweet and slow.

"I'm so sorry Bonnie hurt you, Rodrigo. But because of what she put you through, I think we know we were meant to be together."

His soul soared as if lifted by the wings of a thousand doves.

"If it meant finding you and learning what true love was, it was worth it," he said.

He smiled at her.

"You don't need to worry about that anymore because I love you with all my heart. In fact, it took almost losing you to realize it, but now I know I've loved you since the moment I laid eyes on you, Rodrigo. We've had some ups and downs, but I think we've both finally learned how important it is to trust the one you love."

He looked at her with all the love coursing through his body and nodded. "Yes, we have, and I trust I know where we are going to finish...at the altar."

Ashley stood back, a look of surprise on her face. "Rodrigo, are you proposing to me? Because if you are," she said, her expression breaking into a smile, "I would totally say yes."

They were standing right next to Daphne's Daffodils and Flowers.

Rodrigo plucked a red rose out of one of the containers in front of the store.

"I want to spend the rest of my life with you, Ashley. That became clear the moment I thought I'd lost you. I don't have a ring right now, and I want to propose to you the right way. In the meantime—" He held out the rose. "I'll get you the perfect ring as soon as possible. For now, I want you to know how much I love you."

She gasped and her hands fluttered to her mouth, but in the next breath, she accepted the flower and threw her arms around his neck.

"We almost lost our way once, Rodrigo. I promise

you I'm not going to let that happen again because I want to take this life journey with you."

He pulled her close and they sealed the promise with a kiss.

Step 1: Do not going in for it at last you again because I want to make that the fourth to write with you I... the
He pulled her close and then he laced the picture
within him...

Close would almost not wanted with
has partly... for my muscine welcome... for the
could be dear... happy filled that had been working
have been up there will there... with... the was

Epilogue

Ashley and Rodrigo had decided to have a party at the restaurant. A reverse surprise party of sorts. While the locals who had witnessed the pre-proposal knew about the spontaneous engagement, their families didn't.

Well, except for David Fortune. He knew because, with Ashley's blessing, Rodrigo had gone the traditional route and flown to Fort Lauderdale to ask her father for her hand in marriage.

David hadn't hesitated.

It was short notice, but dozens of Fortunes and Mendozas had descended on Rambling Rose for what they thought was the celebration of Rodrigo and Fortune Brothers Construction's hotel partnership. It was official, even if they were still waiting for the green light to start breaking ground on the hotel. Not only that, another reason to celebrate was Rodrigo and Ashley's joining forces to open the restaurant in the new Hotel Fortune.

Nicole would finally have the opportunity to flex her creative culinary muscles while taking on the challenge of executive chef at the hotel's restaurant once it was up and running. Since it would be a while, Nicole would have plenty of time to hone her culinary chops under Rosemary Allen's tutelage.

To enrich the local culinary experience, Mariana would also be working with Nicole to elevate the comfort food for which she was locally famous to new and original heights.

There were so many blessings to celebrate, including the plethora of possible bone marrow donors for baby Linus.

"I'm so surprised to hear that you're the best donor match, Adam," Nicole said as they waited in the Provisions' lower level bar area. "What's the next step?"

Ashley watched Adam's expression morph from interested to confused.

"I am?" he asked. "This is news to me."

Nicole covered her mouth with both hands. "Oh, no. Was I not supposed to say anything?"

Just that morning, their sister-in-law Becky had learned the results of the latest round of tests performed by Dr. Parker Green. Everything had indicated that Adam was the best match.

"Has Dr. Green not talked to you yet?"

Adam shook his head. Then, looking a little sheepish, confessed, "I hate to admit it, but I've been a little distracted with other things and I'm not fully up on the details of the baby's story. All I knew when they were doing the donor drive was that a baby was in need. Who wouldn't help a baby? So, I submitted to the testing to see if I could help, but until now, I hadn't heard anything. I'm sure Dr. Green will fill me in on everything he knows."

Their conversation was cut short by Rodrigo asking for everyone's attention. With their friends and family finally all gathered around them, each holding a flute of champagne for what they thought was a toast to the new business deal, Rodrigo smiled at Ashley.

A frisson of excitement waved through her. This was it. This was the moment she had been waiting for.

"I am so grateful that everyone could gather here for this celebration," Rodrigo said. "The Fortune and Mendoza families have a long and rich history together. We are so very grateful to be joining forces to bring the Hotel Fortune to this wonderful community. But something else special is happening today. Ashley and I have a very special, very personal, surprise for you."

He held out his hand to Ashley. "Will you please join me, sweetheart?"

An excited murmur went up at Rodrigo's use of the loving endearment.

"A few of you know that Ashley and I formed a very special…partnership after her father hired me to help his daughters open Provisions. But let me say up front that these three ladies needed very little help. They had everything perfectly under control."

Rodrigo pulled a face with pursed lips and big eyes. Everyone laughed.

"No, it's true. I have never met a trio that was smarter, savvier, or more beautiful on the inside and out. But Ashley is the one who stole my heart."

Ashley's heart was pounding as she watched the love of her life reach into his jacket pocket and pull out a small light blue box. Then he dropped down on one knee.

"Ashley, in front of our family, I want you to know how deeply I love you. In the relatively short time that we've know each other, you have changed my life. In that sense, I feel as if we've known each other lifetimes."

Ashley felt a tear that contained all the love she felt for Rodrigo spill over her lower lid and meander down her cheek.

"Will you marry me, *mi amor*?"

She nodded because the happy tears of love were choking back the words.

As Rodrigo slid the gorgeous rock of round diamond onto her finger, Megan and Nicole called out, "Best partnership ever!"

* * * * *

COMING SOON!

We really hope you enjoyed reading this book.
If you're looking for more romance, be sure to
head to the shops when new books are
available on

Thursday 14th May

To see which titles are coming soon, please visit
millsandboon.co.uk/nextmonth

MILLS & BOON

MILLS & BOON

Coming next month

MARRYING HIS RUNAWAY HEIRESS
Therese Beharrie

'It isn't a boat. It's a gondola.'

'My mistake,' she said blandly, and made him smile. She did that a lot. And he was smiling more than he ever had before. That worried him, too. But it didn't stop him from smiling at her. Or from thinking about how different she was now, when she wasn't thinking about the decision she had to make.

What if she didn't have to make it?

He couldn't pay attention to the thought when the gondolier called for them to get in. He did, using the man's help, then gently nudged him aside to help Elena. She smiled brightly, and it became obvious why he'd wanted to help her. Apparently, he would do anything to get that smile. To keep it there, too.

It stuck as they sat down and the gondola began to float down the canal. It was a bright, sunny day, and the blue green of the water around them sparkled as it stretched between buildings. A gentleman began to sing, rich and deep, and Elena sighed at his side. She snuggled closer, not intentionally, he didn't think, but it made him hold his breath.

That might not have been the right description of it. It was more like someone was squeezing his lungs, so he had less capacity to breathe. He'd felt that way the entire day. When they'd been exploring the stores around St Mark's Square. Or when Elena had insisted on feeding the pigeons, then got alarmed when more and more of them came.

'What is it with you and pigeons?' he'd asked. 'I told you this wouldn't end well.'

'I thought you were exaggerating. You exaggerate.'

'You live in Cape Town, Elena. You've been to the Waterfront. You know what pigeons are like.'

'I thought European pigeons would be different.'

He'd laughed, harder when she hid behind him. She'd ended up giving the bag of seeds to a kid before running away, causing the pigeons to scatter. They'd eaten pasta and chocolate crêpes and taken pictures. Once, Elena had photobombed another couple, then apologised profusely and taken about twenty pictures of them alone to make up for it. Now they were here, on the canal, having someone sing to them.

It was a lot to process. Not the experience, but the emotions that accompanied it. And the thoughts. Those insidious thoughts that had popped into his mind all day, then scurried away before he could put his finger on what they were suggesting. They all pooled together now though, growing into an idea that stole his breath.

It was based on never wanting to see Elena as tortured as she had been the night before. To keep her as happy as she was now, as she had been all day. It was built by the memories of how she'd elevated his business banquet that night in Rome because she fitted so perfectly into his world. She went head to head with him when he did something stupid, forced him to think about the way he treated people, and made him feel more like himself than he ever had. If he'd ever encountered his equal, she was it.

She was it.

'This is so nice,' Elena said at that moment, as if sensing his confusing thoughts. And his body, as if confused itself, responding by putting an arm around Elena's shoulders.

He froze. Until she rested her entire body against him. Then he melted.

It was like the hug from the night before. Warm and comfortable. Except there was more now. She was looking up at him, smiling, and he felt himself stumble. Whatever part of him had been standing steady in the face of the onslaught that Elena was unknowingly waging against him broke down. Whatever sanity he had left that told him not to indulge his ridiculous idea fled.

The proposal spilled out of his mouth.

'Marry me.'

Continue reading
MARRYING HIS RUNAWAY HEIRESS
Therese Beharrie

Available next month
www.millsandboon.co.uk

LET'S TALK
Romance

For exclusive extracts, competitions
and special offers, find us online:

 facebook.com/millsandboon

 @MillsandBoon

@MillsandBoonUK

Get in touch on 01413 063232

For all the latest titles coming soon, visit
millsandboon.co.uk/nextmonth

MILLS & BOON

THE HEART OF ROMANCE

A ROMANCE FOR EVERY KIND OF READER

MODERN

Prepare to be swept off your feet by sophisticated, sexy and seductive heroes, in some of the world's most glamourous and romantic locations, where power and passion collide.
8 stories per month.

HISTORICAL

Escape with historical heroes from time gone by. Whether your passion is for wicked Regency Rakes, muscled Vikings or rugged Highlanders, awaken the romance of the past.
6 stories per month.

MEDICAL

Set your pulse racing with dedicated, delectable doctors in the high-pressure world of medicine, where emotions run high and passion, comfort and love are the best medicine.
6 stories per month.

True Love

Celebrate true love with tender stories of heartfelt romance, from the rush of falling in love to the joy a new baby can bring, and a focus on the emotional heart of a relationship.
8 stories per month.

Desire

Indulge in secrets and scandal, intense drama and plenty of sizzling hot action with powerful and passionate heroes who have it all: wealth, status, good looks…everything but the right woman.
6 stories per month.

HEROES

Experience all the excitement of a gripping thriller, with an intense romance at its heart. Resourceful, true-to-life women and strong, fearless men face danger and desire - a killer combination!
8 stories per month.

DARE

Sensual love stories featuring smart, sassy heroines you'd want as a best friend, and compelling intense heroes who are worthy of them.
4 stories per month.

To see which titles are coming soon, please visit

millsandboon.co.uk/nextmonth

JOIN US ON SOCIAL MEDIA!

Stay up to date with our latest releases, author
news and gossip, special offers and discounts, and
all the behind-the-scenes action
from Mills & Boon...

 millsandboon

 millsandboonuk

 millsandboon

It might just be true love...

MILLS & BOON

HISTORICAL

Awaken the romance of the past

Escape with historical heroes from time gone by. Whether your passion is for wicked Regency Rakes, muscled Viking warriors or rugged Highlanders, indulge your fantasies and awaken the romance of the past.

Six Historical stories published every month, find them all at:

millsandboon.co.uk/ Historical

MILLS & BOON
MEDICAL
Pulse-Racing Passion

Set your pulse racing with dedicated, delectable doctors in the high-pressure world of medicine, where emotions run high and passion, comfort and love are the best medicine.